Praise for Leslie Kelly

"Kelly is a top writer,
and this is another excellent book. 4 ½ stars."
—*RT Book Reviews* on *Play with Me*

"A hip contemporary romance
packed with great one-liners! 4 ½ stars."
—*RT Book Reviews* on *Terms of Surrender*

"*One Wild Wedding Night* features sexy and
fun stories with likable characters, only to
end with a sexy story that floors me with how well
it resonates with me. Oh, this one is definitely wild,
but even better, it also aims for the heart."
—*Mrs. Giggles*

"Whoa, baby, *Overexposed* is hot stuff!
Ms. Kelly employs a great deal of heart and
humor to achieve balance with this incendiary
romance. Great characters, many of whom fans will
recognize, and a vibrant narrative kept this reader
glued to each and every word. *Overexposed* is
without a doubt one of the better Blaze books
I have read to date."
—*The Romance Reader's Connection*

Dear Reader,

I'll admit it—I had never read *Lady Chatterley's Lover* until a few years ago. I remember thinking at the time about what a great romance novel it would be...if not for that pesky part about the heroine being married and cheating on her husband with the hero.

When I decided to try to twist this theme into a Harlequin Blaze story, that was probably my biggest obstacle. I don't like cheaters, and could not justify or find any interest in writing about a woman who committed adultery. Then, during a brainstorming session with a good friend, she said something that made everything click in my mind, and I found a way to make *Waking Up to You* work as a sexy, sassy, funny contemporary novel.

I hope you enjoy Candace and Oliver's story. As I did with my June 2012 release, *Blazing Midsummer Nights,* I injected a few Easter eggs into the book. Just the occasional tip of the hat, from the overall theme, to some familiar-sounding names, as well as one very controversial conversation. Hope you enjoy looking for them.

I'm also thrilled that you get another chance to read one of my favorite Blaze novels—and definitely my hottest one—*Overexposed.* My regular readers call this one "The Cannoli Book." Have fun finding out why!

Happy reading,

Leslie Kelly

Waking Up to You
&
Overexposed
—
Leslie Kelly

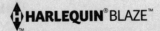

ISBN-13: 978-0-373-79751-6

WAKING UP TO YOU

Copyright © 2013 by Harlequin Books S.A.

The publisher acknowledges the copyright holder
of the individual works as follows:

WAKING UP TO YOU
Copyright © 2013 by Leslie A. Kelly

OVEREXPOSED
Copyright © 2007 by Leslie A. Kelly

Recycling programs
for this product may
not exist in your area.

HARLEQUIN®

Printed in U.S.A.

www.Harlequin.com

CONTENTS

ABOUT THE AUTHOR

Leslie Kelly has written dozens of books and novellas for Harlequin Blaze, Temptation and HQN. Known for her sparkling dialogue, fun characters and depth of emotion, her books have been honored with numerous awards, including a National Readers' Choice Award, an *RT Book Reviews* Award and three nominations for the highest award in romance, the RWA RITA® Award. Leslie lives in Maryland with her own romantic hero, Bruce, and their three daughters. Visit her online at www.lesliekelly.com.

Books by Leslie Kelly

HARLEQUIN BLAZE

To get the inside scoop on Harlequin Blaze and its talented writers, be sure to check out blazeauthors.com.

LESLIE KELLY

WAKING UP TO YOU

Prologue

Pay attention, ladies, it looks like Thomas Shane, hottest young leading man to come out of Sundance, might be ready to trade in his bachelor digs for a cozy cottage for two. The handsome actor, who set female hearts throbbing in his very first picture, is reportedly in the market for a home in the Laguna Beach area.

Shane, who is rumored to be starring in the next big superhero reboot, has been notoriously picky about his lady friends. But he was recently seen house shopping with a hot brunette who, sources say, was the costume designer on his last film.

If it's true that Thomas Shane is leaving the realm of available men, hearts are breaking all over the world.

Don't go, Shane! Don't go!

1

"WAIT, YOU'RE ASKING me to *marry* you?"

Her mouth open, Candace Reid stared into the beautiful, sky-blue eyes that were the dominant feature of the most perfect male face she had ever seen. Thomas Shane, handsomest man on the planet, hottest young up-and-comer in Hollywood, subject of fantasies and object of obsessions, had just said the words every other woman in America would kill to hear from his lips. And he didn't appear to be joking.

"Yes, I am. Marry me, Candace. Say yes."

"But…but…you're a movie star."

"So what? You're a movie costumer."

She grunted. That *so* didn't count. Her check on their last film was smaller than his by at least four zeroes.

"We've known each other since kindergarten."

"Nursery school. Say yes and I will at last forgive you for stealing my Fruit Roll-Ups during nap time the day we met."

She growled. She hadn't taken the damn Fruit Roll-Ups. "That was Joey Winpigler…don't you remember his green teeth?"

"That kid's teeth were always green."

She groaned, realizing they were getting off topic—off this *insane* topic. "I can't marry you…you're my best friend."

"And you're mine. That's why it's so perfect."

Throwing her arms up in frustration, she exclaimed, "But, Tommy, you're gay!"

He waved an unconcerned hand. "Oh, *that*."

"Yeah. *That*."

"It's really no big deal."

"I disagree. I don't have a penis, and they're right up there with raindrops on roses and whiskers on kittens for you."

"Well, I'll admit they *are* among my fav-o-rite things."

Of course Tommy would get the show-tune quip—he'd starred in every musical in their high school and could tap-dance his way around a chorus line of Rockettes. Not that anyone who had seen him in his last film, taking out an entire terrorist camp single-handedly, would believe that.

"But really, penises schmenises, most men are jerks," he insisted. "I *adore* women."

"Not sexually."

He plopped down beside her on the buttery-soft leather sofa in the living room of his Malibu condo. "Sex isn't everything."

"Yeah, right." For him maybe it wasn't, since his career was his entire focus right now. But for Candace, who liked sex a lot, even if she seldom got it, it was kind of a biggie.

"I think maybe I'll just be asexual from now on."

She snorted and rolled her eyes.

"What? I can love from afar. It'll be all tragic and shit."

"Like the mad crush you had on that guy who played your grandfather in your second film?"

He pursed his lips, looking prim. "Every serious actor has a crush on Sir Anthony Hopkins. He's a God."

"But not every serious actor goes trolling for a little

strange cock when he's out of town, away from the cameras."

"Big strange cock," he retorted. "And that's a secret."

"This is nuts. Stop playing around."

"Babe, I've got to keep my personal life on the down-low for now," he said, growing serious. "If I don't, my superhero action-movie days are over. It sucks, but you know it's true."

Part of her wanted to urge him to be true to himself and stop hiding the man he was. She'd known about his sexual orientation for as long as he had, having realized it in middle school when Tommy had gotten pissy about her landing a date with the hottest guy in their class. It hadn't been hard to figure out who, exactly, he was jealous of. The two of them had talked about it, acknowledged Tommy was gay and that was that.

Her sister, Madison, the only person in the world to whom she was closer than Tommy, hadn't figured it out quite as quickly. But once she had, the three of them had become like the Three Musketeers, fighting for Tommy's right to be himself.

And now he wanted to hide who he was for good.

"There have been rumors," he said, not meeting her eye.

She shrugged. "There are always those kinds of rumors about movie stars." Tommy wasn't the first Hollywood celebrity to worry about in-the-closet stories, and he wouldn't be the last.

He rested his head on the back of the couch and stared at the ceiling. "I've also gotten a few veiled threats."

Oh, hell. "What do you mean? Threats from who?"

"Just somebody I had a fling with last year."

"Blackmail?" she said, indignant on his behalf.

"Not yet. But it could get there. He's making rumbles about supposedly having some kind of proof."

Candace glowered at him for being careless. "Tell me you didn't let some dude take pictures."

"Do I look mentally challenged?" He sounded indignant.

"Sorry."

"And before you ask if I left DNA on a Gap dress, let me explain. It was just some text messages."

"They can be faked," she said, waving an airy hand.

"Yeah, but look at what happened to Tiger."

True. Text messages could definitely come back to bite you. She made a mental note. *Next time you're about to break up with someone, borrow his phone to destroy the evidence first.*

He turned to face her. "So you see why this is so important? With that tabloid article hinting I was going to settle down with you, I think I can put out the fires for a while. Once I nail this franchise, I can get haughty and walk away to do high-minded indie films."

Haughty wasn't hard for Tommy, although she knew it was a pretense. He was almost always in character. Right now it suited him to act the part of spoiled Hollywood star. But playing the role of her husband? That would take some Oscar-worthy skills.

"Please, Candy, I'm begging you," he said. "Just give me a few years—five max. You and I both know it wouldn't be the first five-years-to-hide-the-fact-that-I'm-gay marriage in Hollywood."

Five years. Could she really give up five years of her life? Okay, so she was only twenty-six, she wasn't seeing anyone and had no interest in settling down and having babies until she was in her thirties. Still…it was quite a commitment.

"And there'll be no prenup. You'll get half of whatever I earn."

Her eyes nearly popped out of their sockets.

He saw her reaction and pounced. "You know you could use the money, since you won't let me lend it to you. You can help out your parents and your sister, give your grandfather the money to get that broken-down winery he bought last year up and running."

That was all true. Curse him for understanding her well enough to know exactly which buttons to push.

"And it'll be fun. We'll walk the red carpet together." He dropped an arm over her shoulders and pulled her close. "I'll be all romantic when I give my Oscar acceptance speech and thank the wildly sexy woman who made it all possible."

Hmm. That sounded like fun.

"There is still one big problem," she finally said. "I like sex. Five years is a long time to go without it."

"You don't have to," he insisted.

"Eww," she said, shoving his arm off her. "That'd be like having sex with my brother. My gay brother."

"I wasn't talking about me! You can have affairs."

"Tacky. Besides, that'd *really* cause some gossip. I'm already on the radar of those leeches."

She hated that, truly. Being the subject of gossip was infuriating, and she doubly hated the idea that some people might have decided she got her start in Hollywood because of Tommy. If anything, he'd gotten his first break through her. He'd come to visit her at work at one of the studios one day, met a casting director and the rest was history.

"Look," he said, "we both know you've got a gazillion gigabytes of internal memory when it comes to sex. You've already stored up experiences that helped you through dry spells in the past."

She couldn't argue that, but did stick out her tongue at him. It wasn't nice of him to point out all those dry spells, usually caused because Candace had a bad habit of going out with guys who were far more focused on ma-

terial things and their own ambitions than they were on
her. "Your point?"

"My point is, I'll send you on a trip to France for two
weeks. You can boink your way from Bordeaux to Paris,
free from the paparazzi. Once you back up some orgasms
on your libido's hard drive, you can come home and we'll
announce our engagement."

He always managed to make her laugh. "And what if my
vaginal computer crashes? Am I supposed to zip off to a
bordello to do an emergency dump onto my flash drive?"

"I bet you'd make it two years. Then, when you're crawling out of your skin, I'll pay for you to go to Australia and
you can throw a few shrimp on your barbie."

He said the words in a cheesy down-under accent, and
she couldn't help laughing. The whole thing was absurd,
ridiculous.

But, craziest of all, she was seriously thinking about it.

Not just because she loved Tommy, or because it might
be fun playing Hollywood wife. No, because she could really use the money. Her parents were happy in the Florida
home where she'd grown up. But since her dad's heart attack two months ago, they'd been stretched thin financially.

Her sister had just finished grad school and had a mountain of debt. And her wonderful, willful grandfather had,
indeed, been struck by some wild notion and bought an
old run-down winery in Northern California a year ago.
The place had nary a grape in sight, and Grandpa had no
clue how to grow them, much less turn them into wine.
But he was determined to make a go of it.

So, yeah, the money would come in handy. Tommy
had offered to help out, but she wouldn't accept charity.
She always earned what she got. And frankly, if she had
to give up sex for five years, she would earn every penny.
Because, no matter what he said, she'd never risk having
an affair after their engagement was announced, a time

when she'd be more under the paparazzi spotlight than ever. This sowing-her-wild-oats-in-France thing would be it, the full extent of her sexual activity for five long, lonely, vibrator-filled years.

Could she do it? For Tommy? For her family? For the money?

"So what do you say? Pretty please?" he asked, flashing those baby blues and his amazing smile. That grin, that wicked sense of humor and his innate kind streak always made her give in. He deserved the brilliant career within his grasp. No creepy blackmailer should have the right to take it away from him.

"Oh, hell." *Farewell penises of the world.* "I guess I'm in."

"Yes! You are the best friend ever." He pumped both fists in the air, then dropped to one knee. Taking her hand, he stared at her adoringly, playing the man-in-love character. Put him in a Nick Sparks film opposite Emily Blunt and nobody would ever guess he'd once seduced the star football player of their high school.

"Candace Eliza Reid, will you be my bride?"

"Yes, I will. Now get up, idiot. And get your travel agent on the phone because I am *so* taking you up on that Paris thing."

"Or maybe Italy for some spicy pepperoni?"

"Dork," she said as he wagged his eyebrows suggestively.

"Wait…Ireland! I know you've always dug Irish guys."

"Nope, French will do. I don't want my sex toy to speak English. I don't need him for conversation, and I definitely don't want him talking to any reporters who come around."

She doubted she'd come across an absolutely amazing superhunk who would give her five years' worth of orgasms in two weeks, but it was worth a shot. She'd do her damnedest, anyway, and nobody was going to stop her from gorging herself on one last sexual feast before settling in for five hungry years of celibacy.

Before Tommy could make the call, however, her own cell phone rang. She answered, listened and realized that she'd been wrong. Somebody *could* stop her. Something *could* happen that would totally change her mind and her plans. Because, when it came right down to it, her need to stockpile some sexual memories couldn't even begin to compete with family, especially when somebody she loved was hurt and needed her. And her grandfather—whom she adored—was hurt and needed her.

So, within a few hours, Candace was at the airport, waiting to board a plane, not for France and orgasms, but for San Francisco and family. She'd be by her grandfather's side for as long as it took…even if she had to sacrifice any chance she had of meeting a man who might make her most wicked dreams come true.

LYING IN BED in the small groundskeeper's cottage that he now called home, Oliver McKean suddenly found himself wide-awake, wondering what had roused him from his slumber. He was exhausted, his body aching after a long day of hard work, followed by an evening in a hospital. After twenty hours on his feet, he'd been totally wiped. When he'd gotten home, he'd showered, hit the mattress and been sound asleep in minutes.

Until now.

He lay there in the stillness, blinking, looking up at the ceiling that still didn't look familiar, though he'd slept beneath it for four months now. A long silent moment stretched out, broken only by the faint far-off howl of a coyote. Coming from L.A., he still hadn't grown used to the silence up here in Northern California. Sonoma was known for its famous wines, but its landscape was pretty spectacular, with thousands of acres of untamed wilder-

ness. The estate on which he lived sometimes felt like it
was in the middle of a deserted island.

Which was exactly the reason he'd come here, chucking
his old life and heading north, choosing the wine country
both because of his family's ties to the area and his own
love of the region. Being away from the seething mass
of humanity in L.A. had sounded like a good way to re-
group, regain his sense of self. He also wanted to regain his
sense of right and wrong, which had started to slip away
as he'd fallen further into the trap of career and ambition.
He needed to take a year or so, to drop out of the world,
do penance for the wrongs he'd done and to figure out
what he was going to do next. One thing was for sure—it
wasn't returning to the Los Angeles County D.A.'s office.

"Been there, done that, never going back," he whispered. His job as a prosecutor had demoralized him,
savaged his optimistic streak and left him with a strong
distaste for his chosen profession.

Glancing at his clock and seeing it was almost three, he
settled back into his small, lumpy bed, which had come
with the furnished cottage. But right before he closed his
eyes again, he noted the shadows playing across the ceiling. *That's* what had awakened him. Not a noise, a light.

When he'd gone to bed at 1:00 a.m., it had been pitch-
black outside. The sky had been overcast for a couple of
days, leaving the stars and moon—usually brilliant up
here away from the city lights—hidden behind a bank
of clouds. He could hear the soft fall of rain now. But
there was light coming from somewhere. It was notice-
able against the utter blackness, and sifted in through the
uncurtained window.

He got up, walked over and looked toward the main
house. A warm, golden beacon shone from within, shat-
tering the darkness.

Strange. He didn't think he'd left a light on, and the

house was supposed to be empty. The owner, Buddy Frye, was lying in a hospital waiting to have surgery for his broken hip. Frye lived alone, with Oliver occupying the groundskeeper's cottage nearby. Nobody else was within a few miles. Oliver had talked to his boss's daughter earlier, and she'd said she would try to catch a flight from Florida in the next few days. But no way could she have made it this soon. So who was skulking around in the house?

He hadn't been away from L.A., and his job prosecuting some of the most violent criminals in the country, long enough to assume the visitor was simply a friendly, concerned neighbor. Huh-uh. Buddy was pretty new to the area. He didn't socialize a lot; much of the community thought he had to be crazy to buy an old ruin of a vineyard estate that had been on the market for three years.

There had been reports in the news lately about break-ins in some of the outlying areas, even some squatters taking advantage of the abandoned foreclosures. And while Buddy didn't have a lot worth stealing in that glorious old ruin he called a home, no way was Oliver about to let the man get victimized while he was lying helpless in a hospital.

He reached for the jeans he'd taken off a few hours ago. They were crusted with dirt from the long day he'd put in yesterday. He hadn't even had time to change into something else before racing after the ambulance that had taken his kindly old boss to the emergency room. But hell, if they were good enough for the doctors and nurses at the Sonoma Valley Hospital, they were good enough for Mr. Prowler.

He left his small house, following the illumination. His bare feet slipped in the wet grass, and the cold rain jabbed his chest since he hadn't bothered with a shirt. Passing the toolshed, which stood between his place and the main house, he reached out and snagged a rake. He didn't want to have to protect himself, but better safe than sorry.

Strange that anybody would choose *this* house to rob. The place might once have been a showplace—Oliver had seen pictures of it from its glory days, when it had been owned by his own family. It had been passed down from a great-grandfather who'd been a silent movie star. His uncle had sold it a decade ago, and that owner had gone bankrupt. Now Buddy Frye, its current owner, was trying to restore it. Oliver hoped he succeeded—the bones of a beautiful mansion were still there. As for right now, though, it was a falling-down heap, held up as much by the layers of paint on the walls as by any remnants of a foundation.

The porch creaked—the third floorboard being the loudest—so he avoided it as he approached the door. He reached for the knob, which twisted easily in his hand. That wasn't a good sign. He remembered locking it tonight before heading to his place. Buddy often didn't, feeling safe out here in the country, but Oliver hadn't lost that big-city need for security.

Stepping inside, he almost tripped over a small carry-on type suitcase, and was immediately curious about this burglar who carried Louis Vuitton.

Clanging emerged from the kitchen. So the prowler had decided to make himself a sandwich? A little ham and Swiss to go with the breaking and entering?

Nothing about this added up.

The kitchen was at the back of the house. Edging toward it, clueless about what to expect, Oliver paused at the doorway. When he peeked in, he froze in uncertainty.

It wasn't a prowler. At least, it wasn't the sort of prowler he'd ever seen or envisioned, unless prowlers now came disguised as tall young women with thick masses of honey-brown hair that hung in a wave of damp curls halfway down a slender back. She stood at the sink, filling two things: a glass with water, and a pair of jeans with the most amazingly perfect ass he'd ever seen.

His breath caught, his heart lurched and all parts south woke up, too. As he watched, she lifted a shaking hand and swept it through that long hair, weariness underscoring every movement. Her slumped shoulders reinforced that.

He ran down a list of possibilities and lit on the most likely. *A granddaughter.* Buddy had mentioned that one lived in L.A. She must have come up when she heard about her grandfather's accident.

Welcome to Northern California, sweetheart. And thanks for improving the view by bringing that gorgeous ass with you.

He blinked, trying to clear his mind. He'd done enough staring for one night, especially at the posterior of a woman whose grandfather was one of the few men Oliver truly respected.

"Ahem," he said, clearing his throat.

She dropped the glass. It fell from her hand onto the floor, exploding into a volcano of tiny slivers, splashing water on her pants. Spinning around, her eyes wide and her mouth falling open, she saw him standing there and let out a strangled cry of alarm.

"Whoa, whoa," he said, realizing what he must look like, shirtless, wearing dirty jeans and, he suddenly realized, still holding a sharp, threatening-looking rake. The woman, who was beyond sexy, with a pair of blazing green eyes and a beautiful face surrounded by that thick, honey-colored tangle of hair, was eyeing him like he'd popped up in front of her in a back alley.

"I'm not going to…"

He was going to say *hurt you.* But before he could say a word, a pot flew toward his head. He threw up an arm to deflect it, groaning as the metal thunked his elbow, sending him stumbling back into the hallway. He barely managed to stay upright. If not for the rake on which he suddenly leaned, he might have fallen flat on the floor.

But the rake couldn't help him when the frying pan followed the pot.

One second later, he *was* flat on the floor, rubbing the middle of his chest. He focused on trying to catch his breath, which had been knocked out of him as if he'd been KO'd by the love child of Ali and Tyson. That skillet must have been made of cast iron, and she'd flung it like a discus wielded by an Olympic champion.

He held his hands up in surrender, trying to form words, though his body had forgotten how to breathe and his ribs were screaming for her head on a platter. Meanwhile, the rake, which he'd been clutching as he fell, toppled forward. Just to add a little insult to the injury, it landed on his shoulder, then clanged to the floor beside him.

Pain, meet agony, pull up a chair why don't you?

"Get out, I'm calling the police!" she ordered as she scrambled to grab another pot out of the sink.

"Whoa, lady, cool it," he finally gasped. "I'm not… going to…hurt you."

"That's what any sick, raping, ax-murdering psycho would say."

If his chest didn't hurt so damned much, and if he wasn't afraid she would reach for the knife block next, he would have mulled that one over, wondering which she thought him to be: sick, raping, ax-murderer or psycho. All of the above?

Active imagination on that one.

"I'm the…groundskeeper," he said with a groan as the ache in his chest receded, only to remind him of the ache in his elbow. *Funny bone, my ass.* "I work here."

She froze, another pot in one hand, a cell phone in the other, and stared at him from a few feet away. "You work here?"

"Yeah, for Buddy. My name's Oliver McKean. I saw the lights and was afraid somebody had broken in."

She eyed him, her stare zoning in on the blood he could feel trickling down the side of his arm. Obviously she'd broken skin, if not bone, with her mad pot-slinging skills.

Nibbling on the corner of a succulent lip, she whispered, "Oh, dear."

"Yeah. Oh, dear. That's some swing you've got there."

"I'm so sorry. I'm Candace Reid."

"Oliver McKean."

"You said that."

"I know," he mumbled, realizing he wasn't making any sense. The one place she hadn't hit him was his head, but his thoughts were still a whirl as he tried to figure out why on earth he was reacting so strongly to a woman who'd just tried to kill him.

"Are you Irish?" she asked with a deep frown, sounding more concerned than when she'd thought him a maniacal ax-killing rapist.

"My father is. We lived in Cork for a few years when I was a kid," he admitted, wondering if his voice still held a hint of an accent. Also wondering why it mattered.

Not seeing the need to discuss his ethnicity, he staggered to his feet. He was none too steady on them, and his lungs still burned. She'd practically knocked him senseless. Dizzy or not, he was incredibly lucky neither of those flying missiles had hit him in the head. They *really* could have done some damage. But worries about what might have happened dissipated as he stared at her from across the room. Now that he wasn't afraid for his life, he found himself struck into silence by the beauty of her gently curved face. Dark brows arched over expressive jewel-green eyes that were still widened with fear and surprise. Beneath a pair of high cheekbones were soft hollows that invited tender exploration. Her amazing lips were made for lots of deep kisses. Her chin was up, determined and strong, as if she wasn't about to let down her guard completely. He liked that…he especially liked that she remained firm even though her long slender throat quivered and worked as she swallowed down her instinctive anxiety and mistrust.

She wore a delicate, filmy blouse, all cloud and color. It clung to the edge of her slim shoulders, revealing a soft expanse of chest and collarbone. Her skin was creamy, smooth, and his fingers curled together as he imagined touching that softness. The scooped neck of the blouse fell to the tops of her full breasts, revealing a hint of cleavage that left him more breathless than he'd felt after taking a frying pan to the chest.

He continued his perusal, seeing those curvy hips from the front—just as delightful—and the thighs clad in tight denim, on down to the high-heeled boots. Hell, she should have used *those* things for a weapon; the spiked heels could have carved out a hole in his heart.

Hmm. He suspected this woman could carve her name on any man's heart. If, of course, he had one still capable of opening up and being carved.

"You're Buddy's granddaughter, I presume?" he finally asked, once his brain started working again.

His words snapped her out of her long moment of decompression. Apparently realizing she wasn't about to be raped, ravaged by a maniac or ax-murdered, she nodded quickly. "Yes. I'm such an idiot. My mother told me that Grandpa's groundskeeper had been the one to call with the news that he was in the hospital. I can't believe I took you for a home invader." She spun around and grabbed a handful of paper towels, striding toward him, her eyes glued on his bleeding arm. "I really am sorry. Let me help you."

When he saw that she was still armed, he took a step back. "Drop the lethal weapon first, would you?"

Looking down at the pot, she nibbled her lip sheepishly

and did as he asked, opening her fingers and dropping the pot to the floor.

Well, not *quite* to the floor. It had his bare foot to land on first.

The pot fell to the floor with a bang, crushing his toes, then rolling onto the linoleum. "Ow, Jesus," he yelled, grabbing his flattened foot and hopping on the other.

Her beautiful green eyes saucered as she realized what she'd done. With a strangled sound, she reached for him, but he leaped out of striking range and leaned back against the wall.

"Stay back. Please. Just stay away from me." His entire body throbbing, he added, "Jeez, lady, you ought to come with a warning label."

She threw her hand over her mouth in dismay, and bent over at the waist. Sounds like tiny sobs were bursting from her lips and her body trembled.

Great. Just great. Tears.

He quickly shoved away his instinctive reaction, realizing she'd had a hell of a night. Obviously she'd raced up here from Southern California to be with her injured grandfather. She'd been high on fear and adrenaline even before she'd thought she was about to be attacked by a shirtless stranger wielding a rake. Anyone would be a little overwrought.

Realizing she was really mortified, Oliver dropped his foot, praying there were no broken bones, and tried not to wince as he tested his weight on it. "It's okay... I'm all right. Accidents happen."

She straightened and peered at him, those green eyes assessing. But she didn't lower her hand, and her shoulders were now shaking as she made muffled sounds. Funny, her eyes weren't glossy, as if filled with tears. In fact, if he had to guess, he'd say they were almost twinkling instead.

A sneaking suspicion entered his mind. He reached out,

yanked her hand away from her mouth and realized the truth.

She wasn't crying. She was giggling almost uncontrollably.

2

"WAIT, YOU'RE *LAUGHING?*"

Oliver couldn't contain his indignation, not sure whether to retaliate by dropping a pan on her foot or shaking the laughter off her oh-so-kissable lips. She was damned lucky he was not the violent sort, because the shaking thing was definitely winning the internal battle in his mind.

She was also lucky he wasn't the ax-murdering-maniac sort because wringing her neck was a close second.

Then his gaze landed on those kissable lips, and he thought of something else he'd like to do with them. A few somethings, in fact.

She sucked them into her mouth, obviously trying to control herself. "I'm so sorry," she said, her laughter deepening and sounding a little frenzied. "That was just so… so Three Stooges!"

"You break my arm, smash a few ribs, crush my shoulder, pulverize my toes and you think it's hilarious?" His voice was tight with anger. Maybe tomorrow he'd look back and think the situation was funny, but right now he was too concerned about a punctured lung to join in the hilarity.

"I really am sorry," she murmured.

"Yeah, I can tell."

Her laughter fading to the occasional little snort, she explained. "I laugh when I'm stressed. It's awful, I know."

"Awfully strange, anyway," he snapped.

"It's just been such a long day. I was in the middle of a surreal moment even before I got the call about my grandfather. I have been so afraid for him." She swept a shaking hand through her hair, which looked like it had been swept through a lot recently. "The flight up here was a jam-packed nightmare. The kid beside me spent an hour flinging Cheerios and boogers at my head."

Eww.

"The cab ride to the house was an exercise in nausea. I needed a drink, but Grandpa appears to have hidden his stash the way he did when I was a kid. And to top it all off, you skulked into the kitchen, looking all big and bad and scared the shit out of me."

Okay. At some point in that litany of woes, between the boogers, the liquor and the big-n-bad, he got the picture.

She was hysterical.

He understood the reaction. He'd worked with witnesses whose terror had revealed itself via uncontrollable laughter and knew that deep inside, she was churning with anxiety. The laughter had held a tinge of frenzy, her fear and reaction to his presence had been a bit extreme, and now she looked like she was going to… "Oh, hell, please don't," he muttered.

But she did. She segued from snickers to sobs in the drawing of a breath. Before he could even take a second to remind himself how utterly useless he felt around crying women, he saw big fat tears roll from her eyes and drip down those soft cheeks.

"Is my grandfather okay?" *Sniff.* "And are you?" *Sniff sniff.* "Do I need to take you to the hospital? I can't believe I attacked you. Believe me, it was my first assault and battery."

She literally wrung her hands in front of her, clenching and gripping them, as if needing something to hold on to. He had to imagine she was running on empty emotionally and was imagining the worst.

He knew of only two ways to calm her down, to make her stop trying to maim him with kitchen utensils, snort herself to death laughing or sob until she had no tears left.

He started with option one. Reason.

"Buddy is going to be fine, I promise. His doctor said he'll need surgery and then rehab, but when I left the hospital he was high as a kite on pain meds and pinching the nurses."

Her lips twitched, and she managed to lift them a tiny bit at the corners.

"And I'll be fine, too." He eyed the kitchen sink and tried for humor, hoping to coax another laugh, or even a tiny snort out of her. "Just don't ever flash a pot at me or I'll go into post-traumatic shock and instinctively dive for the floor."

The lips curled a wee bit more. But he didn't get his hopes up yet.

"How did it happen? My mother didn't give me any details, just that he'd broken his hip."

He hesitated, before admitting, "He fell down the front steps off the porch."

Another sniff. "Such a short fall and so much damage."

"It happens," he said, knowing brittle bones could easily be broken. "But he's going to get a brand-new hip and come home better than ever. Before you know it, he'll be running marathons."

"Oh, great, then it'll be his other hip or his knees."

He wished he'd quit while he was ahead. She was obviously now picturing her grandfather's much-loved arms and skull being shattered. Sure enough, to prove it, the bottom lip began to stick out the tiniest bit and she welled up again. Those churning emotions just weren't going to let her go without a fight.

"C'mere," he said with a sigh, knowing he had to move on to option two.

Not giving her a warning or a chance to get away, he gently took hold of her shoulders and pulled her closer. She resisted for the briefest moment, as if unsure of his motives.

He reassured her, sighing deeply as he wondered what on earth he'd done to deserve this. Having to act like a wailing wall for a gorgeous woman who was totally off-limits, considering she was his employer's beloved grand-daughter, simply wasn't fair.

"Just let it out, darlin'. You've already maimed and in-jured me, so you might as well use my one good shoulder to cry on."

That elicited a sob that verged on a giggle and she gave in to the invitation. The tall, soft woman melted against him. Burying her face in his neck, she wrapped her arms around his waist, as if it was the most natural thing in the world that she should snuggle up against a half-naked stranger in her moment of need.

He stroked the small of her back, felt the wetness of her tears against his neck and murmured consoling words in her ear. She calmed—her slow shudders growing further apart as she took what he was offering. They swayed a little, as if dancing, and he mentally acknowledged that needing a shoulder to cry on wasn't just an expression. Sometimes that was just exactly the right solution to a problem. Not for nothing was he known as the best brother in the world to his two sisters.

Only this woman was not one of his sisters. Oh, no. She was a beautiful, vulnerable stranger, who, he soon realized, felt incredibly good in his arms. Soft and pliant, warm, all curves and skin and heat and sex appeal. He could feel her gentle exhalations against his bare skin, feel the faint brush of her lips on his nape and was slowly going crazy at the scrape of her nipples through her silky blouse against his chest. He had never been more aware of being shirtless in his life.

He stiffened. Some parts more than others.

He should never have let his mind wander from her mood. Because, while the embrace had started as a comforting offer to a stranger, now he was much too aware that he hadn't had sex in months and a woman shaped like a centerfold had curled up against him like a vine around a trellis.

Shifting back a little, he hoped like hell she wouldn't realize he was getting hard while she wept. But she didn't let him make a gentlemanly getaway. Instead she edged close again, pressing even harder against him. He could feel the warmth at the apex of her thighs, which, with her deliciously long legs, was lined up just perfectly with his groin.

She noticed. She had to notice. Because suddenly, she lifted her head and stared at him. Her soft face was tearstained, but her eyes were wide with shock, confusion and awareness.

Her lips trembled. She licked them, and he held his breath, wondering what on earth she was going to say. Was she about to snap at him and slap his face or issue an invitation? What?

In the end, his wild guesses didn't even come close. Instead, with a soft, regretful sigh, she drew away and whispered, "Why, oh, God, *why* did I not meet you in Paris?"

A SHORT TIME later, after Candace had asked the sexy stranger a dozen questions about her grandfather's condition, she finally allowed herself to think about something else. She now knew for sure that Buddy would be all right. She'd see him tomorrow, but for tonight, she could do nothing else.

Slowly, her fear and worry began to ease away and she let her thoughts drift in another direction. Enough so that, as she sat at the kitchen table and slowly sipped sweet, hot tea with the sexiest man she'd ever seen, she found time to wish two things: that she'd left the pots in the sink, and that she'd never even thought about him in connection with her canceled trip to France.

If she hadn't seen him, reacted like a high school virgin defending her hymen from a horny football team and attacked him to the point of bloodshed, she wouldn't have gotten all giggly, weepy and hysterical. If she hadn't gotten giggly, weepy and hysterical, he wouldn't have taken her into his big strong arms. If he hadn't taken her into his big strong arms, he wouldn't have drawn her against that rock-hard, rippling, sweat-tinged, powerful male body. If he hadn't drawn her against his body, she might not have felt the rigid proof of his virility pressing deliciously against her sex.

And if he hadn't gotten hard, she wouldn't be sitting here vacillating between worrying about her grandfather and wondering when this hot stranger would wake up and smell the estrogen, and realize she was sitting in damp panties.

She shifted in the hard chair. *Seriously damp.*

Of course, fair was fair. He'd been seriously hard.

Yum.

No. Not yum. You can't have him.

Sighing, she inhaled the fragrant tea and murmured, "If you give a mouse a cookie…"

"I don't think your grandfather has any milk," he replied, hearing her. "He's lactose intolerant."

She had to smile that this strong, rugged-looking man understood the reference to a popular children's book. Especially since his voice was all deep and gravelly, sultry and alluring, and completely inappropriate for uttering rhymes to a little kid.

Uttering sexy, needful growls to an adult woman would be much more up his alley.

"I have a niece. She's four," he explained with a shrug. "You?"

Are you asking if I'm single?

She curled her left hand around the cup. The bare left hand. The left hand that was not yet weighed down with the five-carat diamond she suspected Tommy would put on it the minute she got back to L.A.

Remembering Tommy, and everything that ring would entail, she gave a guilty start and dropped her hand into her lap, reaching for the cup with her right one.

"Younger cousins," she finally replied.

There was no point in letting this man know she was single. No possible reason to want him to realize she had gotten all gooey inside the moment he'd pulled her into his arms to offer her some warmth and human comfort. And it would be pure insanity to hope he'd figure out that the goo had boiled into lava once she'd felt the volcanic rock in his pants.

She didn't allow herself to feel terribly flattered. Any bare-chested, slick, hard, virile—*stop with the adjectives*—man would probably stir at the feel of a woman pressing herself against him like she wanted to climb into his skin. That's what she had done, she realized with embarrassment. She might as well have asked him if he could pretty-please comfort her on top of the hard, broad table, or up against the refrigerator. And wouldn't it be nice if the comforting didn't include clothes?

You're engaged, remember?

Right. Engaged. Which meant the Candace Volcano was going to be all Mt. St. Helens from here on out—i.e., dormant. There might be rumbles, but there would be no eruptions for a hell of a long time. Five years, at least. *Oy.*

She would be staying here to help her grandfather for as long as he needed her, which meant there would be no time for a trip to Paris. No chance for a wild fling. Tommy wouldn't want to wait too long to announce their engagement, and she couldn't blame him. She'd have no time to sow any wild oats and bank some sexy memories. But she couldn't truly be upset about it. She adored Grandpa and would do anything for him. Including missing out on her one-and-only chance to be a sex tourist.

So go for the gardener.

She flicked the thought out of her head, not for the first time. That wasn't going to happen. A spring fling in Paris had sounded ideal, but there was no way she was hooking up with someone who worked for her grandfather. She'd wanted someone from out of the country, preferably a stud who didn't speak English. Gorgeous, hung, with a penchant for oral sex and dumb as a rock would have suited her just fine.

This man—as far as she knew right now—had only two of those qualities. He was gorgeous. And oh, had he felt hung.

As for the rest? Well, that mouth looked like it could give a woman incredible pleasure. But he certainly didn't appear dumb. He spoke the language. And, worst of all, lived in her own state. Once she became fodder for the paparazzi, they could easily track him down. They would be very interested to hear that Tommy Shane's beloved fiancée had been having a wild, outrageously sexual affair with a man right before she'd said, "I will."

Mmm. Wild. Outrageously sexual. Oh, did she suspect it would be.

Just her luck that she'd met a man who appealed to her on such a deep, powerful level on the very night she'd agreed to give up sex for five years and marry her best friend.

"Warming up a little?" he asked.

She had been, sip by sip. Grandfather's house was old, damp and chilly, and she hoped her suitcase got here soon with her warmer clothes. "Yes, thanks."

"The nights'll get warmer soon," he said. "Or so I've been told."

"You're not from around here?"

"No." He hesitated, then added, "I moved up from L.A. a few months ago."

Ahh! The plot thickened. Had he been some kind of gardener to the Hollywood elite? She suspected any number of starlets would have been happy to have him trim their hedges and do some deep planting in their gardens.

"Why?"

"It was just time," he explained, his expression and tone telling her that was all he was going to say.

Talk about cryptic.

The silence between them resumed, though it wasn't an uncomfortable one. They both merely sipped their tea, as they had been for the past few minutes. Oliver—that was his name, Oliver, and what a strong, solid, sexy, old-fashioned name it was—had gently pushed her into a chair and insisted on making her some tea. He obviously did know her grandfather well. A cup of Earl Grey was Buddy Frye's solution to soothe all the ills of the world. Tea had cured Candace's scraped knees and hurt feelings, broken hearts and hangovers. And now, it had made her finally relax and brought her tension down a few notches.

She wondered if Oliver had adopted the habit from his employer, of if he was a similar type of man—a calm, deliberate man who always seemed to know how to offer comfort in exactly the right way at the right moment. Whatever the reason, like the hug that had gone from sweet to smokin', it was a nice gesture, one she appreciated.

Of course, she would appreciate it more if the man would put a damn shirt on so she wouldn't have to keep shoving her eyeballs back in their sockets every time he moved.

Deltoids and pectorals and biceps, oh, my!

The last thing she had expected to find when she'd let herself into her grandfather's house, which she'd only ever visited once before, was a hunk of masculine sex appeal showing up in the kitchen. Her mother had, indeed, mentioned a groundskeeper when she'd called earlier today. But she hadn't said anything about a groundskeeper with nearly jet-black hair, thick and wavy and hanging a little long around his stubbled, two-days-past-needing-a-shave jaw. Nothing could have prepared Candace for the dark dreamy eyes, the strong brow, the slashing cheekbones or the powerful body. Absolutely nothing.

She'd met a lot of handsome men in Hollywood. Probably some who were more handsome than Oliver—Tommy among them. But in terms of raw, masculine sex appeal, she'd seen nobody better.

"Better?"

"Not a single one," she mumbled.

"What?"

Realizing she'd spoken aloud, she quickly backtracked. "Sorry, I mean, I am better. Much. Just tired, that's all."

"So, you said you came up from L.A.?"

"Yes. I headed for the airport right after I got my mother's call. I figured I should come and see how Grandpa was doing myself. I'm really hoping I can handle things so Mom won't have to fly out here."

His brow shot up. Knowing he'd been on the receiving

end of her mother's telephone panic, he had to be wondering about that.

"My father had a heart attack two months ago," she explained. "He needs Mom there with him in Florida. So if I can be here for Buddy and set my mom's mind at ease about my grandfather, that's what I'll do."

He frowned, encircling his teacup in his hand. "Buddy might be in rehab for weeks."

Weeks. Well, that wasn't great, but it was doable. She was an independent contractor and was in between movie projects right now. She'd been asked to submit some preliminary sketches for a depression-era drama that could be a major motion picture in a few years, but that was still in the early stages. She didn't have the assignment yet, and she could work on the prelims here. Besides, Leo DiCaprio, who was supposed to be starring in the film, was the easiest guy in Hollywood to dress. The only thing that might call her back to Southern California earlier would be her famous—infamous?—engagement.

"I'll work something out," she mumbled, wondering how long Tommy would be willing to hold off. She wouldn't want to announce anything while she was taking care of her grandfather. The last thing the elderly man would need once he got home was reporters and photographers knocking at the door. "I don't have to be in L.A. right away."

"What do you do?"

Oh, I'm in the movie business. Costume design. Did you see the last Cameron film? That was me.

That was the standard reply, often said with a slightly superior tone, just because that's how everybody in L.A. rolled. But she just didn't feel like playing that game. Not here, in the middle of the night, with a stranger. Not after the day she'd had. "I'm involved with fashion design."

His eyes didn't immediately glaze, the way most men's

would. "My sisters would probably love to meet you. I think they were each born holding a copy of *Vogue*."

She ran the tip of her finger across the rim of her cup. "Not that kind of fashion. I work for some of the production companies doing costuming."

He grunted. "Movies, huh?"

Her back stiffened as he reacted just as she'd expected him to. Most people were awed by her connection to Tinseltown. This one, this earthy, swaggering man, just didn't seem the type. He looked like he could live out some macho, shoot-em-up action film rather than having to sit through one. Of course, what such a man was doing working as a groundskeeper, she had no idea.

"What's wrong with the movies?"

He shrugged.

"You don't like films?"

"Sure I do. I just don't have much respect for the people who make them."

The vision of him being at the beck and call of some spoiled, rich-bitch movie star popped into her head. She had a hard time envisioning this man taking orders from anyone and wondered if he'd gotten tired of being propositioned by his clients. "Interact with a lot of Hollywood types, do you?"

He eyed her then shifted his gaze away, muttering a cryptic, "Not anymore."

Meaning, he had once upon a time?

Something suddenly occurred to her, which could explain why he seemed like such a fish out of water. "Wait. Tell me you're not a method actor up here in the wilds of Northern California getting ready to audition for some back-to-nature film," she said, horrified at the very idea.

He barked a harsh laugh. "Not likely." His lips twitching as he lifted his glass, he added, "What about you? Did you come out here all starry-eyed, looking for your big break, and end up shifting gears into costuming when the acting thing didn't work out?"

"I couldn't act my way out of a speeding ticket if my car was on fire and the cop who pulled me over was my uncle."

His brow scrunched. "Why would you drive a burning car?"

"I…what?"

"If the car's on fire, why would you keep driving it? Why wouldn't you pull over and get out?"

"Are you always so literal?"

"Do you really have an uncle who's a cop?"

She growled, low in her throat. Seeing the twinkle in his eye made the growl louder, so she continued the game of Answer a Question with a Question with a question. "Do you always bait strange women?"

"Only women who specialize in death-by-kitchenware." His tone was deadpan. "And those I make tea for in the middle of the night."

The faintest hint of his smile made her spine relax a bit. He might not look like he had much of a sense of humor, and his gruff voice sure didn't sound like it was used much for laughing, but she suspected there lurked a good-humored man beneath the superhot, strong-and-silent exterior.

She lifted her cup. "Speaking of which, you make a very good cup of tea. It was just what I needed. Thanks again."

"Tea was a staple in our house. It's one thing I have in common with your grandfather—he does like his cuppa."

"So he does."

The way he said cuppa warmed her up inside. She did love an Irish accent, and while his was buried under a couple of decades of blunt Americanism, she still heard the lilt every now and again.

Another sip. The tea was cooling now, her cup nearly drained, and she knew it had to be close to 4:00 a.m. By all rights, she should be tucked in bed in one of the drafty upstairs guest rooms. But something made her stay. She just didn't want to be alone in this big house. Especially because she still couldn't quite reconcile it as being Grandpa's. He'd lived in a condo in St. Petersburg when she'd been growing up, for crying out loud, about as far from this wild, untamed landscape as one could get.

"What's he doing here, anyway?" she grumbled.

"Who, Buddy?"

"Yes. What on earth possessed him to come out here and buy this place?"

"He's living the dream, from the sound of it. He told me he's always loved wine."

"I don't ever remember him drinking anything but Riunite Lombrusco when I was a kid," she retorted.

"I think his tastes have matured a bit."

"Are there even any grapes growing around here?"

"Not yet. That's my department."

"When's that going to happen?"

"It's a long way off. Probably next summer."

"Seriously? You aren't even going to plant for a year?"

His shrug was decidedly rueful. "It takes time to prepare the soil, especially since it's been ignored for so long."

"Have you worked at a winery before? Are grapes your specialty?"

"Not exactly."

"So what did you do before you came here?"

He had tensed during her questioning, and she figured she was being pushy. But asking him about his past was better than asking him how on earth he managed to find shirts that fit over all those muscles.

"Let's just say I've been digging in the dirt a lot in recent years. This job makes me feel a whole lot cleaner."

That was mysterious, but his clipped tone said it was as much as she was going to get.

"Now, your grandfather's surgery is scheduled for 10:00 a.m. Why don't you grab a few hours' sleep and we'll try to get to the hospital at around eight?"

"All right."

Rising, she picked up her cup, and his, carrying them over to the sink. She noted that, while brewing the tea, Oliver had stuck the pots and pans in the dishwasher, as if to get them out of throwing range. Candace still couldn't believe she'd thought a few kitchen items would stop him if he'd really been some kind of villain. With that body—those strong arms and the table-wide chest—he could pick her up and break her in half.

Or, a wicked part of her realized, just *split* her in half with that amazing power tool in his pants. Not having had sex in a while, she couldn't be entirely sure her memory wasn't faulty, but if she had to guess, she'd say that had been a good eight inches of jackhammer straining against his zipper.

"Need a hand?"

She started, not having realized he'd left the table and walked up behind her. It was bad enough to be caught thinking he had an amazing body, but even worse to be standing here wondering about the size of the man's johnson.

"No, thank you," she said, hearing the breathiness in her voice. He was just so close, so big and warm. All she could think about was how it had felt to be pressed against him, his hands on her hips, his salt-tinged skin against her mouth.

It had been a long time since she'd been close to anyone. Honestly, the thought of not being held in a man's strong arms for five years was almost as upsetting to her as knowing she would not be filled and possessed by one in the most raw, sexual way.

Almost.

"Okay, meet you outside at seven-thirty?"

She nodded, turning to face him, hoping her cheeks weren't pink. She was not the blushing type. Still, she feared the heat in her face hadn't been caused by the steam rising off the hot water in the sink.

"Thank you. And again, I'm sorry I attacked you."

He shrugged. "Wasn't the first time."

She quirked a brow. "Incite a lot of women to violence, do you?"

"Not recently."

But he didn't say anything else. He merely nodded good-night and left the kitchen, leaving her wondering what the real story was behind Oliver McKean.

3

CANDACE REID WAS as good as her word. Despite having probably only gotten the same few hours of sleep he had the night before, she was waiting on her grandfather's front steps when he walked out of his cottage at 7:30 a.m.

She looked like crap.

Bloodshot eyes, pale cheeks sans makeup, sopping wet hair slung up in a ponytail—definitely not the Candace he'd met at 3:00 a.m. She wore a shapeless, heavy hoodie that would be much too warm in a few hours when the day shifted into typical Northern California mode, with its wildly swinging night-to-day temperature changes. The jeans weren't designer; in fact, they looked worn and scruffy. And the functional sneakers in no way resembled the spike-heeled do-me shoes of the night before.

He knew he wasn't seeing her at her sexy best, but couldn't help thinking he liked this not-so-put-together version of the Hollywood costume designer. In her real life, with all the feminine trappings women relied on, she probably would have blended into the stylish crowd to which he had become so accustomed when living in L.A. Hell, he'd even been a part of it on occasion. But here, out of her element, obviously uncomfortable and not making any pretentious efforts to impress anyone—including him—he found her vulnerability refreshing.

Huh. Part of him should be a little disappointed that she wasn't making any effort to impress him, considering how thick the sexual tension between them had been the night before. It had filled that kitchen like an invisible fog. He'd definitely thought about her long after he'd gone back to his bed.

But he hadn't come to Sonoma to get caught up with a woman. He'd chosen this area because it was his favorite place to vacation—he loved the scenery, the pace and the people. He'd needed to reevaluate, to recover a sense of peace and tranquility that had been lost during his years running in the rat race with some huge rats. This period of solitude was about regrouping, finding his focus and doing penance for the shitty things he'd done to get ahead in the Orange County D.A.'s office.

Taking a sabbatical from the spotlight hadn't been a bad side benefit, either. The press had had a field day with him when he'd blown the lid off some of the shenanigans taking place in the courthouse. Rising young stars in the prosecutor's office weren't supposed to refuse to railroad an innocent man in order to close a big case, and they definitely weren't supposed to blow the whistle on the misconduct of others. Oh, yeah, he had definitely been front-page fodder, which made him persona non grata with the legal types in L.A., and would for quite some time. Frankly, that was fine with him. He wanted to forget about that period of his life, and wanted everyone there to forget about him.

So, no, having a hot affair just didn't fit in with his plan of atonement. It was just as well Candace had dialed her sex appeal down a notch, even if nothing could really eradicate the beauty of her face or the curviness of her body.

If her appearance today was meant to send him a message, he'd gotten it. Loud and clear. She wasn't interested.

"You sleep okay?" he asked as he walked over, already knowing the answer to his question.

"Sleep? What's that? I feel like the princess from the fairy tale, only there wasn't a pea under the mattress, there were cantaloupes the size of my head."

"I don't think your grandfather has had a chance to re-decorate. A lot of the furniture came with the house, so it's probably pretty old."

"Who owned it before? Fred Flintstone?"

He couldn't contain a chuckle. "The house was built by an old silent movie star, and it remained in his family for several decades until it fell into ruin. He supposedly threw some wild parties with his Hollywood buddies."

"Huh…my kingdom for a Westin heavenly bed. I'd rather be comfortable than sleep on the mattress that once held Charlie Chaplin." She winced and rubbed her shoulder. "And still might, given the bony lumps inside it."

The old Oliver, the one who'd once been young and carefree and had done killer impressions that cracked up his sisters, might have tottered side to side and swung an invisible cane.

The new Oliver—hardened by the things he'd seen, the things he'd *done*—barely even remembered that ide-alistic guy.

"Ready?"

"Sure."

She stepped into the passenger seat of the beat-up old truck as he got in behind the wheel and together, they headed toward the hospital. He could feel her tension and her anticipation. She sat forward on her seat, as if urging the old bucket of rust to go faster.

"Would you sit still?" he grumbled. "Visiting hours don't even start until eight."

"If we keep going negative-two miles an hour, we won't be there until it's time for Grandpa to go in for his surgery."

"If we were going negative-two miles an hour, we'd be going backward."

She smirked. "Now you're just being silly."

Unaccustomed to being called anything of the sort, he tightened his hands on the steering wheel.

"So how did you end up working for my grandfather?"

His grip grew even tighter. "I was just wandering. We ran into each other and he told me he was looking for help to get the old place up and running. Lucky for me, I had some time and experience."

His experience with grounds keeping had been limited to his lawn-cutting business during high school. But that had been enough for Buddy, who, he suspected, had hired him because he wanted the company as much as Oliver's strong back. And it had helped that Oliver was connected to the estate. He also suspected Buddy had sensed Oliver *needed* to be there, to work hard, not think and stay away from most of the world.

The old man had asked him if he was a criminal hiding out from the law. When Oliver had sworn he was not, they'd shaken hands and that had been that. Four months later, after studying everything he could find on the wine business, Oliver had calluses on his blisters, muscles in places he'd never known he'd needed them and the beginnings of a clear head.

"Sorry, but you just don't look much like a gardener," she said, obviously realizing he was prevaricating.

He cast her a sideways glance and let a faint smile lift the corner of his mouth. "You don't look much like a fashion designer, either."

Instead of taking offense, she barked a laugh and lifted a hand to her sopping ponytail. "Touché. I know I'm a mess. Aside from the horrible bed, a cricket kept chirping somewhere inside the house. And the water in the shower ranged from cold to frigid."

"Devastating," he murmured.

She continued, "There's not a hair dryer in sight, because, of course, Grandpa doesn't need one. I almost stuck my head over the stove but figured that might be pushing it."

"Knowing how dangerous things tend to happen when you're in a kitchen, that was probably a good call. And we don't want to tax rescue services with a call about a fire. They were already out here once this week."

"Did I mention that the airline misplaced my big suitcase? I only had my carry-on, which is why I'm wearing the old clothes that my sister left here when she came to visit a year ago."

Judging by the clothes, the sister was a different type of dresser altogether.

"We can run by a store later if you need to shop," he said.

"If the airline doesn't show up with my things within a couple of days, I might have to take you up on that. I had the basic necessities in my carry-on, but I'll be out of stuff pretty soon."

"Are you really going to stick around for a while?" he asked, wondering if she truly intended to stay for weeks. Man, he hoped not. He was supposed to be enjoying a retreat from the real world. But this talkative, beautiful woman had brought it crashing in on him like the winds of a hurricane.

"Maybe. I'm between projects and was supposed to be going out of town for a couple of weeks anyway," she said, crossing her arms and leaning against her window to look out at the passing scenery. "This isn't exactly France, though."

"You were going to France?"

She nodded but didn't look over.

"Why would it have been better if you'd met me there?"

She jerked and swung around to stare at him. "What?"

"You said that last night."

She bit that succulent bottom lip.

He prodded her. "Your exact words were, I believe, 'Why, oh, God, why, didn't I meet you in Paris?'"

She huffed. "Jeez, what are you, a transcriptionist?"

"I have a very good memory."

"Obviously."

"So?"

"So what?"

She was obviously trying to deflect, and he considered letting her get away with it. But something about that sad face and those slumped shoulders made him want to rile her up a little. He'd been raised with sisters, so he knew that nothing worked better to get them out of a sad slump than giving them something to be mad about.

"So, why would it have been better if you'd met me in Paris?"

"I was hysterical. I didn't know what I was saying."

"Not that hysterical. As I recall, you were pretty damned calm at that point. Sedate even."

Her eyes narrowed. "Shall we talk about how *you* were at that point?"

Hell, if she thought he was going to apologize for getting a hard-on when he'd had a gorgeous woman in his arms, she had another think coming. "I have a Y chromosome. And you're beautiful."

Her bluff having been called, she looked away.

"Paris," he reminded her.

Crossing her arms over her chest and harrumphing, she said, "I just meant if I was going to end up in some hot guy's arms this week, it should have been in the city of light, not in my grandfather's kitchen."

He made a mental note of the *hot,* wondering if she

even realized she'd just revealed a little more about her thoughts of last night.

Casting him an arch look, she added, "By the way, it could have been any guy's arms."

"Hot."

"What?"

"You said any *hot* guy's arms."

"It's like I'm riding with a digital voice recorder."

"Like I said. Good memory."

"The point is, I was just speaking in *general* terms about how a run-down old kitchen can't compare to the most romantic city in the world. That's *all*."

He wasn't buying it. "Didn't sound that way."

"Would you stop interrogating me?"

There was fire in her eyes now, and color in her cheeks. Indignation wafted from her, and he congratulated himself on getting her mind off her troubles. Let her be annoyed at him, and engage in a little verbal sparring. At least it would be a few minutes less she spent worrying about her obviously deeply loved grandfather.

"Why were you going to France?"

"Did you miss the part about not interrogating me?"

"It's just a simple question."

"One that's really none of your business."

"So, not for work, then."

She just huffed.

He speculated aloud. "If there was a possibility you'd end up in some random guy's arms, you obviously weren't meeting up with a boyfriend."

"Did you also miss the part where I said it was about kitchen vs. Paris and *not* about a stupid man?"

"Your boyfriend's stupid?"

"Argh!"

Defense attorneys hadn't called him the Honey Badger

of Hollywood for no reason. Oliver had been born with a persistent gene. "Was that an answer?"

"I *don't* have a stupid boyfriend."

"Well he can't be very smart if he lets you come alone up to Sonoma to be stalked by a potential ax-murdering maniac in your grandfather's kitchen."

"There's no boyfriend, okay? Stupid or otherwise!"

He'd known that's what she was saying but was glad for the confirmation, anyway. He couldn't say why that certainty sent a hint of relief gushing through his veins, but it did. "Well, that's good. I'm afraid I'd lose a little respect for you if you liked stupid guys."

"Right now, they're sounding very appealing," she mumbled.

"Low standards, huh?"

"No, I just wouldn't have to be couching every word I say so it couldn't be used against me in a court of law."

That was striking a little close to home. "Because a stupid guy would understand you better?"

"No, because I wouldn't give a damn if he didn't!"

"You calling me smart, and saying you give a damn?" He wondered if she could see his half smirk. "Gee, hot and smart in one conversation. Better watch it, Miss Reid, or you'll make my head swell."

"Shut up, all right? Just. Stop. Talking."

He finally started to laugh. The sound felt a little rusty; he didn't make it very often anymore. And after a few seconds, she slowly joined in.

"You did that on purpose."

"Maybe."

"Women must threaten your life on a regular basis."

"I guess."

They were silent for a moment, then she sighed softly and said, "Thank you."

She didn't have to elaborate. He knew what she meant. So he merely replied, "You're welcome."

A few minutes later, they arrived at the hospital. Seeing it ratcheted up her tension again, and she was yanking the handle and hopping out of the truck the second he parked. He caught up with her at the hospital entrance and escorted her to Buddy's room.

After a soft knock, they entered to find the old man dozing. He was still hooked up to machines and a morphine drip and probably looked pretty bad to his granddaughter. But compared to how he'd looked after he'd fallen yesterday, this was quite an improvement. Oliver wasn't sure he'd ever get over the terror he'd felt when he'd heard the loud cry of pain and he'd run around the house to see Buddy lying on the ground, looking like a fragile, broken porcelain doll.

"Grandpa?"

The eyes shot open and the old man turned to stare at her, his blue eyes shining with vitality and affection. "Candy-cane, what are you doing here?" He cast a glance at Oliver. "I told you not to worry anybody."

"Don't be silly," she said, bending to kiss his forehead. She tenderly brushed away a long strand of silvery hair—used in the ultimate old-man comb-over to cover the sizable bald spot on his pate. "Mom was going to come herself…"

"Ridiculous! She needs to stay in Florida and take care of your stodgy old fart of a father."

Seeing the smile on Candace's face, and the matching one on Buddy's, Oliver could only think theirs was a close-knit family and the joke was an old one. Buddy had to be at least eighty, but he was usually as peppy and energetic as a much-younger man.

"Well, that's why I came, to scope out the situation and see if she needed to visit."

"She doesn't!"

"You certainly seem peppy."

"I'm feeling no pain," he admitted. "You really don't have to stay."

"Of course I'm staying. I'll be here when you get out of surgery, and I'll be at your house waiting for you when you come home."

He didn't argue anymore, looking visibly touched and showing just the faintest hint of vulnerability. Buddy might not want to be a bother, but when it came to being in the hospital, nothing beat having family nearby. The old man hadn't said anything about being nervous about his operation, but considering he hadn't been expecting any such thing twenty-four hours ago, he had to be worried about it.

"I think I'll give you two some time alone," Oliver said. "Buddy, I just wanted to say I'm here and hope everything goes well with the surgery. I have no doubt you'll be kicking up clods of dirt and rocks in no time."

His boss nodded. "Thank you for bringing my grandbaby to see me."

"Not a problem."

"You'll make sure she's okay out there at the house? It's awfully lonely and desolate for a helpless young girl on her own."

He saw Candace roll her eyes at the description. "I'll be fine," she insisted. "I certainly don't need a babysitter."

"Humor an old man. Promise me you'll let Oliver look after you."

She glanced back and forth between them, her mouth opening and snapping closed. Obviously she didn't want to promise any such thing. However, she didn't want to upset her elderly relative, either. Finally, she hedged. "If I need anything, I'll be sure to ask him."

That could range from needing a roll of toilet paper to

needing a spider killed. What it wasn't was an agreement to let him watch over her.

"Promise?"

She obviously didn't like being pressed, and mumbled, "If there's a dire emergency, Oliver is the first one I'll call."

Buddy didn't appear thrilled by the concession, but apparently knew he'd pushed hard enough. "All right." Then he extended his hand. "Thank you again, Oliver."

Oliver walked over for a handshake, but when he tried to end it, the old man didn't let go. Instead, Buddy clutched his hand, while also holding his granddaughter's.

"So, you two are getting along okay?"

If Cupid had ever suffered from a broken hip, he'd probably have taken a day off. Not so for Buddy Frye.

"Grandpa," she said warningly.

"She's already tried to kill me," Oliver said, caught off guard.

Buddy snickered. Obviously the pain meds were still in fine working order. Eyeing Candace, he said, "Did I ever tell you about what your grandma did to me once, back when we were dating? She shoved me in front of a moving car."

"No, you didn't tell me, and I don't believe it," she replied a little primly. Then she gave Oliver a look that said, *Don't you dare make fun of me about this.*

"Yep. She said I was smiling too much at a waitress, so she pushed me into the street. My, that woman loved me."

"She had a funny way of showing it," Oliver couldn't help mumbling. "Imagine if you'd ever really flirted with someone. You'd have been nose-to-nose with a freight train."

Candace obviously heard and her lips quirked.

"I just want you two to get along," Buddy said, settling deeper into his bed and arranging his covers over himself.

He wasn't looking at either of them. "I think you probably have a lot in common."

"I doubt it," Candace said, her tone saying the subject was at an end.

Oliver didn't back her up, or offer her a reassuring glance. He couldn't deny he found the idea of her grandfather playing matchmaker pretty cute, even if the very idea that she'd need him to was ridiculous. The woman was smart, beautiful, funny…she wouldn't need an elderly relative fixing her up. He suspected she could have just about any man she wanted.

She wants a stupid, foreign one, he reminded himself. *Not you.*

Which was just as well. He'd already decided he was not getting personally involved with Candace Reid. So the less time he spent in her company, the better.

She could take care of herself, of that he had no doubt. He would remember Buddy's request and help her in the case of a major emergency, like if the pipes burst or a robber turned up. But as far as spiders and toilet paper went, she was on her own, and he was steering clear.

It was better that way…for both of them.

4

It was the size of a Volkswagen.

Big, hairy, with a million eyes and fuzzy spiked legs and probably a sac full of poison hidden on its bulbous body.

Spiders. God, she hated spiders. Especially spiders who were blocking the only exit from the kitchen, where she stood, wearing a filmy, short little bathrobe, freezing her butt off because she'd come down to put coffee on right after she'd gotten out of the cold-as-ice shower.

"Go away," she ordered in a quivery voice.

The spider ignored her and remained planted right in her path. Beady little pinpoint eyes stared up at her, red and angry—or maybe not, but they looked that way to her—and she knew if he had a mouth, it was smirking.

She edged backward toward the stove, thankful she'd glanced down before walking out of the kitchen, because if she'd placed her bare foot on that furry little beast, she would have screamed loud enough for Tommy to hear her back in L.A. Besides, the little creature looked big enough to have flung her off rather than being smashed flat.

Candace wasn't scared by much. Snakes didn't bother her; she had been skydiving so she wasn't afraid of heights. She'd even bungee jumped off a bridge in Mexico once.

She'd stared down more than her fair share of grubby dudes with cheesy come-on lines on the street.

But bugs? Spiders in particular?

The little bastards terrified her.

"Candace?" a voice called. A voice that was familiar, even though she hadn't talked to him much in the past few days.

She and Oliver, as if by unspoken agreement, had spent little time together since the morning her grandfather had tried to fix them up. When they'd left late that day, after visiting with Grandpa in the recovery room, Oliver had brought her to a car rental place so she could get her own vehicle. She didn't want to have to rely on him to run her back and forth to the hospital, which was where she spent most of her time. They ran into each other there on occasion, had grabbed coffee or a quick lunch and engaged in a little small talk. But as if they both realized they probably shouldn't spend too much time together out at the house, where they were entirely alone, they'd avoided interaction. They exchanged mostly waves as they were coming or going, or when he was working out on the grounds, and she was watching him while pretending she wasn't at all interested.

Any woman would be interested. It was bad enough seeing him inside at the hospital, clothed and respectable. When he worked, when he stripped off his shirt to wipe his sweaty, dirty face, and those muscles rippled and gleamed, he was male beauty in motion. The few times they had talked at home, she'd done everything she could to keep from revealing how incredibly attracted she was to him. Sometimes, though, she caught him staring at her, and suspected she wasn't doing a very good job.

She only wished he would do something to reveal whether or not he felt the same way. So far, he hadn't. He'd been cordial and polite, never more than that, as if she'd suddenly become his employer now that Grandpa was out of commission.

Got a task for you there, Mr. Groundskeeper. How about doing a little plowing for me?

She scrunched her eyes shut, muttering, "Not French, not stupid, off-limits."

"Candace? Are you here?"

"In the kitchen," she said, not sure whether she was hoping he would turn right back around and leave, or that he'd stride in and accidentally squish Mr. Spider so she wouldn't have to (A) deal with the arachnid herself, or (B) technically ask for Oliver's help.

"I just wanted to let you know your suitcase has finally made it. The delivery service just left it on the porch. I signed for it."

Oh, thank goodness. She'd been fighting with the airline about it all week, fearing she would have to put in a claim to replace everything she'd packed for the trip. She'd run out of her sister Madison's left-behind clothes and had had to wash and rewash the few items she'd had in her small carry-on bag. Especially the panties. Hmm. Funny how she'd gone through panties at a record rate since she'd met Oliver. That man ought to buy stock in Victoria's Secret.

"I'll bring it in. Do you want me to haul it up to your room?"

She nibbled her lip, wanting no such thing. Oliver in her bedroom, near her messed bed with the silky nightie tossed carelessly on top? Him filling her private space with that delectable, intoxicating man smell?

Hell, no. She was already having the most intense, erotic dreams about the guy without ever having to picture him near her bed. No way was she going to invite even hotter ones.

"No, it's okay. You can just leave it in the hall."

She waited to hear him bring in the bag and leave.

Waited for an acknowledgment—something. But there was nothing but silence. Frowning, she risked edging a tiny bit closer to the doorway, never taking her eyes off her fuzzy enemy, who showed no signs of moving out of the way. She briefly considered jumping over him, but had the most horrible vision of him launching up while she was split-legged above him. For all she knew, he could be the bug world-record holder at the high jump. Considering she wore nothing but the short robe, she wasn't prepared to even think about where he might land if he leaped. Her vajayjay might have grown cobwebs from disuse, but that was taking things a step too far.

She desperately wanted to go out and make sure Oliver was gone, then dash up the stairs and put some clothes on before he could come back, but it looked like she was going to be involved in a spider standoff for hours. Thinking, she finally grabbed the broom and tried waving it in his general direction. But it wasn't until she got the bristles to within six inches or so that the thing began to move.

Straight toward her.

"No—get away from me!"

A hard pounding emerged from the hallway. She recognized it as running footsteps just as Oliver burst into the kitchen. He didn't hold a rake this time, but the look on his face said he expected trouble.

"What is it?" he snapped as he scanned the room. "What's wrong?"

"Uh, nothing," she said, forcing a smile. Though, when she saw where he stood, she didn't have to force it any further. Because unless the creepy crawly had moved really fast, he was right now stuck to the bottom of a man's thick-soled work boot. Although she loved most creatures, she wasn't about to start playing a dirge for that one, who'd looked like a mad scientist's experimental cross between a bug and a dinosaur.

"Who were you talking to?"

"Nobody. I thought you'd left."

"I was bringing in your suitcase," he explained, walking closer, studying her face to see if she was lying, perhaps covering for a bad guy hiding in the pantry. He obviously wasn't going to go away without an explanation.

Knowing she had to, she admitted in a voice a little above a whisper, "There was a spider."

His frown disappeared. A twinkle might have appeared in those dark bedroom eyes, but he had the courtesy not to smile. "One that speaks English and follows orders?"

"Ha-ha, very funny. That thing was *huge*. I mean, it could have been wearing a mask, swinging from webs and looking for the Green Goblin!"

"Comic book fan, huh?"

"Movie biz, remember?"

And considering Tommy was hoping to be cast as the latest comic hero, he'd made her watch a bunch of them recently. She wasn't a huge fan of the genre, but had to admit, some of those guys did an awesome job filling out their clingy costumes. She'd become a huge Jeremy Renner fan in the past year and fantasized about getting to dress him. Undressing him would be a mighty fine experience, too.

"So where is this huge mutant creature?"

"Gone."

"Where'd he go?"

"I think onto the bottom of your shoe."

"You sure? I didn't hear anything that sounded like the crushing of a colossus."

"Well, he's not…" Her voice trailed off and her eyes rounded as she saw a black leg disappearing behind the table leg. She squeaked, grabbed his arm and ducked behind him. "Oh, God."

"What?"

Keeping her voice low, as if they were facing a ravaging tiger, she replied, "He's right over there."

He followed her gaze and snorted. "That's your monster spider? He's tiny."

"That thing's as big as my hand!" Closing her eyes, she begged, "Please take it away, Oliver. I'll pay you.... I'll bake you a cake, cook you dinner. Just *please* get it out of here."

"Are you a good cook?"

"The best. Excellent. Cordon Bleu. Restaurants vie for my services."

"Are you lying?"

"Oh, hell, yes. Right through my teeth. Now would you please help me?"

"I thought you didn't need any help except in the most dire emergency."

"This is dire."

"Are you an arachnophobe?"

"If that means I am utterly terrified to my bones and feel like I'm going to throw up if I so much as glimpse a spider, then yes, that's me."

"Gotcha."

He didn't tease her anymore, as if knowing she wasn't playing the weak girlie-girl in some effort to entice him. Not, she hoped, that he would ever expect her to. Turning, he grabbed the dustpan, then unhooked her death grip from the broom. Drawing on his primal, caveman-hunter genes, he stalked the monster, deftly swept it into the pan and carried it toward the front door.

"Are you just going to let it go?" she asked, following him. "What if it gets back in?"

"I'm sure he'd be too afraid to risk it. You're pretty intimidating."

"Are you sure you shouldn't squish it?"

"Bloodthirsty, aren't you?"

She thought about it. She wasn't, really. Still, some things were just beyond the bounds of humanity, and sharing a house with a big honking spider was one of them.

"You'll be glad for him during mosquito season."

"Maybe if they're killer mosquitoes carrying the ebola virus. Otherwise, I'll invest in calamine lotion and take my chances."

He opened the door, walked outside and was back with the broom and dustpan a moment later. Leaning them both against the wall, he said, "All gone."

Relieved, she drew in a deep breath and whispered, "Thank you."

"You're welcome. You okay now?"

She nodded slowly. "Oh, sure. Fine."

Her pulse finally stopped racing and her muscles loosened. The nausea receded, as did the panic. Not for the first time in her life, she found herself wondering if an older cousin had dangled a spider in her face when she was a baby or something. Because her phobia about them had been lifelong and was, even she could admit it, a little obsessive. Now that her heart wasn't thumping hard enough to beat out of her chest, she could acknowledge she might have overacted just a teeny, tiny bit.

Feeling almost normal, she waited for Oliver to turn and walk out the door. Considering he usually avoided her, that's what she expected him to do. But for some reason, he didn't leave. He just stood there, two feet away, drawing in slow, even breaths as he studied her.

Finally, he murmured, "Cold in here."

Her spider terror having receded, she paused to remember just what she was wearing—not much.

Her skimpy robe hung to the tops of her thighs, leaving her legs completely bared. The robe also gaped over her breasts, revealing a deep V of cleavage. The whole thing was held together only by a loosely knotted sash.

"Yes, I guess it is," she replied slowly, wondering if he had been making small talk or offering a sideways comment on the fact that her nipples were hard, poking visibly against the silk sliding so sinuously over them.

He continued to stare, falling silent. She knew the answer to that question. He'd finally noticed her apparel—or lack thereof. Oliver was definitely reacting to it. Looking at her. Staring at her.

Visually devouring her.

Her lips parted on a tiny helpless sigh. He didn't acknowledge the sound, instead merely swept that dark-eyed attention over her, from damp-haired top to bare-toed bottom. The gaze was like a touch, lingering here, skimming over there, and she reacted to it instinctively. Here went soft, there went hard, and her most vulnerable places went all hot and wet.

She knew she should yank her robe more tightly around her body and glare him into stopping, or else turn and flounce up the stairs, but she couldn't bring herself to do it. She'd been looked at by men before, of course. By lovers, by potential lovers, by strangers, but she had never felt as thoroughly studied as she did now. It was as if he was examining her, tucking away every detail of her into his prodigious internal memory bank. His dark eyes gleamed, and he made absolutely no effort to disguise his focus or make her think he was doing anything other than memorizing all the things he could see, and imagining all those he could not.

He wanted her. It was stunningly obvious. He was imagining what wild, wicked things they could do together, of that she had no doubt. She knew because she'd been thinking the same thing since the night she'd arrived. So how could she blame him?

A mental voice shouted a warning. But another part of her—the part that had been trying to figure out if he had been avoiding her for the past few days because he *wasn't* attracted to her, or because he *was*—appeared to be calling the shots.

She couldn't walk away from him now. Not just yet.

"This is a really bad idea," he muttered.

She knew what he meant but still replied, "What is?"

He swept a hand through his dark hair. The movement made his arms bulge against the white T-shirt he wore, and drew the thin fabric tight against his shoulders. "You standing there, looking like that. Me standing here, looking at you looking like that."

Her mouth went dry.

Turn around, Candace. Go upstairs. Pray your vibrator is still safely tucked in your suitcase and wasn't pawed over by some luggage guys, dig it out and remember you don't technically need a man to give you orgasms.

But she remained still, as if her feet were glued to the floor. Her vibrator couldn't fill her the way she so desperately wanted to be filled. It couldn't hold her, stroke her, touch her, lick her. It couldn't make her feel as utterly jittery with excitement as she felt just standing here, knowing he wanted her.

Besides, she suddenly realized she *couldn't* run away up to her room. Not while he was standing at the bottom of the steps. Her robe was short and tiny, which was why she'd stuffed it in her carry-on bag, and she had never been more conscious of the fact that she wasn't wearing any underwear. Although she and her sister had done their share of mooning during her younger, wilder days, the only way she wanted to wiggle her bare bottom at this man was if she got on all fours and invited him to make her howl.

Unfortunately, it seemed a bit early in their relationship for that kind of invitation.

No relationship. There's not going to be any relationship. Remember?

"Go upstairs," he ordered, his voice strangled. That was pretty far from an admission of lust.

She instinctively shook her head.

He stepped closer, scowling, almost threatening, as if he could intimidate her into going. "Walk away, Candace. Please."

"No. *You* walk away. The door's right there."

"I can't." His hand rose and he stroked the sleeve of her robe, fingering the silk. He didn't look down, never took his attention off her face, and she wondered if he even realized he'd moved so close. So incredibly close.

"It has to be you," he insisted.

"Why?"

"I need you to turn your back on me, to make it clear that you want me to leave."

He waited. She didn't turn.

"All right, at least say it," he ordered. "Make it clear."

She knew what he was asking, but she couldn't give him what he wanted—a verbal command to go. Not when she suddenly wanted, with every fiber of her being, for him to stay.

"Tell me to go," he pleaded.

She wordlessly shook her head.

He muttered a curse. Reaching for her, as if unable to control himself, he caught hold of the silky bathrobe tie at her waist. He tightened it a little, maybe not even realizing he was doing it, as if he was fighting an inner battle between pushing her away and pulling her close.

But she realized it. Her nerve endings were roaring now, her heart thudding in her chest. There was something almost predatory in his expression, and the tightening of the sash around her waist made her feel somehow claimed.

If he pushed her away, she would be devastated.

If he pulled her close, she'd be lost.

"Go upstairs," he insisted.

"I don't have to."

"God, you're stubborn." He leaned in closer, until his pant legs brushed her bare calves. The fabric was deliciously rough and warm from his body and she couldn't help stepping closer, sucking up that warmth. The early morning air was still chilly but heat wafted from him, like he'd absorbed the first sunbeams of the new day and could now reflect them back.

He inhaled deeply, as if he needed her scent in his lungs. She knew she smelled fresh, soapy and clean, not perfumed or lotioned, but the man looked intoxicated all the same.

"This is not why I came in here." His face was so close to hers, she could feel the gentle fall of his exhalations on her skin. A slight shift and there was the most delicate rasp of his stubble upon her cheek.

"You came to bring my suitcase," she murmured, not really thinking about the words they exchanged, able to focus only on his closeness. His power. The scent of his body, the roughness of his strong jaw. She wanted that roughness scraping all over her, knowing his soft, delicious mouth could kiss away any soreness.

"Right. And now I have." He moved his body even closer. Their thighs came together.

"So you can go." She arched against him, sighing as her hard, aching nipples met that masculine chest.

"You want me to?" One of his hands dropped to her hip and he squeezed lightly, again making her feel claimed.

"The choice is yours." She tilted her head to the side, offering him the bare expanse of her neck.

"I'll go then." He moved his face to her throat, not kissing, not tasting, just breathing in and out, a millimeter from her skin, increasing the tension, heightening her senses.

So close. So incredibly close.

"If you say so." She closed her eyes, swaying slightly

on her feet, willing him not to go, and, for heaven's sake, to just stop talking about it and kiss her.

"I'm going."

"Don't let me stop you."

"Damn it," he muttered as if he'd finally realized she wasn't going to order him to leave, and had finally snapped himself out of the sensual spell. But he still couldn't back away completely, and brushed his cheek against her hair. "Do you always have to get your way?"

"Ask me in an hour."

And she gave up, stopped playing coy and took what she'd been wanting since the night they'd met. Not giving him a chance to fight it anymore, she twined her fingers in his hair and pulled him to her. His eyes flared and he tensed. Then, with a deep groan, he gave in to her and lowered his mouth to hers.

Their lips parted, the kiss hot, sensuous and wet. There was nothing tentative about it, no hesitation, no regret. He simply devoured her and she let him, tilting her head, loving the feel of his tongue in her mouth. Their bodies were pressed together, his hands at her waist, hers tangled in his thick hair, and the kiss went on and on, deep and hungry. She had sensed this man's mouth had been made for kissing, and now she knew. He dined on her, sipped from her, swallowed her exhalations as if he needed her breaths to expand his lungs and fuel his cells.

Against her groin, she again felt the rigid heat that proclaimed his desire for her more than words ever could. Clad only in the robe, with his body slammed against hers, she couldn't help but notice the rock-hard strength of him. She moaned, low in her throat, and rocked toward it, so filled with need she thought her legs would give out.

He suddenly tensed, as if realizing they were one step away from too-far-to-stop. Dropping his hands, he ended the kiss and pulled away, staggering back a step to punctuate the end of their embrace.

The sound of their ragged breaths filled the silent air. Candace felt certain every ounce of blood in her body had pooled in her most intimate places, which now throbbed and boiled with demand. Her breasts hurt, the nipples so sensitive that the scrape of the silk robe was almost unbearable, and she knew nothing would make them feel better but his hands, his tongue, his lips.

But the look on his face said she wasn't going to get any of those things. His hands were shoved in his pockets, his tongue was back in his mouth, his lips were sealed tight and turned down in a frown.

He was trying to pretend he regretted the kiss.

She knew he didn't.

"That was…unexpected," she admitted, hearing the weakness of her voice.

"Yeah." He cleared his throat. "I'm sorry, I didn't mean to…"

"Oh, of course you *meant* to. Just as I meant to."

"Maybe you're right. But that doesn't mean it can happen again, or go any further."

She opened her mouth to argue.

"You're only here for a short time, you're my boss's granddaughter and he trusted me to look after you."

"I think he was sort of hoping you would romance me," she said, her tone dry.

"Yeah, but not bang you up against the front door."

"Is that where we would have ended up? Gee, and the sofa is right in the next room."

"Damn it, Candace."

She held a hand up, palm out, stopping him from saying anything more. "Forget it. I know you're right. I have reasons of my own for not insisting you rip off your clothes and do me until I can't remember my own name."

He coughed and laughed, both at the same time. Then, as if the laughter—and her saucy words—had snapped some kind of spell, he reached out, put his hands on her shoulders and spun her around so she faced the staircase. Gently pushing her, he ordered, "Go."

She spun back around. "I can't."

His jaw turned into granite. "You're being ridiculous."

All because he needed *her* to be the one who walked away and ended this before it really began? As if he had no free will? As if he wouldn't be able to stop himself from doing to her exactly what she'd practically dared him to do unless she removed herself from his presence?

You don't want him to do it, either, remember? You know you can't do this.

Her grandfather was being moved to a rehab facility today. He'd be there for about a week, and then he would be coming home. But coming home to what? Her having an affair with his groundskeeper, then the descent of the paparazzi once her engagement was announced? Did he really need that while he recovered? Did Oliver, who was obviously here for reasons he hadn't yet revealed to her? Did she need the scandal? Did Tommy?

No. She might want Oliver, and having sex with him might even be worth what she would go through afterward if people found out. But nobody else deserved it. She needed to cool this, here and now. She had to be the one who walked away.

Which still wasn't going to be easy.

"I'm telling you, you really don't want to watch me walking up those stairs."

"Yes. I really do."

"And you're honestly not going to get out of here until I do?"

"No."

"You'll regret it."

"Hell, I already regret it," he said, tunneling both his hands through his hair this time, leaving it more tousled than before.

"Not as much as you're about to."

A helping of anger had been heaped upon her sexual frustration. Yes, she'd decided she couldn't have him, but did he have to be so damned insistent about it?

She hadn't been kidding that he was going to regret it. Because she was ready to give him what he was asking for…and wondered if he was ready for what came along with it.

Without another word, she spun around again, squared her shoulders, stiffened her spine and ascended the stairs. He stood below, watching her, and when she reached the fourth one, she couldn't help pausing to glance over her shoulder at him.

"Oh, Oliver, do you want to know why I didn't want to walk up the stairs until you left?"

He didn't reply, just gave her an inscrutable look.

She told him anyway. "Because of this."

Candace took another step, knowing she'd reached the point of no return. Knowing full well he could now see what she was *not* wearing beneath her robe.

She wished she could say his strangled, guttural cry of helpless frustration made her feel better about walking away from what she sensed could be the best sex of her life.

But she just couldn't.

5

EVER SINCE HE'D started getting involved with females, Oliver had known how to handle them. Maybe it was because he'd had sisters, lots of girl cousins and parents with an honest, loving marriage in which nobody held the upper hand. Maybe because he'd had girls after him since he hit puberty. Maybe he'd just been born with the gene.

The point was, he'd always been sure of himself when it came to women. He'd always known when one was interested and when she wasn't, been able to gauge how soon was too soon, or when it was too late and he'd missed his shot. He'd set the pace, led the dance, taken the right steps at the right time.

Until now. Until her. Until Candace.

She had him twisted inside out and upside down, not knowing what to do or say next. He didn't know whether to resist or keep on fighting. Part of him wished she'd never shown up at Buddy's house, and another part dreaded the day she would leave.

"God, what a mess," he muttered that evening as he finished taking inventory in the wine cellar. He hadn't even realized there was one in the house until today, when he'd gone to visit Buddy in the rehab center. He'd watched for

Candace to leave the room, heading to the cafeteria for
lunch, and then stopped by, not wanting to run into her
after what had happened this morning. Coming face-to-
face with her would have been more than his heart could
have taken, even a couple of hours after she'd marched her
bare little fanny up the stairs.

No, not little. Round, supple, perfect.

Just right for cupping in his hands, or pounding against
as he took her from behind, the way he'd been dying to as
he'd watched her sashay back to her room.

He swallowed hard, wishing he hadn't allowed himself
to go back there in his mind. He'd managed to avoid thinking about her most of the day, but now the images came
washing in. He was again overwhelmed by the memory
of the gorgeous, naked ass she'd flashed at him as she'd
ascended the stairs. He suspected he would keep seeing
that vision for a long while, every time he closed his eyes.
"You're a complete idiot," he muttered to himself. "You're
the one who insisted she walk up the stairs while you stood
there like Pavlov's dog, drowning in your own drool."

To give her credit, she had tried to warn him. No, she
hadn't come right out and told him what would happen—
that he was about to be given a free peep show that would
drive a grown man to his knees. And he suspected his
own stubbornness had inspired hers. Still, he wasn't sure
he could ever forgive her for showing him what he could
have had, if not for his own foul temper and his need to
keep punishing himself by not taking anything he truly
wanted. Being noble was all well and good, but if it came
with blue balls, he'd far prefer being selfish.

"Enough," he reminded himself, trying to return his
focus to the task at hand. The wine cellar. He still couldn't
believe it was here, or that it held so much.

Buddy had found a treasure trove in the basement right
before his accident, one he hadn't even realized was there

until he'd started trying out keys to locked rooms. That's what had sent him hurrying down the porch steps to find Oliver. He'd intended to show it to Oliver and ask him to help inventory it.

Now that it looked like Buddy wouldn't be doing any stair-climbing for a while, Oliver had promised he'd get started. Buddy had agreed gratefully, telling him to help himself to anything he found…unless it was worth a king's ransom, in which case he would need it for his medical bills.

He hadn't even thought about that, but now that his employer had brought it up, Oliver couldn't help worrying about it. Buddy had sunk his life savings into this place. God, he hoped this accident didn't bankrupt the man.

Caught up in the old man's excitement, he'd stopped by the store to pick up reference books with grades, rankings and values of old wine. Once he'd found the room and gotten started, he'd been shocked by the sheer quantity of bottles. Obviously, his own great-uncle, who'd bought out his siblings, including Oliver's grandmother, hadn't even realized what he had in his possession. He'd been from back East and never done a proper inventory on the place. The group that had bought the estate from *him* had intended to get investors to renovate it into some corporate retreat, but had never fully investigated, either.

Buddy had bought the whole place—and its contents—out of bankruptcy and was legally entitled to everything here. Including this treasure trove. If the previous owners had realized what they'd had, this stuff would have been on auction blocks around the world, not still stored in this secure room, created solely for keeping wines in pristine condition.

Okay, there was dust. A few cobwebs—Candace would hate the spiders. But for the most part, the setup was ideal and the bottles—more than one hundred of them, possibly close to two—looked sealed and correctly colored. It was very likely many of them were aged to perfection.

This collection could be the answer to Buddy's financial problems. Some of the bottles weren't easily cataloged and an appraiser would have to do it. Many, though, had been listed in the books he'd brought with him as being worth thousands of dollars. There was a small fortune within these walls, and, frankly, Oliver couldn't think of anyone who deserved it more.

They weren't all gems. He had found a few broken ones, dry corks or just plain duds according to the books. Some that *were* good wines still weren't worth much, even if in mint condition. Those included vintages that had been bottled during a surplus production year and just weren't collectible.

It was one of those he was eyeing now. A 1971 burgundy from one of his favorite vintners that was still around today. Buddy had told him to feel free to help himself to anything that wasn't too valuable, and this one wasn't worth more than about a hundred bucks.

He deserved a hundred bucks worth of wine, especially after putting up with Buddy's sexy, infuriating granddaughter.

"How's it going?"

Said sexy, infuriating granddaughter who almost startled him into dropping the bottle. He spun around, seeing her eyeing him from the doorway. "Oh. You're back."

Obviously he had lost track of time down here. It was probably a good thing she'd come looking for him—fully, if sexily, dressed in a pair of slim-fitting jeans and a light-weight pink sweater. With his luck, he'd have consumed the bottle of wine and headed upstairs after she was home and ready for bed, wearing that flimsy little bathrobe and nothing else.

His horny-man brain quickly rebelled at the idea that

that would have been *bad* luck. But he shut that part of his brain down.

"Visiting hours are over. It's after eight. I saw the lights were on upstairs and thought you might still be here. Grandpa told me where to look for you."

She looked like she wanted to come in, but was carefully eyeing the cobwebs and shadowy corners.

"All clear," he told her with a smile, knowing what she was looking for. "I think the mutant spider from outer space is still trying to find his way home."

That was a lie—there were enough webs down here to house the spiders from Harry Potter's Dark Forest. But he wasn't about to tell her that.

She managed a weak smile and slowly entered, her attention focused on shelf after shelf of bottles. She whistled as she walked around the twelve-by-twelve chamber. "Wow. He wasn't exaggerating, was he?"

"Definitely not."

"Amazing!"

"You have no idea."

He quickly filled her in on what he'd discovered, and saw her eyes light up with hope as she realized her grandfather might have actually stumbled into a treasure to help him make this old house into the showplace he envisioned.

"Are you sure?"

"I'm no expert," he told her. "I can only judge by what the books say. Buddy will have to get an appraiser out here. And of course it depends on whether the wine is any good, or if it's gone over." Then he lifted the bottle, holding it up against the milky light coming from the overhead bulb. "I was just about to crack open a bottle of the cheaper stuff and check it out."

She nodded anxiously, looking like a kid agreeing to a dare. "Oh, yes, let's!"

"Are you a wine fan?"

"I'm a woman. Of course I'm a wine fan."

Reaching into his pocket, Oliver drew out a multifunction tool that had a wine opener on it and almost held his breath as he uncorked the bottle. He was careful not to shake it in case of sediment and immediately smelled the air for any scent of vinegar.

Nothing. So far, so good.

Testing the cork and finding it completely moist and not at all crumbly, he began to hope they weren't about to drink a bottle of salad dressing in the making. "This really should be decanted so it can breathe."

Her face fell.

"But there's no point in going upstairs to find a decanter and glasses until we know whether it's worth drinking." He lifted the bottle and extended it to her. "Ladies first."

She didn't put on any fussy airs or complain about drinking out of an old, dusty bottle. Wiping the rim with her hand, she lifted it to her mouth and took a tiny sip.

Her eyes closed. She remained very still. Then she sipped again.

When she opened her eyes, they were sparkling with delight. "Unbelievable. That is the best wine I have tasted in my life! If that's the cheap stuff, I think the really good wine would bring on an instant orgasm."

She immediately caught her bottom lip between her teeth, obviously regretting making that remark.

He regretted it, too. Mainly because, as he took the bottle from her extended hand, and lifted it to his mouth, all he could think about was giving her that instant orgasm.

He could. Of that he had no doubt.

Trouble was, he knew he shouldn't. He didn't have that right. He was in no place to offer her anything and in no condition to take anything. Having sex with her would be about one thing and one thing only—instant gratification. And she just didn't seem like the one-night-stand type.

Nor was that what he suspected his matchmaking boss had in mind for them.

He placed his lips right where hers had been, tasting her lipstick, wishing it wasn't via second degree of separation. Then he sipped, and felt the most delightful burst of flavor in his mouth. He caught smoky undertones, but the tannins were light, unobtrusive. There was also a hint of cherry, or plum. Not sweet, just rich and full-bodied. It went down smooth, the finish just as perfect as the opening, and he couldn't resist taking another healthy sip.

"Fantastic," he said when he lowered the bottle. "Should we go for the decanter?"

"Absolutely!"

She spun around and hurried out the door, leading him up the stairs to Buddy's living room. They were like a pair of kids who'd been given their favorite candy and could hardly wait to dig in.

And they definitely dug.

An hour later, they'd finished off the first bottle, and most of a second one he'd gone down to grab. The second hadn't been quite as perfect as the first, even after a fifteen-minute decant, but it beat anything he'd ever ordered at a fancy California restaurant, hands down. And the book only valued it at forty bucks. Something about age definitely made all the difference.

Dividing what was left between their two glasses, he listened as she went over a list of things they needed to check and do tomorrow. That included finding the closest expert who could come out and do an appraisal. By their own unscientific research, Buddy should come out of this at least two hundred thousand dollars richer. One bottle in particular, a 1945 Château Mouton Rothschild, could very well bring in fifty thousand on its own.

Fifty. Thousand. Dollars. For a freaking bottle of wine.

Damn, he was glad he'd bought the reference books and hadn't dared to just grab a bottle and open it!

Candace sat beside him on the couch. She'd been bouncing with excitement every time he flipped a page and spied a familiar name, pointing to its corresponding mention on his list of Buddy's wine cellar. Her excitement had been infectious. It had also been so spontaneous that, once, she grabbed his thigh and squeezed.

He'd managed to hide a groan, wondering if she was really clueless about the effect she was having on him. And it wasn't just a wine-inspired reaction. Oh, no. Everything about her simply called to something inside him. Her soft scent filled his every breath; her long hair brushed his bare forearm. Their legs touched, hips, too. She filled his every sense, and if he'd thought the attraction was dangerous when they'd first met, he knew he was really in trouble now that he liked her so much.

She was delightful, smart, funny and so sexy it hurt to look at her. Their nearness—and, okay, maybe the wine— made the idea of never having this woman seem not only a shame but a crime against humanity.

"I am thrilled for Grandpa," she said when they'd finally reached the end of the list. She tucked one bent leg beneath her and turned toward him on the couch. "This is going to help him make all his dreams come true."

He nodded, unable to take his eyes off her burgundy-drenched lips, feeling the thrum of excitement that reverberated from her. She was relaxed and happy and he'd never seen her looking so beautiful.

"Thank you," she said, reaching out to grab his hand and squeeze it.

He couldn't resist. Twining his fingers in hers, he lifted her hand to brush a kiss on her palm.

She sucked in an audible breath and edged closer. He continued to kiss his way across her palm, until he reached her wrist. Pressing his lips there, he noted the frantic thumping of her pulse and realized her heart was racing.

He dropped her hand. "I didn't mean to go there."

"Don't stop."

"It's a bad idea, Candace."

"What is? You kissing my hand?" She licked her lips and lowered her voice to a sultry whisper. "Or my mouth?"

Or any other part of her? *Every* other part of her?

"Kiss me, Oliver," she dared. "One real kiss to celebrate. What do you say?"

Intriguing. "Only one?"

"Yes. Just one. I promise I won't ask for more."

He stared into her deep green eyes, wondering whether she was telling him that one would really be enough, or that it would do for a start. Nor could he be sure what he wanted her answer to be.

Not until he spied the list on the table, with Buddy's name scrawled across the top. He was in his friend's home, a little high on his prized wine, contemplating kissing his granddaughter. That alone was enough to convince him he couldn't take any more than the single kiss she'd asked for.

"All right, Candace. Just one."

"You're sure that will be enough?"

Hell, no, it wouldn't be enough. But it was all he was going to allow himself. Period. At least until he didn't feel like the biggest heel in the world for taking advantage of his boss's granddaughter...and for letting himself get close to a woman when he knew he had absolutely nothing to offer her.

He didn't just mean financially. It wasn't just his lack of a career or a house or even his own car, all of which he'd left behind in L.A. He meant himself. He didn't have any emotions to offer any woman. He'd felt adrift for months, and it would take more than a hot flirtation with a beautiful brunette to change that. So he wasn't about to allow himself any more than one small glimpse of the physical pleasure he knew he wasn't entitled to and didn't deserve.

"I'm sure," he finally told her. "*One*. And then we say good-night."

"If you're sure. I mean, remember what we talked about the other night, if you give a mouse a cookie…"

"He's going to say thank-you and walk out the door."

She studied him, gauging his seriousness, and nodded. "All right, Oliver. One kiss, and then we say good-night."

They might have shaken hands given the serious way they made their deal. And a deal was all it was.

One kiss. One and done.

God help him.

ONE KISS? Yeah. Sure. Right.

She couldn't believe he'd really be able to do that, but just in case, Candace was determined to make it a kiss for the ages. She knew from this morning that the man's mouth was ambrosia, and knowing she was going to taste it again was enough to make her whole body shiver and quake in anticipation.

He noticed, and let go of her hand. "Are you cold?"

She shook her head slowly, inching closer to him on the sofa. Untucking one leg, she didn't hesitate to make sure he couldn't change his mind and get up. Giving him a look that was half demand, half plea, she rose onto her knees and slid one leg over his thighs, straddling him.

"Candace…"

"I want my kiss," she insisted as she hovered over his lap. Maybe the wine was making her bold, but she suspected it was pure physical attraction. If she'd been stone-cold sober, she still would have wanted this kiss. This wicked, stolen moment.

"This is a little more than I bargained for," he admitted.

"You're not a very good bargainer," she replied, licking her lips. "You didn't even try to negotiate any ground rules."

"Should I have?"

She smiled wickedly. "Probably."

"I'm guessing it's too late for that?"

"Much too late."

He sighed deeply, but she'd swear his eyes gleamed with excitement and amusement.

"Just one," he reminded her.

"Oh, all right."

She moved down, lowering herself onto him. Her knees rested on the couch on either side of him, the position very intimate. She could feel the heat and power between her thighs and knew he was already aroused. He probably had been for quite a while, judging by the undeniable hardness straining against his zipper.

Yet he wanted only one kiss? The man obviously had an iron will to go along with that iron shaft.

Her blood pulsed and pooled in her groin. She was unable to resist rubbing against him, just a little, taking the heat, the strength and that hardness, and pleasing herself with it. Their clothes were in the way, of course, but she still felt waves of delight pulsing through her as they ground together.

His flexing jaw indicated he was gritting his teeth, as if striving for control, and she made a promise to herself: someday, she'd make him lose it. That control would be long gone before the day they said goodbye. Maybe it wouldn't be tonight. Maybe they would just have one single kiss, as he insisted. But someday, she'd have the rest of him, even if she had to wait five years.

He lifted his hands and twined them in her hair, fingering the strands as he pulled her face down toward his. A quick inhalation, two thudding hearts finding a common rhythm, a last glance of certainty and their mouths finally came together.

It was soft, slow and easy at first, a gentle exploration of lips. Giving, taking, molding, sliding, not a hint of demand in it, just a tender, sexy build.

This wasn't like the kiss they'd shared this morning. It was far more lazy, as if knowing that since one kiss was all they'd agreed on, they both intended to make it not merely the journey but also the destination. It might only be one, but as far as Candace was concerned, this kiss could go on for half an hour and they'd still technically be following the rules.

His warm tongue began to test the corners of her mouth, and she opened for him, sliding hers out in welcome. The kiss deepened, their tongues thrusting together in a deliberate, sultry tango. He tasted warm and spicy, with wine adding even more flavor to his already-delicious mouth. She lifted her arms around his neck, and he dropped his hands to her hips. Digging his fingers into her bottom, he pulled her even more tightly against his erection.

She groaned in the back of her throat, resisting the urge to toss her head back and grind herself into a climax. The kiss deepened as the frenzy increased, and she noticed he was thrusting up slightly, as if making love to her.

Damn their clothes. Damn his conditions.

They might only have one kiss, but he hadn't said anything about what they could and could not touch during that kiss. So without pulling away she reached for his waist, tugging his shirt up so she could touch and stroke that flat, muscled stomach. He sighed against her lips, but didn't resist, merely followed her lead. When his hands tugged her blouse free from her jeans and he encircled her waist with his big hands, she wanted to jump for joy.

She settled for continuing to kiss him, turning her head, going deep then shallow, hard then soft.

His strong hands caressed her, moving up to stroke her midriff, then higher, until his thumbs were resting at the edge of her bra. Whimpering and arching toward his touch, she shuddered with relief when he finally scraped those thumbs over her taut nipples, teasing them through the lace. Sparks erupted as he tweaked and toyed with her.

Her cries of satisfaction seemed to urge him on. Without her asking, he pulled the material down, out of the way, so he could pleasure her more, until she was writhing on his lap, almost desperate with need.

But still the kiss didn't end. It was as if they were both determined to remain true to their terms and see just how far they could go without ever letting their mouths separate.

Pretty damn far, she soon realized as he slid his hands back down her body and unfastened the button of her jeans.

"Oh, yes," she whispered into his mouth.

She suspected he hadn't been waiting for permission.

As he slowly lowered her zipper, she lifted herself up a little, giving him access. He pushed her jeans down just enough to allow him to slip his hand into the steamy crevice between her thighs. When those knuckles brushed against her most sensitive spot, she let out a cry, needing so much more.

He seemed to realize she was right on the edge. Thrusting one hand into her hair to cup her head, he deepened the kiss, making love to her mouth with hungry determination. His other hand remained still, but just as she was ready to pound on his shoulders to demand more, he reached under the elastic edge of her panties. Tangling his fingers in the soft thatch of hair, he moved deeper, until the rough pad of one found her clit and began to work it.

Heaven.

Not being able to pull back and look down was painful. But she didn't want to end the kiss, didn't want to break the spell, for fear everything would stop. All her senses were on overload as she smelled his musky scent, tasted every inch of his mouth, felt his body pressed against hers, saw his handsome face and heard the small groans of pleasure he didn't try to disguise.

Just as she was on the verge of coming, he moved his hand away. This time, she did pound on his shoulder, but he responded with an evil chuckle that she tasted as well as heard. When she realized he was moving deeper into her panties, so that he could slide a long, warm finger into her, she forgave him his every sin.

God, it had been so long since she'd taken anyone into her body. Her muscles clenched him, squeezing, drawing him deeper. He thrust in, drew out, mimicking what he would do when he really made love to her, until she was squirming on his lap.

As if knowing she was desperate for more, he gave her another finger, plunging both deep, stroking her way up inside until she began to shake. And when his thumb moved back up to cover her clit, a warm pulse of pleasure burst out and rushed through her. Every cell in her body felt on fire, from the bottoms of her feet to the tips of her hair, and she could no longer control herself. She threw her head back, gave a long, utterly satisfied cry, and rode out the orgasm that left her quaking and weak.

When she finally came back down to earth, she felt completely spent and collapsed onto him, her head on his shoulders, her arms around his neck. Oliver was kissing her temple, stroking her stomach and then her lower back.

But their mouths had fallen apart. The kiss had ended.

She held her breath, wondering if he was going to say to hell with their deal and make love to her the way his rigid, throbbing cock said he was dying to.

When he gently lifted her off his lap and sat her back down beside him on the couch, she had her answer.

"Seriously?"

She didn't have to say another word. He knew what she was asking; she could tell by the look on his face.

He rose to his feet and tucked his shirt back in.

"Thank you, Candace. Good night."

She gritted her teeth and zipped her jeans, reminding herself that this was entirely her fault. She'd promised one kiss and no more. No, she hadn't exactly invited him to stick his hand down her pants and finger her into oblivion, but it had seemed within reason as long as they were sharing that one kiss.

He was just playing by the rules. Damn the man.

She rose, tucking her blouse back in, and lifting her head, as if she was totally fine about how this whole thing had played out. "Good night, Oliver."

She turned her back to him and began to pick up the bottles and glasses, tidying up the room. He stood there for a moment, watching her, as if waiting for her to throw a fit, call him a jerk or beg him to stay. But she didn't. If he wanted to play this straight, that's what she would do. If he wanted to change the rules of the game, he needed to be the one to say so.

In the end, he didn't say anything. He just nodded, headed to the door and walked out into the night.

6

OLIVER SPENT THE next day wishing he hadn't consumed so much wine the night before, and steering clear of Candace.

He took care of the wine with some aspirin.

Her decision to visit her grandfather for almost the entire day took care of Candace.

That was good. He wasn't ready to run into her again. Not when every time he closed his eyes, he saw her beautiful face, suffused with pleasure, so wanton and gorgeous, he knew she would haunt his dreams forever.

Sometimes, doing the right thing just sucked.

He had thought it was the right thing at the time. Unfortunately, right now, he couldn't remember the reason why.

He'd tried to work out the frustration, spending the day laboring in the storehouse, which still held a number of antique vats. Buddy was hoping to restore and use them. Having tasted the amazing wines aged in antique wood last night, he had to agree that they were worth salvaging. And fortunately, the work was hard enough that he was able to put Candace, and the amazing moments they'd shared on that couch, out of his thoughts. At least, for the most part.

Finally, though, when he glanced at his watch and saw it was after six, he knew he had to call it quits. She would probably be heading back to the estate soon. He intended to go down to the rehab center to visit Buddy. Hopefully, their cars would pass in the night and they wouldn't run into each other, there or here. He just couldn't take another evening of sexual tension with the woman. Not when he knew how sweet she tasted, and how those feminine cries of pleasure sounded when she came apart in his arms. Not when he was dying to slam his cock into her and forget the rest of the world even existed.

As he toweled his hair dry and eyed his jaw in the mirror, he realized he ought to shave. Not because he intended to rub his face on someone sinfully soft and wanted to prepare, but because he was beginning to look a little scruffy. Buddy had made a point of mentioning it·yesterday.

"It's not about that soft skin," he told his reflection. "Not about that stomach. Not about those breasts." God, had he been dying to end the kiss if only so he could look down at the perfect breasts he'd held in his hands. He swallowed, seeing the condensation he left on the mirror as he breathed ever harder. "It's not about wanting to bury your face between her thighs and see if she tastes as good as she feels."

Somehow, though, as he finished shaving and stared at his smooth-cheeked reflection, he knew he was fooling himself.

No, he didn't deserve her. No, he had no business taking up with her. But oh, hell, yes, did he ever want her.

Yesterday, when she'd walked up those stairs, giving him a glimpse of heaven between two limbs, it had taken every ounce of his strength not to follow her. He'd pictured it, a flash of erotic images storming through his brain. He'd seen himself pounding up after her, three steps at a time. Stopping her before she got to the top. Guiding her down onto her knees. Gently pushing her forward until she was on all fours and he could take his place a few steps below. He'd instinctively known how perfect it would be to position her sweet, wet sex above him, to bury his face in it, lick into her until she bucked and cried, then to drive into her before she'd even stopped screaming over the multiple orgasms he'd give her.

Oliver closed his eyes, willing the images to leave his head. But they wouldn't. They were imprinted there, the vision so real it was almost memory.

Then came the images from last night. He could still taste her lips, still feel the softness of her skin, still remember how it had felt to slide a finger into that slick, tight channel and play with that pearly little clit until she whimpered.

He groaned, reached down and found his cock hard and erect.

"Damn it, Candace," he muttered, grabbing himself, squeezing, pumping. His hand was in no way as good— wet, hot—as she would be, but it was all he had. All he would allow himself.

It didn't take long. No longer than it had taken the previous night when he'd gone to bed and let himself replay the moments he'd spent with her on the couch. He came in a hot gush, spewing his essence over his hand, knowing he'd give a year off his life if he could do it in her instead.

"But you can't," he told himself, feeling even more sexually frustrated than he had before his second jacking-off session of the past twenty-four hours.

His hand just didn't cut it. He wanted *her* hand. Her body. Her mouth. More than he'd ever wanted anything.

He tried to forget his sexual needs as he drove down to the rehab center. He definitely tried to disguise his desire as he visited with Buddy and gauged how the elderly man was doing with his new hip. Fortunately, he'd been right about guessing Candace wouldn't be there. She'd apparently stayed until dinnertime, leaving shortly before he'd arrived, so he wouldn't have to pretend he hadn't spent the past twenty hours fucking her senseless in his mind. Hopefully he would get home late, find her rental car in the driveway, see all the lights were out and go to bed, having managed one more day of resisting her.

To make sure of that, he intended to go out for a bite to eat and maybe have a few beers at a local watering hole before heading back. He'd even picked the place.

After they'd spent a half hour talking about the amazing find in the wine cellar, Buddy said something that made him wonder if fate was conspiring to bring him and Candace together.

"You ought to see if you can catch up with Candace at Wilhelm's. I told her they have the best burgers in town and she said she was going to stop there for dinner."

So she could avoid arriving home in time to see him? That was funny, considering she was dining at the very bar at which he'd intended to stop. Now, though, he figured drive-through fast food would do him just fine.

"I should probably get home and make an early night of it. I'm going to get back to work on the old vats tomorrow, see what else we can salvage."

Buddy frowned. "I'd feel better if you swung by and checked on her. Tonight's Monday. Adult softball league night."

"So?"

"So we both know the teams all converge on Wilhelm's for brewskis and wings after their games. It can get a little raucous. I'd hate to think of my girl having to fend off some guy who downs a little too much liquid courage."

Oliver tensed at the very thought of it. No, he didn't have any claim on her, and had told her he didn't want any. But damned if he wanted another man making a move, welcomed by her or otherwise. That was probably pretty selfish, but, frankly, he didn't give a shit.

Since he met her, Candace had been putting off some

strong signals. Her body was dying for some action, she needed sex and she needed it badly. And last night, when they'd kissed and he'd stroked her into an orgasm, she had been like a cat in heat, so obviously ripe and ready that he had smelled her arousal—hence his drooling hunger to bury his face in her sex and eat her like a kid ate an ice-cream cone.

He'd be damned if any guy with less-pure motives and less self-control was going to take her up on what she was silently offering.

"Will you at least go by and check on her, make sure she's okay?" Buddy prompted. He wore a slight frown, but Oliver saw the tiniest hint of a smile on his face, as well. The old man was matchmaking again. Under normal circumstances, that would have sent Oliver running in the other direction, away from the local pub where Candace might now be putting off those vibes he'd been picking up on since the night they'd met.

But because of those vibes, he just couldn't.

"Okay, Buddy. I'll go by and make sure she's all right."

And make sure she wasn't entering into negotiations with any other guy for one tiny innocent little kiss. After giving her that orgasm, he'd left her high and dry last night. Over his dead body would any other man get her low and wet.

HER GRANDFATHER HAD been right. Wilhelm's had great burgers. After Candace swallowed the last bite of hers, she wiped her mouth, reached for her tea and thought about dessert.

Not that she was still hungry. Honestly, the burger had been huge. She never ate like that, and could almost hear her arteries screaming in protest. But she was not ready to call for her check, get up, leave and drive back to Grandpa's place. Not while it was only eight o'clock. Not when there was a good chance Oliver would be up, the lights on in his small cottage, tempting her to find some excuse to wander over to see him.

He'd avoided her all day today. As if his rejection last night and the finality of his goodbye hadn't been enough, he'd made it a point to avoid coming outside at all until she'd left the house this morning.

He had the will of a monk. Or a eunuch. The flash of her cootchie as she'd walked up the stairs hadn't elicited more than a frustrated groan from the man. She couldn't deny she'd slammed the door to her room because he *hadn't* stormed up after her, overtaken by lust. Then, last night after their wild, erotic kiss that had involved a whole lot more than lips and tongues, he'd still stuck to his terms and walked out on her.

She'd gone to bed full of need and hunger, dying to be filled. Thinking about it later, however, she forced herself to concede she'd been lucky. She'd already listed the million-and-one reasons why she couldn't get involved with Oliver right now. A little wine and the offer of a kiss had made her forget them, but there was no harm done. He'd ended it, and she was glad.

Maybe if she told herself that often enough, she would begin to believe it. "This sucks," she mumbled.

"What's that sweetheart?" a voice asked.

She looked around to see a bunch of guys in dusty gym clothes and ball caps, who had just sat down in the booth directly behind hers. One of them was leaning over the back of his seat, invading her space, and her contemplation.

"Nothing, sorry," she insisted, her tone polite but cool.

"Hey, we won our game, how about joining us for a celebration?" said another of the men.

Good grief. Did men really think single women eating alone in restaurants were just praying a table full of sweaty dudes would invite her to join their six-some? The guys looked harmless—stockbroker, businessman types, in matching gym shorts and shirts and pricey sneakers. She didn't feel threatened. Nor, however, was she at all interested. "No, thanks."

Before she had to elaborate, she heard a ringing from her purse. Coming from L.A., where people's cell phones were connected to their heads by magnetic beams or something, she'd developed a loathing for anyone who yakked on one in public. Especially in a restaurant. But now, the excuse to cut short a conversation with some overly friendly jocks was most welcome.

When she saw the name on the caller ID, she was even more grateful. She'd talked to Tommy a few times since leaving home and he always managed to distract her from her troubles…usually by talking about his own.

His were always more interesting, anyway. *Hmm, this sexy rock star or that studly NBA player? Decisions, decisions.*

"Hey, sweetie," she said, her voice louder than technically necessary, just to underscore the point with the on-the-make guys. One of them continued to hover over the back of her booth, so she upped the lovey-dovey factor. "I've missed you so much."

"Missed you, too, sugar lips," Tommy said with a laugh. "Who's listening? Grandpa? Biker gang? Jealous she-hag?"

"Nothing of the sort. I'm at a pub, where I just finished dinner. It looks like it's a popular hangout for the local athletes."

"Any delicious athletes?"

"I honestly wouldn't know."

"Oh, come on, girlfriend, you losing your vision?"

Maybe for some things. She hadn't really been able to see any man since meeting the only one she wanted.

"Maybe just my enthusiasm."

Not to mention her opportunities.

"Any idea when you're going to be able to leave there yet?"

"I suspect I'm going to be here until the day you need me to come back," she admitted.

He grew serious. "Is your grandfather doing that badly?"

"No, he's doing very well. But I want to be around to cheer him on during rehab—it's tedious and painful. Plus I want to be at the house for him when he first comes home."

"When will that be? Will it leave you enough time for a trip? Maybe you could go to Montreal? They speak French. Or hey, there are lots of hunky Spanish-speaking dudes in Mexico. Doesn't Cancun sound awesome?"

"I don't think so. But I won't stay too long after he gets home. He'll have home health aides come in, and Madison said she could fly in from back East to relieve me in ten days or so."

"How is Mad, bad and dangerous to know?"

She chuckled. "Same old, same old. Ready to dive into her career playing hotshot reporter, fighting city hall, exposing corruption and never letting a man get the upper hand."

"The Reid sisters—toughest girls of Blue Lake Elementary."

"And don't you forget it."

"How could I? You two both acted as my beards at one time or another in high school. I couldn't have made it without you."

"Aww, you're such a romantic. How could we resist? You know Madison and I have both always been totally hot for you."

The eyeballs were probably popping out of the heads of the guys behind her now. They were likely envisioning wild threesomes and naughty hook-ups. Huh. Other than the threesome part, she was right there with them. Two would be quite enough for the hook-up that had been on her mind all week.

"Ooh, kinky. Gonna be *that* kind of wife, huh?"

"Don't push it," she muttered under her breath.

She settled into the corner, feeling her tension drift away. Talking to Tommy was like talking to a therapist. But she didn't want to talk to him about Oliver. Mainly because she knew her friend—he'd encourage her to jump the other man's bones or live to regret it later.

She already knew she was going to regret it later. That didn't mean she could do it now. First, because he wasn't the bone-jumping type; he was the type you lost your heart, body and soul to and lived the rest of your days pining for.

He also wasn't interested. Well, he *was* interested; he just wasn't going to act on that interest. So she couldn't, either.

"Sounds like you're really not going to have much time for booty calling your way across North America, much less Europe."

"No. I'm not." She held her breath, wondering if there had been any change, if the urgency had died down. Not wanting him to think she was backing out on him, she didn't ask.

Finally, he said, "Did you catch TMZ last night?"

"No, Grandpa only gets basic cable. Why?"

"Let's just say it's getting a little more uncomfortable down here. I guess me being seen around town without a woman—namely you—on my arm is making those engagement rumors die down. And others spike back up."

Was he asking if he could announce their engagement? Oh, she hoped not. She wasn't ready for that. She hadn't even had a chance to explain it to her family, though she knew they would understand. Tommy had spent just about every summer in her backyard when they were kids. They knew who he was and loved him almost as much as she did. They wouldn't necessarily approve, but they would understand she was marrying him out of loyalty, love and friendship. Still, she wanted to tell them herself before any stupid tabloid got hold of it.

"Why don't you stay home more often then?"

"I'm in demand, hot stuff. Gotta see and be seen."

God, she was not looking forward to being part of that. Except the red-carpet Oscar stuff. That should be an experience. Of course, it would be better if she were walking that carpet as a nominee, rather than the wife of one, but beggars couldn't be choosers. Considering she still hadn't nailed down her next project—she'd done the sketches she was asked for and sent them in, but hadn't heard anything yet—she doubted an Oscar nomination for best costume design would be coming her way very soon.

"Well, gotta go, babe. There's a party with my name on it."

"Be careful."

"I will."

Then, again because she sensed the guys in the next booth were listening, she added, "I love you."

"You know, once you're wearing my ring, guys won't be hitting on you all the time."

"That goes both ways."

"Bite your tongue!"

"Bye, Tommy."

"Bye. Love you, sugarplum."

She disconnected the call, glanced at the time and realized it was now nine. Probably not late enough for Oliver to be in bed, but late enough that she'd look weird and pathetic showing up at his door and thus wouldn't be tempted to find an excuse to knock on it. So she figured it was safe to call it a night.

She lifted her hand to call for the check, but before she could catch the young waitress's eye, her vision was blocked by a big jean-and-T-shirt-clad body. A body she'd know anywhere.

Eyeball to crotch with that familiar body, she swallowed hard and slowly lifted her gaze.

"Can I join you?" Oliver's tone was almost conciliatory, as if he regretted the way he'd ended things last night.

She swallowed hard. Why on earth had he now sought her out when he'd been trying so hard to avoid her?

"Candace?"

"Aren't you afraid I'm not wearing any underwear, or that I'll ask you for one little kiss?" she couldn't help asking.

Behind her, somebody started coughing. She ignored him.

"I guess I deserved that," he said, not cracking a smile.

There was no way to refuse him, and she gestured toward the empty seat across from her. She heard grumblings from the baseball team and could only imagine what they thought. She'd shot them down, then had a romantic phone conversation and now invited a gorgeous man to take a seat. They probably thought she was a bored housewife on the prowl, cheating on her poor spouse.

"What are you doing here?" she asked after he sat down.

"Your grandfather asked me to check on you."

Her brow shot up. "You two think I need babysitting?"

His scowl deepened, and he nodded toward the table full of guys behind her. "When I came in and looked over, one of those bozos was right above you, just waiting for you to move enough so he'd have a clear line of sight down your shirt."

She jerked her head around and looked over her shoulder. The amateur ballplayers all immediately ducked their heads together, as if realizing they'd been caught out.

"So you came storming over to defend my honor?"

That was rich, considering he was the only man who'd

come even close to sullying it lately. And oh, had she liked being sullied.

"No. They're men, they're out drinking beer and you're beautiful. Of course they're gonna look."

The *beautiful* part echoed in her ears.

His jaw tensed, and he crossed his arms over his chest and raised his voice slightly. "But if any of them even thinks about touching you, he'll be drinking his beer through a straw."

She should resent this he-man protector stuff. But instead, she found herself feeling all warm and soft at the realization that he felt protective of her. Mainly because it meant he somehow felt possessive of her.

He could have possessed you yesterday—twice—and twice he turned you down.

Right. She straightened in her seat, determined not to relax her guard around him, or let him know she was still smarting over what had happened. She was determined to forget all about yesterday, pretend she'd dreamed the whole thing. Well, except the orgasm. She wanted to remember that. She wanted to hug and hold that memory because, as far as she could remember, it was the only time her head had completely blown off her shoulders and then settled back into place.

The waitress sauntered over, lazy and laid-back as she'd been all evening. But when she reached the table, she did a double take and offered Oliver a much bigger smile than she'd offered Candace. "Hey, there, Mr. McKean. Nice to see you again!"

The woman practically simpered. Ugh.

"You want the usual?" the woman asked.

"Sure."

She was back with his beer in record time. "Can I get you something else? Anything at all?"

Candace gripped her hands together under the table,

determined not to react. It wasn't easy, especially when the woman responded to Oliver's request for a menu by leaning over him to grab a paper one standing between two condiment bottles on the back of the table. Her ample breasts rubbed his shoulders. He didn't appear to mind.

Once the waitress had walked away, after telling him to think about what he *wanted,* Candace said, "Gee, who's going to defend *your* honor?"

His jaw may have softened a bit. "You offering?"

"You didn't look like you needed—or wanted—any help."

"If I didn't know better, I'd say you sound jealous."

"How fortunate that you know better."

She reached into her purse, tucking her phone back inside. Before he'd shown up, she'd been planning to pull out some cash, pay her bill and leave. Now that he was here, though, she found herself wanting to stay.

"Have you eaten?" he asked.

"Yes."

"Okay, let me order, then I'll walk you to your car."

And leave him here to be the blue plate special for the big-boobed waitress? Not a chance.

"I'm fine," she replied sweetly. "I was thinking about ordering dessert." She grabbed another menu, skimmed over the offerings and decided on her very favorite: a dish of ice cream. Simple, easy, nonsuggestive, delicious vanilla ice cream.

After they'd ordered, they spoke briefly about her grandfather, and his reaction to their find in his wine cellar. The old man had been ecstatic, and had immediately started making plans for what he would do with the money. Most of his ideas had to do with helping out his family—her included—and for a moment, Candace had allowed herself to think she would not have to marry for money. Then she remembered. She wasn't really marrying for money. She was marrying for friendship. And no amount of money could ever replace Tommy in her life.

However she felt about Oliver as a man—and potential lover—she had to give him credit: he was a conscientious employee, though she suspected the relationship between the two men had moved beyond professional to personal. Grandpa liked him…that was quite obvious, and the feeling appeared to be reciprocated.

She was a little surprised by their conversation. Once they'd turned the focus away from them—the sexual tension that was so thick between them she was surprised she could see him across the table—she found Oliver very easy to talk to.

They chatted about the wine, and the results of the phone calls Candace had made today to an expert in the region. He had given her the number of an auction house in San Francisco, saying if she really did have the bottles she'd mentioned, they'd be begging for the chance to sell them. If not rich, Buddy was at least going to be a lot more comfortable soon.

The waitress returned with Oliver's hamburger a short time later, and brought Candace's ice cream. She waited until the woman had left to pick up the spoon and help herself to a small amount. Lifting it to her lips, she almost cooed, seeing the tiny black flecks of vanilla bean. This was her favorite treat. Not terribly decadent or exciting, but she had always had a thing for plain vanilla.

"You gonna marry that stuff or eat it?"

Startled, she almost dropped the spoon. She'd apparently been oohing and aahing over it before she'd even brought a spoonful to her lips. And, for a change, there had been absolutely nothing deliberate about it. She wasn't trying to tease him, taunt him or make him regret walking away from her yesterday. She just liked ice cream.

"I don't usually eat dessert."

"Don't let me stop you."

She inserted the spoon into her mouth and sighed in pleasure, closing her eyes as the creamy sweetness hit her tongue and made her taste buds burst to life. "How can something so plain and simple taste so incredibly good?"

The question had been a rhetorical one, but Oliver looked like he was giving it serious thought. Very serious. He appeared contemplative and stared at her, hard. Some devil within her made her dip the spoon into the dish and draw more toward her mouth, knowing he was watching, rapt and attentive.

"Mmm." She licked every drop, loving the tingle as the cold refreshment slid over her tongue and down her throat.

Okay, so now she was being deliberately provocative. But he so totally deserved it.

He grabbed his burger and started to eat it, not looking toward her again. Which made eating the ice cream a little less fun, though no less delicious.

She knew she shouldn't mess with him, shouldn't play with fire, but he'd been sending her mixed signals since the moment they'd met.

Takes one to know one.

True.

She scooped more, making another sound of satisfaction.

"You're such a brat."

She smiled. "I don't know what you're talking about." She licked the spoon clean, wiggling with delight.

"Would you stop it?" he asked after she'd swallowed.

"Stop what?"

"Stop licking that spoon like you're thinking about sex."

"I am thinking about sex," she admitted, licking again. She saw no reason to be coy and wasn't about to let him off the hook. "I've been thinking about it since last night. How could I not?"

He leaned over the table, coming closer, making everything around them disappear. "You're playing with fire."

"Funny, I don't feel like I'm getting burned. In fact, it's quite chilly."

He took another bite of his burger, chewing the thing like he had to wrangle it into submission. When she began to help herself to another spoonful of her dessert, he cast her a warning look. "Time for either a subject change or a table change. Your choice."

Meaning he would get up and leave her here alone if she didn't stop tormenting him? How cute was that? She honestly hadn't realized he would be that affected by her engaging in a little food foreplay. But she didn't want him changing tables. Not when the waitress might very well decide to take a break and plop down on his lap.

"Okay, subject change. Grandpa mentioned that you had a connection to the estate. *Your* great-grandfather was the silent movie star who built it?" That had surprised her, especially given Oliver's apparent disdain for the movie business.

"Yeah." He looked relieved she'd done as he asked. "A million years ago. I never knew him."

"Have you ever seen any of his movies?"

"Sure. My great-grandfather bought a bunch of them when his studio went bankrupt. My father has a box of them. We sometimes had family nights watching them when I was growing up."

"How very Norma Desmond," she murmured.

He nodded, getting the *Sunset Boulevard* reference.

"When he found out I was living here, he mailed me a few so I could show them to Buddy. I haven't had a chance to do it yet."

"What a fascinating era it must have been. So much more mysterious and glamorous than today, given the 24/7 coverage of every gruesome detail of a famous person's life." She knew her voice contained a hint of bitterness, on Tommy's behalf, but he didn't question her on it.

"They sure knew how to party, from the sound of it."

"I'd love to see one of those films."

He reached for his beer. "They're on big reels. A pain to operate, but they certainly make for an authentic experience. Buddy borrowed a projector from somebody, but we never got around to showing them."

Meaning he couldn't just give her a disk to pop into her laptop. He'd have to come in and set up a whole viewing room. Stay and operate the machine. Spend time with her, watching it. Like one of his family movie nights growing up, only it would just be the two of them.

"We can watch one some evening if you're bored."

This was sounding a little like a movie date, and she suddenly wondered if he would live to regret having her change the subject. She could eat all kinds of ice cream while watching a movie. And if he dared to offer her *two* kisses, she might finally get that multiple orgasm she'd been craving.

"I'd love that," she murmured. "It might make you feel like you're at home. Speaking of which, where does your family live now?"

"San Diego. I was born and raised there."

"Big family?"

"Parents, two sisters, one brother-in-law, one niece."

"All in Southern California?"

"Yes."

"So why aren't you there with them?"

"I was close, in Orange County, until four months ago."

Finally she was getting somewhere. "What on earth made you come up here?" she couldn't help asking. "I'd normally guess one of the three biggies—romance, legal trouble or job. But you appear to be single and don't look like the law-breaking type."

"I am. And I'm not."

She went over the answer in her mind, realizing he was admitting he was single—hallelujah—and an honest guy.

"Okay. So, number three. Job? I don't mean to offend you, but it seems to me your field isn't necessarily one that would require you to move so far away."

He sipped his beer again, not meeting her eye. She didn't push, sensing he was trying to reach a decision about how much to say. Finally, with a sigh, as if he realized she wasn't going to back off and would be around long enough to wear him down if she chose to, he admitted, "I was with the district attorney's office in L.A. until earlier this year."

"With...wait, you mean you're a *lawyer?*"

She shouldn't have been surprised, considering she'd already seen evidence of his intelligence, his memory and his darned interrogation skills. But it was just so strange to think of a big Los Angeles attorney moving up here to work as a laborer for her grandfather.

"It's a long story."

She merely stared.

"I don't want to get into it."

"Come on, you've got to give me more than, *I was a lawyer, quit and came up here to plant grapes.*" She suddenly remembered what he'd said the night they met, about feeling cleaner digging in the dirt here than he had in his previous life. Then she thought about the kinds of cases he must have been involved in. Los Angeles was a glitzy haven to starry-eyed actors and actresses. But anyone who actually lived there knew it could be incredibly seedy. Ugly, violent, with crimes and murders happening often enough to immunize its residents to the shock of them, unless they involved a movie star.

"One crappy case too many?" she speculated.

"Yes," he replied, staring straight into her eyes, looking a little surprised she'd understood so easily.

"I can see why you'd want to come here, then, if you needed a change. Better hard manual labor than a mental breakdown."

A smile appeared. "I don't know that I was near that point, but I was definitely feeling on the verge of a moral one."

"Oh?" Now he had her really curious.

He idly rubbed the tip of his finger on the rim of his beer mug. "You might not believe it, but criminal law is one hell of a competitive place."

"Well of course I believe it. I read John Grisham."

"Multiply that by a hundred and you might have an idea of how brutal the atmosphere can be, especially in a place like Hollywood, with the money and the star factor added in. There's a winner-take-all attitude, a score-points-on-the-other-guy mentality. It's not about guilt or innocence, not about finding the truth, not even always about justice. More than anything it's about winning."

That surprised her. She'd always been one of those idealists who believed in the justice system. But it sounded like Oliver no longer did.

"Oh, my God," she whispered, suddenly remembering some of the news coverage she'd seen last winter, about corruption uncovered in the district attorney's office. She didn't remember seeing Oliver's picture, or hearing his name, but she hadn't really been paying attention, and the timing certainly made sense. "Were you the whistle-blower?"

He stared into her eyes, not looking surprised she'd remembered the story. She didn't recall any of the details; she just knew the media had had a field day with the previous D.A., whose own employee had accused him of judicial misconduct, including hiding evidence of innocence in a high-profile murder case.

"Yeah," he said, lifting his mug and downing his beer.

"You were involved in that case where the kid in the gang was accused of murdering the pregnant mother?"

"It was my case. I was all set to go to trial when I found proof that he hadn't done it."

"And your boss buried it," she murmured, remembering more.

"Tried to." He leaned back, dropping his napkin onto his plate. "The kid was a punk, but it was mostly swagger. Maybe the close call will make him clean up his act." He frowned. "Or he could get worse and end up killing somebody after all."

"But he didn't kill that woman?"

"No, he didn't. I'd let myself go along with some of the crap you have to do to score convictions. Did stuff I'm not proud of. But I couldn't be a part of convicting an innocent young man of murder, no matter what he might do in the future."

Stepping forward and doing the right thing had been noble and admirable. But it had also probably cost him his job.

"Were you blackballed?"

"Blackballed, dumped by the woman I'd been seeing, shunned by people I'd thought were friends," he said with a harsh laugh.

"That's awful," she muttered, focused more on the dumping than anything else. How could any woman do that to this gorgeous, amazing man?

He went on. "I can never go back to any D.A.'s office in California, and I'm not ready to switch sides just yet."

"Defense attorney, you mean?"

"Right. I'm too jaded, too quick to see the bad side of humanity to start defending people I automatically assume are guilty. So for now, I dig, I shovel, I fertilize, I test pH, I till, I haul, I study. And I drink wine."

"I think that last one's my favorite."

This time, his laugh wasn't angry...it was soft and genuine.

Candace sat there and let the masculine sound wash over her. She'd seen him angry and tense, seen him sexy and aroused, seen him concerned. This was the first moment, though, that she truly believed she was seeing the real man, with his guard completely down. Seeing the Oliver he had been before his world had fallen apart last fall. She liked this man. Liked him a lot.

And oh, God, did she ever wish she had met him before she'd agreed to marry her best friend.

7

OLIVER WASN'T CERTAIN what had caused that warm, tender look to appear in Candace's lovely eyes, but he figured it was bad news. He liked it better—felt safer—when she was snapping at him, taunting him, even flirting with him. This softness, this sweetness, this emotion he saw in her now, was way outside of his comfort zone.

He should have kept his fat trap shut. He should never have told her anything about himself—his past, his regrets, his shame. Because now, he greatly feared, he'd opened up a window through which she could climb, going around his instinctive defenses.

So let her.

Huh. Maybe he should. He still wasn't ready for a relationship, still hated the idea of messing around with Buddy's granddaughter while the old man was laid up. But he had to admit, he found Candace incredibly easy to talk to. She had heart and brains to go with that boatload of sex appeal, which made her a triple threat. He couldn't deny he was tempted to take what she'd offered yesterday morning and last night. Maybe hooking up with someone who would be leaving in a week or so was exactly the right way to get back in the game of life.

Unfortunately, now that he'd realized he liked her as much as he wanted her, hooking up seemed less appetizing than it had before. He sensed it would satisfy him physically, but would just make the emotional strings that much harder to untangle. And emotions were still not his strong point.

"Will you excuse me a minute? I need to run to the ladies' room," she said.

He pushed his plate to the edge of the table so the overly flirtatious waitress, who'd come on to him every single time he walked into this joint, could pick it up. "Sure. I'll ask for the check."

She reached into her purse.

He waved a hand. "Forget it. It's on me."

"No way. You don't bring down the big bucks anymore."

He lifted a brow in challenge, remembering she'd said she was between jobs right now. "At least I'm employed."

"Good point. But I think I can spring for one hamburger."

Frankly, it was worth every penny to pay for her meal, if only for the pleasure of watching her eat that cursed ice cream.

He watched her walk away, again noting the changes in her wardrobe since she'd stopped wearing her sister's more loose, casual ensembles in favor of stylish, extremely colorful and bright stuff. Her jeans were fire-engine red. She wore them with spike-heeled black ankle boots, and a silky blouse that fell off one shoulder. Every guy in the place watched her go, Oliver included.

He would bet every other guy in the place would give his left nut to have kissed her, and touched her the way he'd touched her twenty-four hours ago.

You're a brainless bastard to have walked out on her like that.

If he had the day to do over again, he sensed yesterday

would have ended up very differently. He only wondered if it was too late to change things.

After she'd left, Oliver signaled for the waitress, cutting her off when she tried to engage in small talk. It had been fine that she'd flirted when Candace was around to see and get a little tight-lipped, but now that she was gone, he couldn't be bothered to play along. He hadn't been interested in this woman, or any of the others he'd met since coming here four months ago. Only one interested him.

So what are you going to do about it?

He honestly didn't know. But the more he got to know Candace, the more he wanted to do something.

"Hey, dude, you better watch it. She's toxic."

Startled, he looked up to see one of the jocks from the next table leaning over the back of his booth. He gave Oliver a look of manly commiseration that looked a little fake, as if he enjoyed spreading tales. "She's messing around on you."

"What?"

"Your girl. I heard her on the phone before you got here. She was all into whoever she was talking to. Just sayin', you should watch your back, man."

His muscles contracting, he realized he should tell the guy to go screw himself, that he and Candace weren't a couple and if she had been on the phone with anyone else, that was her business. Not his.

Instead, he simply ignored the jock, tossed some bills on the table and got up. No, he had no business questioning who Candace talked to. But she'd sure made it sound like she was single, and she'd certainly acted that way yesterday during their erotic encounters.

Could she really have a lover somewhere? Was she the type who got bored easily and was simply killing time with Oliver while she was stuck up here in Sonoma?

The thought bothered him more than he cared to admit.

So much so that he couldn't even force a tight smile when she got back and walked over to him.

She spied the bills on the table. "I told you I'd pay for mine."

"Forget it," he insisted, his tone brusque to match his attitude. "Are you ready to go? Because I'm leaving."

He didn't plan to walk out and leave her here, not now that he knew just how closely the table full of men had been watching her. But he didn't need her to know that.

"Sure," she said, blinking in surprise at his here's-your-hat-what's-your-hurry attitude.

He didn't enlighten her. Telling her what the nosy softball player at the next table had said would only open up a conversation he really didn't want to have. The only reason he'd need to know if she was available was if he intended to sleep with her.

He didn't.

Right?

They walked outside to the parking lot. While they'd been inside, the early signs of a storm had blown in. This area didn't get a whole lot of rain, and what it got usually came in the winter. But sometimes the spring brought wicked storms and it looked like they would have one tonight. The air was wildly alive, with gusts that had the trees bouncing and a whistling sound coming from under the eaves of the building.

Instead of tightening her jacket, ducking against the weather and racing to her car, Candace tilted her head back, smiled and closed her eyes. She apparently liked the feel of the wind battering her body. Liking it, too, he understood. There was something freeing about being in a climate so variable and elemental. L.A. and San Diego were pretty standard all year round—sunny, warm, beautiful. In the winter and spring months he'd been up here, he'd realized you couldn't really count on anything. You never knew when the winds would change and the air would crackle with electric excitement.

"I love this," she said, raising her voice to be heard.

"I can tell."

The gusts kept catching wispy strands of her honey-brown hair, blowing them across her face. She didn't even try tucking them behind her ears or restraining the long curls. The longer they stood outside, the more primal and tangled it became. She was beautiful, sultry, exotic…he had a sudden image of being back at the estate with her, outside, naked, letting the wind batter them as they came together in an explosion as powerful as a spring storm.

Unable to take it anymore, he looked away, not wanting to be utterly entranced by the wild, erotic picture she presented, all windblown and sexy, with her lips moist and parted in exhilaration as she breathed in the cool night air.

"It's going to break over us pretty soon," he said. "And it won't be a fun drive once it starts pouring. We should go."

Her shoulders slumped. "All right."

When they reached her rental car, she said, "It seems like a good night to stay inside. Maybe I could pay you back for dinner by picking up some candy and popcorn for our home movie night?"

He frowned. "It's late." It wasn't that late, maybe ten o'clock. Ten minutes ago he might have leaped at the chance. But the fact that he didn't know enough about her had been hammered home by the jock inside.

"Tomorrow maybe?"

"I don't know if I'll have time for that before you leave."

Disappointment flashed across her face. "Oh."

Part of him wanted to take it back, especially seeing the flash of hurt in her eyes. But it was better this way. Better that he put the walls firmly in place again. She'd be gone in a week, returning to her life and her…whoever the guy on the phone had been. Buddy would be home.

Oliver would descend back into his self-imposed purgatory. Everything would be as it should. Hell, maybe once he'd gotten his shit together, he'd go back to L.A. and look her up. Find out if she was single or not. But who knew when that would be?

"Well, thanks for dinner," she said as she got into her car. She wasn't meeting his eyes. Embarrassed? Angry? He wasn't sure.

Muttering, "You're welcome," he pushed the door shut. He strode to his own truck, not turning around as she revved up her car's engine, threw it in gear and tore out of the parking lot like she had a dragon on her tail.

Okay, so she was angry.

Hell.

It's better this way, he reminded himself.

Somehow, though, he didn't feel better. In fact, he felt like crap. Crappy enough that, rather than heading right for the Sonoma Highway and home, he stopped at a liquor store and bought a six-pack. Not just because he had the feeling he could use a second beer, but because he didn't want to get back to the estate until he knew she would be safely tucked inside Buddy's house.

But after his stop, as he began driving home, leaving the highway and hitting some of the twisty back roads, he couldn't get the image of her standing there, enjoying the wind in her face, out of his mind. Especially because that wind threatened to take the steering wheel out of his hands a couple of times. And now it had started to rain.

"Shit. You should have followed her home."

Candace wasn't used to driving in this area, with hilly roads full of dangerous switchbacks and steep drop-offs. The bad weather made it even worse. If he hadn't been such an ass, he could have made sure she was safe, and he practically held his breath until he got to the estate and saw her rental car in front of the main house.

He parked his truck outside the cottage, breathing a deep sigh of relief that she'd made it, too. Replaying their conversation back at the bar, he knew he'd behaved badly. So much for the smooth gentleman he'd always been praised as being in his old life. He'd been a total dick to Candace half the time. He'd been like a kid who knew he couldn't play with the toy he most wanted, so he'd pretended he didn't want it at all.

Tonight, he'd reacted like a prosecutor instead of like a man who was getting to know an honest, refreshing, bright and sexy woman. He hadn't given her the benefit of the doubt. Was he so jaded, so used to being lied to and manipulated that he no longer had the capacity to give someone a chance?

He owed her an apology. And if all the lights hadn't been off in the main house—the place utterly pitch-black in the windy night—he would have gone over and offered it up, even though he'd have had to run through the driving rain. But the building was obviously shut down. She'd come home, turned off every light and gone to bed, probably sending him a silent message to stay away from her.

"Message received," he said as he hurried to the door of his cottage, getting soaked along the way, and pulled out his key.

Buddy always laughed at him for locking the door since they were out in the middle of nowhere, but the big-city habit was too ingrained. He found himself wondering, though, if he'd really been out of it when he'd left earlier this evening for the hospital. Because the knob twisted easily in his hand. He must have forgotten to lock it.

Letting himself in, he reached for the switch on the wall and flipped it up. Nothing.

"Oh, God," he mumbled, suddenly realizing why the world was so dark. The power was notoriously unreliable in high winds, and his was probably out.

He waited for his eyes to adjust, before making his way across the big room that dominated the main floor of the cottage. It served as both living room and kitchen, the two separated by a stone fireplace that opened on either side. It was a great feature and he'd used it and nothing else to heat the place during the winter. Looked like it was going to come in handy tonight, too, both for heat and for illumination.

Before he moved to light it, he thought about Candace. She was alone in that huge house. That huge drafty house with its spiders, crickets, cracked window casings and frigid tile floors. No lights, no heat, no hot water—which was pretty well par for the course—and he'd bet the phones were out.

"Better go check on her," he mumbled.

Grabbing the coat he'd just placed on the hook, he began to put it on. But he hadn't even gotten one arm in a sleeve when he heard a soft, feminine voice coming from the sofa on the other side of the room.

"You don't have to check on her. She's right here."

CANDACE HAD ONLY been waiting for Oliver for a few minutes—since just after she'd gotten back, realized the power was out and decided his cozy cottage with the fireplace would be a better place to ride out the storm. But that had been long enough for her to decide she'd made a mistake.

Sitting here in the dark, in his space, had been more disturbing than comforting. The whole place smelled like him—all musky, spicy and hot. Utterly masculine. Her body reacted to the scent even before her mind could put it together and figure out it wasn't just the cold making her nipples hard.

She also worried how he would react to finding her there, in the dark, and what he would make of her presence. He was a private person; it had taken him days to even admit to her that he was really an attorney. He probably wouldn't take kindly to her using Buddy's keys to let herself in and make herself at home. She suddenly felt a little like Goldilocks. Add a broken chair and a few bowls of porridge and she might come face-to-face with an angry bear.

She'd decided to leave, to brave the cold and the darkness in the main house, when she heard him pull up outside. Her chance to escape was gone. She had to stay and brazen it out.

"Candace?"

"It sure isn't Goldilocks," she muttered.

He hung his coat back up and approached, moving carefully in the darkness. She'd been here longer; her eyes had adjusted, so she could easily see him moving toward her. His hair was wet, dark strands sticking to his unsmiling face.

"How did you get in?"

"I'm sorry. I used Buddy's key. I know it was rude."

"And illegal."

Twisting her hands in front of her, she rose from the couch. "I was freaked out. That place is spooky enough when it's daylight. I kept picturing spiders lurking in every corner."

"Not the ghost of Fatty Arbuckle stalking you?"

"Oh, great, thanks. That makes me feel tons better!"

"I'm surprised you know who I was referring to."

"Hello, movie biz, remember? Was he one of your great-grandpa's cronies?"

"They did a few films together," he said.

Very cool.

"Let me brighten things up a little in here."

He headed for the kitchen. She heard him fumble with something, and a moment later, a soft light spotlighted his handsome face. He came back carrying a thick candle, which he placed on the coffee table.

"So, do you want me to leave?"

He hesitated, then shook his head. "It's coming down in buckets. You'd be soaked to the skin with no way to warm up."

True. "I can stay?"

"Yes. Sit down. I'll light a fire."

"That would be wonderful."

She curled up on the couch again, watching him. Fortunately he'd had logs and kindling already set in the fireplace, and they sparked quickly. Within minutes, the small space was benefiting from the heat created by the blaze, and the room was enveloped in a lovely golden glow.

She took the opportunity to look around a bit, knowing he'd only been here a few months, but sensing he'd taken steps to make the place his own. There were some nonfiction books on the mantel, along with a few thrillers. No pictures on the walls, but a couple of framed family type snapshots stood on the end table. Some colorful pillows were tossed on the furniture, and the thick rug in front of the hearth looked new and cozy.

She'd definitely seen worse bachelor pads.

"Better?"

"Much, thank you."

He fell silent again, and she felt that tension between them that had appeared in the restaurant, after she'd gone to the ladies' room. Compared to his friendliness before she'd left, she couldn't help thinking something had happened. As she'd driven home, she'd half wondered if he'd made some assignation with the waitress and just wanted to be rid of her. She couldn't deny she'd held her breath waiting to hear him come home, and was pleased he had, even if it had meant she was trapped and busted as a home invader.

He finally broke the silence. "I think I owe you an apology."

"Oh?"

He sat on the floor, near the fireplace, on that thick rug. His long jeans-clad legs were stretched in front of him, booted feet casually crossed. The jeans pulled tight on those powerful thighs. She again noted how built he was, obviously not from any L.A. gym lifestyle but from his physically demanding job.

"Yeah. Earlier tonight, at the bar, one of the guys in the next booth told me you'd been on the phone before I arrived, having a very intimate conversation."

She laughed. "Of course I was—intentionally! My best friend called, and I was trying really hard to make it sound like he was my boyfriend, so they would stop pestering me."

He dropped his head back, shaking it and mumbling something under his breath. Something that sounded like, *idiot.*

Well, yeah, he had been. Being all macho-aloof instead of asking her about it had been the typical male reaction.

"Is that why you were such a jerk in the parking lot?"

He straightened to look at her. "I'm sorry."

"Were you angry about it?"

"Not angry. Jealous as hell," he admitted.

That sent warm shivers of excitement rushing through her. There was no reason for Oliver to have been jealous if he didn't want her for himself.

"I know it's none of my business, but you said you didn't have a boyfriend...."

"I don't," she insisted. "No boyfriend, no husband, no lover."

Just a fiancé.

The thought stabbed into her head like a brain freeze, shocking and painful. She was so used to not being involved with anyone, it was hard to remember that now, she technically was.

Oh, hell, what a mess.

She knew she should just tell him the situation, be honest and let him know what was happening. But in order to do that, she'd have to tell him why she'd agreed to a sexless marriage, and why it was okay for her to cheat on her fiancé.

She couldn't out Tommy to somebody he didn't know. Nobody had that right. Especially because, even if she didn't reveal the name of her future husband, once the press got hold of her engagement and marriage, Oliver would realize who she'd been talking about. It wasn't like he was some foreign, overseas stranger who would never give her another thought. He lived right in California, worked for her grandfather. His family lived in San Diego, and he probably still had plenty of work ties to L.A. No, he wasn't the type who would run tattling to the press the minute he heard the news, but what if he accidentally said something to the wrong person? Tommy could be hurt—badly—because of her. She just couldn't risk it.

Telling him the truth was out. But lying was just against her nature.

Was there a happy medium? Could she walk the tightrope and take what she wanted more than anything in the world—a wild affair with Oliver—without jeopardizing her best friend's reputation?

Oliver watched her from the floor, his dark eyes catching glimmers of firelight, reflecting them. He cast a long deliberate stare over her, gazing from her face, down her throat, to the single bare shoulder revealed by her blouse. She'd been wearing a raincoat when she came in, but hadn't wanted to get his couch wet. At least, that's what she'd told herself. Actually, the thought of him looking at her, like this, hadn't been a small part of the reason she'd taken the coat off.

Something was happening between them. Heat—quiet but intense—flared. But the problem bore repeating: what a mess.

"This has been pretty inevitable, hasn't it?" he asked, his tone simple, to the point. As if he'd given up resisting something they had both known was going to happen.

"Yes, I think so."

He wanted her. That was obvious. He'd been fighting it, as had she. But it seemed they'd both had enough of playing games. The attraction between them had been thick from the moment they'd met. They were always headed to this moment. Always.

Find the happy medium, an inner voice urged.

She couldn't let it go that one last step toward becoming this amazing man's lover until she'd clarified a couple of things. No, she couldn't reveal Tommy's secret, but she had to be as honest as she could be. "You need to know something."

He didn't seem to be paying attention. Instead he got on his knees, crawling closer to the edge of the couch. His glittering eyes were narrowed, his lips parted, his hair was damp and hanging in his face. He looked earthy, primal and...hungry.

"Oliver..."

"Unless you need to tell me you're a virgin or a nun, I don't think there's anything else I absolutely have to know right now."

She couldn't help laughing a little at his vehemence. "What if I needed to tell you I was gay?"

He moved closer, dropping his hand on her calf. "Then I'd tell you you're a liar."

She swallowed hard, feeling the heat of his palm through her jeans. He squeezed lightly.

Quivering in reaction, she managed to insist, "I really do need to make something clear."

He hesitated. Her heart ached as she thought of doing anything to sabotage what she sensed could be one of the most sensual, erotic nights of her life, but she had to at least try to make things as open as possible.

"Whatever happens can't go beyond this week."

He smiled a little, looking relieved. Okay, maybe he had just wanted a one-night, or one-week, stand. Which shouldn't have bothered her, since a week was all she had. But her insides twisted, anyway.

Stop overanalyzing. Maybe he's just relieved you didn't say you were transgendered.

She forced herself to go on. "I meant it when I said I don't have a lover or a boyfriend, but that doesn't mean I'm free. I have made a serious commitment and I intend to keep my word. Once I leave here next week, when Grandpa gets home, this is completely over."

He eyed her intently. "You want to tell me what the commitment is?"

"I could try, but it wouldn't be easy for me to say too much without breaking someone else's confidence," she said, hoping that wouldn't be a deal-breaker.

"Understood," he said with a nod. She already knew he valued integrity and wasn't totally surprised he hadn't insisted she spill everything.

"You're an adult, you want me and you're not married. As long as all three of those things are true, then, honestly, right at this moment, I don't give a damn about anything else."

He fell silent. So did she. Their stares locked.

Finally she spoke. "All those things are true."

He moved closer.

"But I do have a request to make. Can we just agree

that, if we, uh…" She could feel her cheeks warming. "If we enjoy tonight…"

His spontaneous laugh made her smile. The man did not suffer from any lack of confidence.

"If we do, and we want to spend the rest of the week together, that's great," she explained. "After that week though, it's never mentioned again, never referred to. You don't contact me…. I don't contact you?"

"No strings? Absolutely no regrets?"

"Exactly."

He didn't jump for joy the way most men probably would have at hearing a woman admit she wanted a no-strings sexual affair with him. "You're serious?"

"Very."

He didn't answer for a moment, considering. Then, at last, he slowly nodded. "My life's too crazy now to even consider getting tangled in any strings. If that's really the way you want to play it, that's the way it'll be."

Another long stare. A silent assent.

Then an exchange of slow, sultry smiles.

They'd made a bargain. They would be lovers.

She had a week. And she intended to enjoy every minute of it.

8

ONCE THE WORDS had been said, the deal struck, Candace let all her questions, doubts and worries fade away. She might not have a long-term future with Oliver, and her life might be taking her in directions she could never have imagined, but for now, for tonight at least, she intended to enjoy herself with a man who made her whole body come alive.

"I have a bed upstairs in the loft," Oliver murmured, sliding his hand down her calf.

"I like it right here," she said, not willing to waste the time moving, not when she was finally going to get what she'd so desperately wanted.

His approving nod said he agreed. When he reached into his pocket and withdrew a condom, she knew he'd been anticipating this moment. Considering she'd picked up a box at the drug store and had a few tucked into her purse, she couldn't pretend to take offense. She could only be grateful.

The man was gloriously handsome at any time of day, in any lighting. But when he tugged at his shirt and pulled it up and over his head, tossing it to the floor, she had to admit he did amazing things for firelight.

His body was perfectly shaped. The shoulders so broad,

the chest beautifully sculpted. Months of hard, physical labor had obviously eradicated any sign of the L.A. lawyer and turned him into a muscular god, with incredibly defined abs, a lean waist and slim hips. A light swirl of hair encircled his nipples, trailing down into a thin line that disappeared into the waistband of his jeans.

She licked her lips, wanting to see where that happy trail led. But after kicking off his shoes, he stopped, leaving his jeans in place.

She pouted. "Keep going. You definitely don't have to stop on my account."

"We'll get there. But fair's fair. You're still fully dressed."

"You can fix that for me."

"I'd be happy to."

He tugged the boots off her feet, then gently palmed and massaged her arches. When his fingers slipped up under her pant legs, the brush of skin on skin made her internal temperature soar. An hour ago she'd been freezing. Now she knew a spark had just ignited and she was going up in flames.

Her skinny jeans were tight, and he couldn't move his hand nearly high enough to satisfy her, so she stretched out and began to wriggle, reaching for her waistband.

"No. Let me," he insisted.

Still kneeling on the floor, he touched his way up her limbs, slowly, deliberately. By the time those talented fingers reached the tops of her thighs, she was groaning. She couldn't begin to imagine what it would be like when he finally got her undressed. Fortunately, she knew she wouldn't have to wait long to find out.

"Please, hurry," she whispered when he traipsed his knuckles up the strip of fabric covering the zipper.

"You're not the patient sort, are you?"

"If you go negative-two miles an hour I might just have

to kill you," she admitted, whimpering when he reached for the button and unfastened her jeans.

"We have all night," he insisted, not sounding the least bit prodded to speed up. "I've been thinking about this—dreaming about it—since the minute we met. There's no way in hell I'm rushing through it."

"Ditto," she admitted. Then, being honest, she added, "The thinking and the dreaming part, I mean. I'm all about rushing."

Fast and hard. Deep and wild. She was dying to be filled by him, possessed, pounded into and taken.

"Sorry, beautiful. It's not happening."

He slid the zipper down slowly. She could practically hear the teeth separating, the faint hiss competing with the roar of the wind outside, the crackling of the fire and the pounding of her blood in her veins.

When he'd finished unzipping her, she lifted her hips, shimmying to help him as he pulled the pants down, peeling them off and baring her legs. To her disappointment, he didn't slide his hands down the front of her groin, didn't take the skimpy panties with the jeans. But she really hadn't expected him to. Aside from what he'd just admitted, Oliver had already proven himself to be a very patient man. He was going to take his time, go slow, wring every ounce of pleasure out of each and every experience they shared.

"I will, too," she told herself, whispering it aloud. "I can do this."

"You will and can what?"

"I'll go slow," she promised. Then he traced the tip of his finger along the elastic edge of her panties and she whimpered. "Oh, God, yes, please, rip them off. Take me!"

His chuckle was pure evil. "That's not going slow." He slid his finger below the elastic, scraping it into the soft tuft of curls nesting at the top of her sex, then away again.

"I said slow, not in slow motion," she groaned, her hips thrusting up as a nameless but very familiar need took over.

"We're just getting started," he insisted, moving his hands to the bottom hem of her blouse.

Okay, that detour she could allow. Her breasts were aching, her nipples pointy and so sensitized her own shirt was giving her a thrill. His mouth and hands would likely send her out of her mind.

"God, you're beautiful. It killed me not to be able to look down at you last night when I touched your breasts," he whispered as he pushed the blouse up, revealing her tummy and her midriff. "Stay still. Let me explore you."

Being explored sounded good. Very good. She could be the wilds of undiscovered America and he could go all Lewis and Clark over every hill, valley and stream. She just hoped those hills were her breasts, the valley her pelvis and the stream the flood of creamy desire filling her sex.

He lowered his face so he could press a kiss on her hip bone. She felt the warmth of his breath on her skin, so close to her panty line, and instinctively rose to offer him more, praying he was eschewing the hills and valleys and going for the stream.

He moved in the other direction, though, kissing his way up the indentation of her pelvis, to her belly button.

She let out a groan that was half pleasure, half frustration. Ignoring her, he continued to push her blouse up, moving his mouth after it. Inch by inch, he explored her body, licking into each hollow between every rib, testing her, tasting her, breathing her in. It was wonderful, erotic…and frustrating. She was whimpering and twisting below him, wanting him to hurry up, but not ever wanting this to end.

He reached her bra, which opened with a front clasp. She held her breath, tensing as he touched the fastener with his thumb and finger, and deftly flicked it open, revealing her curves for his most delicious attention. He paused for a moment, staring, as if memorizing every line and dip. Her nipples were tight buds, pink and pointy, obviously begging for some attention.

But when he again began to trace his mouth over her, he focused on her sternum, kissing his way right up between her sensitive breasts, his smooth cheeks brushing against the sides but making no effort to suck away some of her tension. Nor did his teasing hand offer any relief, as he simply continued those light, delicate strokes over her belly, her pelvis and her upper thighs, never giving her what she really needed.

"Oh, God," she groaned, every inch of her burning. Her senses were so deliciously heightened the pleasure was almost pain. She'd never felt anything like it, never been so totally keyed up and ready.

Shudders coursed through her body, her muscles tensing, every inch of her aware and anxious. But he didn't give her any relief. He was entirely focused on what he was doing. He seemed to love the curve of her collarbone, which he sampled and scraped his teeth across. He found something delightfully kissable in the hollow of her throat. Here he licked. There he pressed his face and breathed her in. Here and there, there and here.

It was wonderful. Erotic. The anticipation was beyond anything she'd ever experienced.

But she was dying. Just dying. Because every tender caress he placed on one part of her body only sent more currents of hot, electric desire to her core. Her clit was so hard it ached, her sex was throbbing, all her nerve endings seemed to have bunched between her thighs.

Maybe because she'd only ever been with guys her own age, and those in the movie business, who were always on a schedule, she'd never had a lover take so much time, be so deliberate in every caress. Oliver seemed to savor every part of her he uncovered. He appeared determined to pay full, glorious attention to every inch of her body, leaving the choicest bits for last.

Her tummy and throat and, oh, the nape of her neck, adored him for it.

Her choicest bits were screaming for his attention.

"Shh," he ordered.

"I didn't say anything," she groaned.

"Your thoughts are very loud, Candace." He lifted his head to look at her, a smile of pure wickedness on his face. "I know what you want."

"Well, mind reader, if I've been so obvious, why..."

"Oh, you've been very obvious," he insisted with a low, sultry laugh. "And I'm looking forward to meeting your every demand." He bent to slide his lips over her jaw, moving up until he reached her ear and traced the lobe with the tip of his tongue. "But I'd like to at least kiss you before I slide my tongue into your pussy and lick you until you don't remember what planet you're on."

Bam. Explosion.

"Oh, God!"

She climaxed, just like that, from those words, from the weight of his hand on her thigh and the slide of his mouth on her cheek. Her whole body quaked, hot bolts of pleasure rocketing through her. This wasn't a slow, pulsing wave; it was a tsunami, hitting her hard in every direction. As he'd insisted he wanted to, Oliver moved his mouth over hers, catching her gasps of pleasure with his lips, taking them in and swallowing them down.

When she finally regained a brain cell, she realized Oliver had somehow managed to tug her tiny panties off her hips and push them out of the way. They were tangled around her legs, and she kicked and bucked to get free of them. He helped, drawing them all the way off her.

His wickedly erotic words still echoed in her ears, and she held her breath, wondering if he would now go back to some of those choice bits for more attention. When he began to kiss his way down her body, she suspected that's exactly what he intended.

"Oh, yes," she groaned.

He ignored her, his mouth moving down between her breasts. But this time, thankfully, he detoured and pressed hot, openmouthed kisses on her breast. She was whimpering by the time that wonderful mouth moved to cover her nipple and cried out when he sucked it. He caught her other one in his fingers, teasing and tweaking, plumping her breast in his hand while continuing to suckle her into incoherence.

Not until he'd paid equal attention to her other rock-hard nipple did he continue his downward journey over her body. He licked a line straight down, tasting her inch by inch. He nibbled her belly, nipped at her hip bone, his lips grazing the hollow above her groin. His face brushed against the curls concealing her sex and she couldn't stop her hips from thrusting up in welcome.

He turned her to face him, then tugged one leg over his shoulder, opening her to his hungry gaze.

"Oliver," she whimpered as embarrassment warred with utter lust. The look on his face was so covetous, so admiring, she decided to go with the lust.

"You are absolutely mouthwatering." He traced his fingertip over her clit, then down, separating the lips of her sex, opening her for his most intimate perusal. "So pink and shiny. I love how wet you are."

She gulped. No lover had ever examined her so frankly, or spoken so bluntly. That thick note of hunger in his voice said he meant every word he said. This man knew how to use language, all right—he seduced her with every word he said. She'd bet he was wicked in the courtroom. And more wicked in the bedroom.

"This is so pretty," he mused as he thumbed her clit, rolling it around. He slipped a finger into her channel, drawing a low gasp from her. "And so is this. I can't decide which I want to taste more."

He was apparently the decisive sort. Because not ten seconds had passed before he moved his head between her thighs and went down.

When he buried his face in her sex and began to devour her, she saw stars. She clutched him, twining her fingers in his hair as he lifted her other leg and draped it over his shoulder. Her limbs were practically wrapped around his neck, but he didn't seem interested in going anywhere else, so she left them there and focused on the incredible sensation of his mouth against her plump, swollen lips.

He devoured her, licking into her, making love to her with his tongue. She was gasping as he moved up to her clit and gently sucked and stroked. Back and forth he went until she was arching, twisting, helpless against her body's intense reaction.

This time, when she came in a heated rush, he didn't stop what he was doing. He went right on pleasuring her, focusing on her clit while he slid his fingers deep into her and worked some magic on a spot high inside. Tears formed in her eyes, and she was whimpering as another orgasm washed over her.

Now he finally seemed satisfied. He gently lowered her legs and kissed his way back up her body. Still dazed, she only regained her senses when she realized he was pulling away to stand up and unfasten his jeans.

This was worth her full, utmost attention.

She caught her lip between her teeth and watched him, feeling like a kid on Christmas morning who was finally going to get to open her biggest present.

"Wow," she whispered when he peeled away his boxer briefs.

Because big didn't quite describe him. His cock could be described with three of her favorite adjectives: *long, thick* and *rock-hard*. It jutted out, proud and male and hot. That river between her legs threatened to turn into an ocean just at the sight of him.

"I've been walking around like this since the night you slammed me with the frying pan."

"Feel free to get even by slamming me with that," she whispered.

He chuckled softly, but he soon stopped laughing. Because Candace wasn't satisfied with just looking. She had to touch him, feel all that silk-encased steel.

She sat up straight. Scooting to the very edge of the couch, she parted her thighs to make room for his legs and leaned close to his naked body. Close enough to cast warm breaths of air over him, her lips hovering an inch from all that luscious maleness. But she didn't go further, not quite yet. She wanted him as out of his mind with desire as she'd been.

Groaning, he twined his hands in her hair. Candace knew she was tormenting him, but knowing from very recent experience that anticipation was wonderful, she didn't give him what he wanted. Instead, she reached up and traced her fingers over his cock, from the top down the long back, to the sacs beneath. She cupped them gently, hearing his gasp and feeling his hands tighten in her hair. The position was incredibly intimate. He was as physically vulnerable as a man could make himself, and she was conscious of the trust that must require. Obviously, given how men loved to be blown, the benefits had to outweigh the risk. And this time, she was finding herself truly looking forward to something she'd usually viewed as an item to check off a list during foreplay.

Not with him. Him she wanted to taste. Oliver she wanted to please.

She continued to breathe deeply, evenly, loving the musky scent of man that filled her nostrils. Wrapping her hand around as much of him as she could hold, she stroked him, up and down, squeezing lightly, knowing by the way his pulse pounded in his groin that his heart was racing.

Needing to smooth the glide, she lifted her hand and traced her fingers across the top of his cock, moistening them with the arousal seeping from the tip. Curious, she drew a finger to her mouth and licked the moisture from it.

"Jesus!"

She heard pure desperation in his voice. Casting a look up through her bangs and seeing Oliver's hungry expression, she knew she'd pushed him to his limits, and finally licked her lips and moved in for a deeper taste. He was definitely too big for her to take him all the way, but she did her best, taking the bulbous tip into her mouth and sucking gently.

"Oh, God, yeah," he groaned, pumping the tiniest bit, as if a slave to his body's demands.

She didn't mind. He tasted delicious—warm, a little salty, ever-so-smooth. The act was incredibly intimate, and she loved hearing his groans of pleasure as she sucked him as far as she could, laving him so he could glide more easily.

He didn't allow it to go on too long, not nearly as long as he'd pleasured her. Within a few minutes, he'd gently pushed her away.

"I want in."

The blunt demand made her shiver with excitement. He reached for her, drawing her to her feet, and she wasn't quite sure where they were going. When he lifted one of her legs so she could rest her foot on the arm of the couch, she got the picture.

He paused to tear open the condom packet and slide it

on—it was a wonder the thing fit. When he was sheathed, he drew her into his arms, covering her mouth and kissing her deeply. His erection was a powerful ridge between their bodies, and she arched toward it, needing him desperately.

"Please, Oliver," she insisted.

He gave her what she wanted, tilting her toward him and nudging into her curls. She was slick with want, her body opening in welcome. He eased into her, bringing ecstasy with him. Candace began to breathe in shallow little gasps as he filled her, inch by delicious inch. He was so thick, hard and hot that she felt every bit of him as he possessed her.

As if he realized that her whole body was melting, he grabbed her by the hips and lifted her. She wrapped her legs around his waist, allowing herself to sink fully onto him. As he impaled her, she threw her head back and let out a low, guttural cry of pleasure.

He began to thrust slowly, sinking deep, then drawing away. The man's strength surprised her. He seemed completely comfortable bearing her weight as they gave and took. She answered every stroke, clenching him deep inside, knowing by his shudders that he felt and enjoyed every squeeze.

Soon, the frenzy built. He drove faster; she cried louder. She clung to his shoulders, and he backed her against the wall. The leverage made things deeper, hotter, and he drove into her again and again, losing himself to the passion.

She was lost to it, too. Lost to everything but this moment, this man, this act, and giving all she had to bring them both to the pinnacle of delight. When she reached that peak, climaxing yet again, she held on tight and let him drive deep to attain his own.

WAKING UP THE next morning and seeing his bedside clock flashing, Oliver realized the power had come back on at some point during the night. Honestly, it wouldn't have mattered if it had remained off. He and Candace had created plenty of heat on their own, both down in front of the fireplace, and again later in this bed.

This small bed.

He had never been more aware of its size until now, when he felt her curled up against him, one slim leg entwined with his, her arm draped across his waist, her head on his shoulder.

He liked small beds, he decided.

He liked them a lot.

And he especially liked waking up to find her in bed with him, twined around him like she needed to touch as much of him as she could while she slept.

The light sifting in through the window said the storm had passed and the day appeared sunny and bright. There were a million things he could work on, but he had the feeling he was going to want to skip them in favor of making love to this beautiful woman again.

He had her for one week and one week only. He had no idea why those had been her terms, or what the secret was that she hadn't wanted to share. Last night, in the heat of the moment, he hadn't given a damn. Now though, he couldn't deny he was curious. But not curious enough to push her and risk losing out on what time he had left with her.

It was going to be a week he would never forget. And one she would never forget. He'd make absolutely certain of that.

"Mmm…good morning," she murmured.

He glanced down to see her looking up at him, yawning and blinking against the bright sunlight.

"Hi."

She curled her arm tighter, tucking her leg a little more intimately, and cuddled close. "How did you sleep?"

"Like a man who'd run a marathon," he admitted. "Something zapped all my strength last night."

"I think that was me." She might have been a cat for the satisfied purr in her tone.

"I told you the night we met that you should come with a warning label."

"What would it say?"

"Caution: combustible female. Approach only when wearing protective gear."

She giggled against his chest and traced a lazy hand down his stomach. "You wore protective gear last night."

True, though he wished he hadn't had to. The very idea of being buried inside her, skin to skin, was incredibly appealing. Unfortunately, he might never get that chance. Their relationship was very new, and short-term, and that kind of trust and intimacy usually didn't happen right away.

"What are you thinking?"

He had to be honest, so he told her the truth.

She quivered delicately and he saw a warm flush suffuse her cheeks. "Mind reader."

"Really?"

"Yes. I'm all for being responsible, but the truth is, I'm on the pill and I thought about throwing those condoms into the fireplace last night."

"It was probably best for us to talk about it first. I'd never put you at risk—you know that, right? I'm as healthy as a horse."

"After last night, didn't I prove I trust you?"

Oh, she definitely had, lowering her guard and surrendering herself to him in every way a woman could. Of course, he'd done the same. It was the most intimate he had ever been with anyone, which made the idea of him only having her for another week all the more untenable.

No strings. No emotions. That was the deal. And really, it was for the best.

Somehow, though, it was getting harder to remember that.

"And for what it's worth, I haven't been around the block a whole lot myself. In fact, before last night, it had been over a year since I was with anyone."

"Have men in Los Angeles gone blind, deaf and lost their sense of smell, taste and touch since I was away?"

She giggled, the sound cute and unusual for her. "Well, I don't usually go around asking guys to sniff me, and when I tell them to bite me, it's not a genuine invitation."

He couldn't resist sliding down and nibbling her neck.

"So you're saying?" he asked as he moved lower to kiss her chest, delighting in those perky, pouty nipples that cried out for attention.

She groaned and wrapped her legs around him. "I'm saying I want you inside me. Right now. Unless that's a problem for you."

It wasn't.

He immediately moved between her parted thighs and tested her readiness with his fully engorged cock. She was wet and warm, soft and yielding. So ready.

"Absolutely not a problem," he muttered as he buried himself to the hilt.

The sensation was blissful, all sweet heat and moisture, and he closed his eyes, giving in to the pleasure. Then they began to rock together, bathed in the morning light, connected in every way possible.

And not for the first time, he began to wonder how on earth he was ever going to let her go.

9

OVER THE NEXT couple of days, Candace found herself falling into a routine. She would get up early, and spend the morning with Grandpa, cheering him on with his rehab. Then she would come back to the house, have lunch with Oliver, have sex with Oliver, have orgasms with Oliver, do a little drawing, then go back to have dinner with Grandpa. Often Oliver accompanied her for dinner, though they left the sex and the orgasms at home.

She couldn't remember a time when she'd been happier. Oh, she was still very worried about her grandfather, and was now busy dealing with her newest assignment. The studio had called, saying they loved her sketches and wanted her for the project. She knew as well as anyone that this could be the film that got her some major attention. Aside from that, she was also busy talking to appraisers and auctioneers about the wine collection. And surrounding all that business and activity, a happy glow of personal contentment swirled around her just about every minute of the day.

She and Oliver did more than just have the most amazing sex. They cooked together, walked together, laughed together. She'd gotten him to open up a little more about his savaged career, and even got him to admit that, with his change in lifestyle, he probably could afford to put out a shingle and take on only the clients he truly believed were innocent.

Only one thing could pierce her glow of contentment: thinking about what awaited her back in L.A.

"Hey, chickie, whatcha doing?" Tommy asked when she'd answered the phone late one afternoon.

She hadn't told him about Oliver. The only person she'd even hinted to about her relationship with him was Madison, to whom she talked every other day or so. Her sister had been her other half since birth. They had the kind of bond few people ever experienced with a sibling. Madison knew how to keep a secret, so they usually told each other everything. But even Madison didn't know the whole story. Candace had kept some things from her, the most intimate things. She'd protected the relationship, wanting to keep it private for as long as it lasted. But the fact that it couldn't last much longer was crushing her.

"I'm shopping," she admitted. "I've got to buy a new dress."

"For?"

"There's a big winery owner's ball tomorrow night," she said, still wondering if she'd made the right decision in saying she would attend with Oliver.

Their relationship so far had been mostly about sex. Drinking wine, talking about Grandpa and him teaching her what he'd learned so far about the wine business had taken up some time, too. But other than that one dinner/dessert they'd shared at Wilhelm's, they'd never actually gone on a date. So last night, when her grandfather had told them he wanted the two of them to go to the event, since he had already RSVP'd for himself and Oliver, her first instinct was to refuse. Then she'd met Oliver's eye from across the hospital room and had seen the gleam of interest there.

She couldn't deny being curious. She'd gotten to know him as a working man. This formal, black-tie event might be her only chance to catch a glimpse of the man Oliver had been before his life imploded. Not that she didn't adore the man who'd taught her things about her body she'd never even known, but she wanted to learn as much about him as she could, while she could. She wanted to discover all his facets and imprint them on her memory, to tide her over for the long and lonely years that stretched ahead.

It was getting harder to think about those years, harder to envision the life she'd chosen for herself. Even the sound of Tommy's voice, which usually made her happy, twisted the knife in the wound. For a few days, she'd been able to pretend she was at the start of a relationship that could change her life.

Maybe it still would. Maybe she'd change from a normal, happy woman to a heartbroken, never-able-to-love-again sad case.

Love? What the hell are you thinking, girl?

"Sounds fancy."

She was still too busy tripping over the word *love* in her mind to respond.

"Where is it?" he asked.

She finally shook her head, forcing away thoughts she wasn't ready to deal with, and replied, "At a hotel in San Francisco."

"Nice. I love that city."

A faint smile tugged at her lips. "I can't imagine why."

"Do you think anyone would notice if I walked in the parade? I could blend in with the crowd."

"Maybe…if you covered yourself with gold body paint from head to toe and wore a rubber gorilla mask on your face."

"Party pooper."

She shrugged as she walked around the square in Sonoma, eyeing the windows of various boutiques. "Have you been behaving?"

"Define behaving."

"Staying out of the news?"

"Babe, I'm always in the news. I can't take a piss in a restaurant bathroom without some jackass trying to snap a picture he can sell to the tabs."

"That really sucks, Tommy," she said, hearing the note of sad resignation he couldn't disguise.

"Yeah, poor, poor me," he said, his dark mood lifting quickly, as always. "Remind me of that next time I get a contract for a ten-mill picture."

"Will do."

"Considering half of it will be yours, I'm sure you will!"

Right. His millions would be her millions. Somehow, that had meant something to her once upon a time. It just didn't now.

"Hey, have you heard from the studio?"

One bit of bright news. "Yes. I got the job."

"Congrats, girlfriend!"

"Thanks. They sent me the script and I'm starting on some prelims."

"Excellent. We should celebrate."

"We will. When I get back."

"When's that going to be again?"

She swallowed hard, knowing she had to say the words aloud—not just for his sake, but for hers.

"I'm coming home in a few days. Grandpa gets out of the rehab facility on Sunday. The last time I talked to Mad, she was booking a ticket to come out and spend some time with him. She should be here sometime this weekend."

"So there's nothing keeping you there?"

No. Nothing keeping her.

Nothing at all.

She wished she could talk to Tommy. Other than her sister, he was the one to whom she could always spill her darkest secrets and woes. And since her sister lived clear on the other side of the country, and they seldom saw each other, it was Tommy who she usually relied on.

But she couldn't talk to him about this. Couldn't admit anything about her amazing relationship with Oliver. It was too personal, too vulnerable, and she had to concede, too heartbreaking. Telling him would mean revealing her feelings—she could never keep those from him. If she revealed how she really felt, she would be putting Tom in a hell of a position.

Would he urge her to follow her heart, tell her he'd deal with the fallout?

Maybe.

Or maybe he'd panic and beg her not to bail on him.

Either way, she'd end up feeling like the worst friend in the world. Because she'd promised. Agreeing to marry him was not the kind of promise she could go back on, not when so much was riding on it for him. If she didn't follow through, his career could be over, and so could their friendship. So no matter how deeply she feared she was falling for Oliver McKean, her old friend had to come before her new lover.

Even if hers was the only heart in their strange triangle that ended up getting broken.

HEARING A CAR pull up that evening, Oliver walked to the front room of Buddy's house and gazed out the window. Candace had just returned from town, and as she got out, she pulled a plastic-wrapped bundle on a hanger with her. Her shopping trip had apparently been a success.

He still couldn't believe he'd agreed to escort her to the ball. The whole hobnob-with-the-wealthy-set had never been a big part of his life, though he'd attended a few events when he was with the D.A.'s office. But he sure hadn't hauled his tux with him when he'd moved; the thing was moldering in a storage unit along with most of his suits and a mountain of law books. He'd had to stop by a rental place to order one, which was always a pain in the ass. In fact, the whole thing was a bad idea all around.

But when Buddy had suggested it, he simply hadn't been able to resist. He wanted to take Candace out, to have her on his arm, at least once. Wanted to show her a great time that didn't include them being in bed.

Well, it would probably end up with them in bed. In fact, considering he'd booked a room at the hotel, he was counting on it ending up there. Still, the point remained. He didn't want her just for the phenomenal sex. He liked being with her, and wanted her to know it.

Why, he had no idea.

Because you don't want her to leave, jackass.

Oh. Yeah. That.

Oliver had set up a special evening for them and looked forward to seeing her reaction when she walked in the door. Candace had appeared happy since the moment they'd become lovers, but every so often a shadow would appear. Her lush mouth would pull down, her brow would furrow with worry, and he knew she was stressing over something. He had a feeling it was because she was hearing the ticking of the clock. Frankly, he was stressing over it, too.

When he'd agreed to her one-week-only terms, he hadn't been thinking about much beyond getting her naked. Saying goodbye hadn't sounded so painful if it meant a week of mind-altering sex. But now that he'd become addicted to that mind-altering sex, and, he greatly feared, the woman with whom he was having it, her imminent departure weighed on him heavily.

So ask her to stay. Or to at least keep the lines of communication open when she leaves.

The thought had definitely occurred to him. He just wasn't sure he was ready to broach the subject with her. He didn't want her to go, but he also didn't want to spoil the last few days of the week she'd allotted them by pushing for more before she was ready.

She reached the porch, and he opened the door before she could even grasp the knob.

"Hi."

The furrow and the frown disappeared, as did the faintly slumped shoulders that hinted she bore some heavy weight. He would like to help her with that, but whenever their conversations turned too personal, she changed the subject by dropping an item of clothing.

Somehow, that always worked.

She draped what looked like a glittery, siren-red dress— God help him—over the railing at the bottom of the stairs. "Hi, yourself."

Stepping into his arms, she lifted her face for a kiss, and he welcomed her. It felt as right as everything else about them, this easy, coming-home embrace, as if they'd always walked into each other's arms at the end of a day.

"Success?" he asked.

She nodded. "A little out of my price range, but some of those boutiques are amazing. I think you're going to like my pretty new outfit."

The way she said it made it sound like the thing was sweet and innocent. He knew, however, judging by that color and the scantiness of the material, that it would be anything but.

"You're messing with me, right?"

"Oh, absolutely. You're going to love my wicked new take-me-now dress."

He could hardly wait. But considering he'd made other

plans for this evening, wanting to show her they could be more to each other than just incredibly erotic sex partners, he figured that would have to wait.

"Did you eat?"

"Nope."

"Good." He took her arm and steered her toward the living room, which he'd set up for tonight's surprise.

When she saw the large, old-fashioned movie projector, and the screen he'd erected against the far wall, she clapped her hands together. "Movie night?"

"You got it."

Smiling broadly, she walked over to the couch, then saw the feast he'd spread out on the coffee table just beyond it. He had never taken her to a movie, so he'd had to guess what her favorite candy would be. Covering all the bases had seemed like a good idea at the time.

"Hot dogs, nachos, popcorn…oh, my God. Dots? You bought me Dots? They're my absolute favorite," she gushed, hurrying over and plucking that box from among all the other junk food he'd piled onto the table. "If there's a wedding ring in this box, I'll say yes on the spot."

She was laughing, her eyes sparkling, but the moment the words left her mouth, she winced and bit her bottom lip. Obviously sheepish, she mumbled, "Sorry, I was just…"

"I know," he said, waving off her explanations. To be honest, he didn't want to discuss that topic any more than she did. Not because he was upset she'd mentioned it, but because the idea wasn't as immediately horrifying as he'd have thought a few weeks ago. No, he was in no way ready to get married. But since meeting Candace, he no longer considered *marriage* to be a dirty word.

He couldn't help wondering if costume designers could telecommute. How strange would it be if it turned out that he'd come up to Sonoma to find out what he wanted from the rest of his life and discovered what he wanted lived back in L.A.?

"So, what are we watching?" she asked as she kicked off her shoes and plopped onto the couch. "One of your great-grandfather's hits?"

"I don't know if it was a hit," he said, eyeing the metal case in which the movie reel had been packed. He walked over to the projector, through which he'd already threaded the film, and flipped it on. Dimming the lights, he explained, "I haven't seen this one before myself. Judging by the title, *Master of the Heated Sands,* it's either about a sheikh in a desert or a pimp in Miami."

She snickered, opened a box of her favorite candy and popped three of the juicy, colorful little treats into her mouth. "Num num," she murmured as she chewed, her grin as wide as a kid's.

He'd never developed a taste for gummy candy, but he couldn't deny he suddenly wondered how the confection would taste when devoured off Candace Reid's tongue.

"What?" she asked, obviously catching him in his stare as he returned to the couch and sat down next to her.

"I'm suddenly developing a sweet tooth."

She clutched the box to her chest. "Mine."

He snorted a laugh. "You weren't watching *Barney* the day they went over that whole sharing thing, huh?"

"Are you kidding? I was forced to share from the minute I drew breath. Madison and I had to split everything fifty-fifty."

"Your sister?" She'd mentioned Madison, who would be coming in from the east coast this weekend, always speaking fondly of her only sibling.

"Yep. Believe me, I never had a thing to call my own."

"Close in age, huh?"

Her grin was infectious. "Uh, yeah. You could definitely say that."

Before she could elaborate, the movie began to play. The image flickered on the screen, grainy and gray, and the credits began to roll.

"Where's the music?" she asked, looking confused. "Didn't they always have that really dramatic music underscoring everything?"

"The music wasn't imprinted on the movie any more than dialogue could be—hence the term *silent picture*."

She smacked her palm against her own forehead. "Duh."

"Hey, don't be too hard on yourself. I asked exactly the same question the first time I watched one of these with my family."

"Whenever I see clips from these old movies, there's always music. Where'd it come from?"

"The written score always accompanied the reels when they were sent out to the big movie houses." He reached for the bucket of popcorn. "In-house organists would play along as the movie ran."

"Live?"

"Yes. I've seen some pictures from some of my great-grandfather's movie openings. There were huge, elaborate organs."

"Guess the musicians had to be fast studies."

"I suspect a lot of it sounded alike.It was the cue to the audience about how they were supposed to feel."

"Have you ever seen any of those YouTube videos people make with clips of horror movies set to the soundtrack from a comedy? Or vice versa? The music definitely makes the moment."

"So, should I hum?" he asked with a grin.

"Are you any good?"

"I'm told I have the perfect voice for singing in the shower. Or on a deserted island."

Laughing, she curled up against him on the couch, watching as the credits finished and the action started. He draped an arm over her, amazed at how natural this was, how laid-back and comfortable. He found her so easy to talk to. There was no pretension with her, no subtext that he'd often experienced with other women, when they'd say one thing but mean another.

Candace was nothing like that. She was honest—refreshingly so—and utterly open.

Except about her secret.

Yeah. Except about that.

Forcing himself not to think about it, he focused on the screen, immediately recognizing his ancestor, who rode in on a beautiful Arabian horse.

"Not exactly politically correct," he said, noting the heavy makeup.

"Shh."

"Why do I have to shh when there's nothing to hear?"

She elbowed him in the ribs. "I'm reading."

"And you need to hear to do that?"

"Yes, so I can create the voices in my head."

She sounded a little testy, and he couldn't resist baiting her. "Hearing voices in your head…do that a lot, do you?"

She sat up and glared at him. "Shut up or I'm going for the pots and pans."

He held up a self-protective hand before making a zipping motion over his lips.

Leaning over and brushing a quick kiss on his lips, she settled back against him, her arm around his waist, her head tucked against his shoulder. She fit perfectly against him and this little scene of domestic tranquility seemed somehow right, even though it was against everything he'd expected for himself in recent months.

As they watched the story unfold, he found himself getting immersed in it. Something about watching without the music made it more dramatic. It was easier to focus on the images, the way the actors emoted. The plot was easy to follow, and probably typical of the era. Handsome sheikh rescues beautiful blonde American woman from the dangers of the desert and whisks her off to his sensuous silk-swathed palace. Their people try to tear them apart, but in the end, true love triumphs over all.

Once the film ended, Candace murmured, "It's just like that line from *Sunset Boulevard.* They didn't need words, they had faces."

"I think you're right."

"Your great-granddad was a handsome dude."

"He was apparently quite the rogue."

"Like grandfather like grandson?"

He grunted and slipped his arm out from under her so he could go turn off the projector.

"Come on, Oliver, spill," she said, leaning over the arm of the couch to watch him. "Did you leave a trail of broken hearts throughout Hollywood when you moved up here?"

"Hardly." He swallowed visibly. "Just the one."

The teasing light faded from her eyes. "You mentioned that at the bar. She left you because of the scandal?"

"Yes. She bailed right around the time the newspapers started sucking my blood."

He flipped the projector off, not bothering to turn on the floor lamp in the corner. It was cozy in here, with enough illumination spilling in from the nearby kitchen to cast warm streaks of light on her beautiful face.

He hadn't necessarily intended to have this conversation, but figured it had probably been inevitable. So he admitted, "We worked together. When I started making waves in our little office pool, she swam for the shallow end and left me there, treading water."

Looking indignant on his behalf, she sat up and crossed her arms over her chest. "Bitch."

"Maybe. She was ambitious and didn't want to go down with a sinking ship."

"Then she obviously didn't care very much about you. She could have, at the very least, thrown you a life preserver."

Nobody had. None of his colleagues, anyway. Nobody he worked with had wanted to come anywhere near him once he'd made himself a marked man by going up against the powerful D.A. Yes, eventually the media, the public and the judicial system had started calling him a rare man with integrity. A hero. But behind closed doors, he had been vilified. He was finished in Orange County, and he knew it. Unless, as Candace had suggested, he kept on living simply and started taking some jobs on his own. He couldn't deny he'd been thinking about it since she'd suggested it. His experience as a prosecutor had made him view most defendants as guilty, but he knew in his soul that some were not. It was just a matter of finding them.

Candace rose to her feet, crossed to him and put her hand on his chest. "I'm sorry you had to go through that, Oliver. But can I also say I'm glad it brought you here? I honestly hate to think of what my life would be like right now if you hadn't been here waiting for me when I arrived."

He put his hands on her hips and drew her close, pressing a soft kiss on her mouth. She wrapped her arms around his neck and kissed him more deeply, parting her lips, sliding that delicious tongue out to play with his. God, how he loved kissing this woman. Loved the way she molded against his body, every curve of her fitting into some hollow in his.

After a long moment, she said, "Want to head over to your place?"

By unspoken agreement, they'd confined their lovemaking to the cottage, as if neither of them wanted to take advantage of Buddy by making love in his house. "Yeah."

"Give me a couple of minutes," she said with an impish smile. She walked toward the stairs. "I want to throw a few things in a bag."

He didn't think she meant luggage since his place was all of a hundred yards from here. He could only hope she meant she wanted to pack something sinfully sultry...or wickedly erotic.

"Am I going to like what you're packing?"

"You're going to love what I'm packing," she promised with a saucy wink. Then she turned and hurried up the stairs.

Figuring he'd have a few minutes, Oliver carefully took apart the old projector. He placed the components back in the case, and collapsed the screen. Buddy had kept the things in a small storage room adjoining the kitchen, so he carried them back there, carefully setting the antique equipment in a corner where it wouldn't be tripped on. Afterward, he cleaned up the food and their drinks and carried the leftovers to the kitchen, finding places for them in the cabinets.

The Dots he kept. He tucked the half-empty box into his pocket, envisioning a few places he'd like to put them... just so he could pull them back out with his teeth and his tongue.

Before the night was over, he might end up liking gummy candy after all.

With that thought in mind, he was smiling as he walked back toward the front of the house. Candace was standing at the bottom of the stairs, her back to him, looking up. She'd changed her clothes and had slipped into something a little more comfortable. Not a sexy nightie, unfortunately, just a loose-fitting pair of jeans and a sweatshirt. He couldn't stop a tiny stab of disappointment that she wasn't wearing leather and screw-me heels, but figured it was chilly out and she'd have more to strip off in front of him when they got to his bedroom.

"I can't wait to get these off you," he murmured, coming up behind her and sliding an arm around her waist.

She gasped, obviously startled. Oliver held her tighter, spreading his hand across her belly, pulling her hard against him so her curvy butt pressed against his rapidly hardening cock, and bent to nibble on her neck. "You make me crazy, Candace. All day long, I think about nothing but getting you naked and wet."

Rather than lifting her arm over her shoulder and encircling his neck, or tilting her head to give him more access, she cleared her throat and slowly turned around to face him. His hands dropped lower, cupping her backside, and he looked down at her.

Then he blinked, wondering what was wrong. Something was…off. She wore a look of amused speculation that he couldn't remember ever seeing before and her lips were curled up in a tiny, jaded smile that was half sneer. Candace's grin was usually far more sexy—or, occasionally, sweet. Never jaded. Not Candace.

Tilting his head in confusion, he stared at her, slowly drawing in a breath. Because the truth finally landed in his befuddled brain.

"Son of a bitch," he whispered. "You're not Candace."

10

WHEN SHE HEARD Oliver speak, Candace thought for a moment he'd called out to her from downstairs. She strode to the top of the staircase and glanced down, expecting to find him looking up at her.

Instead, she saw the man she was falling for, with his hands on her sister's ass.

"Whoa!" she called, charging down the stairs, taking them a couple at a time as she descended.

Oliver, his mouth agape, stared at her, then at Madison, then back at her. He dropped his hands and took a quick step back, almost tripping over his own feet.

"Twins? You're twins?"

Realizing what had happened—that her lover had mistaken her sister for her and obviously copped a feel—Candace felt her flash of jealousy disappear. She bit down on her lips to prevent a giggle, knowing Oliver was incredibly embarrassed.

Madison stuck her hand out, as if he hadn't just been gripping her butt, which had always been just a wee bit curvier than Candace's. "I'm Madison Reid. It's nice to meet you. You're Oliver, I presume?"

He didn't take her hand, continuing to stare back and

forth between them, as most people did when they first realized they were seeing double.

Finally shaking off her shocked amusement, Candace threw her arms around her twin's shoulders. "What are you doing here? I didn't expect you until at least tomorrow."

"I caught an earlier flight."

Madison squeezed her tight, and they held each other for a long minute. Neither seemed willing to let go first.

Ever since Candace had moved out to L.A. to try to break into movie costuming, missing Madison had been the hardest thing to deal with. Oh, of course she missed her parents and her friends, but she and her twin had a special bond. The only person who'd ever come close to coming between them was Tommy, and that was only until Madison had clued in to the fact that he was gay and wasn't someone they ever had to compete over.

Before the move, they hadn't ever been apart for longer than a few weeks, since they'd both gone to colleges in Central Florida and shared an apartment throughout. Mad had been Candace's best friend since the day they were born, and until this moment, when tears started pouring out of her eyes, she honestly hadn't realized how long they'd been apart. It had been months since she'd flown to New York to help Mad move into her new place after she'd landed her first big-city reporting job.

"I've missed you so much," her sister whispered.

"Right back at you."

She heard sniffling—not her own—and realized she wasn't the only one who'd turned on the waterworks. Finally, knowing Oliver had to be standing there, gaping, wondering when somebody was going to explain, she let Mad go and took a step back. They both wiped their eyes, probably looking like a pair of saps.

"Uh…does somebody want to tell me what's going on?" Oliver still looked a little stunned.

Candace walked over and took his arm. "Didn't I ever tell you that Madison and I are identical twins?"

"I think I would have remembered." He didn't sound happy. "How do you not mention something like that? And I can't believe Buddy didn't."

She shrugged, a little sheepish. "I guess it never occurred to him. When we were younger, we were both pretty adamant about not being thought of as just the Reid twins. We wanted to always be known as individuals."

"Right," Madison interjected. "Individuals who had each other's back no matter what, switched places all the time and sat in on each other's classes for the subjects one or the other of us didn't like. But everybody had to call us by our given names, not, 'the twins.'"

Candace exchanged a smile with her sister, both of them obviously remembering their stubborn insistence during childhood on being unique people, not part of a duo. Of course, they'd been inseparable anyway. Oh, how she'd missed her.

"I really wish I'd known," Oliver said. When he rubbed his hands over his eyes and shook his head, she realized he was more embarrassed than anything else. He confirmed it. "I was an ass. I'm sorry, Madison, I truly thought you were Candace."

Her sister, who prided herself on chewing men up and spitting them out, both romantically and in the cutthroat world of journalism in which she'd immersed herself, offered him a wide smile. "Are you kidding? I loved every second of it."

Wondering just how much she'd missed, Candace shot a pointed stare at her sister that silently said, *Back off. He's mine.*

Madison put her hands up, palms out in a conciliatory gesture, but ruined it when she wagged her eyebrows up and down. "Candace wasn't quite as descriptive about you as she might have been."

Wishing her twin hadn't mentioned the fact that she'd been talking about him, she changed the subject. "Come on in, sit down, relax. Do you want something—coffee? A glass of wine?"

"Is it from a fifty-thousand-dollar bottle?"

Candace grinned. She'd filled her sister in on the treasure in the basement. "Sorry, no. We figured we'd better leave everything else that's down there for the appraiser. I have horrible visions of accidentally misreading something and breaking open a bottle that would pay off the mortgage on this place."

"Ah well," Mad said, waving a hand. "I guess I'll make do with cheap swill for tonight."

"I'll see if I can find something up to your New York City tastes," she replied with a chuckle.

Mad followed them into the living room and plopped down on a recliner, flipping the handle to lift the footrest. She kicked off her comfortable shoes and flexed her feet, making herself at home.

Candace went to the bar, grabbed a bottle she'd picked up at a nearby store and popped it open. Oliver, meanwhile, sat on the couch, trying unsuccessfully to hide the fact that he was looking back and forth between them, trying to find differences that were hard even for family members to spot. Candace's second piercing in one ear, a freckle on her left hand, the tiny scar on Madison's chin, which she'd split open in nursery school—those, and their vastly different wardrobes, were all that really told them apart now that Mad had given up her redhead experiment and gone back to her natural color.

"You doing okay?" she asked Oliver after she'd given Madison her wine. She touched his shoulder lightly. "I'm really sorry I didn't say anything. I meant to."

"It's all right," he said. "As long as I'm not going to get charged with groping a stranger."

Her brow went up. "Groping?" She cast an arch look at her sister. "Just how long did you let him think you were me?"

Mad smiled sweetly. "Long enough to be impressed, little sister."

Little by virtue of being born twenty-seven minutes after her twin.

Candace sat down and dropped a possessive hand on Oliver's leg. He covered it with his own, squeezing her fingers, and she knew his embarrassment was fading.

As she sipped her wine, Madison asked a million questions, mostly about Buddy. She was just as fond of their grandfather as Candace and was looking forward to seeing him tomorrow. Deciding his heart probably wasn't up to any pranks right now, she agreed not to sneak into Candace's closet and try any identity swaps.

"So when is he going to be able to come home?"

"The day after tomorrow," Candace replied.

"I'm sure he's looking forward to it." Madison dropped her gaze, eyeing the ruby liquid in her glass. "Are you, uh, still planning on leaving as soon as he's released?"

Her stomach lurched. That had been the plan all along. Mad had promised to come visit her in L.A. once Grandpa was back on his feet, since she knew Candace had already been here for almost two weeks.

She had to do it, knowing real life was waiting for her. But oh, God, she did *not* want to go. She wasn't ready to end this wonderful interlude. The time she'd spent here, her days with her grandfather, as well as the long heated nights with her lover, had been the happiest she could remember for a very long time. She loved the climate, loved the country, loved being involved in the excitement of her grandfather's collection.

She loved Oliver.

That realization had been creeping up on her a little more every day, but she hadn't allowed herself to really believe it until now. While her first inclination was to continue to shove the very idea away, pretend it had never occurred to her, she knew she wasn't that good at denial.

Somewhere between her first night here, when she'd attacked him with a pot and fifteen minutes ago, when she'd seen him holding her sister, she had lost her heart to him. All her mixed-up feelings toward the man had cemented into pure and simple love.

"Yeah, Candace," Oliver asked, his tone serious and his stare intense. "Are you leaving?"

She swallowed, but since her mouth had gone so dry, it didn't help. "I, uh…I'm not sure yet."

He nodded slowly, then cast a glance between her and Madison. "Listen, it sounds like you two haven't seen each other for a while. I'll get out of here so you can catch up."

"You don't have to…" she protested.

"Don't go on my account!" added Madison.

He stood anyway. "Tomorrow's going to be a long day." He cast a glance toward Madison. "Candace and I were supposed to go to a winery owner's event down in the city tomorrow evening. Why don't you take my spot?"

That was the courteous offer to make and she wasn't surprised he'd extended it. But her heart twisted anyway. She'd been so looking forward to an evening out with him, being on his arm, dancing with him. Spending the night in an opulent hotel room where they didn't have to share a small, lumpy bed or sneak out of Buddy's house like she was a teenager getting it on with her high school football player boyfriend.

Especially if it was to be the last night they'd have together.

The last night ever.

Tears formed in her eyes again. She blinked them away, willing him not to notice.

"Not a chance!" Madison replied with a visible grimace. "I've been working fourteen-hour days lately. I'm so burned-out I think I'll do nothing but sleep and visit the old guy for at least a week."

"It really isn't…"

"Forget it," Mad said, cutting him off. "I'm not being nice—ask Candace. I don't do nice. I'm just being honest. I really don't want to go."

True. Mad didn't play nice for niceness's sake. She was blunt and honest. Still, seeing the twinkle in her sister's eye, and knowing Madison had to realize by the way she'd been talking about him that Candace was crazy about Oliver, she couldn't help thinking that this time, her sister's crusty heart was speaking for her.

"If you're sure," Oliver said. He turned to Candace. "So will you be ready to leave by three o'clock tomorrow?"

Spoken as if he didn't think he'd see her tonight. Ha. She had a key to his cottage and she wasn't afraid to use it. She'd proved that to him already.

But, figuring she'd surprise him later by showing up in his bed without a stitch, she merely smiled. "Of course."

Bidding Madison good-night, he left the house. They were silent for a few minutes, then without saying a word, her sister got up, went to the bar and poured two glasses of wine. She came back, handed one to Candace and sat beside her on the couch.

"You're in love with him."

Candace could only nod.

"I think he's in love with you, too." She chuckled. "He's definitely in lust. Whoa, girl, that man has some plans for you. He's totally delish, by the way."

"I know."

She didn't go on, feeling that deep well of sadness rise

up within her. Because yes, she suspected Oliver had developed feelings for her. But no, she was not going to have the happily ever after her twin seemed to be envisioning.

It was silly, really. Most women would be envious, thinking she'd be blissfully happy when her engagement to one of the most eligible bachelors alive was announced. In truth, her heart would be shattered, knowing she'd given up her only chance at happiness with the lawyer-turned-groundskeeper who had made her entire world come alive.

"So why are you miserable?" Mad asked, sensing her mood. Her mouth twisted into a frown. "Has he done something to hurt you? Jesus, he's not married is he!"

"No, of course not."

"Then what is it?"

She sighed deeply. "I can't keep him."

Her sister snorted. "Of course you can."

"I have to get back to my life in L.A."

"Bullshit. You can work from here."

"It's not the job," she admitted. "I've made a commitment and I can't back out on it."

Madison leaned forward, dropping her elbows onto her knees. "There's no commitment in the world that's more important than figuring out if this guy is the love of your life."

"Yes, there is." She sighed heavily, glad to be able to reveal her secret to someone. Madison would understand, of that she had no doubt. "I'm engaged."

Her sister spit out her mouthful of wine. It dribbled down her chin, landing on her sweatshirt. She grabbed Candace's left hand, noted the absence of a ring and gaped. "What the hell are you talking about?"

"It's true," she insisted. "I've made a promise. I'm going to marry Tommy."

THE NEXT AFTERNOON, Oliver walked up to the main house, knocking on the door for the first time in as long as he could remember so he didn't make any more identity mistakes. Candace answered right away, holding a small suitcase in her hand. She looked beautiful, as always, wearing slim-fitting tan slacks and a bright pink blouse, the color of cotton candy, cut low over those delicious curves. His mouth watered with the need to taste her, because oh, did she ever melt on his tongue.

Judging by the way her nipples pebbled beneath the fabric, she'd seen his expression and read his thoughts. Those dusky points were prominent against the material, and he wondered if she'd eschewed a bra. Candace was generously built, with breasts that invited lots of deep sucking, which he knew she loved. The thought that she was bare beneath her clothes would torment him throughout the whole drive into the city.

His pants tightened across his groin. He couldn't even look at her without wanting her. If they weren't on a timetable, he'd have her on the couch and be between her thighs, cock-deep in heaven, within ninety seconds.

She'd left his place maybe seven hours ago, after a long night filled with eroticism. But seeing her now, he wanted her all over again. He didn't think he could ever possibly get tired of making love to this woman. For all the years that he'd scoffed at friends who'd fallen victim to the love-and-marriage trap, he suddenly repented. Because the very idea that she might leave tomorrow, that this might all be over, had him ready to offer her just about anything if only she'd stay.

Hell, he'd even follow her. And considering his loathing of Southern California right now, that was probably the biggest sacrifice he could offer, the most sincere declaration he could make of his feelings for her.

Love. That's what he felt for her. He'd never experienced it before, with any woman, but Candace Reid had crept into his heart and planted a flag, claiming it as her own.

Unable to resist, he slid a hand into her thick, beautiful hair, and drew her close for a kiss. He didn't for a second worry that he was kissing the wrong woman. Now that he knew there were two of them, he allowed his senses and his instincts to tell him this was his lover. His woman. He'd never mistake anyone else for her again.

They kissed for a long, sultry moment, before finally drawing apart. Candace was pink-cheeked, her lips parted and her breaths shallow.

"Hello to you, too," she murmured.

"I've missed you."

She didn't demur or wave that off with an it-was-only-seven-hours comment. Instead, she simply nodded. "I know."

They stared at one another, exchanged a slow smile, then he reached for her bag. "Ready to go?" he asked, knowing he'd be hard and hungry for her the entire forty-minute drive to the hotel.

"Yes."

"Where's your sister?"

"She stayed with Grandpa. The two of them are old backgammon enemies. She brought his board and I doubt either of them will be willing to quit until they've played a half-dozen games."

He would definitely have bowed out if her sister had wanted to attend tonight's function, but Oliver couldn't deny he was glad Madison had declined his offer. No, he didn't give a damn about some fancy party, during which the big wineries would pat themselves on the back. But getting away with Candace for a night sounded like pure heaven.

They made the drive in her rental car. The old farm truck he used was not exactly formal ball material, and he couldn't imagine driving it up to the valet stand and handing over the keys. Since her car was a convertible, they put the top down for the drive. It was breezy, but there wasn't a cloud in the sky. A perfect day. She seemed to delight in it. Her long hair whipped behind her and she closed her eyes, obviously savoring the feel of the sun on her face.

Of course, when they hit the city, that changed. Downtown San Francisco was, even on a Saturday afternoon, a busy mass of humanity, and traffic was a bitch. They didn't arrive at the hotel until late afternoon and weren't ensconced in their room until after five.

She whistled as they entered and spied the plush room, the huge bed and the great view of the bay out the window. "Nice. You sure you can afford this, groundskeeper?"

"I've got a few dollars tucked away," he said, reaching for her and drawing her into his arms.

She twined hers around his neck. "Seriously. You didn't need to pay for all of this. I'll pitch in."

Laughing, he refused the offer. "Do you really think I'm working for your grandfather because I need the money? For that matter, do you really think I've ever actually cashed one of the checks he's given me?"

Her mouth fell open. "He's not paying you? Good grief, Oliver, you work like a maniac!"

"I don't think he's figured it out yet. I don't need the money, sweetheart. I needed the escape. Needed a place to stay, and hard work to do, so I could figure things out."

She stepped out of his arms, taking his hand and pulling him toward the bed. Unfortunately, rather than stripping naked and leaping onto him, she sat down, patting the space beside her for him to sit, as well.

Oh. Great. They were going to talk.

"And have you?" she asked. "Figured things out, I mean?"

"I'm getting there."

She lifted her hand and cupped his jaw. "Are you going to be all right, Oliver?"

He turned her palm toward his mouth and kissed it. "I am. I promise."

There was only one thing that could derail him from being all right, something over which he had no control. But he couldn't push her, couldn't force her. Hell, right now, he couldn't even bring himself to ask her, not if it meant spoiling the last full day they would have together. By this time tomorrow, her grandfather would be home and Candace would be packing to leave for Los Angeles.

Maybe he could convince her not to go. But maybe he couldn't. Which meant today might be all he had, all he would ever have of her, for the rest of his days.

"What do you…"

"Later," he insisted, pressing his mouth to hers for a deep, hungry kiss. She twined her hands in his hair. Oliver continued to kiss her, breathing her in, memorizing her scent and her taste and the way he felt at this moment. God, did he ever hope he wouldn't have to bank these memories for a long time, and that she wasn't really going to walk away from him tomorrow. Whatever this promise was that she'd made, surely she could get out of it. No way could she feel about him the way he suspected she did and not stay here and fight for a real relationship.

When the kiss ended, she persisted. "I want to know what you're thinking."

"Shh," he insisted, kissing his way to her wrist. He flicked his tongue out on the pulse point, then continued moving up her arm, pushing her sleeve as he went. "Enough talking."

"Mmm," she said as he abandoned her arm and moved to her neck, nuzzling the hollow. "You don't play fair."

"Lawyer."

"But…"

"No buts. We have to be at that ball in two hours, and I intend to spend the next one-hundred-and-five minutes giving you many, many orgasms. After that, you'll have exactly fifteen minutes to wipe my cum off your thighs and get into your dress."

"Oh, my God," she groaned, her voice thick with hunger.

Candace always got off on his more blunt expressions of need for her, growing even more inflamed when he whispered in her ear the kinds of words a polite man usually didn't say to a nice woman. She loved it, always growing wetter, wilder, when he talked about how much he loved eating her pussy and the fantasies he had about her gorgeous ass. They'd even gotten into a conversation about the most forbidden word in the female lexicon, and he knew she now looked at it in a whole new way, knowing if he ever used that word, it would be because he was out of his mind with need for her. What was once offensive had become incredibly erotic to her.

"Any more arguments?" he growled as he nipped her earlobe, dropping a hand to her thigh.

She gasped. "No arguments."

"Good. Now take off your clothes, Candace," he ordered as he nibbled her collarbone.

"Why don't you make me," she said, her tone sultry, provocative. She was daring him, egging him on, testing the boundaries.

He stared at her, narrowing his eyes, giving her a moment's warning. Then he reached for the front of her blouse, grabbed two handfuls and yanked.

Buttons flew. She gasped. Two gorgeous, perfect, pink-tipped breasts spilled out.

As he'd suspected, no bra.

All was right with the world.

"I'll buy you a new one," he said as he pushed her back onto the bed, bending for a taste of one succulent nipple.

"To hell with the blouse." She cooed as he sucked one

breast while tweaking and toying with the other. They were made for pleasure, big and sensitive, and as he played with them, he wondered if every other man in the world was as hopelessly addicted to sucking the breasts of the woman he loved.

Twining her hands in his hair, she rose toward his mouth, holding him where she wanted him, whimpering with pleasure as he suckled her. Her hips were rising in tiny thrusts, as if every pull of his mouth sent sparks of heat surging to her groin.

After he'd paid lavish attention to those beauties, he kissed his way down her belly to the seam of her pants. Unbuttoning them, he pulled them off her, taking her shoes and panties, too, until she was naked, spread out like a feast for the devouring.

He stood up beside the bed, slowly stripping off his shirt, his hands shaking with need. He never took his eyes off her. Candace lay there, writhing, stretching, running her hand over her own body, from her breasts down to that perfect little tuft of curls between her thighs.

"Touch yourself," he ordered her as he unfastened his pants.

She did, slipping a long, slender finger deeper into her crevice to stroke the tiny nub of flesh that perched at the top.

"Like this?"

"Oh, yeah. I definitely like that."

She laughed softly. "I do, too," she admitted, her voice filled with feminine power. She knew what she did to him, knew he went a little crazy every time they made love.

He shoved the rest of his clothes off, smiling with male satisfaction as she stared avidly at his erect cock. She licked her lips, whimpering, her body twisting even more restlessly as her need overtook her.

He didn't reach for her yet. Reaching for his cock, he

stroked it, knowing he could bring himself to climax by just standing here watching her.

But he wouldn't. Because that wouldn't even come close to the sensation of coming inside her body.

"How do you want me, Oliver? What's your fantasy?"

His mouth went dry as he pictured all the ways he'd had her, and the ways he hadn't. He could make love to her every day for a month and find something new to try, some new place on her lush body to explore with his hands and his mouth.

But one thing immediately came to mind.

"Turn over," he told her, his tone silky.

"With pleasure."

She smiled up at him, her eyes gleaming with anticipation, and did as he'd asked. Oliver groaned at the sight of those pale, round globes, his hands tingling with the need to squeeze and stroke them.

"Have I ever told you how much I love your ass?"

"I don't believe so."

"Ever since that morning when you walked up the stairs, shaking it at me, all I've been able to think about was getting you on your hands and knees and slamming into you from behind."

She didn't hesitate, rising onto her knees, her bottom perched up invitingly. When he caught sight of that glistening pink slit, he forgot everything else. Nothing mattered except the need to get inside her and pump wildly, to imprint himself on her, body and soul.

"Come and take me," she ordered. "Take me and come."

He knelt on the bed behind her, nestling his cock between her cheeks, sliding up and down to wet it with the cream seeping from her sex. She was whimpering, pushing against him, silently begging for more. Unable to resist a moment longer, he nudged her legs farther apart and moved his cock to her slick opening.

"Yes. Now, please!"

He didn't need any further urging. Giving in to her demands, and his own body's, he thrust into her. Sensation battered him, and he was left stunned at how good the angle felt, how much deeper he got, and how fucking erotic it was to look down and see his cock buried balls-deep in her body.

He grabbed her hips, pulling out, thrusting back. Candace met his strokes, groaning, begging, going mad.

It was wild. Hot. Incredibly pleasurable. When he bent over her to cover her back, and reached around so he could toy with her clit, she came with a loud cry.

He almost followed her, but something made him stop. Yeah, he loved this. Yes, he knew it would go down as one of his favorite things in the entire world.

But he wanted to see her face. Wanted to memorize how she looked when racked with pleasure and totally lost to everything but him.

So without saying anything, he pulled out of her, gently turned her over and settled back between her thighs. She reached for him, encircling his neck, smiling as she pulled him down for a long, slow kiss.

"Amazing," she whispered against his lips when the kiss ended.

"Yeah. We are."

She tightened her hold on him, wrapping her legs around his hips as he slid back into her. Their bodies melted together, each of them giving and taking by turns. He lost all sense of time and place, sure only of one thing.

He couldn't lose her. He'd do whatever it took to keep her in his life forever.

11

OLIVER HAD TAKEN pity on her and given her thirty minutes to get dressed rather than fifteen. Other than that, though, he kept his word, giving her more orgasms in an hour and a half than she'd thought humanly possible. As they rode the elevator down to the ballroom where this evening's event was being held, Candace had to shift back and forth on her feet, incredibly aware of how tender and well used she felt.

He apparently noticed. Stepping close, he slid an arm around her waist and ducked his head toward hers. "Are you okay?"

"Perfect," she whispered back, conscious of the other people on the elevator, another couple—middle-aged and well dressed—and a duo who looked like a mother and daughter. Neither of whom could take their eyes off Oliver, who did things to a tux that James Bond would envy.

Good heavens, the man was handsome. Not just hot and sexy, but so amazingly handsome he turned heads—male and female. Tonight she thought he could outshine Tommy, routinely called one of the top ten sexiest men in the world.

Tommy.

Hell.

She hadn't thought much about him today. Nor had she

answered when he'd tried calling a little while ago. She'd been busy, using all of her thirty minutes to clean up, fix her hair and makeup and get dressed. She would call him tomorrow, once she'd willed herself to pack up and head home. Tonight, she didn't want to think about anyone or anything but Oliver.

When they reached the ballroom, Oliver removed two tickets from his breast pocket and handed them to the person at the door. The minute they walked in, a congenial older gentleman with a barrel chest and very little hair walked over and greeted them. When he heard who she was, he enquired after her grandfather.

"I heard he was laid up—some kind of accident?"

"Yes, I'm afraid so. But he's recovering nicely. He's supposed to come home from the hospital tomorrow."

The man nodded absently, then moved on to what she suspected was his real topic of conversation. "Say, I've been hearing some stories. Something about a fabulous secret collection of antique vintages?"

The Northern California wine community was a small one. She was not at all surprised rumors were already being bandied around. Considering these growers and vintners were also wine drinkers, she would bet most of them would be attending the auction once it was set and advertised.

But not wanting to reveal too much, she merely shrugged and pasted on a vapid smile. "I don't know about that. Actually, I'm afraid I don't know anything about wine at all," she said, forcing a giggle. "Just that I like to drink it!"

"Oh, yes, of course." He patted her hand, condescension dripping from him, and wished her a nice evening.

As they walked away, she heard Oliver's deep chuckle. "Well played."

"Hey, no point in getting the vultures circling until Grandpa gets home and decides what he wants to do. If word spreads too much, we're going to have to start locking the door to the house."

"Buddy would never stand for that."

As they walked across the already-crowded room, Candace looked around, noting the decorations. Vines that looked quite real climbed and wove around some free-standing arbors, while beneath couples danced and chatted. The softly lit chandeliers cast a gentle glow over the well-dressed attendees, and laughter and wine were in abundance.

Oliver smiled pleasantly at several people who said hello. Although he wasn't technically one of them, he'd apparently met and impressed Buddy's colleagues and neighbors. In fact, one of them, a beautifully gowned, attractive woman in her fifties, approached them before they got halfway across the room.

She leaned in close to Oliver, not looking like the typical partygoer interested in exchanging gossip and feigning ennui. "You're Mr. McKean, aren't you?"

He nodded. "Yes. I'm sorry, have we met?"

"I'm Doris Gladstone." She stuck out her hand. "I work with Ben Harmon."

He dropped her hand. "Oh."

"Hear me out."

"I'd rather not."

This was getting more and more interesting. Oliver obviously knew who this Ben Harmon was, and didn't want to talk to his associate.

Candace stepped the tiniest bit closer, wishing the nearby string quartet would quiet down so she could eavesdrop more easily.

"Look, I know the whole story," the woman said. "Everybody knows. You might have made some enemies in the southern part of this state, but I promise you, everywhere else, people are well aware that you did the right thing and got royally screwed for it."

The truth dawned. Oliver hadn't said anything about his past following him up here. But it obviously had. Hearing the way the woman was speaking, it wasn't hard to gauge her respect for him, nor her interest in engaging him in shoptalk. Since Oliver almost never talked about his old life, she found herself intensely curious, wondering what he'd been like in that other world. Had he been as sexy, as thoughtful, as sweet? Had he exhibited flashes of that sardonic wit? Had he been a wildly erotic lover to lots of women?

She swallowed, not wanting to consider that. Knowing how fast-paced life in Los Angeles could be, and how shallow some of the wealthy set was, she had to wonder if he'd ever been the flavor of the week for some socialite who'd heard about the rising hotshot of the D.A.'s office.

"Ben is still dying for you to come in and talk to us. It's a small practice, with just the office in Napa, but we're both horribly overworked and we think you'd be a great fit."

Tension poured off him, and his hand tightened on Candace's waist. She imagined he didn't even realize it.

"I don't do that anymore."

"You don't prosecute," the older woman said. "But come on, you wouldn't have made it in the L.A. district attorney's office for four years, much less with a nearly perfect conviction record, if criminal law wasn't in your blood."

His jaw was growing stiffer, his hand tighter, and Candace feared this Doris Gladstone person was pushing too hard. She wanted Oliver to think about what the woman was saying, but, like most men, he wouldn't want to be forced into it.

She caught the other woman's eye and narrowed her eyes, warning her off with a small, negative shake of the head.

The attractive blonde got the message. Smiling brightly, she said, "Well, anyway, I won't bother you and your lovely friend. I just wanted to reiterate what Ben told you. We'd love to talk to you." Ignoring his silence, she reached into her purse and drew out a business card. She held it out and for a moment, Oliver just stared at it. When Candace nudged him, though, and he realized how rude he was being, he took it and dropped it into his side pocket.

"Guess I should get back to my husband. We have a small place. He produced a thousand bottles last year and now thinks he's ready to go up against Mondavi."

Smiling pleasantly, she walked away. A few other people stood nearby, all engaged in loud conversation, but Candace kept her voice down anyway.

"They want you to come work with them?"

"It's been mentioned."

"But you declined?"

"Her partner didn't offer me a job or anything. Just asked me to lunch one day and broached the subject."

"You're not even tempted?"

He swiped a hand through his thick, dark hair and shook his head. "I don't know, honestly. I just don't want to think about it tonight."

"Understood," she said, meaning it. The subject was closed for now, and she would respect his wishes by dropping it.

Smiling his thanks, he turned toward a corner. "How about a drink? Red, white or an appallingly sweet combination of the two?"

"Let's go with red, and see if anything measures up to that bottle we shared from Grandpa's cellar."

He twined his fingers with hers and squeezed, obviously appreciating that she'd let the subject change. Oliver had come up here to think about what he wanted to do with his life, including whether that life included a career in law.

For four months, he'd buried himself in hard work and had allowed himself to believe he had no supporters, nowhere else to turn. So seeing that wasn't true was probably good for him. An occasional nudge was probably in order. But any more than that was out of line. He would have to decide for himself what his future should be.

Whatever it is, it won't include you.

She had to forcibly control a wince of sadness that thought caused. She'd done a pretty good job of avoiding reality all day, well, for the past several days. But now that it was bearing down on her, each tick of the clock bringing her closer to the moment when she would have to say goodbye, the pain within her was sharpening.

Tomorrow is soon enough. You've got tonight. Make it a night worth remembering.

Forcing a smile to her lips, determined not to let him see her sadness and question it, she let him lead her to the nearest bar. There were several set up in the room, each offering glasses of the various vintages being feted tonight. They let themselves be drawn into a brief tasting, and Candace managed to hide another wince, this one caused by some pretty crappy wine. Fortunately, another bar had much better offerings, and she accepted a full pour.

Carrying their glasses, they worked their way around the room, meeting many people who knew her grandfather, or at least had heard of him. Almost all of them brought up the subject of the rare collection Buddy Frye had reportedly found, and she changed that subject every single time.

"Good grief, these people are like bloodhounds," she said after she and Oliver ducked another busybody, who'd actually followed them across the dance floor, weaving between swaying couples. They'd evaded him by slipping into a private corner beneath a cozy arbor, a tiny oasis in the crowded ballroom.

"Want to dance?" he whispered.

She didn't want to go back out into the crowd. But apparently that hadn't been his intention. Before she could assent, he slid an arm around her waist and caught her hand, drawing her close to his body. They began to sway to the music, moving in a small circle within the arbor, oblivious to the other people who wandered in and out.

She didn't know what she expected, but it wasn't that he could dance, or that she would be so swept away by the music that she almost forgot where they were. Though surrounded by hundreds, she felt like they were entirely alone, swaying to the soft strains coming from the talented musicians, and to the gentle gurgle of water from a nearby fountain. He bent his head close to hers, brushing his lips against her temple, breathing her in, holding her as if he would never let her go.

Oh, God, she wished he didn't have to.

The moment was so beautiful, and the thought so distressing, that she suddenly felt tears well in her eyes. "Will you excuse me?" she said, abruptly stepping out of his arms. "I need to visit the ladies' room."

He raised a curious brow, his expression skeptical, but she smiled broadly and spun around, hurrying away from him before he could offer to escort her. Smiling at a few people who offered friendly greetings, she didn't pause but moved through the ballroom as quickly as she could, practically bursting out of it into the hotel corridor. She sniffed a couple of times and wiped away her tears with the tips of her fingers, looking around frantically for the nearest facilities.

She'd just spied a restroom across the hall and a few doors up when she heard something that made her freeze in utter shock.

"There she is! My gorgeous bride-to-be. Hey, honey, are you surprised?"

The walls seemed to spin around her as she slowly

turned on her heel, knowing that voice, hearing the words, but not really able to process anything.

"Tommy?" she whispered, seeing her friend approaching from the main lobby.

He was here? Not just in San Francisco, but in this very hotel? More importantly—he was claiming her as his fiancée? Now, in public, when the man she loved was waiting for her in the next room?

Immobilized by shock, she watched him approach, seeing the familiar grin, the bright blond hair, the dazzling blue eyes glued to her face. As he drew closer, she noted a tiny frown appear between those eyes. Tommy always recognized her moods and realized she was not exactly overjoyed to see him.

Nor was she thrilled about who was following him.

A person holding a microphone. Another holding a very large camera.

No. Oh, please no.

But she knew it was true. He'd brought a camera crew here to "surprise" her. He'd gone public with their engagement.

"Didn't I tell you she was gorgeous?" Tommy said as he slipped his arms around her waist and lowered his mouth to hers for a friendly kiss. Thank God he didn't try to make it a passionate one or she might have instinctively shoved him away.

"What are you doing?" she whispered.

"Crisis mode, babe," he said under his breath. Then he raised his voice, wanting others to overhear. "I'm surprising you because I've missed you so damn much. I couldn't stay in L.A. one more day without you."

Her smile pasted on, she managed to bite out a few words in a low, angry voice. "I'm going to kill you."

His arm tightened around her waist as he leaned close, as if nuzzling her neck. "Hell's breaking loose, babe. When

I ran into these media types in the lobby—they're here covering this event, I guess—I figured the time was right to let the world know our happy news."

"I can't believe you didn't warn me."

"I've been trying to call you for hours!"

She couldn't argue that, realizing she'd turned her phone off, not wanting any interruptions to spoil their special night.

Glancing over his shoulder at their growing audience, Tommy went on, his voice a little louder, intentionally so. "You left town so quickly to come to your grandfather's hospital bed that I hadn't even had time to make our engagement official."

With that, he reached into his pocket and drew out a ring with the most enormous, gaudy, ostentatious diamond she had ever seen. On either side of it were rows of tiny rubies—her birthstone.

Tommy must have seen her grimace because he chuckled. "Figured we might as well go all out with it."

Her brain wasn't functioning, and she couldn't figure out what to say. Her hand lay limply in his as he lifted it and slid the ten-pound rock onto her ring finger.

"There, now you're fully dressed," he said, leaning down to rub noses with her.

She clenched her fists in his leather jacket—no black tie for the sexy movie star—and whispered, "Get me out of here. Now, Tommy, I mean it."

"Five minutes. Then we split."

But, she suddenly realized, she didn't even have five minutes. Because word of the superstar's arrival had apparently spread, and people were coming from all over the hotel to gawk at them. Sure, San Francisco had its share of celebrities, but Tommy was the "it" guy of Hollywood right now, having starred in two blockbusters in the past eighteen months. Directors courted him, women threw panties at him, men clapped him on the shoulder. Of course people would come and stare. Including a few from the ballroom.

Panic rose within her. She had to get out of here, had to escape and find a quiet place to sit down and figure out how to handle this nightmare. What on earth was she going to say to Oliver? Yes, of course he would someday find out she was marrying Tommy. But oh, God, she did not want it to be like this. Not tonight, on what had been, up until a few minutes ago, one of the most magical she had ever experienced.

Suddenly, she spied a face in the shifting crowd. Her worst fears were coming true. Her heart thudded in her chest and sweat broke out on her brow. This couldn't be happening!

But it was. As fans drew closer, asking Tommy for autographs, she saw Oliver's face in the crowd. He stood about twenty feet away, his attention glued on her, his face expressionless. How long he'd been standing there, she had no idea. Considering Tommy was hugging her to his side like she was his prized possession, she could only imagine what he was thinking.

The worst.

"No," she whispered.

Tommy, probably thinking she was nervous about the growing hysteria of his largely female fan riot, dropped a possessive arm over her shoulder and hugged her tightly against his side. "Hey, folks, don't freak out my fiancée, okay? I don't want to scare her off before I get her down the aisle."

The words caused a stir in the hallway, and every whispering person in the hallway gaped at her, most of the women eyeing her with jealousy, the men assessing her looks.

And then there was Oliver. She watched as shock

washed over him, his dark eyes widening, his mouth moving, though she couldn't hear a word he said. Of course, she really didn't need to. Because, as the truth of the situation hit him—at least, the truth as he saw it—he drew himself up stiffly and thrust out his jaw. His shoulders squared, his eyes cold, he nodded briefly in her direction. Then he turned and walked away, heading for the lobby and, she imagined, the exit.

"Tommy, let go," she insisted, knowing she had to go after Oliver and try to explain.

"It's okay, honey, we'll get up to our room soon," Tommy said, overplaying the part of horny lover. She would bet he'd rather be chatting up the superhot waiter who was hovering near the banquet room door.

Just as she was ready to pound on his chest and scream at him to let her go, she saw another familiar face. It was Madison. She stood in the lobby and was jumping up and down, waving her arms over her head, trying to be seen above the crowd.

Her sister. Her twin. That was just who she needed.

"I, uh, need to use the facilities," she said to Tommy, knowing her face was red with frustration and anger. Hopefully his adoring fans would think she was blushing over the behavior of her flirtatious fiancé, or at least because she'd had to make a public issue out of needing to use the damn john.

He finally let her go, but pressed a quick kiss on her lips before she could escape. "Hurry back sweet cheeks."

She growled at him, and for the first time since he'd arrived, he finally looked her fully in the face and realized she was absolutely furious. And positively devastated.

"Babe?"

"I'll deal with you later," she snapped, pushing her way through the throng, who continued to converge on Tommy, gushing over his films. Nobody paid her much attention, and she slipped away, hugging the wall, until she reached the lobby.

She didn't see Oliver anywhere. But she did see her twin's head as Madison ducked down another hallway. She followed her, rounding a corner as Mad disappeared into what turned out to be a ladies' room.

Hurrying in after her, she bumped into her sister, who'd been waiting anxiously by the door.

"Oh, God, Madison!"

"I know, I know," she said, grabbing Candace and hugging her.

"How? When…"

"I was at the center and went to the cafeteria to get Grandpa some ice cream. When I came back, he said Tommy had called, looking for you because you weren't answering your cell. He had just landed at the airport and wanted to know where you were."

Of course Grandpa would tell him. He'd known Tommy since they were kids and probably thought his surprise would be a wonderful one for Candace.

"As soon as he told me, I started trying to call you."

"I forgot to turn my phone back on," she admitted.

"Where's Oliver? Did he…"

"Yes. He saw. He turned around and left." She sniffed, trying to hold in a sob as she imagined how he was feeling. "He'll probably never speak to me again."

Madison stepped back, gripping Candace's shoulders, looking into her face, her expression serious. "Is that for the best, do you think? I mean, if you're going to really go through with it and marry Tommy, maybe you should just let him go."

"No!" The very idea was abhorrent. Yes, she'd intended to leave, to remind him of their agreement, fly back to Los Angeles and move on with her life. But at no time had she envisioned him being so publicly slapped in the face with the decisions she'd made before she'd ever met him.

He deserved an apology, and as much of an explanation as she could give him. He also deserved the right to tell her off, even if she had kept the truth from him out of loyalty to her oldest friend.

She understood now, though, that her loyalties were more torn than ever. She loved Oliver. If she were free, she would want to make a life with him. She wouldn't choose marriage to a movie star, with all the money, fame and glamour it included, over Oliver. Not a chance.

But Tommy? Her lifelong friend? The one to whom she'd given her word?

"Oh, God, Mad, what am I going to do?"

Her sister scrunched her brow, then nodded. "Take off your dress."

Her jaw unhinged. "What?"

"Come on, hurry up. Somebody might come in." She pushed Candace toward the stalls, shoving her inside one. "Get out of it. We'll switch clothes. I'll go back and play adoring fiancée while you get out of here and find Oliver."

"Are you serious?"

"Of course I'm serious. Hell, it'll be an adventure. I can't stand reporters—it'll be fun putting one over on them."

Candace simply stared.

"I know, I know," her sister said, waving an airy hand. "I'm a reporter. That doesn't mean I necessarily like myself. I think I chose the wrong field."

"Nice time to decide that, Ms. Columbia Master's Degree."

"You want me to change my mind?"

"Oh, hell, no!"

Thankful there was a way out of this, at least for right

now, she immediately leaped on her sister's offer. It wasn't, after all, the first time the two of them had traded places.

"Thank you so much," she said, yanking down her zipper and flinging the dress over the wall of the stall.

Madison, who'd shoved off her jeans and shirt, took the dress, doing a double take. "Whoa, Candy, that's some serious underwear you've got on there."

She looked down, seeing the incredibly sexy set of lingerie she'd bought especially to wear under tonight's dress. A red bra with cutouts over her nipples, and a skimpy thong. She'd envisioned Oliver being the only one seeing her in them for the few minutes it would take to rip them off. Right now, though, she was too anxious to be embarrassed.

"Where do you think he went?" Madison asked as she yanked the dress on over her head and struggled to smooth it over her slightly larger butt.

"The keys to the rental car are in my purse," she said, buttoning the jeans. "So he either got a cab or walked."

"Walked, I'll bet. Men like to go walk out their frustration over this kind of stuff. It seems like the guy thing to do."

She had no idea whether that was true or not, but was ready to take any help she could get. She'd try walking, and was very glad she had her sister's flat shoes in which to do it.

Yanking her hair into a ponytail and wetting a paper towel to wipe away some of the heavy makeup from her face, she shoved her purse toward Madison. "Lipstick. Eye shadow. Now."

Her sister went to work, applying cosmetics with a heavy hand, a look that was most unusual for her. Candace took the pins she'd pulled from her own hair and used them to twist her sister's into a quick updo, hoping nobody would notice it was a lot less intricate than Candace's had been.

When they were finished, they stood side by side and looked in the mirror. Madison looked so close to the way Candace had earlier tonight—she had no doubt most people would be fooled.

Her sister took her hand and squeezed.

"It'll be okay."

"How?" she whispered, not seeing a happy ending here. Maybe she could find Oliver. Maybe he'd stand still and listen to her enough so she could apologize. Maybe he'd even forgive her.

But that didn't change the fact that they couldn't be together.

12

As Oliver stalked out of the hotel, needing to get away and deal with the truth, he vacillated between anger and devastation. His emotions churned one way, then the next. One minute he wanted to punch something, the next, he was tempted to go back to the hotel, haul her into his arms and ask her why in hell she was marrying a pretty boy movie star who could never make her happy.

"Married," he muttered out loud, drawing a curious look from a passing couple, dressed for clubbing, who looked like every other couple he'd passed. Saturday night in San Fran was when all the hipsters came out, and he felt entirely out of place. Although, not as out of place as he would feel in Candace's world, now that she was engaged to one of the sexiest men alive.

Bastard.

When he'd first walked out of the ballroom to look for her, having grown concerned when she didn't come back right away, since she'd looked on the verge of tears when she left, hadn't believed his eyes. Seeing Candace there, standing in the embrace of another man, he'd had a sudden certainty that he was seeing Madison. Not Candace. Not his Candace.

But the dress was the same. The hairstyle. The pale face, trembling lips, damp eyes.

It was her. He'd known that even before she'd met his stare and silently pleaded for understanding he wasn't sure he'd ever be able to offer.

The farther away from the hotel he walked, the more he tried to understand.

That she was really engaged seemed beyond doubt. She'd let that guy slide that big ugly ring on her hand. She hadn't laughed it off as a joke or shoved him away. In fact, the two of them looked pretty comfortable and cozy together, and he had to wonder how long they'd known each other.

Probably longer than the two weeks she'd been here. But damned if he'd let anyone tell him he didn't love her more than anyone else could. She'd become a part of him. He couldn't fall asleep if she wasn't in his arms, and was edgy every day until he heard her voice. She was the one he wanted to talk to about his plans for the future—maybe going back to work in a local law office, maybe getting married and having a family. Those things had seemed impossible—and he hadn't really wanted them—until she'd crept into his life and turned it completely upside down.

She's marrying someone else. She always planned to, and you know it. She warned you.

Yeah, she had. That first night when he'd made love to her, she'd laid down her conditions, stated her terms. He tried to remember exactly what she'd said, though his brain had been foggy with lust and he'd had a hard time thinking of anything except how much he wanted to be inside her.

She'd made a promise to someone, he remembered that much. A commitment. One that meant she and Oliver could have no more than one week, and would have to part ways, no questions asked, not seeing each other again.

He'd sort of believed she meant it. But a part of him really hadn't. And once they'd started sleeping together, once the physical connection had wrapped them up in such strong emotional bonds, he'd had an even harder time with the idea.

He should have pressed her when she'd offered to try to explain. Maybe then he wouldn't have been so blindsided when she turned out to have a fiancé.

She hadn't lied. She'd answered him truthfully when he'd laid out his three deal-breaking conditions. She'd wanted him, she was an adult and she wasn't married.

Just engaged to a freaking movie star.

"Oliver, please wait!"

He froze, spinning around and seeing a woman hurrying after him. His heart leaped as he thought for a moment it was Candace, that she'd walked away from the crazy promise she'd made to marry a man she didn't love, and had come after him. But he noted her clothes, and realized that was impossible.

"I'm not in the mood, Madison," he told her, striding away before she got to within ten feet.

"Oliver, wait, it's me."

He stopped again. This time, when he turned around, he studied her more closely, noting the full lips so recently well kissed, the faint circles under her eyes and streaks on her cheeks that said she'd been crying.

"Candace?"

She nodded and came closer, stopping about three feet away.

He clenched his hands by his sides, not reaching out for her, though he very much wanted to.

"Can we please talk?"

He looked around, seeing a few bars, but also a small coffee shop that was still open. He gestured toward it, and she nodded in agreement, walking with him across the street.

They didn't speak while they walked, and the tension built. Oliver wanted to ask her what had happened, what her coming after him meant and how the hell she'd gotten hooked up with Thomas Shane. But he didn't know where to start, and she didn't break the silence.

Not until they were sitting across from each other at a small booth, waiting for the waitress to return with their coffee did she attempt an explanation.

"I'm so sorry," she whispered.

"Excuse me?"

She was looking down at her own hands, which she kept twisting together on the table, and cleared her throat. "I'm so sorry you had to see that."

He was about launch into a barrage of questions when he realized what he was not seeing on that hand.

The ring. That big ugly ring.

His heart flipped in his chest. Had she ended it? Broken off with the golden boy?

"I didn't mean for that to happen. I had no idea Tommy was coming up here or I would never have put you in that position. Or myself, for that matter." She rolled her eyes, disgusted. "He's a publicity hound."

"How the hell could you even think about marrying someone like that?"

She opened her mouth to answer, but before she could, the waitress returned with two steaming cups of coffee. She chatted a little, offering them dessert, but they both declined, waiting for her to leave.

Once she had, they both sat silently for a minute, stirring their coffee, searching for words.

Eventually, Candace began to explain.

"I've known Tommy since I was a toddler. He and Mad have been my two best friends my entire life."

He blinked in surprise, but didn't interfere.

"Tommy and I had a lot in common. We were both artistic and emotional and very theatrical, while Mad was the calm, blunt one who evened us out and kept us steady. We made a good trio, spent our entire childhoods together. Every school year, every summer break, every birthday party, Tommy was with us."

He didn't doubt anything she said, having heard that the breakout star had come from Florida, just as Candace had. He had never really thought about the young lives of the rich and shameless, but it sounded like Shane's had been pretty normal.

"So what happened when you grew up?"

"I studied design in college, he went into theater. Madison decided to move to New York to go to grad school, so we thought we'd give our starry-eyed dreams a shot and moved to L.A."

"You lived together?"

She nodded.

He clenched his teeth so tightly his jaw flexed. He had to busy himself lifting his coffee cup to his mouth, sipping it though it remained very hot, just to avoid saying something he shouldn't. She'd said they hadn't been lovers, yet they'd lived together? Was it even possible for a woman as beautiful and sexy as Candace to live with a man and not tempt him into bed?

"It's not what you're thinking," she insisted. "We weren't lovers, Oliver. I never lied to you. Tommy and I have never had a physical relationship, and we never will. I think of him as a brother. Period."

A hint of relief washed through him. It didn't last long.

"Brothers and sisters don't usually exchange wedding vows," he objected, unable to keep his anger as tightly controlled as he'd like.

"There are other reasons to get married, aside from romantic passion."

"Not any better ones," he snapped.

She sagged back in her seat, sighing deeply. "I know."

"Then why?" A thought occurred to him. "Is it because he's rich and famous?"

"Yes, although not in the way you might imagine. I don't know if I can make you understand…."

"Try."

She nibbled her trembling bottom lip, casting her eyes away, still twisting those hands. Her anguish as she tried to figure out how to explain something he already found unfathomable made his chest tighten, and he nearly reached out and covered her hands with his, wanting to stop that desperate, heartbroken clenching.

He didn't. She might have taken the ring off, but she still hadn't said whether she'd broken this sham engagement.

"As you said, Tommy is a star. He's under a microscope, his every move dissected, every part of his life spied upon and discussed." She shook her head sadly. "He doesn't deserve it. He's a good guy, one of the best, and his world is coming apart because people can't mind their own damned business."

"If he's such a good guy, why did he put on that ridiculous performance back there? Why did he back you into a corner and talk you into marrying him when you're not in love with each other?"

"I was single. I hadn't been seeing anyone in a long time…. We're best friends. I never envisioned…never thought I would…"

"Fall for someone else?"

A stark nod.

It was the closest she'd come to admitting she had feelings for him. He waited for her to say more, but she didn't.

"This doesn't make any sense," he mumbled, still unable to follow everything. "Shane is the bachelor of the damn year—he could have any woman he wants. Why the hell does he have to have you?"

"He needs me. I...I understand him."

"What's that mean?"

She dropped her gaze, not meeting his eye.

Oliver continued to mull it over, until a thought began to form in his brain. It was small at first, a crazy possibility. But he focused on it, developed it. And while it shocked him, given the fact that he'd caught a couple of Thomas Shane's movies and seen him in person, he finally had to ask, "Is he gay?"

She bit her lip even harder, refusing to say a word.

Oh, Christ. Now everything made sense.

He leaned his head back against the booth, looking up at the ceiling, wondering how things had ever gotten this screwed up.

Her lifelong best friend had asked her to help him hide his sexuality from the press and the public who would rip him apart over it.

That's why she'd said yes. That's why she'd told Oliver they could have only one week and he could never try to contact her afterward. That's why she wouldn't explain what her secret commitment was all about.

She was displaying all the character traits he most admired in a person—the ones he'd seen so little of during his years as a prosecutor. Loyalty, compassion, integrity.

Yet, right now, with his heart pounding over the fact that he really might lose her to a guy who could never make her body sing—and didn't even want to—he wanted her to give up all those things. Break her promise, betray her friend, come away with him.

If she loves you, that's exactly what she should do.

Maybe. But the choice had to be hers. He couldn't ask

it of her, couldn't make things any more difficult than they already were.

He only owed her one thing: honesty about his feelings.

"What are you thinking?" she whispered.

He wrapped his hands around his coffee cup, realizing they were shaking when a little of the lukewarm liquid sloshed out.

"Tell me. Please."

Unable to resist, knowing it might not matter, knowing it might even hurt her, he still went ahead and told her the only thing he could. The truth.

"I love you, Candace."

She sucked in an audible breath.

"I don't mean to hurt you, or make this any worse than it already is. But I love you." He reached for one of her hands, catching it in his and holding tight, knowing he would soon have to let it go for good.

"Oliver, I…"

"You don't have to say anything. I just thought you should know. Believe me, I want to fight for you, keep you, but I know I can't. You've got to do what your heart tells you is right, and I can't be the one who makes you betray a friend or go back on your word." One more tight squeeze, then he released her fingers. "So I have to let you go."

Tears were spilling from her eyes and running down her cheeks, and he wanted more than anything to take her in his arms and comfort her, kiss the tears away, assure her everything would be all right.

He didn't, though. Everything wouldn't be all right. He didn't know if things would ever be all right for either of them again.

Knowing he needed to go now before he changed his mind and kissed her until she admitted she could never really leave him, he slid out of the booth and stood.

"Goodbye, Candace," he said.

Stiffening his resolve, he headed for the door. But right before he exited, he heard her murmur his name.

"Oliver?"

He turned back and looked at her.

"I love you, too."

Their stares met and locked, a thousand more words hung in the silence, questions asked and answered, promises offered and lost. All the might-have-beens held in that one long, steady stare.

Until he looked away, opened the door and walked out into the night.

CANDACE SAT AT the table at the all-night café until her coffee was cold and her tears had dried. The kindly waitress had brought her some tissues, patted her on her shoulder and then left her alone. She spent the next hour sitting there, going over everything that had happened, marveling at how her life had changed so very much in just a few short weeks.

And wondering what she was going to do about it.

Finally, seeing it was almost midnight and knowing her sister would be worried, she pulled her phone out of her purse and texted Madison, telling her where she was.

Her sister wrote back immediately. On my way.

She hadn't asked her twin to come, but of course she'd known she would.

She just hadn't known she wouldn't be coming alone. When Madison walked into the café, with Tommy hot on her heels, Candace threw herself back in the booth and groaned. She just wasn't up for a dramatic scene.

"Oh, honey, are you okay?" Mad asked, sitting beside her and pulling her in for a hug.

"I don't know," she admitted.

"Jeez, Candy, why the hell didn't you tell me what was going on?" Tommy took the seat across from her, frowning. "You know I never would have showed up here to-night and made that scene if I'd had any idea you were with some dude."

"He's not some dude," she retorted.

"You really are in love with him," Tommy said, sounding stunned.

She couldn't speak; she could only nod.

"Madison said you were, but I didn't believe her."

"I can hardly believe it myself," she admitted. "But it's true. I'm crazy about him. He's brilliant and fun and wonderful." Sniffling, she added, "So wonderful that after he told me he loved me, he gave me up rather than ask me to break my promise to you!"

Tommy's mouth fell open. "Seriously?"

She nodded.

"Oh, Candace, he really is a keeper," her sister said, gently smoothing her hair back from her tear-streaked face.

"Yeah." A humorless laugh spilled from her mouth. "And I just threw him back."

"I'm so sorry," Tommy said.

She looked at him, her dear friend, seeing in that handsome face the funny little boy who'd liked to do puzzles with her for hours every day. She would do just about anything for him.

Anything but rip her heart out of her chest and let it be completely shredded.

She couldn't lose Oliver. She just couldn't.

It was on her lips, a plea for Tommy to understand and let her change her mind. She loved him…he was family, but if she didn't give her relationship with Oliver a chance, she knew she would regret it until the end of her days.

"Tommy, I…"

"Oh, hell, I'll do it," her sister said, cutting her off mid-sentence.

They both stared at Madison, who was rolling her eyes

and crossing her arms over her chest, which looked a bit more impressive than Candace's had in the glittery red dress.

"You'll do what?" Candace asked.

"I'll take your place with Tommy."

Her heart thumped. "What did you say?"

Tommy's eyes widened. "Huh?"

"I said I'll be this big jerk's fiancée. I'll move in with him and play the part to the hilt."

"You can't be serious," Candace said. "What about your job? Your new apartment?"

Her sister shrugged. "Actually, I've been shifting gears a little. I thought I'd try my hand at screen writing. What better place to be than at all the best parties with all the right people?"

Stunned, Candace tried to wrap her mind around the whole thing. "But who will believe it?"

Waving her left hand, still weighted down by that ring Tommy had slipped on Candace's hand earlier, Madison said, "He never did introduce me—or you—by name, right? Nobody will know any different. Heck, since I've known him just as long as you have, we could say we were childhood sweethearts or something." Then she stared at her potential bridegroom. "By the way, this is an engagement. Not a marriage. I'll wear your ring for a year and play adoring wife-to-be. That should take the heat off until you straighten your shit out."

Tommy's sparkling eyes said he was seriously considering the offer. Then he confirmed it, saying, "Two years."

She pursed her lips. Mad was nothing if not a negotiator.

"Eighteen months. We break up Christmas of next year."

He grinned. "The tabloids will love it. I'll be all heartbroken and tragic. The Academy will ask me to present."

"If they do, we're getting back together," Madison warned. "And you're so buying me a Vera Wang gown."

"Done!"

Tommy stuck his hand out toward Mad. She took it, they shook and sealed the deal.

Candace's thoughts were reeling. Had that really just happened? Had her sister truly just agreed to take her place in Tommy's life, leaving Candace free to pursue the man of her dreams? Had the offer really come in the nick of time, so she hadn't been forced to hurt Tommy by telling him she wanted out of the deal?

She looked at her sister. Mad looked back, a sweet, tender expression replacing her usual blunt, take-no-prisoners one.

"Thank you," she whispered as the truth of it finally sank in. More excited by the second, she threw her arms around her sister, then reached across the table and dragged Tommy into a group hug. "Thank you both!"

They squeezed for a moment, until Tommy said, "Okay, now get out of here and let me make googly eyes at my wife-to-be. I'll bet some paparazzi asshole followed us from the hotel and is taking pictures from across the street."

Madison concurred. Tossing her a set of keys, she said, "My rental car's at the curb. Mr. Hollywood will get me back to the hotel safely." She reached up and touched Candace's cheek. "Go claim your man."

That was the best suggestion Candace had heard all night. And she immediately stood up and strode out of the restaurant, determined to do just that.

She didn't waste time going back to the hotel, knowing Oliver wouldn't have gone there. She would bet money he had called a cab and paid a fortune for it to take him back to Sonoma. That's where she headed, hoping her instincts were right.

During the entire forty-minute drive, she clutched the steering wheel, tense and anxious, trying to find the words to make things right, wondering how he would react when he saw her. She had so much she wanted to tell him, so many things to explain, secrets to share, wishes and dreams to whisper. She just hoped he didn't slam the door in her face when she showed up at his cottage.

Arriving at the estate, which was dark and silent, she drove up the long, windy driveway, glad Madison's rental car was a hybrid with a very quiet engine. She didn't want to give Oliver too much warning so that he could put his defenses too firmly in place.

She parked in front of the house, slipped from the car and hurried to the cottage. Reaching for the knob, she thought twice, knowing if this was the beginning of the rest of their lives, she needed to start on the right foot.

She knocked.

This wouldn't be about coercion, letting herself in, seducing him—although she hoped she'd get that chance later. She wanted him to let her in, to give her a chance.

Just one chance to win him.

A light flipped on and she released the breath she'd been holding. She'd guessed correctly.

The door slowly opened, and he saw her there. His eyes widened a tiny bit, but his mouth remained set in a firm line. No smile tugged at it, no welcoming glimmer of happiness. He merely waited. Watching, assessing. But she'd bet the wheels were churning away in his mind as he tried to figure out what she was doing at his door.

"May I come in?"

Stepping out of the way, he gestured for her to enter, still not speaking.

"I thought I'd find you here."

He finally spoke. "Why did you come?"

"To claim you."

That surprised a flinch out of him. "Huh?"

Though she desperately wanted to slide her arms around

his neck and pull him down for a warm kiss that would
do a better job of explaining why she was here, she knew
she had to give him the gift he'd given her earlier—utter
and complete honesty.

"I love you, Oliver."

He nodded slowly. "You said that earlier."

"Yes. But I didn't say that I want to be with you, for
as long as you'll have me. I want to stay here and build a
life with you. To help you figure out what you want to do
with your life."

He looked stunned.

"Maybe you'll want to go back into law, or maybe you
won't. Maybe you'll want to stay here and help Grandpa
turn this into a premiere winery. You can grow grapes, I
can draw costumes and we'll drink wine and live."

He stepped closer, not reaching for her, but looking
more hopeful by the second. "What about your engagement?"

"It's over."

His relief was visible. Because she'd known he hadn't
wanted her doing anything purely for his sake, she explained the whole story, telling him about her sister's plans
to stay in L.A., which, frankly, made her very happy on
many levels.

"But you didn't ask her to?"

"No, I swear. I was just about to tell Tommy we needed
to find another solution because I couldn't give you up. But
before I said anything, Madison jumped in and offered to
be the phony fiancée for a while."

She wasn't entirely sure Madison had been serious
about the screenplay-writing thing. It was possible, though.
Her sister had recently hinted that she wasn't happy with
her job, despite how hard she'd worked toward a career
in journalism. Mad had always loved to write, and had
thought hard-hitting news articles would be her forte. She'd

also been great at creative writing, so perhaps this idea of hers hadn't been just a throwaway offer meant to make Candace not feel so guilty. Maybe she really wanted this shot at a new career. Candace certainly hoped so anyway.

"So she's not giving up her dreams so you can have yours?"

"No, I really don't think she was."

They fell silent, staring at one another. She saw him processing everything, that keen mind evaluating all that had happened…what she'd said, what she'd done, what it meant.

"I love you," she repeated, holding nothing back, her voice thick with emotion.

He took a step closer. Then another, until he stood a foot away, close enough for her to feel the warmth of his body. Far enough away for her to miss it.

"Say something," she said.

His perfect mouth widened little by little, until that sexy grin appeared, stopping her heart and chasing away all her misgivings.

"Something."

Laughter spilled from her mouth. "Jerk."

He didn't torment her anymore, didn't hesitate. He reached for her, wrapping his arms around her and drawing her hard against his body. His mouth covered hers, lips parting, in a kiss that seemed like a very long time coming, though they'd only been apart for a few hours. With that kiss, she told him again and again how she felt, and knew he was saying the same thing.

Eventually, he picked her up in his arms and carried her to the steps. Carrying her up them, he began to whisper the sweetest things—promises, dreams, hopes for the future.

All she'd ever hoped for. All she'd ever wanted.

"I love you, Candace. I want you with me always. I want to go to bed with you every night and wake up with you every morning. And I promise I'll do everything I can to make you happy."

This time the wetness in her eyes was brought on by pure joy. She knew he meant what he said, knew she could trust him with everything—her heart, her body, her life.

He was her present and her future.

Her everything.

And she was his.

Epilogue

The Hollywood Tattler: She's Landed The Big One!

Well, it's official. Superhunk Thomas Shane has announced his engagement to his childhood sweetheart, a private, reclusive journalist from New York, who has recently moved with him into a new oceanfront home. A certain Ms. Reid is sporting an enormous ring that even Jennifer Aniston would covet, and has quickly settled into life on the West Coast.

The happy couple has been seen romancing all over town, with cozy dinner dates in exclusive restaurants, and late nights dancing at all the hot spots. Sources say these two put off some major heat—theirs is obviously a real love match.

Shane's future wife is also rumored to be writing a screenplay adaptation of a recent blockbuster, with an eye toward her future husband landing the leading role. Sounds like the birth of another Hollywood supercouple!

Don't you just love happily-ever-afters?

* * * * *

LESLIE KELLY

OVEREXPOSED

Prologue

THEY CALLED HER the Crimson Rose.

As her name was announced in sultry, almost reverent tones at Leather and Lace, an exclusive men's club, an awed quiet began to slither through the crowd. The room stilled, noisy conversation giving way to quiet expectation.

Businessmen in open-collared shirts stopped their whispered flirtations with waitresses wearing tiny black skirts and skimpy tops. Attendees of an entire bachelor party returned to their table, elbowing the groom to watch and weep. Single men who came every week just to see *her* sat back in plush leather chairs and stared rapt at the stage through hooded eyes. The ice tinkling against their glasses was soon the only sound in the lushly appointed room, even the servers knew better than to interrupt the clientele when the Rose was on stage.

She danced only twice a week—on Saturdays and Sundays—and since the night she'd started, the Crimson Rose had become one of the hottest attractions in the Chicago club scene. Because while the jaded city had long been used to hard-looking dancers taking off their clothes and gyrating to the heavy beat of sexual music, they simply hadn't seen anything like *her*.

She wasn't hard-looking, she was elegant. Her delicate

features and natural curves made every man who saw her wonder what it would feel like to touch her creamy skin.

She didn't strip…she undressed. Slowly. Seductively. As if she had all the time in the world to give a man pleasure.

She didn't gyrate, she swayed, moving with fluid grace. Every gesture, every turn an invitation to gaze at her.

Her sound wasn't sexual, it was sensual, erotic and soulful enough to make a man close his eyes and appreciate it. Though, of course, when she was onstage none ever would.

While her job might have diminished some women in the eyes of those around her, the Rose *owned* it, embraced it, lifted it up to a level of art rather than pure sexual titillation.

She liked what she did. And they liked watching her.

The low, sultry thrum of a smoky number began, but the stage remained dark as the workers put final placement on a portable red satin curtain, used only by her. It had been a recent addition by the management, who'd realized that the high-class, stage-performer feel was part of the Crimson Rose's appeal. As was the mystery.

While most of the other dancers at the club performed under bright overhead light and full exposure, the Rose danced in shadow and pools of illumination provided by precisely timed spotlights. Her red velvet mask never came off. Most figured the management was playing upon the popularity of the aura of secrecy surrounding the Rose.

Finally the music grew louder, the gelled spotlights, ranging in color from soft pink to bloodred, illuminated the stage, dancing back and forth, each briefly touching on one spot: the seam of the closed satin curtain.

"Now, for your viewing delight," said a smooth male from the sound system, "Chicago's perfect bloom, the Crimson Rose."

No one clapped or whispered. No one *moved.* All eyes

were on the center of the curtain, where a hand began to emerge.

It was pale. Delicate, with long fingers and slender wrists. A colorful design—painted-on body art—began at the tip of one finger, with a tiny leaf. It connected to a vine, which wound up her hand, around her wrist. As her arm emerged, more of the leafy vine, complete with sharp thorns, was revealed. It glittered, sensuous and wicked, alluring and dangerous.

Sinuous, slow, unhurried, she emerged from the drape, until she was fully revealed. But her head remained down, her long reddish-brown hair concealing her face.

The tempo throbbed. The dancer stayed still, as if completely oblivious to the crowd. Finally, the spotlights changed color, the vibrant reds giving way to a soft morning-yellow. And, as if she were a tightly wound blossom being awakened by a gentle dawn, the Rose began to move.

Her head slowly lifted, the delicate beauty of her pale throat emphasized by more body art. Her hair fell back as she turned toward the light, as if welcoming the morning.

Her full lips—red and wet—were parted, sending vivid images and erotic fantasies into the mind of every man close enough to see their glisteny sheen.... This was a woman made for the art of kissing. And sensual pleasure.

There the view of her face stopped. A soft red velvet mask covered the rest. The mask glittered with green jewels like those in the vine, leaving her audience certain that the temptress's eyes must be a pure, vivid emerald. Most already knowing the mystery of her face would not be revealed, her admirers refocused their attention to the rest of her.

She wore layers of soft fabric, cut in petal shapes. Still like the flower being awakened by the sun, she began to indulge in the spotlight's warmth. Swaying, she stretched lazily like a cat in a puddle of light. Her movements were unhurried, revealing a length of thigh, a glimmer of hip.

Then the tempo picked up. So did her pace. She arched and swayed across the stage with feminine grace. But to most, she appeared lonely—removed from her surroundings—revealing a sensual want that begged for fulfillment that would never come.

Anyone in the audience would have fulfilled it for her. *Anyone.*

Every move she made set the billowing layers of her costume in motion, until the petals nearly danced around her on their own. They parted to reveal her slender legs, providing a peek here and a glimpse there.

And then they started to disappear.

Every man in the place leaned forward. Wherever she turned, another bit of fabric hit the floor. Her hands moved so effortlessly that the layers seemed to fall by themselves. The light pinks and puffy outer veil went first, followed by the heavier satin pieces. Soon her long, perfectly toned legs were revealed up to the thigh. A drape of satin covering her stomach fell next, torn away from the strings of a bikini top.

She continued her siren's dance as the fabric fell away, the tempo pushing harder, her hips thrusting in response. Finally, when she wore nothing but a sparkly red G-string and two tiny delicate pink petals on the tips of her breasts, she glanced at the audience, deigning to give them her attention. Normally, at this point, she would offer a saucy smile, pluck the petals off her nipples, then duck behind her curtains. She'd give them a glimpse—quick, heart-stoppingly sexy—then disappear into the dark recesses of the club until her second performance of the night. But tonight…tonight, she hesitated. No. Tonight, she *froze.*

Because as she cast a final glance at her audience, seeing a number of familiar faces in the crowd, her attention was captured by a shadowy figure standing in the back of the room, beside the bar. Ignoring the expectant hush from those familiar with her performance, all of whom were waiting for the payoff moment they'd come to see, she focused all her attention on *him*.

She couldn't see much at that distance, both because of the mask she wore and the spotlights still shining in her face. But she saw enough to send her heart—already beating frantically due to her performance—into hyperdrive.

From here, he appeared black-haired and black-eyed and black-clothed. She could make out none of his features, just that tall, dark presence—broad of shoulder, slim-hipped. He might be dangerous, given his size and the shadowy darkness swallowing him from her view—but now, at this moment, she felt lured by him. Entranced. Captivated.

Their eyes locked. He knew he had her attention. And in that moment, she desperately wanted to walk off the stage, across the room, close enough to see if his face was as handsome as his shadowy form hinted. Then closer— to see what truths lay in the mysterious depths of those inky black eyes.

But suddenly someone whistled…someone else cat-called. She realized she'd lost track of the music and the dance and the audience and her reasons for being here.

Titillation. Seduction. Those were her reasons for being here. Which made it that much more strange that, right now, the Rose was the one who felt seduced.

Enough. Time to finish.

Sweeping her gaze across the crowd, she gave them all a wickedly sexy look, as if her pause had been entirely purposeful. And entirely for their personal delight. In it, she invited them to imagine just who had her breathing hard—licking her lips in anticipation. Who had her skin flushed and her sex damp and her nipples rock hard.

She only wished she knew the answer.

With one more sidelong glance through half-lowered lashes, she reached for the tiny petals—pink, to match the tender skin of her taut nipples—and plucked them off.

The crowd was roaring as she disappeared behind the curtain. They cheered for several long minutes during which she regained her breath and tried to force her pulse to return to its normal, measured beat.

When it did, she took a chance and peeked through the curtain, her stare zoning in on that dark place by the bar.

But the shadowy stranger was gone.

1

FOR THE FIRST two weeks after he'd returned from the Middle East, Nick Santori genuinely didn't mind the way his family fussed over him. There were big welcome-home barbecues in the tiny backyard of the row house where he'd been raised. There were even bigger dinners at the family owned pizzeria that had been his second home growing up.

He'd been dragged to family weddings by his mother and into the kitchen of the restaurant by his father. He'd had wet, sticky babies plopped in his lap by his sisters-in-law, and had been plied with beer by his brothers, who wanted details on everything he'd seen and done overseas. And he'd had rounds of drinks raised in his honor by near-strangers who, having suitably praised him as a patriot, wanted to go further and argue the politics of the whole mess.

That was where he drew the line. He didn't want to talk about it. After twelve years in the Corps, several of them on active duty in Iraq, he'd had enough. He didn't want to relive battles or wounds or glory days with even his brothers and he sure as hell wouldn't justify his choice to join the military to people he'd never even met.

At age eighteen, fresh out of high school with no interest in college and even less in the family business, entering the Marines had seemed like a kick-ass way to spend a few years.

What a dumb punk he'd been. Stupid. Unprepared. Green.

He'd quickly learned…and he'd grown up. And while he didn't regret the years he'd spent serving his country, he sometimes wished he could go back in time to smack that eighteen-year-old around and wake him up to the realities he'd be facing.

Realities like this one: coming home to a world he didn't recognize. To a family that had long since moved on without him.

"So you hanging in?" asked his twin, Mark, who sat across from him in a booth nursing a beer. His brothers had all gotten into the habit of stopping by the family owned restaurant after work a few times a week.

"I'm doing okay."

"Feeling that marinara running through your veins again?"

Nick chuckled. "Do you think Pop has ever even realized there's any other kind of food?"

Mark shook his head. Reaching into a basket, he helped himself to a bread stick. "Do *you* think Mama has ever even tried to cook him any?"

"Good point." Their parents were well matched in their certainty that any food other than Italian was unfit to eat.

"Is she still griping because you wouldn't move back home?"

Nodding, Nick grabbed a bread stick of his own. For all his grumbling, he wouldn't trade his Pop's cooking for anything…especially not the never-ending MRE's he'd had to endure in the military. "She seems to think I'd be happy living in our old room with the Demi Moore *Indecent Proposal* poster on the wall. It's like walking into a frigging time warp."

"You always did prefer *G.I. Jane*."

Nick just sighed. Mark seldom took anything seriously. In that respect, he hadn't changed. But everything else sure had.

During the years he'd been gone, the infrequent visits home hadn't allowed Nick to mentally keep up with his loved ones. In his mind, when he'd lain on a cot wondering if there would ever come a day when sand wouldn't infiltrate every surface of his clothes again, the Santoris were the same big loud bunch he'd grown up with: two hardworking parents and a brood of kids.

They weren't kids anymore, though. And Mama and Pop had slowed down greatly over the years. His father had turned over the day-to-day management of Santori's to Nick's oldest brother, Tony, and stayed in the kitchen drinking chianti and cooking.

One of his brothers was a prosecutor. Another a successful contractor. Their only sister was a newlywed. And, most shocking of all to Nick, Mark, his twin, was about to become a father.

Married, domesticated and reproducing…that described the happy lives of the five other Santori kids. And every single one of them seemed to think he should do exactly the same thing.

Nick agreed with them. At least, he *had* agreed with them when living day-to-day in a place where nothing was guaranteed, not even his own life. It had seemed perfect. A dream he could strive for at the end of his service. Now it was within reach.

He just wasn't sure he still wanted it.

He didn't doubt his siblings were happy. Their conversations were full of banter and houses and SUVs and baby talk that they all seemed to love but Nick just didn't get. And wasn't sure he ever would…despite how much he knew he *should*.

I will.

At least, he *hoped* he would.

The fact that he was bored out of his mind helping out at Santori's and hadn't yet met a single *appropriate* woman who made his heart beat faster—much less one he wanted to pick out baby names with—was merely a product of his own re-adjustment to civilian life. He'd come around. Soon. No doubt about it.

As long as he avoided going after the one woman he'd seen recently who not only made his heart beat fast but had also given him a near-sexual experience from across a crowded room. Because she was in *no way* appropriate. She was a stripper. One he'd be working with very soon now that he'd agreed to take a job doing security at a club called Leather and Lace.

Forcibly thrusting the vision of the sultry dancer out of his brain, he focused on the type of *normal* woman he'd someday meet who might inspire a similar reaction.

He'd have help locating her. Everyone, it seemed, wanted him to find the "perfect" woman and they all just happened to know her. The next one of his sisters-in-law who asked him to come over for dinner and *coincidentally* asked her single best friend to come, too, would be staring at Nick's empty chair.

"Do you know how glad I am that your wife's knocked up?"

"Yeah, me, too," Mark replied, wearing the same sappy look he'd had on his face since he'd started telling everyone Noelle was expecting. "But do I want to know why *you're* so happy?"

"Because it means she doesn't have time to try to set me up with her latest single friend/hairstylist/next-door neighbor or just the next breathing woman who walks by."

Mark had the audacity to grin.

"It's not funny."

"Yeah, it is. I've seen the ones they've thrown at you."

"You seen me throw them back, too, then."

Nodding, Mark sipped his beer.

"Doesn't matter if she's a blonde, brunette, redhead or bald. Any single woman with a pulse gets shoved at me."

"And Catholic," Mark pointed out.

"Mama's picks, yeah. But *none* of them are my type."

Deadpan, his brother asked, "Women?"

"F-you," he replied. "I mean, I do have a few preferences."

"Big—"

"Beyond that," Nick snapped.

Mark relented. "Okay, I'm kidding. What *do* you want?"

That was the question of the hour, wasn't it? Nick had no idea what he wanted. It was *supposed* to be someone who'd make him want *this*. This sedate, small-town-in-a-big-city lifestyle.

"I don't know if I'm cut out for what all of you have."

When Mark's brow rose, Nick added, "I wasn't criticizing. You all seem happy. The couples in *this* family don't seem as…"

"Boring?"

"I guess."

"Thanks," his brother replied drily.

"No offense. But you're all the exception, not the rule."

Mark murmured, "That's a lot of exceptions."

It was. Which meant Nick was out of luck. How many great, happy marriages could one family contain?

But damned if he wasn't going to give it a try. He'd been telling himself for the last three years of his active enlistment that once he was free—once he was home—he was going to have the kind of life the rest of his family had. The dreams of that normal, happy lifestyle had sustained him through some of the wickedest fighting he'd ever seen.

He would not give them up now. Not even if they suddenly seemed a little sedate.

"Face it, they won't rest until you're 'settled down.'"

"Like *you?*" he asked, raising a brow. His twin was a hard-ass Chicago detective who could hardly be described as "settled down." The man was as tough as they came, despite his occasionally goofy sense of humor.

"Yeah. Like me."

Nick rolled his eyes. "You are in no way *settled down*." He glanced at the cuts on his twin's knuckles.

Mark smiled, a twinkle in his eyes. "Guy resisted."

"Does Noelle know?"

The smile faded. "No, and if you tell her I'll pound you."

"I'd like to see you try."

Leaning back in the booth and crossing his arms across his chest, Mark nodded. "I guess you might be able to hold your own now that the Marines toughened you up and filled you out."

It had long been a friendly argument between them that Nick had inherited their mother's lean, tall build like Luke and Joe. Mark and Tony resembled their barrel-chested father. But after many tough, physical years in the military, Nick was no longer anybody's "little" brother. "I think I could take you on."

"I think you could take *anybody* on. So why don't you come down to the station and talk to my lieutenant?"

"Not interested in your job, bro. I've had enough of rules and regulations for a while." They'd talked about the possibility a few times since Nick had returned home, but he wasn't about to relent on that issue. He'd done his time on the battlefields of Iraq; he didn't want to add to them in Chicago.

"Yeah, okay," Mark said, glancing around the crowded restaurant. "I can see why *this* is so much more up your alley."

Nick followed his glance and smothered a sigh. Because Mark was right. Helping at the pizzeria was no problem in the short term, heck he'd helped run the place when he was in high school, putting in more time than any of his siblings. But did he really want to become a partner in the business with his brother Tony, as he used to talk about… and as the family was hoping?

Seemed impossible. But Mark was the only one who would understand that. "I'm getting into protection," he admitted.

"You gonna mass-produce rubbers?" Mark sounded completely innocent, though his eyes sparkled with his usual good humor.

"I can't *wait* to tell your kid what a juvenile delinquent you were. Like when you put the *Playboy* magazine in Father Michael's desk drawer in sixth grade."

"Believe me, my kid will know Dad's on the job from the time he's old enough to even *think* about swiping candy bars. Now, what's with this protection business?"

"I'm going to work part-time as a bodyguard."

"No kidding?" Mark said, sounding surprised.

"Joe did some renovation work on a nightclub uptown and got friendly with the owner. Turns out they need extra security, so he set up a meeting. I went in Sunday night to talk to them."

"Bet Meg *loved* big brother Joe working in a nightclub."

Like the rest, their older brother Joe was happily married. Nick knew he'd never even *look* at another woman.

"So," Mark asked, "why does a club need a bodyguard?"

Nick knew *exactly* why this club needed a bodyguard after watching the erotic performance by a dancer called the Crimson Rose. The sultry stranger had inhabited his dreams and more than a few of his fantasies ever since he'd seen her onstage, revealing her incredible body while still remaining, somehow, so *above* it all. He imagined men with less control might try to do more than fantasize about the woman.

"The performers attract a lot of unwanted attention," he said, not wanting to get into details. Not because he was embarrassed about his job, but because he didn't want to start talking about the rose-draped dancer and her effect on *him*.

Nick didn't need that kind of distraction in his life. A hot stripper definitely did not fit in with the nice Santori lifestyle he kept telling himself he wanted. Not one bit. Which meant working with her was going to be a trick.

But he'd handled bigger challenges. Besides, meeting her—talking to her—would take the bloom off that rose. Intense fantasies were meant for women who were untouchable, mysterious, unknown. It was, he'd come to believe while living in the Middle East, part of the allure of veiled women living in that culture. The unknown always built high expectations.

The Crimson Rose soon would *not* be an unknown. He'd see the face that had been hidden behind the mask and her secrets would be revealed. Which would make her much less intriguing.

Wanting his mind off *her* until it had to be when he started work, he changed the subject. "This place is hopping."

"So why aren't you out there taking orders from women who'd like to order a side of *you* with their thick crust?"

"Even the help gets an occasional night off."

He cast a bored glance around the room. A line of patrons stood near the counter, waiting for carry-out orders. Every table was full. Waitresses buzzed around in constant motion, all of them overseen by Mama. Nothing caught his attention…until he spotted *her*. And then he couldn't look away.

She stopped his heart, the way the dancer had, though the women couldn't be more dissimilar.

The stranger stood near the door, leaning against the wall. Looking at no one, her eyes remained focused on some spot outside the windows. Her posture spoke of weary disinterest, as if she'd zoned out on the chattering of customers all around her. She was separate, alone, lost in her own world of thought.

Not fitting in.

That, as much as her appearance, kept Nick's attention focused directly on her. Because he, too, knew what it was like to not fit in among this loud world of family and friends and neighbors who'd known one another for years.

She was solitary, self-contained, which interested him.

And her looks simply stole his breath.

From where he sat, he had a perfect view of her profile. Her thick dark brown hair hung from a haphazard ponytail, emphasizing her high cheekbones and delicate jaw. Her face appeared soft, her skin creamy and smooth. Though her lips were parted, she didn't appear to be smiling. He suspected she was sighing from her open mouth every once in a while, though out of unhappiness or of boredom, he couldn't say.

Dressed casually in jeans and a T-shirt, she also wore a large baker's type apron over her clothes. That made it impossible to check out her figure. But judging by the length of those legs, shrunk-wrapped in tight, faded denim, he imagined it was spectacular. With a lightweight backpack slung over one shoulder, she looked like she'd stopped off to grab a pizza on her way home from work, like everyone else in line.

Only, she was so incredibly sexy in her aloof indifference, she didn't *look* like any other person in line.

Across from him, Mark said something, but Nick paid no attention. He continued to stare, wishing she'd turn toward him so he could make out the color of her eyes. Finally, as though she'd read his mental order, the brunette shifted, tilted her head in a delicate stretch that emphasized her slender neck and turned. Sweeping a lazy gaze across the room, she breathed a nearly audible sigh that confirmed she was bored.

Then her eyes met his…and there they stopped.

Hers were brown, as dark as his. As their stares locked, he noted the flash of heated awareness in her stare. She made no effort to look away, watching him watch her. As if she knew he'd been checking her out, she returned the favor, looking him over, from his face down, her stare lingering a little long on his shoulders, and even longer on his chest. Nick shifted in his seat, his worn jeans growing tight across his groin, where heat slid and pulsed with seam-splitting intensity.

Though he was seated and there was no way she could see her effect on him, the stranger began to smile. One corner of her mouth tilted up, revealing a tiny dimple in her cheek. But it wasn't a cute, flirty one…nothing about this woman was cute and flirty, she was aggressive and seductive.

Needing to know her—now—he pushed his beer away and slid to the end of the bench seat without a word.

"Nick?" his brother asked, obviously startled.

"I have to meet her."

"Who?"

Nick didn't answer, he simply rose to his feet, never taking his eyes off the stranger.

Mark turned around. *"Her?"* his brother asked, sounding so surprised Nick wondered if marriage had made him entirely immune to the appeal of a hot, sexy stranger. "You have to *meet* her?"

Already walking away, Nick didn't answer. Instead, he strode across the restaurant, determined to not let her get away. He had to meet the first *real* woman—not a fantasy dressed in rose petals—who'd made his heart start beating hard again since the day he'd gotten home from the war.

IZZIE NATALE HAD A SECRET.

Well, she had *many* secrets. But the secret she was trying to disguise right now was one that would get her thrown out of the windy city for life.

She preferred New York–style pizza to Chicago deep-dish.

Shocking, but true. In the years she'd been living in New York during her dancing career, she'd fallen in love with everything there, including the food. But she'd be taking her life in her hands if she admitted it. Because, man, they took their pizza *very* seriously here. Her grandfather would turn over in his grave if he found out she'd gone to the dark—thin-crust—side. Her father, at whose request she'd made this stop at Santori's, would disown her. And her sister, whose husband ran this place, would never speak to her again.

Hmm. That might be a blessing. Considering her sister Gloria never had mastered the art of shutting up when the occasion demanded it, Izzie felt tempted to tell her that not only did she like her crust thin, but she also preferred the Mets over the Cubbies. That would get her stoned in the street.

How am I going to get through this?

It wasn't the first time she'd wondered that in the two months she'd been home, taking care of her family owned bakery while her father recovered from his stroke. If her friends in Manhattan could see her—covered in flour, wearing an apron, working behind a counter—they'd think she'd been kidnapped.

This could not be Izzie Natale, the former long-legged Rockette who'd had men at her fingertips. Nor could it be the Izzie who'd gone on to land a spot with one of the premiere modern dance companies in New York, short-lived though that spot may have been after her ACL injury had required major surgery seven months ago.

But it was. *She* was. And it was driving her *mad*.

It wasn't that she didn't love her family. But oh, did she wish one of *them* could run the bakery. Because she was not happy being once again under the microscope, living in this big-geographically, but small-town-at-heart area of Little Italy.

Before she could groan about it, however, something caught her eye in the crowded pizzeria. Make that someone caught her eye. As she cast another bored look around, half wishing she'd see someone she'd recognize from her *other* life here in Chicago—the one nobody else knew about—she spotted *him*.

A dark-haired, dark-eyed man was staring at her from across the place. Even from twenty feet away she felt the heat rolling off him. An answering sultry, hungry fire curled from the tips of her curly dark hair down to the bottoms of her feet.

God, the man was hot. Fiery hot. Global-warming hot.

His jet-black hair was cut short, spiky. *A military man*.

His dark eyes matched the hair. They were deep set, heavily lashed…bedroom eyes, she'd have to say. His lean face was more rugged than handsome. The strong jaw jutted out the tiniest bit, and his unsmiling mouth was tightly set, as if intentionally trying to disguise the fullness of a pair of amazing male lips.

His shoulders were Mack-truck wide and his chest was football-field broad. And his attitude was all 100 percent Santori male.

Because Izzie knew it was Nick Santori who'd met her stare from across the room. Nick Santori who'd risen from his seat and was winding his way across the room toward her. Nick Santori who was making the earth shake a little under her feet, just as he always had when she was a teenager.

She told herself to breathe and not let him get under her skin. He sure had once…like at Gloria and Tony's wedding, when she'd been a bridesmaid of fourteen and Nick had been a groomsman. He'd had to escort her down the aisle, and his big bad going-into-the-Marines-eighteen-year-old self hadn't liked it. And that day was one she would *never* live down.

Somehow, though, that memory didn't steady the floor. Nor did it cool her off as he came closer. Those dark eyes of his were locked on her face as he effortlessly cleared his way through the crowd with a look here or glance there. Everyone made way for him. The men out of respect. The women… well, the women looked like Izzie imagined she did: dumbstruck. All because of the simmering sensuality of this one sexy man.

The one she'd wanted since the first time she'd felt heat between her legs and understood what it meant.

"Hi," he said when he finally reached her.

"Hey." She felt almost triumphant at having achieved that note of casual aloofness. She even managed to keep slouching against the wall, probably because she needed the support. She might have learned to handle men but she'd never gotten over feeling like Izzie-the-geek around this one.

"Is there something I can do for you?"

Oh, yeah. She could think of several somethings. Starting with her getting some payback for him ignoring her when she was a chubby, lovesick kid. And ending with him naked in her bed.

But getting naked in bed with Nick Santori would involve serious complications. Her sister was married to his brother. The families were old friends. If she so much as looked at the guy with interest the neighborhood would have them married off with her popping out brown-haired Italian babies within a year.

Uh-uh. No, thanks. Not for Izzie. Sex with Nick would be delightful. But it came with *way* too many strings.

"I don't think so," she finally answered.

He didn't back off. "I'm sure there's something."

"What, are you a waiter now?" she asked, amused at the thought of him waiting tables. Especially since that chest of his could probably double as one.

Nick had, like all the Santori kids, worked in the restaurant in high school. Just as Izzie had worked in the bakery—often eating her paycheck to sweeten her teenage angst.

But he'd been in the Marines for years. She didn't see him slinging pizzas now that he was back in Chicago. Not after he'd been slinging Uzis or whatever those macho soldier guys carried.

"Maybe. Why don't you tell me what you want and I'll let you know if I can get it for you?"

Thin and cheesy New York–style pizza was the first thing that came to mind, but Izzie didn't want to get strung up at the corner of Taylor and Racine. "I already placed my order."

He smiled slightly. "I wasn't just talking about pizza."

God, was that…it *was*. There was a flirtatious twinkle in those blackish-brown eyes of his. He'd been throwing some subtle innuendo at her and it had gone clear over her head.

"Oh" was all she could manage.

Cake flour must have clogged her femme-fatale genes in the past two months. It was the only way someone with her experience with men could have missed his double meaning.

"Want to sit while you wait for your order?" he asked, gesturing toward a few chairs in the waiting area.

"No, thanks." She fell silent. If she opened her mouth again, she might do something stupid like throw out a dumb, *"Wow, what I wouldn't have given for you to look at me like that when I was a teenager"* line, which she so didn't want to do.

She zipped her lips. She'd be Izzie the uninterested mute. Which was better than Izzie the lovesick mutant.

"How about at a table?"

"At a table…what?"

He smiled again, that sexy, self-confident smile that had probably had woman on five continents dropping their panties within sixty seconds of meeting him. "We can sit at a table while you wait for your order."

God, she was an idiot. "No, I'm fine here, thank you."

She had to give herself a break for being so slow. After all, Nick Santori had been scrambling her brains since she was ten—right around the time her sister Gloria had started dating his brother Tony. And though he'd always had a way with females, he'd never looked twice at *her* that way.

Especially not since Gloria and Tony's wedding. The one where she'd tripped on her ugly puce gown—which hugged her tubby hips and butt—while they were dancing the obligatory wedding-party waltz. She, the kid who'd been in dance lessons since the age of three, had tripped.

Maybe it wasn't so shocking. She'd been worried about what he'd think of her sweaty palms. She'd been *terrified* that her makeup was smearing off her face and revealing that she'd had the mother of all breakouts that morning.

Nervous plus terrified times the pitter-patter of her heart and the achy tingle in her small breasts from where they brushed against the lapels of Nick's tux had left her dizzy. So dizzy she'd stepped off the edge of the slightly raised dance floor and crashed both of them onto a table full of cookies and pastries made especially by her parents for the wedding.

It hadn't been pretty.

Colorful candy-covered almonds had flown in all directions. Her butt had landed on a platter of cream puffs, her elbows in two stacks of pizelles. Her dress had flown up to her waist to reveal the panty girdle she'd worn in an effort to hide her after-school-cookie-binging bulge.

The icing on the five-tiered Italian cream wedding cake—which she'd *somehow* managed to not destroy—had been Nick. He'd gotten tangled up in her dress, and had landed on top of her, sprawled across her chest.

And right between her legs.

It was the first—and last—time she'd figured Nick Santori would be between her legs, which both broke her heart and fueled some intense fantasies throughout her high-school years. Shocked by the unexpectedness and the *pleasure* of it, she'd been slow to part those legs and let him up. Slow enough for the moment to go from embarrassingly long to indecently shocking.

She'd thought her mother was going to kill her afterward.

But that wasn't all. Because Izzie had the luck of someone who broke mirrors for a living, the incident had also been the money shot of the whole day. The videographer caught the whole thing on film, creating a masterpiece that would taunt her throughout eternity.

She'd been a laughingstock. Everyone in the crowd had whooped and clapped and teased her about it for months afterward. She might as well have worn a banner proclaiming herself "Lovesick pubescent girl who crushed the cookies and dry humped the groomsman at the Santori-Natale wedding."

"I haven't seen you in here before," he said, finally breaking the silence that had fallen between them.

"I come here a couple of times a week," she replied.

He shrugged. "I've been gone a long time."

"In the military."

"Right. Things have definitely changed around here in the past twelve years."

"Maybe in some ways," she said. Then she glanced around and saw a minimum of five people she knew— all watching intently as she talked to Nick. Frowning, she muttered, "In some ways it's still the same small-town hell it always was."

She surprised a laugh out of him. "I somehow think we have a lot in common."

His laughter softened his tanned face, bringing out tiny lines beside his eyes. It also made him utterly irresistible, as several women sitting nearby undoubtedly noticed.

Nick had been incredibly hot as a teenager. Lean and wiry, dark and intense. As a thirty-year-old man he was absolutely drool-worthy. Not that he'd changed a lot—he'd just matured. Where he'd been a sexy guy, he was now a tough, heart-stopping male, big and broad, powerful and intimidating.

She didn't suspect he'd changed on the inside, though. Once a Santori male, always a Santori male. The men of that family had always been good-hearted.

Honestly, looking back, if Nick had been a jerk about what had happened at the wedding, she might have gotten over her crush a lot sooner and this moment might be a lot simpler. She could tell him to f-off, remind him he'd once laughed at her and added to her humiliation. Only... he hadn't. Curse the man.

He'd been very sweet, carefully helping her up—once she'd released her thunder-thigh death grip from around his hips. He'd gently wiped powdered sugar and cream off

her cheek. He'd helped her pull her dress back down into
place without making one crack about her chubby thighs
or her panty girdle. He'd pretended she hadn't practically
assaulted him. And he'd helped her back up onto the dance
floor and continued their dance. Absolutely the only an-
noying thing he'd done was to start calling her Cookie.

As her mother often said, he'd been raised right. Just like
his brothers. He was every bit a gentleman—a protector—
and he'd never given her a sideways glance that hadn't been
merely friendly. In his eyes, she'd always been Gloria's
baby sister—the chubby ballerina who looked like a little
stuffed sausage in her pink tutu and tights and he'd treated
her with nothing but big-brotherly kindness.

Until now.

Fortunately, though, she wasn't sweet Izzie the cookie-
gobbling machine anymore. He hadn't seen her for almost
a decade…she no longer blushed and stammered when a
hot guy teased her. And she no longer even tried to imagine she could have been a ballerina with her less-than-
willowy figure.

Once she'd stopped eating pastries and hit brick-shit-
house stature at age eighteen, she'd known her future as a
dancer would come from another direction than the ballet.

She'd also learned how to handle men.

Now, *she* was in the driver's seat when it came to seduction. She'd been running the show with men for years.
And it was high time to let Nick Santori know it.

"So, when you offered to serve me…what *were* you talking about?" she asked, swiping her tongue across her lips.
It was a move she'd perfected in her Rockettes dressing
room. Men used to come backstage, trying to pick up the
dancers and they all went for the lip-licking. God, males
were so predictable. She held her breath, hoping for more
from this one.

And she got it.

GET FREE BOOKS and FREE GIFTS WHEN YOU PLAY THE...

Just scratch off the silver box with a coin. Then check below to see the gifts you get!

SLOT MACHINE GAME!

YES! I have scratched off the silver box. Please send me the 2 free Harlequin® Blaze™ books and 2 free gifts for which I qualify. I understand I am under no obligation to purchase any books, as explained on the back of this card.

151/351 HDL FV7L

FIRST NAME

LAST NAME

ADDRESS

APT.#

CITY

STATE/PROV.

ZIP/POSTAL CODE

7 7 7 Worth **TWO FREE BOOKS** plus 2 **FREE Mystery Gifts!**

Worth **TWO FREE BOOKS!**

Worth **ONE FREE BOOK!**

TRY AGAIN!

Visit us at: www.ReaderService.com

HB-L7-05/13

DETACH AND MAIL CARD TODAY!

HB-L7-05/13

© 2012 HARLEQUIN ENTERPRISES LIMITED
Printed in the U.S.A. ® and ™ are trademarks owned and used by the trademark owner and/or its licensee.

"I'm talking about me serving you with a line and you tipping me with your number. But since it's crowded and I'm rusty at that stuff, why don't you just give me the number?"

Izzie had to laugh. If he'd come back with a smooth line, the laugh would have been at his expense—because she doubted there was one he hadn't heard. But Nick had been completely honest, which she found incredibly attractive.

She also laughed to hide the nervous thrill she'd gotten when she realized Nick Santori really did want her number. That he really was trying to pick her up.

Her...the girl he'd once complained about having to dance with at a wedding. What were the odds?

"I think I've got *your* number." She'd had it for years.

He didn't give up. "Use it. Please."

He meant it. He wasn't teasing, wasn't trying to make her blush, wasn't treating her the way he treated his kid sister, Lottie, who'd been one of her classmates.

Nick Santori was trying to pick her up. Which shouldn't have been a big deal, but, for some reason, had her heart fluttering around in her chest like a bird trapped in a cage.

"My name's Nick, by the way."

No, *duh*. She was about to say that, then she saw the look in his eyes—that serious, intense look. He wasn't kidding. He wasn't pretending they were just meeting.

She sagged back against the wall, not sure whether to laugh or punch him in the face.

Because the rotten son of a bitch had no idea who she was.

2

THE WOMAN HAD flour in her hair. She smelled like almonds. Her apron was smeared with icing and whipped cream. Food coloring stained the tips of two of her fingers.

And she was utterly delicious.

The hints of flavor wafting off her couldn't compete with the innate, warm feminine scent of her body, which assaulted Nick's senses the way no full frontal attack ever had. Though they were in a crowded restaurant, surrounded by customers and members of his own family, hers was the only presence he felt. He'd been drawn to her, captured in an intimate world they'd created the moment their eyes had locked.

"You're name's Nick," she said as if making sure. Her voice was a little hard, her dark eyes narrowing.

Worried she had an ex with the same name, he replied, "I'll answer to anything you want to call me."

"Anything?"

He nodded, unable to take his attention from that bit of flour in her hair. He wanted to lift his hand and brush it away. Then sink his fingers in that thick brown hair of hers, tugging it free of its ponytail to fall in a loose curtain around her shoulders. His fingers clenched into fists at his sides with the need to tangle those thick tresses in his hands and tug her face toward his for a brain-zapping kiss.

She had the kind of mouth that begged for kissing. One that promised pleasure. God, it had been a long time since he'd really kissed a woman the way he *liked* to kiss a woman. Slowly. Deeply. With a thorough exploration of every curve and crevice.

Recently, his sex life had been limited by proximity and his active status. He hadn't had any kind of relationship in years. And the sex he had was usually of the quick, one-night variety, where slow, indulgent kissing wasn't on the agenda.

He could kiss this woman's mouth for *hours*.

Nick didn't understand why he was so drawn to her. All he knew was that he was attracted to her in a way he hadn't been attracted to anyone for a long time. Not just because she was beautiful under the apron and that messy ponytail. But because of the wistful, lonely look she'd worn earlier that said she didn't quite belong here and she knew it. Just like the one he'd had on his face lately.

"You're single?" he asked, wanting that confirmed.

She nodded, the movement setting her ponytail swinging. It caught the reflection of a candle on the closest table, the strands glimmering in a veil of browns and golds that made his heart clang against his lungs.

"What's your name?" he finally asked.

She arched one fine eyebrow. "We haven't settled on what we're going to call *you* yet."

He turned, edging closer to her as a group came into the restaurant. The brunette slid along the wall, farther away from anyone else. Nick followed, irresistibly drawn by her scent and the mystery in her eyes. "I guess you have a Nick in your past?"

"Uh-huh."

"It didn't go well?"

"I'd have to say that's a no."

"Bad breakup?"

"No. We never even dated." One side of her mouth tilted up in a half smile. It held no happiness, merely jaded amusement. "He barely even noticed my existence."

"Then he was an idiot."

The other side of her mouth came up; this time her genuine amusement shone clearly. "Oh, undoubtedly."

"He didn't deserve you."

"Absolutely not."

"You're better off without him."

"Nobody knows that better than me." She sounded more amused now, as if her guard was coming down.

"Enough about him," Nick said. "If you don't like my first name, call me by my last one. It's Santori."

He watched for a flare of surprise, a darting of the eyes to the sign in the window, proclaiming the name of the place.

Strangely, she didn't react at all. "I think we've already determined what I should call you. You said it yourself."

Puzzled, Nick just waited.

"Idiot," she said, tapping the tip of her finger on her cheek, as if thinking about it. "Though, honestly, it doesn't quite capture you now. It might have sufficed years ago, but for today, I think we'll have to go with…complete shithead."

Nick's jaw fell open. But the sexy brunette wasn't finished. "By the way, that number you wanted? Here it is, you might want to write it down…1-800-nevergonnahappen."

And without another word, she shoved at his chest, pushing him out of the way, then strode out the door. Leaving Nick standing there, staring after her in complete shock.

"I'd say *that* didn't go well." Mark stood right behind

him, watching—as was Nick—as the brunette marched off down the street like she'd just kicked somebody's ass.

Well, she had. Namely his. He just didn't know *why*.

"No kidding."

"I see you haven't lost your touch with women."

"Shut up." Shaking his head in bemusement, he lifted a hand and rubbed his jaw. "I don't know how I blew that so badly."

"But you sure managed to do it."

Hearing his twin chuckle, Nick glared. "At least I'm not wearing a ring. I can still *try* to pick up a hot stranger."

Mark just laughed harder. Which made Nick consider punching him. Only, Mama was standing behind the counter, glancing curiously at them as she waited on the customers. If Nick went after his twin, she'd come around and whack them both in the head with a soup ladle.

"Hot stranger…oh, man, you are going to hate yourself when you figure out what you just did."

His eyes narrowing, Nick waited for his twin to continue.

"You really didn't recognize her, did you?"

Oh, hell. He should have recognized her? He *knew* her?

"Still not getting it?"

"Tell me how much trouble I'm in," he muttered, praying he hadn't just come on to a cousin he hadn't seen in years. If they were related—and he *couldn't* have her— that would be a crime worthy of a military tribunal. So he prayed even harder that she'd been some girl he'd known in high school.

"Pretty big trouble."

He waited, knowing Mark was enjoying watching him sweat.

"She *is* family, you know."

Damn. All the blood in his body fell to his feet out of

embarrassment…and disappointment. "Why didn't you stop me?"

"You shot out of the booth like your ass was on fire."

Rubbing a hand over his eyes and shaking his head, Nick mumbled, "Who is she? Mama's side or Pop's? Please tell me she's not one of Great Uncle Vincenza's thirty grand-daughters. Otherwise I just might have to re-up and hide from him and his mafia buddies for the next decade."

Mark's eyes glittered in amusement. The guy was enjoying this. "Not Great Uncle Vincenza. Think closer."

Closer. Christ. "There's no way she's a first cousin…."

"Not a cousin."

Oh, thank heaven. "So who?"

"I'll give you a hint. Did you happen to notice the icing and flour all over her apron?"

Had he ever. He didn't know if he'd ever smelled anything as good as all that messy, sugary stuff combined with the brunette's earthy essence. "Yeah. So?"

"You're not usually this dense."

"You're not usually this close to death."

"Think…the bakery…."

"Natale's? Gloria's folks?" And suddenly it hit him. "No."

"Oh, yes."

No. Impossible. It was out of the question. "Not Gloria's baby sister. *Tell* me that wasn't chubby little Cookie."

"She ain't chubby and I think if you called her Cookie to her face she'd slug you." Mark threw a consoling arm across Nick's shoulders, his chest shaking with laughter. "To answer your question, yes, my brother, that was Isabella Natale."

Nick couldn't speak. He was too stunned, thinking of how she'd changed. It had been at least nine—ten years, perhaps—since he'd seen her. She'd still been in high school and he'd run into her at a Christmas party at Gloria and Tony's when he was home on leave. She'd still blushed and stammered around him. And she'd still been girlishly round—pretty but with such a baby face he'd never taken her crush on him seriously.

Oh, he knew about the crush. *Everybody* knew about the crush. His brother Tony had threatened to break his legs if he so much as looked at her the wrong way at the wedding.

Huh. He hadn't looked at her the wrong way. He'd just landed on top of her in a pile of cookies. And had been unable to get up because she'd wrapped her limbs around him like she was drowning and he was a lifeguard trying to save her.

He started to smile. "Izzie."

"Izzie. Formerly chubby sister of our sister-in-law, turned sexy-as-hell woman, now back in town working at the bakery."

"Her parents' bakery up the block?"

"That's the one."

"Is she here for good?" he asked, already wondering how things could have turned out this perfectly.

"I don't know. She's been home for a couple of months, since Gloria's father had a stroke. With the new baby, Gloria couldn't help much, and the middle sister's a lawyer."

"So the youngest one came home to take over." Not surprising. The Natales were much like the Santoris—family meant everything.

It almost seemed too good to be true. He'd finally come across someone who not only made his nerves spark and his jeans grow a size too tight, but who also came with a premade stamp of approval from the neighborhood. She was gorgeous. She was feisty. Her smile nearly stopped his heart. She'd had a crush on him forever—and was obviously still affected by him, judging by the way she'd taken off in a huff.

And she was *not* a faceless stripper behind a mask.

Enough of that. The Crimson Rose was every other man's fantasy. At this point in his life, Nick wanted *reality.* He was ready for what his brothers and sister had. And he had just stumbled across a *real* woman who he sensed could both drive him absolutely wild with want and be someone he could truly like.

"I think I'm feeling a need for some fresh cannoli," he murmured, smiling as he looked out the window at the sky, streaked orange by the setting sun. Izzie was no longer in sight…she obviously wasn't too desperate for pizza.

Maybe he'd deliver it to her.

"Judging by the way she bolted, you'd better think again."

Nick shrugged. He wasn't worried. After all, Izzie had had a thing for him once upon a time…she had practically chased him down. He just needed to remind her of that.

And to let her know he was ready to let her catch him.

"I SWEAR, BRIDGET, you should have seen his expression. It was as if it was the first time in his life a woman has ever turned him down." Izzie didn't even look at her cousin as she spoke. She was too busy punching into a huge ball of dough, picturing Nick Santori's face while she did it.

Though it had been nearly twenty-four hours since she'd run into him, she hadn't stopped thinking about him. Drat the man for invading her brain again, when she'd managed to forget him over the past several years. Ever since she skipped out of Chicago to follow her dancing dreams, she'd been convincing herself her crush on him had been a silly, girlish thing.

Seeing him had reminded her of the truth: she'd wanted Nick before she'd even understood what it was she wanted. Now that she *knew* what the tingle between her legs and the heaviness in her breasts meant, the want was almost painful.

"Didn't Nana always say the secret to a flaky crust was not to overwork it?" her cousin said, sounding quietly amused.

Izzie shot her cousin—who sat on the other side of the bakery kitchen—a glare. "You want to do this?"

Bridget, who was pretty and soft-looking, slid a strand of long, light brown hair behind her ear. "You're the baker. I'm the bookkeeper." She sipped from her huge coffee mug. "So why did you walk away? You've wanted him forever."

"Maybe. But I don't want *forever* in general," she reminded her cousin as she floured the countertop and began to work the dough with a rolling pin. "You know I don't want *this* for any longer than I'm forced to have it." She glanced around the kitchen, where she was working alone to finish up the dessert orders for their restaurant clients. Including Santori's.

Not that she'd be the one delivering their order…no way. Her delivery guy would be in to take on that task shortly.

"I know. You'll be gone again once Uncle Gus is well enough to come back to work." Bridget didn't sound too happy about that, which Izzie understood. Her sweet, gentle-natured cousin was an only child, and she'd practically been adopted by Izzie and her own sisters. They'd been very close growing up.

Izzie missed her, too. But not enough to stay here. As soon as her father recovered, and her mother no longer had to nurse him at home full time, Izzie would be out of here for good. Whether she'd go back to New York and try to reclaim some kind of dancing career she didn't yet know. But her future did not include a long-term stint as the Flour Girl of Taylor Street.

It also didn't include becoming the lover of any guy who her parents would see as the perfect reason for Izzie to stick around and pop out babies. Even a lover as tempting as Nick.

"So how's your life going?" she asked her cousin, wanting the subject changed. "How's the job?"

Bridget leaned forward, dropping her elbows onto the counter. "I guess I'm not very good. My boss obviously doesn't trust me, there are some files he won't even let me look at."

"Weren't you hired to keep the books at that place?"

Bridget, who'd gone to work three months ago for a local used-car dealership right here in the neighborhood, nodded. "They're a mess. But every time I ask him for access to older records, he practically pats me on the head and sends me back to my desk like a good little girl."

Izzie assumed her cousin meant her boss *figuratively* patted her on the head. Because, though Bridget was in no way a fireball like Izzie and her two sisters—she wasn't a pushover, either. It might take her a while to get her steam up, but Izzie had seen glimpses of temper in her sweet-as-sugar Irish-Italian cousin. That boss of hers obviously hadn't gotten to know the *real* Bridget yet. Because she was about the most quietly stubborn person Izzie had ever met…as anyone who'd ever tried to beat her in a game of Monopoly could attest.

"Why don't you quit?"

Her cousin lifted her mug, leaning her head over it so that her long bangs fell over her pretty amber eyes. She looked as if she had something to hide. And if Izzie wasn't mistaken, that was a blush rising in her cheeks.

A blush. Cripes, Izzie didn't even know if she *remembered* how to blush. The last time her cheeks had been pinkened by anything other than makeup was when she'd burned herself while lying out too long on the deck of a cruise ship a year ago.

Trying to hide a smile, she murmured, "Who is he?"

Her cousin almost dropped the mug. "Huh?"

"Oh, come on, I know there's a guy."

"Um…well…"

"For heaven's sake, you're looking at a woman who used to schedule two dates a night, just come out with it."

Chuckling, her cousin did. "There's this new salesman."

"A used-car salesman?" Izzie asked skeptically.

Frowning, Bridget asked, "Do you want to hear this or not?"

Izzie made a lips-zipped motion over her mouth.

"His name's Dean," Bridget continued. "Dean Willis. And Marty hired him about a month ago. He's got cute, shaggy blond hair and big blue eyes—well, I assume they're big. They could look bigger because of the thick glasses he wears."

She watched Izzie, as if waiting for a comment. Izzie somehow managed to refrain from making one.

"He's sold more cars than anyone else because he's just so…quiet. Easy to talk to. Unassuming." Sighing a little, Bridget added, "And he has the nicest smile."

Izzie had never heard her cousin go on like this about a man. Must be serious. "So, have you gone out with him?"

Bridget shook her head and sighed again—only, much louder. "He's never even noticed I'm alive."

Snorting, Izzie replied, "I doubt that. You're adorable."

Bridget's bottom lip came out in a tiny pout. "Fluffy teddy bears are adorable. I want to be…something else."

Sexy. It was obviously what Bridget had in mind. Izzie eyed her cousin, considering making her over. Bridget had the basics—she just needed to bring them out a little. But she didn't think Bridget needed much. She was so quietly pretty, so gentle and feminine…any guy would be an idiot to want to change her.

Then again, she'd known a ton of guys, few of whom were Einstein material. "So ask *him* out. *Make* him notice you."

"I couldn't."

"Just for a cup of coffee."

Her cousin snagged her lip between her teeth.

"What?"

"Well, he *did* ask me to go for coffee once, but I was so flustered and nervous, I told him I didn't drink it."

Raising a brow and staring pointedly at the industrial-size mug in front of her cousin's face, Izzie grunted.

"But it wasn't a date," Bridget added. "At least, I don't think so." Sounding frustrated, she added, "Maybe I should get a collagen injection. I've heard men like big lips."

Ridiculous. Bridget's beauty was the natural kind that needed no false crap like the stuff Izzie had seen other dancers do to themselves. But before she could say that—or threaten to lob a handful of ricotta cheesecake filling at Bridget if she did something so dumb—she heard the bell over the front door.

Glancing at the clock, she bit back a curse. It was nearly five—an hour after closing time. She must have forgotten to lock the door after her part-time lunch workers had left for the day and some customer had wandered in for a snack.

She doubted there was much left to serve. Mornings were their busiest time, with regulars and passersby coming in for pastries and muffins. During the lunch hour, when Natale's served light sandwiches and salads along with decadent deserts, they were busy, too. Since Izzie had come up with the idea to offer free wireless internet access to anyone with a laptop, some customers parked themselves at one of the small café tables and remained there until closing time. They drank a lot of coffee…and ate a lot of sweets. By 4:00 p.m., Natale's display counter was generally wiped out, as this late customer would soon discover.

"Hello?" a voice called.

Grabbing a towel, Izzie wiped her hands on it and tossed

it over her shoulder. "Be right back," she told her cousin as she walked down the short hallway to the café. "Sorry, we're closed for the…" The words died on her lips when she saw who stood on the other side of the glass display case, looking so hot she almost shielded her eyes from the glory of him.

"I know." He shrugged slightly. "But the door was unlocked, so I thought I'd take a chance and see if you were here."

Nick stood inside the shadowy café, illuminated by the late-afternoon sunlight streaming in through the front window. The light reflected in his dark eyes, lending them a golden glow that seemed to radiate warmth. She felt it from here.

"You found me," she murmured.

"You didn't exactly need to leave a trail of crumbs, Cookie…this place has been here forever."

"*Don't* call me Cookie," she snapped.

He held up his hands, palms out. "Sorry."

Ordering her heart to continue beating normally, Izzie tossed the towel onto the counter, then crossed her arms over her chest to stare at him. "Are you trying to tell me you *knew* I'd be here because you *knew* who I was? Try again."

Nick cleared his throat, averting his gaze. Wincing in a cutely sheepish way, he said, "No, I didn't know you at first."

So, he'd recognized her after she had left?

"Mark told me who you were."

The jerk.

"I'm sorry I didn't recognize you. It's been a long time."

Not long enough to erase *him* from *her* mind, that was for sure. She'd recognize Nick Santori if she bumped into him blindfolded during a blackout. Because his scent was imprinted in her brain. And her body reacted in one in-

stinctive way whenever he was near—a way it didn't react
with anyone else, even men with whom she'd been intimate.

He made her shaky and achy and weak and ravenous all
at the same time. Always had, for some unknown reason.

"Yeah. A long time," she mumbled, walking over to
wash her hands in the small sink behind the counter.

Damn, she hated that he flustered her. She had known
more handsome men. She'd been to bed with more handsome men. Maybe none who were as rugged and masculine, or so sensual. But she had dated drop-dead gorgeous
actors and millionaires who wanted to notch their bedposts
with a professional dancer who could kick her leg straight
up above her head. None of them had ever affected her the
way this one—who she'd never even kissed—did.

"I have to run, Izzie," a voice said. "I don't want to
be…in the way."

Izzie had almost forgotten Bridget was in the kitchen.
Seeing the grin on her cousin's face, she blew out a deep,
frustrated breath. She'd intended to use Bridget as an
excuse—or at the very least as a five-foot-five chastity belt,
to keep Izzie from doing something stupid. Like smearing
rich cheesecake filling all over Nick's body, then slowly
licking it off.

But her cousin was bailing on her, already heading toward the exit. "Nice to see you, Nick," she said.

"How's your family?"

They fell into a brief, easy conversation, like most
people who'd grown up in the neighborhood usually did.
Except Izzie—who hadn't yet rediscovered that easy cama-
raderie with all the people she'd grown up with. While the
two of them chatted, Izzie tried to regain her cool, forcing
herself to look at this guy like she looked at every other
guy. As nothing special.

Fat chance. She couldn't do it. He *was* special.

It had to be because he was the first man she'd ever wanted. Never having had him made the intensity of her attraction build. With no culmination—no explosion when she finally had him and got him out of her system—she'd remained on a slow, roiling boil of want for Nick for years.

So take him and get it out of your system.

Oh, the thought was tempting. Very tempting. Part of her desperately wanted to ask him to go with her to the nearest hotel and *do* her until she couldn't even bring her legs together. If she thought he would, and that he'd then forget about it, never expecting a repeat and never—*ever*—breathing a word about it to anyone, she'd seriously consider it.

But he wouldn't. Not in a million years. She knew that just as surely as she knew he'd never have even *kissed* her when she was underage, not even if she'd leaped on him and held him captive. Which, to be fair, she had…at the wedding.

He was a Santori. With everything that went with the name. His upbringing, his family, his own moral code meant he would never have a meaningless sexual encounter with his sister-in-law's younger sister. The daughter of his father's friend. The girl up the block. No way in hell.

He was the kind of guy who would have to *date* a woman he slept with. Dating—neighborhood style—as in hand-holding and miniature golf and pizza at his family's place and cannolis at her family's place. The whole deal. *Gag.*

Not that he'd actually asked her on a date. If he did? Well… that might have thrilled her once—years ago when she had actually thought the bakery and her family and Little Italy were all the world she'd ever need. Now, however, it just made her sad, because as she'd already realized, dating Nick equaled strings. Strings could very well choke her.

"Well, see you tomorrow," Bridget said as she walked out.

Izzie hadn't even noticed Bridget and Nick were finished talking. Cursing her cousin for bailing on her, Izzie
cleared her throat, about to tell him she had to get back
to work.

He spoke first. "So, do you forgive me?"

"Yeah, sure, no big deal," she replied, forcing a shrug.

A tiny smile tugged at those amazing lips of his and the
dark eyes glowed. "No big deal? You seemed pretty mad."

Damn. He'd noticed.

"I wasn't mad. More…amused."

"Sure. That's why my chest is bruised where you shoved
me."

Her jaw dropped and she immediately began sputter-
ing denials. Then she saw his wide grin. "You're an ass."

"And a shithead," he replied, his grin fading though
the twinkle remained in his eye. "I really mean it, Iz, I'm
sorry I didn't recognize you." Stepping around the counter
to see her better, he cast a slow, leisurely look at her. From
bottom to top. Then down again. "But you have to give me
a little bit of a break. You don't look much like you did."

"I'm not addicted to Twinkies anymore," she snapped.

"You weren't chubby."

"I was the Michelin Man in pink tights."

He shook his head. "You were just baby-faced the last
time I saw you. A kid. Now you're…not."

"Damn right."

He didn't say anything for a moment, still watching
her as he leaned against the counter. The pose tugged his
gray T-shirt tight against his shoulders and chest, emphasizing the man's size. Lord, he was broad. But still so
trim at the waist and lean at the hips. It was the hips that
caught her attention—the way his faded, unbelted jeans
hung low on them, the soft fabric hugging the angles and
planes of his body.

It really wasn't fair for a man to be so perfect.

"So…about our conversation last night."

When staring at him—overwhelmed by his heat—she could barely remember her own name. Much less any conversation. "Huh?"

"What do you say? Will you give me your number?"

Oh, what she wouldn't have given to hear those words from him ten years ago. Or hell, even two *months* ago—if she'd happened to run into him in Times Square and he'd proposed a sexy one-night stand for old times' sake. One nobody in Chicago would ever have to know about. She would have leaped on the offer like a gambler on a free lottery ticket.

"I don't think so."

"Come on, you know you can trust me. I'm not some stranger stalking you. We've known each other since we were kids."

Well, he'd known *her* since she was a kid. From the time she'd met him, Izzie had only ever seen the glorious, hot, sexy *man*. Even if he had been no more than fourteen.

"Just a night out for old times' sake?"

He was so tempting. Because the only old times she recalled were the heated ones of her fantasies. And the incident at the wedding. He'd ended up between her legs during both. "Well…"

He moved again, coming closer, as if realizing she was wavering. Dropping his hand onto the counter near hers, he murmured, "No pressure. We could just go grab a pizza."

She stiffened, any potential wavering done with. The last thing she would consider doing is having a public meal with Nick Santori at his own family's restaurant. Not when her sister would hear about it and tell their parents, who'd then get their hopes up about Izzie remaining safely in the nest, as they'd so desperately wanted her to do when she was eighteen.

Leaving home after high school had been a struggle.

She'd been an adult, legally free, but she'd still had to practically run away in order to pursue her dream of dancing professionally. Especially because she was the only one of the Natale daughters who'd inherited their father's gift in the kitchen.

Probably because she loved food so much. As evidenced by every one of her porky-faced school pictures from kindergarten through tenth grade.

Her father had been crushed that she didn't want to work with him. But she had known she had to escape—had to take her shot while she could or risk regretting it the rest of her life.

So she'd gone. She'd hopped a train, determined to stay away until she'd given her dream of being a professional dancer everything she had to give.

Making it at Radio City hadn't eased her parents fears of her being "out there all alone." It had actually increased them once they'd realized she was unlikely now to *ever* come back.

If they knew just how wild her life had been for the first few years she'd been on her own, they'd have felt justified in their fears. Like any good girl kept on a tight leash, she'd taken great pleasure in breaking every rule in the book once she was free and able to make her own decisions. Especially once she had men surrounding her and money to do whatever she wanted.

It had been wild. It had also been reckless—so in the past couple of years, she'd settled down. Stopped partying, stopped hooking up, stopped blowing every dime. She now had a nice nest egg…which she hoped to use to re-establish her life in New York. She'd been approached about going back to work at Radio City, as a choreographer this time. And she knew she'd probably get the same offer from her other modern-dance company.

Or she could teach. She could open her own school….

She had the money to at least give it a shot. That was among the things she'd been considering doing when she got back to reality.

Her parents, however, would give anything for her to stay here and never go back to that other life, the one that didn't include them beyond the weekly phone call and twice-yearly visit. Openly dating a local guy—a friend of the family—would raise their hopes unfairly and hurtfully. So she couldn't do it.

Before she could say so, however, he stepped closer. Close enough to stop her heart. "You're a mess," he murmured. He lifted a hand, touching a strand of hair that had fallen across her cheek. Closing his fingers over it, he slowly pulled, wiping away flour or cream or whatever had happened to be there.

The brush of his fingertips against her cheekbone almost made her cry. Almost made her whimper. Almost made her lean forward to press her mouth onto his.

"A sweet, delectable mess," he added, his fingers still tangled in her hair. He touched her face, rubbing her skin as if he'd never felt anything so smooth, so soft.

Every muscle in her body went warm and pliant, until Izzie wondered how she could still be standing upright. As if sensing her weakness, he moved closer, sliding one foot between her legs, slipping one hand into her tangled hair to cup her head.

"I have to see how sweet you taste," he muttered, sounding as helpless as she felt. "If only once…I have to taste you."

Drawing her forward, he bent closer. Even knowing it was crazy and could go nowhere, Izzie prepared for a kiss she'd wanted for more than a decade. She'd cried over that mouth, had fantasized over those lips for more nights than she could count.

And she wanted it, God how she *wanted* it. Even if it was all she was ever going to get to have of him.

But rather than a simple kiss—the soft brush of his mouth on hers—he shocked her by immediately sampling her lips with his tongue, tasting her, as he'd said he must.

She whimpered, low and helpless.

"Oh, very sweet," he whispered, licking at the seam of her lips again, boldly demanding entrance rather than asking for it with a more typical, closemouthed first kiss.

Izzie couldn't deny him *or* herself. With a hungry groan, she opened to him, welcoming his tongue in a deep, sensual exchange that she felt from her head to the tips of her toes.

He'd thought she tasted sweet. She thought he tasted like irresistible sin. He was warm and spicy, his mouth just moist enough to whet her appetite. Just hot enough to send her temperature rocketing higher.

He sunk his other hand in her hair and held her close. Sagging against him, Izzie gave herself over to pleasure, wondering how it was possible for something to be as good as a dozen years of dreaming had promised it would be. It was a kiss more intimate than any she'd had even when making love. Because it was like making love. It was hot and sexy and powerful.

Their tongues found a common rhythm and tangled to it as their bodies melted together. Her nipples ached with need as they pressed against his broad chest. She arched harder against him, easing her legs apart to cup him intimately, whimpering again when she felt his huge erection.

He wanted her. Badly. As much as she wanted him.

The realization was almost enough to shock her into doing something stupid like ending the kiss. This was Nick—the guy she'd always wanted—hot and hard and hungry for *her*.

"Don't say no to me, sweetheart," he whispered as

he finally—regretfully—drew his mouth from hers. He moved it to press kisses along her jaw, then down to the throbbing pulse point below her ear. "Say yes."

Yes, say yes! a voice screamed.

Oh, he was so tempting. And she wanted him desperately— wanted him to pull off her clothes, back her up against the counter and make love to her right on top of it. It would be incredible, the culmination of all her dreams and secret fantasies. She could finally put an end to all the years of restless, hopeless wanting.

But it wouldn't be the end. It would be the *start* of something, rather than the end of it. He'd make incredible love to her, make her come with a few more touches of his hands and a few more of those incredible kisses and she'd be alive and happy and completely fulfilled for the first time in her life.

But then he'd want to take her out for a pizza. Or get together with friends. And she'd be caught so deep in a quagmire of family and home that she'd *never* be able to get free of it.

"Say yes, Izzie," he ordered, sucking her earlobe into his mouth and nibbling it—a tiny bite that she felt clear to the floor. "Give me your number and let's finally get this started."

Get this started. Get *everything* started.

She just couldn't do it. Izzie had always been strong and determined and had taken what she wanted. But she couldn't take *him*. Not now. It was much too late.

Yanking away, she winced as her tangled hair got caught in his fingertips. Her breathing ragged, her body crying out at the injustice, she shook her head, hard. Then she backed away, wrapping her arms around her waist in self protection. "No."

He started to follow, his dark eyes glittering…predatory. "You don't mean it."

She held a hand up. "Yes. I do," she said with a firm shake of her head. "Now, if you'll excuse me, we're closed and I have work to do in the kitchen." Taking a deep breath and striving to keep her voice steady, she added, "I want you to leave."

3

ON HIS FIRST NIGHT working at Leather and Lace, Nick showed up in a bad mood. He'd *been* in a bad mood for two days—since Izzie Natale had shot down his efforts to get closer to her.

The woman was unbelievable. Ten years ago, she might as well have taken out an ad in the Trib declaring her devotion to him. Now she wouldn't throw dog drool on him if he was on fire.

Damn, she was feisty. Had she always been that way? He figured with Gloria for a sister she had been. But considering he'd never seen her as a woman—just as a cute, lovesick kid—he'd never noticed. *Until now.*

Oh, yeah, now he'd noticed. He'd noticed everything about her. And he was not going to give up on her yet. Not when she'd become the first thing he thought of every morning and the star of his dreams every night.

Especially since that incredible kiss they'd shared.

Who would ever have guessed that the cute, pesky girl with the obvious crush on him would prove to be the most sensual, kissable woman he'd ever known? He'd suspected he could kiss her for hours. Now he knew better. He could kiss her for *ever.*

After she'd ordered him out of the bakery the other

evening, he'd decided to play dirty, going right to Gloria
to ask her for her sister's phone number. His sister-in-law
had been glad to oblige. She'd also been more than candid
about how Izzie had felt about him in the old days.

Not that Nick had needed her to tell him about it. He'd
been well aware—as had everyone else.

"Not anymore," he muttered as he parked his truck—
which he'd purchased right after getting home a couple of
weeks ago—behind the club. He frowned, wondering how
much of a jerk it made him now to be disappointed that a
girl who'd had a wild crush on him as a kid didn't give a
damn about him anymore. Probably a pretty big one. But
he couldn't help it.

Knowing little Izzie had been crazy about him had been
a constant during his teenage years. A given. Just another
part of his reality. Certainly nothing he'd ever taken advantage of or embarrassed her about. It had just been…
kinda cute, thinking there was a girl out there doodling his
name in her school notebook. Innocent. Simple.

Man, he hated that that girl wouldn't even look at him
now. Especially because he didn't think he'd done anything
to deserve her coldness. No, he hadn't recognized her. But
he also hadn't recognized the kid who had delivered the
newspaper and now ran a newsstand on the corner. Or a
couple of guys he'd played basketball with at St. Raphael's.

Mark thought he *did* deserve it. Not because he hadn't
recognized her, but because he'd counted on her childhood
feelings to give him an edge with Izzie the adult.

Hell, maybe he was right. Maybe he shouldn't have
teased her, been so sure of her. He'd known enough women
to know how they felt about being taken for granted. He
should have taken her out to dinner before kissing her like
he needed the air in her lungs to keep on living.

So he needed to start over with Izzie. Start slow, like
he would with any other woman he'd just met.

It might not be easy. Because she already affected him more than any woman he'd ever met. He'd dreamed about her this week, thought about her, gone out of his way to walk past the bakery in the hope of bumping into her.

"Tables have definitely turned," he muttered aloud when he walked through the private employees' entrance into the back of the club. "Which is probably just the way she wants it."

Yeah, she could be stringing him along out of revenge. But somehow, Nick didn't think that was the case.

She hadn't been able to hide her feelings behind those incredibly expressive brown eyes. Though she'd sent him away after their kiss, she still wanted him. But something was preventing her from doing anything about it.

He just had to find out what.

"Nick, you're right on time!" The club owner, a beefy, good-natured guy with a Santa Claus–like belly laugh, emerged from his office and extended his hand.

Nick shook it. "Mr. Black."

"Call me Harry."

"Harry, then. Thanks again for the opportunity."

The other man waved a hand in unconcern. "Your big brother, he's one of the few honest contractors I've met in this city. Did beautiful work at a fair price. And if he says you're up to the job, I trust him completely."

Nick had already bought his brother, Joe, a beer in thanks for setting up his interview. He wished he'd made it a pitcher.

"All the paperwork's done, you check out exactly like Joe said you would," Harry said as he gestured Nick toward a seat in his office. "Now, you're clear on what I need from you?"

Nick nodded. "Have there been problems recently?"

Harry tapped his fingers on the desk and nodded. "The

Rose has made a stir. Men want to see her and there have been a few *incidents*."

Nick stiffened reflexively, even though he hadn't met the woman yet. "Incidents?"

"Nothing too serious, thank God. But a couple of grabs, dressing-room prowlers. A few disturbing notes." Harry shook his head, looking disgusted. "Can't imagine any man saying stuff that crude to any woman. But she was a sport about it, laughed it off." Staring pointedly, he added, "That's one reason I hired you—she tends to not take it seriously. And I want someone else to."

"I will," Nick replied, confident of his own words.

Harry nodded, obviously convinced. "Other than that, there's not too much trouble on a nightly basis. A guy'd have to be drunk as a skunk or just plain stupid to think he could go after one of the girls at the risk of taking one of the bouncers on. But we don't let anybody get drunk as a skunk in my joint." He chuckled. "And stupid people can't afford it."

That wasn't a surprise. When Nick had come in last weekend, he'd noticed the upscale feel of the club. Far from being seedy or shadowy, like most strip joints, this place was elegantly comfortable, from the earth-toned leather furniture to the framed pieces of classy-looking art on the walls. The prices reflected the ambiance; this was no after-work beer joint.

"I wanted to introduce you to the Rose, but she called and said she's running a little late tonight. I don't imagine there'll be time before her first number."

Nick stiffened, realizing he'd soon be seeing the woman behind the mask. Somehow, during the past few days when he'd been so focused on Izzie, he hadn't let the thought of the sultry stripper drift into his mind. Now, however, knowing he was about to see her again, he couldn't help but remember the way she'd made him feel last weekend.

Hot. Hungry. Needy.

So would any sexy, naked woman after such a long dry spell.

"She's something else."

"I noticed last weekend."

Harry Black shrugged. "Yeah, she's a looker, but there's something special about her even when she's not onstage. Got her head on right—a smart one. But that doesn't mean I'm not worried about her. She could get herself in trouble."

Nick could certainly understand that. Considering how attracted he'd been to her, he could see how a much more desperate man might react to her sultry performance.

"She's not going to like me hiring someone to mainly look out for her," Harry cautioned. "So we'll leave that part between us, okay? As far as she knows, you're just another bouncer."

"Fine." In fact, it was more than fine. He wanted as little interaction with the woman he was supposed to be protecting as possible. Not that he was truly worried about her effect on him—it had been a one-time thing, that was all.

He'd been telling himself that for days. He'd also been ignoring the fact that none of the other strippers he'd seen that night had so much as caused his heart rate to increase its regular, lazy rhythm. Only *her*.

Meeting her would take care of that, he was sure of it. She wore a mask, meaning her looks were all from the neck down. She'd have muddy eyes or crooked teeth or a hooked nose. Or a voice like a truck driver. Or she'd snort when she laughed. Something would be wrong. Something would break the spell.

That would be the end of his interest. No doubt about it.

THE CRIMSON ROSE spotted the dark-haired man in black the moment she peeked through the curtains on the stage. And the moment she saw him—immediately recognizing

him by his height and the power of his shadowed body—
her heart began to beat harder.

He'd come back. For *her*.

This was the first night she'd been back to the club
since last Sunday night, when she'd first seen him during
her last performance on this stage. Inexplicably, she suspected this was his first night back, too. When she'd asked
the other dancers about him, all had denied seeing such a
man in the club during the past five nights.

She had drawn him back. Just as he—the very thought
that he might be in the crowd again tonight—had worked
to draw her here, as well.

Not that she needed much of a draw. She loved what she
did. She positively came alive while moving under a spotlight. The fact that her clothes were falling off her body as
she did so was completely incidental.

She honestly didn't care.

"He came back," she whispered, almost bouncing on
her toes, so excited she could hardly stand it.

Not just excited. *Relieved.*

Because though she'd only seen him from a distance,
she already felt incredibly attracted to him. He'd be a mar-
velous distraction from the *other* man who'd been occupying her thoughts lately.

The one she couldn't have.

She began to smile, feeling, for the first time in days,
a little upbeat. Working at the club was her one outlet,
her only escape from the life she had so wanted to avoid
coming back to here in Chicago. She loved these secret,
wicked weekends.

And now that she'd realized there was another man—
someone else—who could cause an instant, aching sort of
want deep inside her, Izzie Natale sensed those weekends
simply wouldn't come fast enough.

"You're not the only man in Chicago, Nick Santori,"

she whispered while the stage crew finished stripping the stage for her signature solo number.

When she'd first seen the ad in the paper for dancers for a Chicago gentleman's club, Izzie had had no illusions about what the job would entail. She wasn't some young dance ingenue who'd turned up for an audition only to be shocked at the very idea of taking off her clothes for a bunch of men.

Izzie had taken off her clothes for plenty of men. Sometimes even groups of them.

It wasn't as if the Rockettes danced in a whole lot of clothes. And during the three months she'd performed with the Modern Dance Company of Manhattan, she'd done two nude artistic performances.

The dancing she did at Leather and Lace wasn't *exactly* artistic. But, then again, she wasn't *exactly* nude, either. After all, she never took off her G-string.

Yes, her audience in Chicago was after sexual titillation rather than cultural stimulation. But, honestly, judging by the way some of the modern-dance aficionados had come backstage and tried to pick up the dancers, she figured the motivations were, at heart, exactly the same.

Dancing was dancing. After the dire prognosis she'd received when having her torn ACL repaired several months ago, she didn't care where she was performing, or what she was wearing when she did it.

Honestly, now, having had a taste of it, she realized she couldn't have chosen a better venue. Because here, hidden behind a red velvet mask, she was free to be everything Izzie Natale of the famous Taylor Street Natale's Bakery was not.

Sexual. Uninhibited.

Free.

Before she'd even dragged her mind into readiness, she was introduced and her music had begun. Izzie moved onto the stage, dancing for herself and herself alone, as she always did, letting the petals fall where they may. She remained above everything, even oblivious to the money being tossed onto the stage—the crew would pick it up when she was finished. She also ignored the gasps and avid stares of the crowd.

Except one man's avid stare. His, she wanted to see, though it would prove difficult with him standing in the most shadowy area of the place and her nearly blinded by the spotlight. But when the choreography moved her downstage right—closest to the bar, and *him*—she risked it and looked.

And nearly fell off the stage.

Oh, my God, oh, my God, oh, my God.

She lost the beat of the song and got a little tangled on her own feet. She also had to throw down an extra couple of petals a few measures too soon to try to cover her misstep.

Because in that quick flash when the light had hit him just right, she'd recognized the face, those shoulders, that hair.

It was Nick Santori who stood near the bar. Nick was the same dark, shadowy stranger who'd had her blood pumping through her veins, throbbing between her legs both last week when she'd first seen him here and a few moments ago when she'd glimpsed him again.

The bastard. Was she never going to be free of him? Would no man ever make her feel that crazy/excited/hungry feeling she got whenever he was in the vicinity? And what in the hell was he doing here, anyway?

Worse—what was he going to do about it if he realized she, the woman who'd shot him down in the bakery two days ago, was the Crimson Rose?

Her mind awash with the ramifications of Nick's presence, Izzie finished her number. As soon as it was over, she darted behind the curtains and stuck her arms into a short, silky robe hanging right backstage. Barely noticing the crew members, who immediately got to work resetting the stage for the more typical dancers, she hurried down the back stairs toward her private dressing room.

Normally, all the dancers would share one and Izzie was no prima donna who required her own space. But the owner of Leather and Lace had insisted on giving her a private, coat-closet-size room because of how serious Izzie was about protecting her identity. Once he'd realized just how much the "mystery" of the Crimson Rose enhanced the club's reputation—and brought in more customers— he'd upgraded her to one the size of a small bathroom.

Before she could duck into it, she heard his voice. "There you are! Hold up a second, I want you to meet someone."

She was in no condition to meet anyone—especially not another one of Harry's cousins or old fishing buddies. There was always someone ready to play on old friendships or family connection to meet the dancers.

On the positive side, Harry was as protective as a papa bear and the introductions never went further than a quick handshake or a signed autograph. Despite how much some of the men he brought around seemed to want it otherwise.

Pasting on an impersonal smile behind the mask she hadn't yet removed, she turned around.

"This is Nick Santori. I've just hired him to beef up our security."

Izzie sagged against the wall. If it hadn't been there, she might have just fallen sideways onto the tile floor, but thankfully, her shoulder instead landed on some hard wood paneling and it kept her vertical.

More than she could say for her heart. It had gone rolling down and had landed somewhere in the vicinity of her stomach, which was now churning with anxiety.

"This is…"

"Rose," she quickly interjected, cutting Harry off before he could say her real name. She cleared her throat, seeking the sultry, husky tones she'd always used when greeting fans backstage at Radio City. The one that was quite different from the voice Nick had heard at the bakery just a couple of days before. "Nice to meet you."

He held out his hand. She took it. Time didn't stop or anything, and the floor didn't buckle beneath her feet. But, damn, his touch did feel *fine*.

He had big hands. Strong hands. A soldier's competent hands. They were capable of brute force. Yet equally capable, she knew, of tender care. Like when those hands had helped her pull her ugly bridesmaid dress into place, then gently lifted her back onto the dance platform and back into their waltz so many years ago.

"Nick's brother Joey Santori sent him in. You remember him, don't you? He did all the work upstairs. You met him last month."

Yes, she had…and it had been a closer call than this meeting with Nick, who could see almost nothing of her face because of the mask. She'd barely had time to duck behind a changing screen before coming face-to-face with Nick's older brother.

Now she had to wonder…had Joe seen her? Recognized her? And was he now playing Mr. Neighborhood Protector by sending his baby brother in to watch out for the girl up the block?

Possible.

God save her from Italian men.

One plus—he hadn't told Tony. Because no way would her overprotective brother-in-law have let Izzie's new job go undiscussed. He'd have come down on her with some big-brother lecture about how she simply had to quit now, immediately, if not sooner. Either that or he'd have told

Gloria, who would have had a shrieking meltdown over what the neighbors and her sweet, impressionable boys—wild little maniacs, in Izzie's opinion—would think.

"Harry, help! Some CEO's at the door saying he had reservations for ten," a frantic voice called from the top of the stairs. The hostess who worked the front desk came clattering down three stairs and spotted him, relief evident in her face. "You need to get up here."

Muttering under his breath, Harry offered Nick an apologetic shrug. "Sorry. Never fails. Tell you what, why don't you talk to…Rose…get an idea of what her routine and schedule are like and then meet me upstairs in thirty minutes?"

Nick nodded and they both watched Harry walk away. Well, Nick watched Harry. Izzie watched Nick.

She hadn't noticed at first—she'd been too frazzled herself—but Nick appeared tense. The muscles in his neck were rock hard, his jaw jutted out stiffly. Beneath his wickedly tight black T-shirt, his broad shoulders were squared in his military posture and his hands were fisted at his sides.

Interesting.

If she had to guess, she'd say he wasn't particularly happy to meet her. It was as if he actively disliked her… which didn't make much sense.

The only reason he could have for *already* disliking her was that he had somehow recognized her. That he'd looked into her eyes, revealed behind the mask, and seen something familiar. Or heard a note in her voice that he'd heard before. He certainly hadn't seemed very happy with Izzie-the-baker when she'd practically pushed him out of the bakery the other evening and imagined he'd convinced himself she was at best a pain in the ass and at worst a complete tease.

But if he looked at her and saw only a complete stranger…

what could he dislike about her after knowing her for all of two minutes? Nick wasn't the judgmental type. She couldn't see him working here if he had some kind of problem with women stripping.

Besides, his dislike seemed personal, directed only at her. He'd been perfectly fine with Harry.

"So, is tonight your first night?" she asked, keeping her tone low and thick. She sounded sultry—wicked—but that couldn't be helped. She needed to disguise her voice, at least until she knew for sure whether Nick had recognized her. Or if he'd been tipped off by his big brother.

"Yes."

"How do you like the club?"

He shrugged, noncommittal.

"Come now, you're not shocked are you? I imagine you've been in places like this all over the world."

His dark eyes narrowed. "How would you know I've been all over the world?"

Oh, man, that was stupid. She'd just tipped her hand. "I mean…you look like the military type, with the hair and the all-black commando look you have going on. Am I right?"

He nodded once, still not unbending one iota.

Izzie had to force herself not to react to all that simmering, intense male heat. Nick had been adorably sexy when flirting with her and trying to pick her up. And incredibly sensual when seducing her with his kiss.

Now…when he was all dark, intense business, he was absolutely devastating. Dangerous, almost, and though she'd never feared him, she couldn't contain a tiny shiver.

If he decided to kiss her now, it wouldn't be with sweet, sultry persuasion. It would be with raw, overpowering hunger.

She wanted that kind of kiss from him.

"I saw you here last weekend," she said, not even realizing she was going to admit such a thing until the words had left her mouth. That probably wasn't smart. She needed to keep the upper hand here—letting Nick know she'd been aware of him from first glance wasn't a good way to do that.

"I came in to talk to Harry about the job."

"And you watched me dance." She dared him to deny it.

He nodded once. The jaw flexed.

"Did you like it?"

"You're talented."

Oh, if only he knew.

"You're not…uncomfortable around me, are you?" she asked, trying not to laugh. "I mean, having seen so *much* of me?"

He shook his head. The shoulders tensed. "This is a job, Miss…"

"Rose will do."

"As you wish. The point is, I want to keep you…all of you…safe. Meaning we need to implement some new security procedures." He sounded impersonal, but every movement or flex of his body screamed that his tone was a lie. He was definitely reacting to her and Izzie would lay money it had nothing to do with him knowing her real identity.

If he knew who she was, he'd never remain stiff and unyielding, trying to keep up this professional act. He'd be either seducing her—finishing what he'd started the other day—or else he'd be lecturing her for doing something so out of character for a nice Italian girl from the neighborhood.

Nope. He didn't know who she was. No way in hell. So why he was being so stiff and gruff, she really didn't know.

"Would you like to come in while I change?" she asked, gesturing to the closed door behind her. It had a cheesy little tinfoil star on it—a joke from one of the other dancers, who'd been remarkably welcoming after the first week or two. Considering their clientele had increased significantly since she'd been performing at the club, she figured they were all benefiting from the "mystery" of the Crimson Rose.

He hesitated for only a moment. Then nodded. "Sure."

Opening the door, she walked in and ushered him in behind her. "Sorry for the mess."

The space was crowded—one mirror, surrounded by bright lights, covered an entire wall. A long, sturdy vanity, connected to the wall, ran the width of the room, reducing the floor space to about a three-foot-wide aisle. The vanity was covered with makeup and hair products. Not to mention G-strings and pasties.

He saw those and blanched, quickly looking away. Shifting uncomfortably, he moved back the tiniest bit, but was stopped from going far by the door, which Izzie had closed behind him.

A muscle worked in his cheek and he crossed his massive arms tightly across his chest. His feet spreading a little apart, he looked like a sturdy, unmovable sea captain standing on the deck of a ship. Unapproachable, unweatherable, unflappable.

Only, he *wasn't* unreachable. Because she'd seen that look at her sexy, glittery underthings. And his reaction to them.

Which was when Izzie started to get an inkling of what was bothering him. It wasn't a matter of him liking her or disliking her. Of him recognizing her or not recognizing her.

He wanted her. She just *knew* it.

Nick wanted to have sex with a stranger—a stripper—and he didn't like that about himself. He didn't like that weakness. She could practically hear his thoughts now, since she'd been raised exactly the way he had.

It wasn't good. It wasn't nice. It didn't quite fit the wholesome neighborhood-kid image.

It was, however, very honest. And despite how *he* felt about it, Izzie liked that very much. As a matter of fact, she *loved* that he wanted her. Not quite as much as she'd loved that he'd wanted Izzie—the invisible girl—but pretty darn close.

Trying to hide her smile, she walked around behind a changing screen and slipped the silky robe off her shoulders. Tossing it over the top of the screen, she murmured, "You're not…uncomfortable in here with me, are you?"

He didn't reply at first. Glancing at the mirror, she saw his reflection—saw him shake his head. Then he cleared his throat, answering aloud, "I'm fine."

He was turned toward the wall—away from the screen, away from the mirror. Which was probably a good thing, considering the reflection ran all the way to the far wall… even on her side of the changing screen.

If he looked in that mirror, the screen would prove to be completely superfluous. He'd see every bit of her…except her still-masked face.

She took her time getting dressed.

"That's good. If you're going to be working here, I suppose you're going to have to get used to seeing a *lot* of your coworkers." She licked her lips and almost purred as she added, "Much more than you'd see in a normal job."

"I'm not easily shocked," he muttered.

Turn around and we'll see.

But he didn't. Curse the luck.

"Can we talk about your routine, how you drive to work, what time you usually arrive?"

Bending over, she slipped out of the tiny G-string, then straightened and draped it over the top of the screen, answering his questions as she undressed. She never took her eyes off him, waiting for him to turn around, imagining how his eyes would widen and his mouth would drop when he realized he could see every move she made in the mirror.

He remained in the same position; however, the flash of movement must have caught his eye. Because his gaze shifted over—quickly, almost imperceptibly—but he definitely glanced.

She watched his reflection, seeing the way his body grew harder. His black trousers highlighted the clench of his muscular thighs and that tight butt. Though he made no sound at all, he dropped his head forward and slowly shook it, desperation rolling off him though he remained entirely silent.

Triumph surged through her as she realized what was happening. He was dying for her. And desperate to resist her.

Izzie continued to take her sweet time as she pulled on a pair of tiny panties—not much bigger than the G-string she'd just discarded. Then she added a matching lacy bra, cut low, almost to her nipples. Not the type of underclothes one would expect of a baker…they were the types of silky things she wore beneath her clothes to remind herself that she was *not* a sweet Betty Crocker wannabe.

Through it all, Izzie was careful not to dislodge the mask. She was also careful of her clip-in hair extensions. They took her shoulder-length dark brown hair down to the middle of her back, and added reddish highlights that worked well in her act. If he recognized her, the game would be over. And right now, Izzie was enjoying the game too much to let it end.

Particularly because she'd begun to see exactly how it could be played.

With no rules. No restrictions. Complete anonymity.

As the Crimson Rose, she could have him—take him—completely free of the repercussions that would surround her if she dared to do such a thing as Izzie Natale. She could have incredible sex with him, enough to get her deep-rooted need for him out of her system for good, then walk away, without anyone ever knowing the truth.

Including, if she was very lucky, *him.*

The question was—could she pull it off?

Catching sight of movement, Izzie realized Nick had finally turned around. He was reaching for the doorknob of the dressing room, his mouth open as if he was about to tell her he was leaving. Then he glanced toward the mirror and caught sight of her.

Nick's defenses dropped. He looked utterly helpless as he completely devoured her with his eyes. Visible hunger—primal and urgent—rolled off him in nearly tangible waves.

And in that moment, Izzie knew she could, indeed, pull it off. She was finally going to have the man she'd wanted for half her life.

4

HE SHOULD NEVER have come in here. Should never have walked into a small room with a woman who already had his head reeling and his body taut with anticipation. One he was *supposed* to be protecting from guys who'd already threatened her.

Nick had been handling things okay up to now. Even while watching the dancers perform—while watching *her* perform—he'd felt in control of the situation. Yeah, she'd affected him. Any man not affected by the Crimson Rose had to have been castrated or born with no libido. But her effect was purely physical—not mental, not emotional. In his head, he still only saw one woman. Wanted one woman. And that was Izzie Natale.

He'd been feeling cool and confident when Harry had brought him downstairs to meet her. A little of that confidence had disappeared when he'd gotten close enough to her to smell the light, delicate perfume she wore—so at odds with her surroundings and her profession. His coolness had gone right out the window when she'd ushered him into her small dressing room where he'd felt like a bear trapped in a telephone booth.

And now…this…seeing her in the mirror?
Madness.

He'd seen her almost naked onstage and she'd stunned him. Now, close up, she blew his mind. Even wearing something that might pass for clothing on a sun-drenched beach, she was every bit as seductive as she'd been during her naked dance.

She was tall and she was curvy and she was soft and she was breathtaking. Her full breasts were contained by a bra that cupped the bottoms but left the tops nearly bare. Her cleavage spilled over the seam and the dark, pointed tips of her nipples thrust against the white lace, demanding attention.

Every man in the room had seen her breasts upstairs minutes ago, but now, up close, Nick was able to truly appreciate their perfection. How perfectly they'd fit in his hands, how delightful her nipples would taste against his tongue.

Nick drew in a deep breath, letting his attention drift lower. His gaze skimmed over the midriff, the slim waist. It lingered on the generous hips highlighted by the strips of white—the strings of her panties—slung over each one. The elastic top of her panties skated across the pale, vulnerable-looking skin below her hip bones. A tiny tuft of pretty brown curls peeked out from the top of them, the dark shadow behind the white silk was all he could see of the rest.

This was *more* than she revealed in her dance, and every male cell in his body reacted to the glorious sight. His heart rate slowed, the way it did when the world around him became dead serious. He swallowed—his mouth flooding with hunger. And his cock leaped, raging for release against his zipper.

The vanity interfered with the rest of his view, leaving him ripped with curiosity as his mind filled in the blanks of what he was not seeing. Those long legs. She had legs that could wrap around him twice, he knew that much from her dance.

It was all too easy to imagine lifting her onto that strong, flat surface, spreading her legs, then pulling up a chair to sit between them. He'd push her back, then loop her knees over his shoulders. Dipping his head in close for a thorough exploration, he'd sample those pretty curls and the shiny folds that they concealed. He'd pleasure her completely, devour her until his face was wet with the slickness of her arousal. He'd take the edge off his hunger, then focus only on her, giving himself a long time before he'd look up to watch the pleasure on her face as her orgasm rolled through her.

But in the vision, it wasn't the masked face of a stranger he saw. It was *Izzie's* face. This stranger had aroused him. Izzie was the one he wanted to fulfill him.

He needed to get out of here. Now. Because even if Izzie *had* shot him down—if there was absolutely nothing between them—she was still the one he really wanted. The one he'd dream about tonight, whether he got his rocks off right now or not.

He could do this stranger…and it might even be good. But it wouldn't get rid of his hunger. And it sure as hell would complicate things here in his new job.

Logically, he knew all that. The good Santori son who couldn't imagine bringing a woman like this around his traditional family should have been gone long before now.

Something made him stay. Maybe it was the *other* Nick. The one who'd grown predatory on the battlefield and bored in the real world. The one who'd been shot down by the reluctant woman he craved and was face-to-face with a willing one he desired.

They just locked eyes, hers mostly hidden behind that mask she still wore. Her lips slowly curled up into a sensuous smile and her chin came up in pure visual challenge.

Nick couldn't help it. He started to smile, too, a tight, dangerous smile that few would have recognized on the face of one of the affable Santori boys. "I don't think that screen works very well," Nick managed to say, his voice throaty.

"I'd say that depends on what I want it to do."

Knowing better, he asked, "If not giving you privacy to change, what is it you want it to do?"

The smile widened, a glitter of pleasure appearing in those shaded eyes. "Perhaps just heighten the anticipation. It's amazing how much more arousing it is to see some… but not all."

"You show almost all onstage."

"Almost," she conceded. "But if you noticed, it's mostly flash and petals, and only a tiny glimpse at the end."

His jaw clenched. "I noticed."

"Did it make you want more? Did a glimpse make you hunger for a look…which in turn made you ravenous for a touch?"

Which would make him insane for a taste.

He didn't answer, he didn't need to. She saw the answer in his face. As if tired of the game, she stepped out from behind the screen, still wearing only three things: the minuscule panties, the skimpy bra and the red velvet mask, which was bigger than either of the other two.

"Why don't you take that off?" he asked, needing to see her face. He needed to find something about her that turned him off so he could get upstairs where his boss was waiting. So he could put her out of his head and get his libido back under control.

Quirking a questioning brow, she pointed to her bra, which startled a small laugh out of him. Because hell, yes, he'd like to see her without the bra—up close—but he knew he couldn't let that happen. Not if he wanted to keep his job. Not if he wanted to have the kind of life his brothers had.

Not if he wanted to work things out with Izzie.

"No. I mean that." He nodded toward the mask.

"I don't think so."

"You really take this anonymity seriously?"

"More than you know."

She moved closer and Nick honestly didn't know which pleased him more—feeling her warmth as she approached, or seeing her both in the flesh and reflected in the mirror. The woman's panties were not only tiny, they were thong-style and he could see the succulent curves of her ass in the mirror. His hands clenched with the need to fill them with those curves.

She reached for his left hand and lifted it. "No ring."

He shook his head.

"So there's no one…special?"

He hesitated a second before answering. A week ago the answer would have been an unequivocal no. Right now he wasn't so sure. He hedged. "That one's in the air right now."

Her bottom lip edged out in a tiny pout, glistening and wet against the red velvet cupping her mouth.

He wanted to bite it. Suck it into his mouth and lick the plumpness of it, then pull her down on his lap and explore all those curves and soft angles of her body.

"I'm unattached, too," she murmured, licking her lips as if she'd read his thoughts. "And frankly, in my line of work, I don't have much use for dating and get-to-know-you chats."

He suspected he knew where she was going. With some other woman—just about any other woman—he'd watch for signals, wonder if she was trying to pick him up. With this one, he knew she'd be very frank about what she wanted.

Her hand came up, she trailed the tips of her fingers across his shoulder, her nails scraping the cotton of his shirt. He felt the touch *everywhere*. Her scent overwhelmed him. Her heat screamed to him in pure sexual invitation.

She made it even more clear. "I want to have sex with you."

His heart skipped a beat. His pants shrunk across his groin and if the woman looked down, she'd know he could quite easily accommodate her. Several times, if she'd let him.

Before he could say a word, she quickly continued, "Despite what you might think since we just met, I'm not making this suggestion lightly. As Harry could confirm… I'm not in the habit of letting men in my dressing room. You are, in fact, the first one I've been alone with since I started working here."

Interesting. She sounded as if she was worried he'd question her morals or think she was trashy. He'd known trashy women. But in his experience, they were women with low self-confidence and lower self-esteem who grasped at sex with anyone in an effort to feed their egos and fill their empty hearts.

He could already tell Rose wasn't like that. She was *incredibly* self-confident. She could lift a finger and have any man upstairs ready to give her anything she wanted… and she knew it. She didn't need physical devotion to feed her self-esteem. In fact, he suspected it was her unshakeable self-esteem that enabled her to take off her clothes in front of a room full of men and yet remain so completely out of reach of all of them.

She could strip for them, entice them, seduce them… but never lower herself to a level that said she'd *ever* give them what they wanted.

But now, that's exactly what she was doing. Offering herself…to him. "I'm flattered," he said, his tone husky.

She reached for him, scraping the tips of her fingers along the waistband of his pants, tugging a little at his shirt.

"But it's not going to happen."

Her hand stilled. "You said you weren't attached."

"That's not the only issue."

"You're attracted to me."

He couldn't deny something so obvious. "We work together."

Shrugging in unconcern, she stepped closer, sliding one bare foot between his so that her leg scraped against his thigh. "Working together is what makes it so very… convenient."

She tilted her head, glancing toward the sturdy-looking vanity, and Nick knew she was picturing a very similar scenario to the one that had filled his mind earlier.

It would be shockingly easy to lift her onto that surface, step between her legs and drive into her body. Or to turn her around, lay her over it and come into her from behind. Their eyes would meet in the mirror…but he wouldn't see the passion in their depths. He could barely make out their color behind the fabric of her mask. And he knew one thing for sure—he would never make love to the woman as long as she wore the thing.

"I'm sorry, Rose. You're very attractive and sexy, but you're just not who I'm looking for right now," he said. "I've done the one-night-stand thing and I've had enough of it."

"Who said anything about one night?" Her words were flippant. Her husky tone was not.

The idea of having more than one night appealed to him. But it didn't change the basics: she was not the kind of woman he needed to get involved with right now. Not even on a purely sexual basis. "I'm sure there are a hundred guys upstairs who'd take you up on this in a heartbeat."

"I don't want any of them," she murmured. "I want you."

"You don't even know me."

"I don't have to know you to want to have sex with you."

"I'm not wired that way."

She made a sound of disbelief. "You've never had raw, wild, uninhibited sex with someone just for the sake of feeling good?"

"Just to get off, yeah," he muttered, making no effort to be delicate. "But only because time and expediency demanded it. I don't operate that way anymore."

"I could make it so good for you." She lifted his hand again, this time putting it on her bare hip.

Nick couldn't help squeezing it. "I don't doubt it."

"*Let* me," she ordered. "Let's see how good it can be."

His jaw stiff, he pulled his hand away. "I *know* how good it could be. I don't doubt we could screw ourselves senseless and make each other come a dozen times in an hour."

Her eyes closed behind the mask. He could see her pulse fluttering in her neck. Still talking in that throaty, sultry whisper, she asked, "And what would be so bad about that?"

Nothing would be so bad about that. In fact, it would be incredible. But he'd feel like shit afterward. He knew it as sure as he knew his brother Mark was never going to let him forget he'd been born twelve minutes before Nick had.

Some things were inarguable.

Like the fact that he couldn't have sex with this woman tonight and still look Izzie—the woman he sensed could be right for him for all the *right* reasons—in the eye tomorrow. So glancing at his watch, he found some nugget of resolve and said, "Harry's waiting for me upstairs. I'll see you later."

Without giving her a chance to try to stop him, he turned around and walked out of her dressing room. Judging by the way something went flying in that tiny room once the door was closed behind him, he knew he'd left a very angry woman in his wake.

"So HOW YOU DOIN', little brother?" Nick heard a woman's voice ask as he sat in a booth at Santori's the next day. It was early Sunday afternoon and the church crowd hadn't yet shown up for their traditional Sunday big midday meal, so he'd taken advantage of the lull to grab some lunch. Glancing up, he saw his sister-in-law, Gloria, Izzie's older sister.

They didn't look much alike. Gloria was pretty— especially for a thirtysomething mother of three—but she didn't have Izzie's flamboyant looks. Her face was sweet, not dramatic. Her mouth soft, not sensual. She didn't have Izzie's amazing figure. Nor had she inherited her sister's desire to escape from here.

Gloria personified the world in which he'd grown up. She'd worked in her parents' business, gone to high school right here in the neighborhood. Married an Italian boy up the block. Gone to work in *his* family's business. And proceeded to produce lots of little Italian babies who looked just like her husband.

Though they were both hardheaded and volatile, and had been known to shout the street down when they got going, Tony and Gloria were absolutely crazy about each other. They had the kind of marriage anyone would want to have. The kind he would be lucky to have…once he figured out if he really wanted it.

Not knowing what he wanted was proving to be a real pain in the ass. Made more painful by the very sexy distraction called the Crimson Rose. He'd been able to avoid her for the rest of last night while working at the club, but every time their eyes met, she reminded him that she knew he was attracted to her.

"Nick?" Gloria prompted. "Everything okay?"

"I'm good, where are the boys?" he asked, looking past her for his two older nephews, or the carriage holding the baby one.

"I came in through the back…Tony Jr. and Mikey are in the kitchen with their father." She raised her voice, never shifting her eyes toward the swinging door leading into the kitchen. "Who had *better* not be giving them candy outta Pop's candy jar if he wants to *live* another day."

From the back room came the sound of Tony's deep laughter. Nick would lay money the boys were already high on Pop's secret stash of gummy bears. "What about the baby?"

Gloria frowned, glancing toward the door of the restaurant. "He should be here any second. It's hard enough bringing the boys to mass without Tony there to help me. No way could I handle three of them. So he stayed with Auntie Izzie." Smiling in relief, Gloria nodded. "Here they are now."

Something about seeing Izzie pushing a baby carriage into the restaurant made Nick's stomach twist. Not because she looked like an absolute natural doing it…but because she looked miserable. Uncomfortable as hell.

He had to laugh. The woman was *so* unlike anyone else around here. Maybe that was why he couldn't get her off his mind.

"Hey, Iz, how'd you do with my little prince?"

"He puked in my hair. Twice."

Gloria swooped in and lifted the three-month-old out of the stroller, cuddling him close. "Aww, what'd you do to him?"

"I told him if he puked on me again I'd take him to the zoo and drop him in the bear cage," Izzie muttered. "What do you think I did to him?"

Gloria patted the baby on his back. "It's okay, Auntie

Izzie's just grumpy because she doesn't have a sweet man to cuddle up with…much less four like Mommy's got."

Nick almost choked on his water at that one. If Gloria had been facing her sister, she would have seen the death ray that had come from Izzie's eyes. Apparently she heard him… because suddenly that death ray was sent in his direction.

Nick held up his hands, palms out, in a universal peace gesture. "I'm with you. Don't drop me in a bear cage."

Her glare faded and she half smiled. "Don't tempt me."

"Careful, Nick," Gloria cautioned, still focused on the baby, "our Izzie's not quite the sweet young thing you remember. You don't want to tangle with her."

Oh, yeah, he did want to tangle with her. Tangle his hands in her hair and his tongue in her mouth and his arms around her body and his legs between her thighs. Mostly he wanted to tangle in her life…and tangle her in his. At least enough so she'd give him a chance to win back some of that interest she'd once felt toward him.

Before Izzie could say anything, the door opened and more family members poured in. His parents and his brother Joe—with wife and baby in tow—led the way. Folks from the neighborhood followed. Next came lots of cousins and aunts and uncles, all of whom came to the restaurant every Sunday for a big family meal.

Izzie's whole body went tense. He could see it from five feet away. She didn't want to be part of this—didn't *feel* a part of this. And Nick, more than anyone else in the room, understood. So without saying a word, he got up, took her hand and tugged her toward his table.

She resisted. "What…"

"Come on, it'll be okay," he whispered as he pulled her down to sit beside him. "I'll tell you who I recognize, you tell me who you recognize and we'll get through this together."

She stared at him, her eyes wide, her mouth trembling.

Looking for a moment like a trapped deer, she seemed on the verge of fleeing. She appeared unable to deal with something as innocuous—yet painful—as a neighborhood gathering.

"It's okay," he repeated. "You can do it."

It took a few more seconds, but that panicked look slowly began to fade from her eyes. As family friends and neighbors greeted her, he felt her begin to relax beside him. She even chatted a little, smiling at people she hadn't seen in years.

Everything went fine. Right up until the minute some old lady from the block clapped her hands together, then pinched Izzie's cheek. "Oh, you're a beautiful couple!" she exclaimed. "At *last* you've got your man, Isabella Natale. All those years and you've finally landed him!"

Everyone fell silent, immediately turning in their direction. Especially Gloria. And Nick's parents.

"Shit," Izzie mumbled under her breath. Her face turned as red as a glass of the chianti Pop loved so much.

Nick put a hand on her leg under the table. But she pushed it off. And with a quick goodbye to her sister and the family—and a glare at Nick—she strode across the restaurant and stalked out the front door, not looking back. Not even once.

Over the next couple of days, Izzie gradually began to lose her mind. Began? Heck, she'd been losing her mind since the night she'd toppled onto a table full of cookies and Nick Santori had landed on top of her. The man had been consuming her for *years*. This week, however, he was on track to win the gold medal in the Let's Drive Izzie Crazy games.

After her failed seduction attempt at Leather and Lace, he'd avoided her as much as he could when on the job. They hadn't been alone at all the rest of Saturday night, or when they'd both worked again Sunday. Just as well. She was still ticked about what had happened at the restaurant that afternoon.

He did take his job seriously, making sure she went nowhere alone. But *he* hadn't been alone with her for one minute. It was as if he feared "Rose" would make another move on him the first chance she got, and was making sure she didn't get the chance.

Grr...men. So untrusting.

But if Nick was frustrating her with his aloofness at the club by night, he was absolutely killing her by day. He'd come by several times in the past few days, popping into the bakery for a muffin and a coffee. Every time he was all cute and sweet and sexy. So different from the dark, brooding guy at the club that she'd have thought they were two different people.

She honestly didn't know which man appealed to her more. Probably whichever one she happened to be with at the time. Funny...he knew her as two different women. And while his name was Nick either way, she knew him as two different men, too.

Both of them were messing with her head. She'd been making all kinds of stupid mistakes at the bakery today—like using peppermint extract instead of almond in a batch of cookies.

Giving up in the kitchen since she had several hours before the restaurant orders had to be delivered, she decided to do some paperwork before closing. It was well after lunch, she was working alone but could hear the bell if anyone came in.

But even that didn't go well. She'd added up a column on a deposit slip four times and still hadn't gotten it right. She was tempted to call Bridget to ask her cousin to straighten out her books. But judging by the conversation they'd had earlier in the day, Bridget had finally worked up the nerve to ask her shaggy-haired used-car salesman out. And Izzie didn't want to do anything to distract her.

Izzie just wished *she* had a distraction. Because she couldn't get Nick out of her head. He'd invaded her life. No, *both* her lives. When he stared at her across the club and devoured her with his eyes at night while physically spurning her, she felt ready to howl in fury.

Showing up here by day—the handsome guy next door who wanted to lick the cream out of her cannoli—and her having to refuse him? It was pure hell.

She wanted Nick the bodyguard at night. Not Nick the sexy guy up the block by day.

She wanted sex. Not romance.

Wanted temporary. Not ever after.

Wanted to *do* him. Not date him.

It was simply a matter of wills to determine which of them got what they wanted first. God, she hoped it was her.

"Izzie?"

Startled, Izzie yelped and spun toward the front of the shop, seeing a customer at the counter. So much for thinking she'd hear the bell—she'd been deafened by her own thoughts.

Recognizing the woman, a weary smile curled her lips. Lilith was a regular, who could supposedly read the future. A bit out there, but a good customer, and a nice one. "I'm sorry." She wiped her hands on her apron. "My head was in the clouds."

"If the clouds all smell like this bakery, that's not a bad place to be."

Maybe for the customers. But after practically living in this place for two months, Izzie was *over* the nauseatingly sweet smells that invaded her nostrils from morning till night. "Believe me, it's not so great going home from work with hair scented like anisette and clothes that reek of ginger."

"On the positive side, they say the scent of licorice is great for dieters because it controls your appetite."

Didn't seem to her that the sexy, short-haired brunette had anything to worry about in that regard. Frankly, neither did Izzie. She'd long since lost her taste for sweets… no more cookie-induced panty girdles for her. "Twizzlers can keep it. I try to ignore the smells unless someone burns something."

"Oh, come on, no one at Natale's ever burns anything."

Quickly washing her hands, Izzie had barely dried them before Lilith pointed with impatience at the lone cannoli remaining in the front display case.

When Lilith told her she'd be eating in, rather than taking the cannoli to go, Izzie asked, "Got a reading?"

While she didn't entirely believe in that stuff, Izzie knew a lot of regulars swore by Lilith's spiritual readings. Though she'd never considered it before, Izzie half wondered if the other woman could help her figure out the quagmire that was her life. Especially the Nick part of that quagmire.

"Nah, I'm taking a break from the medium world right now."

"Just my luck. For the first time in my life I think I'd actually *pay* to have someone tell me who the heck I'm going to be next week."

Izzie the baker? Izzie the stripper? Izzie the New Yorker? Izzie the Chicagoan? *Izzie the horny?*

That was the one she really wanted an answer to. Was she ever going to get laid again, and oh, please, please, please, would it actually be Nick Santori who did the laying?

She didn't ask Lilith any of those things, though the medium promised she'd try to help her as soon as she was "back in business"—whatever that meant. But that might be too late. She might already have done something stupid—like having sex with Nick the bouncer as the Crimson Rose. Which would be fabulous but would make him hate her if he found out the truth.

Or something *more* stupid, like going out on a date with Nick, the guy up the block, which would have her parents planning their wedding. Then she'd hate *herself.*

Ordering a cappuccino to go with her treat, the mysterious brunette made herself at home at a front table, firing up a laptop. After making the frothy cappuccino, Izzie carried it over. "Doing some surfing?"

"I'm going to try. The most I've ever used the web for is updating my website and answering email."

"Don't forget shopping. Or maybe you're going to start haunting chat rooms?"

"No, I'm doing research."

Leaving the woman to it, Izzie went back to work. Concentrating on cleaning out the display cabinet, she was surprised to hear the bell jangle as another late-day customer came in. This one she didn't recognize—and she definitely would have, if she'd seen her before. The leggy brunette was dressed entirely in sleek, black leather and she looked like a predatory cat. The sexy little motorcycle parked outside the door suggested the woman was a risk taker and a rule breaker.

Izzie liked her on sight.

"Hey, Izzie," Lilith called, "what do you know about computers?"

Offering the new customer a quick smile, she answered, "Well, I don't know how to find any naked pictures of Heath Ledger, and I haven't figured out how to send a death ray to spammers, but I do the website for the bakery." It was a basic one, but Izzie was pretty proud of it.

"I hear ya. So you know how to enlarge pictures? Other than ones of naked movie stars?"

Izzie grinned. "Yeah, give me a sec." She looked at the newcomer. "What can I get you?"

"Espresso and a cannoli."

"Sorry, Lilith took the last."

Settling for just the espresso, the woman paid her and waited for her drink. After making it, Izzie went over to Lilith to see what help she could offer.

It wasn't much. It turned out the medium needed to enlarge a grainy newspaper picture in order to see a ring on some guy's finger. And Izzie just didn't have the know-how to do it.

The newcomer in black leather, however, did. Joining them, she asked a few questions, then bent over Lilith's computer and went to work. Watching her type, her fingers flying on the keys, Izzie figured she was experienced at this. But when the woman acknowledged that she was hacking into the newspaper website to try to find the original photo, she suspected there was a lot more than simple ballsiness to the woman.

She was mysterious. Maybe even a little dangerous.

They *both* seemed that way, really. Lilith with her supposed psychic abilities. This woman with her risky, who-gives-a-damn attitude. So unlike little Izzie of the bakery.

Maybe, however, not too unlike the Crimson Rose. She wondered what these two would think if they knew she wasn't quite the sweet, simple bakery worker she appeared to be.

"Who is this guy, anyway?" the stranger asked. "Don't tell me you're trying to figure out if that ring is a wedding band and he's the asshole you've been dating for the past three months."

"Ew."

"So he's not your lover."

"Say that again and I'll dump the dregs on you. He's a jerk I'm investigating."

"A jerk?" The stranger snorted. "What makes him different from every other man on this planet?"

"Good question," Izzie muttered, though her heart wasn't really in it. Nick had always been one incredibly good guy. The fact that he wouldn't have sex with her as a stripper didn't mean he was a jerk.

Even though he was.

She wandered away from the other two, cleaning off the empty tables in preparation for closing. As she worked, she kept up with the other women's conversation, trying to stay out of it, but unable to when she heard who Lilith was currently dating. Hearing that the sexy medium had hooked up with Mac Mancuso, a nice boy-next-door type turned Chicago cop, she had to put her two cents in. Mainly because their situations—whether Lilith would believe it or not—were very similar.

"Mac's not a jerk. He grew up just a few blocks from here. Our families know each other. I'd think any woman would love to catch a good, honest cop like him."

The stranger in black immediately stopped typing. "You're sleeping with a cop." Somehow, Izzie suspected the woman was allergic to anyone official—especially the police.

"I'm sleeping with him, not married to him," Lilith insisted. "Trust me when I say that my definition of right and wrong varies from his by huge degrees."

Huh. Sounding more and more like Izzie's situation. She almost wished she and Lilith were alone so they could talk.

"Keep working and your next ten espressos are on me," Lilith told the other woman.

"I won't be around that long, but thanks for the offer."

"Add her to my tab," Lilith told Izzie. "Any time she stops in, coffee's on me." Glancing at the stranger, she asked, "What's your name?"

"Seline."

Amused since Lilith's tab currently took up two pages in her accounts book, Izzie asked, "Does that mean you're actually going to pay it someday?"

Lilith shrugged in unconcern, watching as Seline kept working. When she finally struck pay dirt and got Lilith the information she wanted, they both seemed triumphant.

Izzie only wished her problems with Nick could be solved with an internet search. Unfortunately, if she searched for the stuff she wanted to do with Nick Santori on the internet, she'd probably get inundated with spam from sites like bigpenises.com from now till eternity.

Finishing up her cappuccino and shutting down her computer, Lilith thanked Seline for helping her out, then turned to Izzie. "Thanks for the sugar boost and the wi-fi."

"Anytime." Unable to help it, Izzie called out, "Lilith, don't be so quick to write off a great guy like Mac. Maybe you and he can find a way to make it work, even if you think there's no way it ever could."

And maybe she was a sucker who should still be reading fairy tales. But hey, it didn't hurt to dream, did it? Even if she was dreaming on behalf of someone else.

Once Lilith was gone, the other woman, Seline, approached the counter. Even her walk was feline—sultry—and Izzie wondered if she'd ever danced before.

"Here," Seline said. She put a one-hundred-dollar bill on the counter. "For her tab. I sense that she needs the money more than I do. And I don't have to be psychic to figure that out."

Stunned, Izzie murmured, "Thanks." She opened her mouth to say more—to offer the money back—but the mysterious woman in black had already turned toward the door, her coffee in hand. She walked out into the bright sunshine without another word, got onto her sleek motorcycle and roared away down the street.

BRIDGET DONAHUE HAD always known she would never be wildly sexy and self-confident like her cousin Izzie. But there were times when she allowed herself to think that, maybe, since they were related, Bridget had a tiny bit of Izzie-power trapped deep inside her. So ever since she was a kid, she'd played a game. WWID, aka *What Would Izzie Do?* And then she'd try to do that.

Asking Dean Willis to go out with her one day at lunchtime had definitely been a WWID moment. And Bridget still couldn't believe she'd gone through with it. But if she hadn't, she wouldn't now be sitting at a coffee shop, looking across the table at his handsome face. Make that staring at his face.

Staring. Izzie wouldn't stare. Bridget ducked her head down, focused on her cup of Earl Grey tea. Not the double-shot espresso she probably needed—because of her "I don't drink coffee" fib—but okay…mainly because of the company.

"You ready for a refill?" Dean asked.

Bridget shook her head. "I'm fine, thanks."

They weren't at her uncle's bakery, but at a big chain place not far from her apartment. Bridget had chosen the spot, which seemed safe, neutral and impersonal. Not the kind of place that said she thought they were on a date. Not the kind of place where a date would be absolutely out of the question.

God, she sucked at this. Izzie would have met him at a hotel bar.

Small steps, she reminded herself. Asking a man out was a first for her. It wasn't that she'd never dated—or that she was completely inexperienced. But if Izzie was on the top rung when it came to dealing with men, Bridget was still pulling the ladder out of the cellar.

They sat in an alcove by the front window. Bridget had her chair pushed back from the table, to accommodate the length of his legs beneath it. He looked crowded—bunched up in the small chair and the small corner—but he hadn't complained.

"You must be tired of hearing me rattle on about my landlord problems," she said as the conversation lagged. "I haven't seemed to shut up."

He shook his head. "You're easy to talk to."

"You haven't been doing much talking…just listening."

"You're easy to listen to," he replied with a small smile.

Nice answer. And it was mutual, because he was also very easy—easy to like. But she still didn't feel like she knew anything about him. "So how do you like working for Marty? You've sold more cars in the month you've been there than any other salesman has sold in the past three."

He shrugged. "It's not hard when you have good products to sell." Lowering his gaze, he reached for his cup. "I guess you'd know that since you've worked for Marty longer than I have."

Sighing, Bridget shook her head. "Not much longer."

"Really?"

"I started just a couple of months before you did so I don't know much of anything, either."

He frowned. "But you keep the books, surely you know how things are going. I bet the place is raking in the bucks, huh?"

Grunting in annoyance, she admitted, "I have no idea. I see just enough to keep the books balanced and not much else."

Dean stopped stirring his tea and lifted his eyes to hers. Leaning forward over the table, he asked, "You don't know *anything* about what's going on at Honest Marty's Used Cars?"

"I know Marty's a bit of a con artist," she said tartly. "Honesty is just one of his…embellishments."

She suspected her boss also embellished some other

things—like stuff he told the IRS. But she didn't have proof and was not about to say such a thing to anyone else.

He persisted. "But you must make the deposits, pay the invoices, keep an eye on the accounts receivable."

"I take what he gives me and do what I can." Shrugging, she added, "Honestly, I don't know much of anything about the business, it's all I can do to keep the checkbook balanced."

He held her stare, his blue eyes looking searchingly into her face, as if he was trying to find the answer to some question. She couldn't imagine what. She had no idea why he was so interested in the financial dealings of their employer.

Then she thought of something. It *could* be a matter of job security. Dean was personable and a good salesman, but he didn't exactly dress like someone who had a lot of money. The sports coats he wore to work usually didn't fit well across his broad shoulders, and his pants were sometimes a little shabby.

Dean hadn't said a lot about what he'd done before coming to Honest Marty's. For all she knew, he'd been put out of work by poor management at his last job. That would certainly be enough to make anybody ask questions, especially somebody who lived paycheck to paycheck, as she suspected he did.

Not wanting to embarrass him, she carefully tried to set his mind at ease. "Look, I don't know specifics, but I know the dealership's doing well. I see the number of cars coming onto the lot and the number leaving it. You don't have to worry."

He frowned, as if not understanding what she meant. Some impulse made Bridget reach across the table and put her hand on his. She almost pulled her hand back right away, surprised to feel a warm tingle where skin met skin.

But, swallowing for courage, she left it there. *Like Izzie would.*

If this was a date, he'd interpret her touch as a signal that she wanted more. If it was *not* a date, he'd interpret it as concerned friendship. Bridget considered it a little of both. "Your job is secure."

He was staring at their hands, still touching. "My job?"

He sounded—distracted. As if he was as affected by their touch as she was, which gave her a little thrill. "Marty would be a fool to let you go. You're the best salesman he's got."

He said nothing at first, he just slowly twined his fingers in hers, rubbing at the fleshy pad of her palm with the tip of his thumb. Her pulse raced and she wondered if he could feel it throbbing right there below her skin.

She somehow managed to concentrate on getting a positive message across, ignoring the tingling in her fingers and the flip-flopping of her heart. "It's okay, I know what it's like to worry about making ends meet, but please don't worry about the company. I'm sure you're not going to lose your job."

He looked up at her, his jaw dropping. "Lose my…"

"I thought that's why you were curious."

Dean's mouth snapped and he mumbled, "It's okay." He pulled the hand she'd been touching away and dropped it onto his lap. "Well, they probably want this table for other customers. I guess we should go."

Oh, God, she felt like a fool. She'd ruined this, he probably thought she had been pitying him or something. "Dean, I really didn't mean anything…"

"Hey, don't worry about it. I just wasn't sure what you meant at first. It's good to know the company's doing so well," he said, still sounding distracted. "Thanks again for meeting me. I'm glad we got the chance to get to know each other better, since we'll be working together."

Bridget managed to suck her trembling lip into her mouth, recognizing a brush-off when she heard one. Either he'd never intended this as a get-to-know-you date at all, or he *had* and she'd blown it. But whatever the case, it was finished now. He was not interested in seeing her again.

WWID...Izzie wouldn't cry. So she blinked. Hard.

"Bye, Bridget," he said as he escorted her outside.

She somehow managed to sound perfectly normal when she said goodbye, too. But deep inside, she felt anything but normal.

In fact, Bridget felt a little bit broken.

5

OVER THE NEXT WEEK, Nick went out of his way to change Izzie's mind about going out with him. He stopped by the bakery, phoned in orders for stuff he didn't really want and made sure he was the one to sign for any deliveries at the restaurant, just in case she happened to be the delivery person.

She never was.

But he wasn't giving up. While at first she'd been a sexy stranger who'd caught his eye, she'd now become something of a challenge to him. He wanted to work his way around her protective wall and see if the smiling, funny girl was still there behind that to-die-for woman exterior.

Maybe it was just as well that Izzie consumed his thoughts by day. Because it made it easier to resist temptation by night. It definitely had on Saturday and Sunday night.

He'd worked at Leather and Lace for a second weekend. This time, knowing what he was in for, he'd been careful to avoid being alone with Rose, the club's sultry star performer, and hadn't even exchanged a word with her. Even still, it had been impossible to keep his eyes off her.

Especially when she danced.

Especially when she watched *him* while she danced.

If she'd made another move on him, he honestly didn't know that he'd have been able to refuse. So ensuring he was never alone with her was probably a good thing.

Hell, he honestly wasn't sure why he was resisting. As long as he kept the woman safe, he didn't see Harry Black being the kind of man who'd have a problem with it. After all, he was married to one of his own former star performers.

And letting off a little sexual steam didn't have to have anything to do with Nick's normal, daytime life. In fact, nobody in his family ever needed to know about it. There was no law that said an unattached man couldn't have sex with a willing woman, just because he was interested in another woman.

One who wasn't interested in him.

Damn. That's why he hadn't done it. Because it was driving him crazy that Izzie wasn't interested in him.

Frankly, he'd never worked so hard to get a woman's attention in his life. The fact that Izzie was the woman in question made the whole situation that much more challenging.

She'd been crazy about him once. He'd get her to see him that way again if it was the last thing he did. Even if it meant doing stupid, sappy shit like showing up at her bakery with a handful of flowers.

Like he was right now.

God, how the guys in his unit would laugh to see him, standing on a street corner on a hot August day, holding a brightly colored bouquet he'd bought off a guy on the corner.

"What are you doing?" she mouthed through the glass late Thursday afternoon when he knocked on the locked front door.

"I'm bringing you flowers," he yelled back. "Open up."

"Don't bring me flowers."

Shrugging, he flashed her a grin. "Too late."

"I mean it."

"Like I said, too late. Come on, let me in. They're thirsty."

She glared at him. Seeing pedestrians stopping to watch the show, she went a step further and bared her teeth.

Man the woman was *hot* when she was hot.

"Go away!"

Tsking, he shook his head. Then he looked at the closest woman who'd paused midstep to see what was going on. "Can you believe she doesn't want my flowers?"

A teenager and her girlfriend, who'd also stopped nearby, piped in together, "We'll take them!"

The older woman, an iron-gray haired grandmother, frowned. "What did you do?"

Good question. He wasn't *entirely* sure. "I didn't recognize her after not having seen her for ten years."

The grandmother's eyebrow shot up. Pushing Nick out of the way, she marched up to the glass, stuck her index finger out and pointed at Izzie. "Take the flowers you foolish girl." Rolling her eyes and huffing about youth being wasted on the young, she stalked down the street.

Izzie, still practically growling, unlocked the door, yanked it open and grabbed his arm. "Get in here and stop making a fool of yourself."

"I wasn't making a fool of myself," he pointed out. "You were making a fool of me."

"You don't require much help."

Shaking his head and smiling, he murmured, "What happened to the sweet, friendly, eager-to-please Izzie?"

"She grew up."

She yanked the bouquet out of his hand, stalking behind the counter and grabbing a glass to put it in. Watching her, he noticed the surreptitious sniff she gave the blooms, and the way she squared her shoulders, as if annoyed at her own weakness.

Nick didn't follow her, tempted as he was. Instead, he leaned across the glass counter, dropping his elbows onto it. "The flowers are a peace offering."

"Are we at war?"

"It's felt that way to me ever since I was stupid enough to not recognize you that night at Santori's."

Ignoring him, she finished filling the glass with water, turned off the tap and plopped the flowers in.

"I still can't believe you're punishing me over that."

"Don't flatter yourself. I'm not punishing you over anything. I'm just not interested in you, Nick."

"Yeah, I got it." Only he didn't. He was in no way ready to concede that. Something had caused Izzie to put a wall up between them…and he was going to find out what it was. "But there's no reason we can't go back to being friends, is there? We were once."

"No. We weren't. You were the stud of the known universe and I was the puppy dog with the big humiliating crush. You can't seriously think I'd go back to that."

"I tell ya, Izzie," he said, hearing the frustration in his voice, "I don't know for sure *what* I want from you. I just know I can't stand that you won't even look at me."

She finally did just that. Looked at him, met his direct stare. In those dark brown eyes he saw stormy confusion. It was matched by the quiver of her lush lips and the wild beating of the pulse in her throat.

"You liked me once," he said softly. "And we did pretty well helping each other out at the neighborhood-prying-session disguised as lunch last Sunday. Can we at least try being friends?"

She opened her mouth to reply. Closed it. Then, sighing as she pushed the vase of flowers to the center of the counter, slowly nodded. "I *guess*."

It was a start. Maybe not the start he wanted to make with her…but at least the start of something.

"Do you want some coffee?" She didn't sound particularly enthusiastic about the invitation.

He glanced at the industrial coffeemaker, scrubbed clean for the night, and shook his head, not wanting to put her to the trouble.

"I have a small coffeemaker in the back."

"Sounds good."

Nick followed her down a short hallway between the café and the kitchen, trying to remember that it wasn't very polite to stare long and hard at the ass of someone who was just a friend. It didn't work. Because though she wore loose-fitting khakis and an oversize apron, the woman had a figure to die for. Every step pulled the fabric a little tighter across her curves, and the natural sway in her hips made him dizzy.

Friends. That's it. And *not* friends with benefits.

"How do you like being back in Chicago?" he asked as he sat at a tall stool beside a butcher-block work counter.

Izzie ground fresh beans. At last—a woman who knew how to make coffee. One more thing to like about her, aside from the cute way her ponytail wagged when she moved and the way she smelled of sugar and butter and everything nice. "About as much as I like getting a root canal."

"That bad? You don't like being back in the family business?"

She glanced around the kitchen, immaculately clean and stocked with every baking supply ever invented. "My prison smells like anisette."

"Mine smells like marinara," he muttered, meaning it.

She nodded, not asking him to elaborate. She obviously knew exactly what he meant. "Not easy to come home, is it?"

He shook his head. "Not easy at all. My parents still

haven't forgiven me for moving into an apartment, not back into my old room. It still has my high-school posters on the walls."

She snickered. "Mine, too. Though I don't suppose yours were of ballerinas and Ricky Martin."

"Uh...definitely not." A grin tickling his lips, he admitted, "Demi Moore and *Lethal Weapon 3*."

Izzie laughed softly. There was a twinkle in those dark brown eyes of hers and a flash of a dimple he remembered in one cheek. At last.

"Are you..."

"What?" he asked.

"I'm sorry," she said, "it's none of my business."

"What's none of your business?"

"I guess I was just wondering if you felt...a little...out of place with your family."

"I feel like I belong with the Santoris about as much as that kid in *The Jungle Book* belonged with the dancing bear."

She nodded, as if in complete agreement. "But if I recall correctly, I think he *wanted* to belong with the dancing bear and couldn't understand why he didn't quite fit in."

Nick said nothing. She'd made his point for him.

Izzie seemed to realize it. "Yeah. Me, too."

"Something else we have in common," he said.

"Don't get too excited about it," she muttered, "I'm still not giving you my phone number."

"You must know I already have it."

She rolled her eyes but didn't frown. "Gloria. Dead sister walking." The coffee had finished brewing, so she poured two big cups. "Cream or sugar?"

"Neither." Taking the cup from her, he inhaled the steam. "My mother makes lousy coffee. So does your sister, who seems to have decided even the *smell* of caffeine can make our hooligan nephews bounce off the walls."

"Decaf's for quitters," she muttered.

Startled, Nick barked a laugh. This was no sweet little Izzie, the girl he remembered.

"I lived on coffee in Manhattan," she admitted. "It was the only way I could maintain my schedule."

He sniffed appreciatively, allowing the rich aroma to fill his head. When combined with all the other scents permeating this room, it was making him weak with physical hunger.

Or *she* was. He honestly wasn't sure which.

"I think I would have killed for something this good even when it was one-hundred-twenty degrees in the desert."

Izzie sat on one of the other stools across from him, her cup on the counter between them. Watching him intently, with a bit of trepidation, she forecast her curiosity before the words left her mouth. "How did you make it through every day?"

What a good question—and one nobody had asked him yet. Oh, he'd been asked about the action and the things he'd seen. Asked if he'd shot anyone, killed anyone, saved anyone. Asked what he'd done to relieve the boredom, to accomplish his mission.

But nobody had asked him what it was that had held him together every single day. Not until now.

"I'm sorry, that's probably none of my business."

"It's okay. If you want to know the truth, it was *this* that held me together." He gestured around the room.

She frowned skeptically.

"I don't mean the bakery. I mean this lifestyle. Home, family, all the safe, secure stuff I grew up with that I thought would be exactly the same when I got back. Only, it wasn't."

Staring at him, Izzie revealed her thoughts in her expressive brown eyes. She understood what he meant—got it, exactly. Nick didn't look away, liking the connection even though they were separated by several feet of sweet-smelling air. Mentally, though, they were touching. Bonding. Sharing the unique brand of estrangement they had each been feeling from the world they'd grown up in.

She finally shook her head. "Well, obviously you have some things to figure out, man-cub."

He grinned, remembering what he'd said about *The Jungle Book*. "Yeah, well, so do you, right? You didn't get what you bargained for when you came home, did you?"

She shook her head.

"What'd you do in New York, anyway?" he asked, never having gotten the whole story. He knew she'd had a good job but had given it up to come home and help her family.

"I was…in the arts," she murmured, lifting her cup to her mouth. She blew across the surface of the coffee, sending steam curling up into the air. It colored her cheeks, already flushed a delicate pink from the heat of the yeasty kitchen. "On the stage."

An actress. The idea stunned him for a second, though it made sense. Izzie had looks and personality and a lot of self-confidence. He suspected she was amazing onstage.

"But I got hurt last winter and haven't worked since."

He lowered his cup, waiting.

A tiny frown line appeared between her eyes as she explained. "I tore my ACL in my left knee and had to have surgery. It required a lot of rehab."

"And you're on your feet working in a kitchen all day?" he asked, appalled at the idea of how much pain she had to have experienced. He knew guys who'd had those injuries during his high-school sports days. They were not fun.

"I'm better." She pointed down to the stool on which she sat. "And I work sitting down a lot."

Nick wanted to know more. Lots of things. Like what kind of life she'd led in New York and whether anyone had shared it. And what her neck tasted like. And what she planned to do once her father was well enough to come back to the bakery. And what she'd eaten today that had left her lips so ruby red. And why she was resisting something happening between them.

And when she was going to be in his bed.

But the phone interrupted before he could ask, much less get any answers. Excusing herself to answer it, she revealed her frustration with the caller with every word exchanged. Nick heard enough to understand what was going on—her part-time delivery person was calling in sick.

"I can't believe this," she muttered after she hung up the phone. "All these orders and he bails on me." Almost growling, she added, "Are the Cubs playing today? It sounded like the little bastard was at the ball park."

Fierce. He liked it.

"Don't sweat it, Iz. I'll help you out."

Blinking, she replied, "Huh?"

"I'll help you make the deliveries." Hopping off the bench, he walked over to a tall cart, laden with cardboard boxes labeled with the names of several local restaurants. "After all," he said, offering her a boyish smile over his shoulder, "what are friends for?"

FRIENDS WERE FOR going to the movies with. Sharing bad date stories with. Getting through boring reunions with. Crying over breakups with. Dieting with. Drinking with. Clubbing with.

Friends were *not* for having sex with. Or lusting over. Or inspiring lust simply by the way they handled a few heavy boxes and filled out their soft, broken-in jeans.

Nick Santori was no friend of hers. Because oh, God, she had already broken every "friend" rule in the book and she'd only agreed to his terms a few hours ago.

When they'd talked in the kitchen, he'd been friendly

and warm. That boyish smile he'd flashed her when he'd offered to help her with the deliveries had made him seem so charming and endearing. Completely the *opposite* of the brooding, simmering hunk of male heat she'd watched through covetous eyes at the club last weekend. It was like he was two people in one body.

And she wanted both of them desperately.

She couldn't believe she'd thought she could handle being merely his friend. Now, having been closed up in a delivery van with him for the past couple of hours, she was definitely having second thoughts.

He was being so damned *wonderful*. Not just offering to help her, he had refused to let her lift a single box. They'd gone to a dozen shops and restaurants, delivering cakes, pies and pastries to some places for their dinner customers tonight, and muffins and coffee cake to others for their breakfast crowds tomorrow. He'd charmed her customers, and *her*. He'd even driven, since Izzie hated dealing with the traffic. She'd sat in the passenger seat of the bakery van, reading off the list of stops, trying not to notice how big he was and how small the van felt with him in it.

She also tried not to notice how wonderful he smelled. How the sound of his low laughter rolled over her, more warm and sultry than a summer breeze. How his short hair curled a little behind his ear. How strong his lightly stubbled jaw was and how thick his body was beneath his tight T-shirt. How he warmed her from two feet away.

And how very, very much she wanted him.

Especially after the cannoli. It was the damn cannoli that put the nail in her coffin…and the wetness in her panties.

They had an extra box. Izzie had been so wiped out from working so many hours, both at the bakery Tuesday through Saturday, and at the club Saturday and Sunday nights, that she'd miscounted. She'd boxed up an extra two dozen of the decadent ricotta-and-cream filled treats. Once they'd finished all the deliveries, thanks mostly to Nick's strong back—oh, heavens, that strong back—she'd noticed the extra box and realized her mistake.

So, when they'd gotten back to the bakery and parked in the small private lot behind it, she'd offered him one. He'd immediately taken her up on it, not even getting out of the van before digging in. And seeing him eat it with such visceral, sensual appreciation, was making her a quivering, shaking mess.

"God, these are amazing. No wonder they sell out every day at Santori's," he said as he licked at the creamy center of the tube-shaped pastry.

Izzie shifted in the seat. Licking. It was not a good thing to watch a man do if you wanted to have sex with him but couldn't.

He nibbled some of the flaky crust.

Nibbling. Also bad. She added it to her mental list of no-nos to watch.

Then he bit in and closed his eyes in rapturous delight. Oh, Lord. Biting—anything that put that look of intense pleasure on his face—was absolutely out of the question.

Thankfully, he finished the thing so quickly—devouring it in three bites—that she didn't have time to do something foolish, like, say, offering him her tongue to lick and her breast to nibble and her inner thigh to bite.

"You are going to let me have another one, aren't you?" he asked. Not waiting for an answer, he got out of the driver's seat and bent over to step into the back of the van. Metal racks were attached to each side of it, with an aisle down the middle. Opening the lone box remaining on one shelf, he held it toward her. "Come on, have one."

She hadn't voluntarily eaten a cannoli since tenth grade, the day after she'd split her pants while trying to do a sit-up in gym class. They'd torn with a resounding flatulent sound and she'd almost dropped out of school then and there. "Uh-uh."

He smiled, his eyes glittering in the near darkness. Dusk had fallen while they were out making the rounds, and it was now after eight o'clock. The book shop next door was also closed, their private parking spots empty, and the small lot was entirely quiet and deserted. Very private.

She really should hop out of the vehicle and go inside. Being out here, in the near-dark, alone with Nick, was not a very good idea. Of course, being inside the closed shop, in the light, alone with Nick, probably wouldn't be much safer.

"One little taste. How can you tell how good you are at doing it if you never give it a try?"

Nearly choking, she repeated, "How good I am at *doing* it?"

"You know. Making them."

Yeah. Sure. That's what she'd thought he meant.

A small smile continued to play on those incredible lips of his as he watched her, as if he knew what she'd been thinking. And had intentionally put those thoughts into her head.

Get out. Now.

But she didn't reach for the door handle. Instead, like a kid lured by the ice-cream man, she ducked into the back of the van with him. There wasn't room to stand, but Nick had already sat down on the carpeted floor. One leg was sprawled out in front of him, the other bent and upraised. He was carefully picking his way through the open box of pastries, as if searching for just the right one to satisfy his craving.

Izzie sat down across from him, cross-legged, wondering whether the temperature in the van had just gone up forty degrees or if it was her imagination. Considering it was a breezy summer evening and the front windows were open, she somehow doubted the air had gotten hotter...only *she* had. In fact, being this close to Nick was setting her on fire.

"You going to let me tempt you with one?" he asked, still looking down at the box, not at her.

They did look good. *So* good. "I really shouldn't."

"Just a taste," he whispered. Not waiting for her to answer, he lifted one out, then put the box back on the shelf. He scooted forward...close, so close she felt his heat wash over her and his warm, masculine scent fill her lungs. He lifted one of his legs over her crossed ones, until her right knee brushed his hot, jean-covered butt.

She didn't move. Not one inch.

"Won't you have one little lick?" he murmured, lifting the cannoli to her lips.

Staring at it in his hands—the flesh-colored cookie, the pale creamy cheese oozing from the end—she suddenly realized just how phallic the thing looked. Her mouth flooded with hunger—she wanted to lick, to taste, to devour.

Not the pastry. *Him.*

Almost whimpering, she lowered her mouth to it, scraping her tongue along the flaky crust, brushing his finger as she did. He shifted a little in response, as if no longer comfortable sitting the way he had been. The way they were sitting, she quickly realized why.

He was rock hard, his erection thick and long against her leg. She almost drew her legs together, the pressure in her sex demanding relief.

Izzie could hardly think or breathe. Unable to resist, she moved her leg a little, rubbing it against him, and got a low groan in response.

"Taste, Izzie."

She tasted. Imagining it was him she was sampling, she nibbled at the filling, brushing her lips against it.

She didn't need to invite Nick to share it. He was already there, kissing the corner of her mouth, his tongue flicking out to clean some of the sweetness off her lips. "Good," he whispered.

Oh, *very* good.

She licked again, dipping her tongue inside the cookie shell for a deeper taste. Nick tasted deeper, too. He covered her lips with his, stealing some of the cream right out of her mouth, their tongues tangling over it for a long, delicious moment.

"Get your own," she whispered with a soft laugh when he pulled away to offer her another lick.

"I'd rather have yours," he murmured, moving his mouth to her cheek, then lower. He nibbled her jaw, scraping his lips along it until he could nuzzle the sensitive spot just below her ear. "Actually, I'd rather have *you*."

His words washed over her, echoing in her head. With his warm breath on her neck, his mouth on her skin, his hard body radiating heat just inches from her own, she couldn't remember a single reason why she shouldn't have him.

"I noticed." She shifted back far enough to uncross her legs. Without thinking or considering, she draped them over his thighs, scooting close—so close—that that thick ridge in his jeans pressed against the damp seam of hers.

He arched forward reflexively, grinding against her, and Izzie gasped. Moisture flooded her and her sex swelled almost painfully against her clothes. Her clit felt as if it had doubled in size and she bucked into him, needing to come so badly she could almost taste it.

"More?" he asked.

She arched harder. She definitely wanted more.

He lifted the cannoli. She shook her head, then let it fall back. She wanted to *be* the dessert now. Right or wrong, stupid or not, she wanted Nick Santori too much to resist him again.

When they stepped out of the van, the real world would return. He'd still be the great neighborhood guy she couldn't publicly date. But for now—oh, for now—she wanted him desperately, with a longing that had built in her for more than a decade. "Have me, Nick," she whispered, saying yes to the question he hadn't quite asked.

He made a low sound that might have been unrestrained—want or might have been triumph. Honestly, Izzie didn't care. Especially when he nibbled her earlobe, then worked his way down her neck. "Mmm, you taste like sugar and almonds." He kissed his way down to her collarbone, lightly biting her nape, and she shivered.

Never taking his mouth off her, he reached up and pulled her ponytail holder off. Her thick hair fell around his hand and he twined it through his fingers. Cupping her head and supporting her, he pushed her back a little so he could have better access to her neck.

When she felt the cool wetness touch the hollow of her throat, she gasped. The ricotta filling felt good against her heated skin. When Nick licked it off, it felt amazing.

Dropping back to support herself on her elbows, she watched through heavy-lidded eyes as Nick began slipping open the buttons of her sleeveless blouse. After every button was freed and another bit of skin revealed, he dabbed filling on her. Soon there was a trail of dots from her throat, down her chest, in the middle of her cleavage and all the way down to her belly.

He wasn't tasting them. Not yet. She twisted and arched up, desperate for him to, but he ignored her silent plea.

Once he tugged the top free of her jeans, it gaped open. Shrugging, she let it fall off her shoulders, then watched him devour her with his eyes. His breath grew audibly choppy as he saw the way her breasts overflowed her skimpy bra. Bent back as she was, she could barely keep the thing in place, and one nipple was actually peeping freely above the lace.

"Beautiful," he muttered hoarsely. He lifted the pastry and dabbed some of the filling on her nipple.

This time he didn't move on. He stopped for a taste.

"Oh, God," she groaned as Nick bent over and covered her nipple with his mouth, licking and sucking at the cheesy filling. He lapped up every bit, pushing her bra all the way down so he'd have complete access to her breast.

"You are glorious," he said as he lifted a hand to cup her. His fingers were dark and strong against her pale skin, and she literally overflowed his hand. "You hide a lot behind that apron you usually wear."

She hid a lot more behind the mask she sometimes wore. The thought flashed through her head, but she thrust it aside. This was not the time to be thinking about her alterego…or what Nick might do if he ever found out they were one and the same.

Now was for savoring. Indulging.

Reaching for the clasp of her bra, he unfastened it and pulled it off, catching her other breast as it spilled free. Scooping out a large fingerful of filling, complete with tiny chocolate chips, he smeared it all over the taut tip, then devoured it as completely as he had the other side.

Her legs clenched, heat shooting from her wet nipples down her body, straight between her legs. She jerked up, dying to be freed of her jeans. "I need…"

"I know," he whispered. He dropped his mouth to hers for a deep kiss that shut her up and zapped her brain. He tasted sweet and hot and decadent.

Izzie worked at Nick's shirt as they kissed, pulling away so she could tug it up and off him. Then she sagged back, staring in disbelief at the perfection that was his body.

In his clothes, he was an incredibly well-built man.

Out of them he almost defied description.

He was rock hard, not an ounce of excess on him, with a massive chest and thickly muscled shoulders. His huge arms rippled as he moved, highlighting a sizable tattoo—a Marine Corps logo. Just the perfect amount of dark curly hair emphasized the breadth of him before narrowing down to his waist and hips, where he was incredibly lean.

"I'm not finished my dessert yet," he muttered when she reached for his waistband.

He tossed the tiny bit of cannoli away and grabbed another one out of the box. Taking her hand, he pushed her arm over her head until she had to lie flat on the floor. Then he worked his way down her body, kissing, nibbling and licking off all those spots of cream he'd deposited on her earlier.

"It tastes sweeter now," he said when he dipped his tongue into her belly button and swirled it there. "It just needed one more ingredient to make it absolutely addictive."

Her. It needed her.

And she needed *him*.

His hands. His mouth—oh, heavens, his mouth. His amazing body. And that big hard erection she could feel pressing against her leg as he slid farther down her body.

He didn't even move his mouth off her as he undid her pants and pushed them down her hips. Izzie lifted up to help him…and unintentionally offered herself to him *much* more intimately.

He was *on* her immediately.

"Nick!" She gasped and panted when he covered the front of her tiny panties with his mouth, breathing through the fabric, sending warm tendrils of pleasure right where she needed them most. "Please."

"I bet this will taste even sweeter," he whispered as he tugged the satin away.

Izzie barely breathed as he pushed her clothes down and off, until she lay naked beneath him. And she absolutely flew out of her skin when he took the new tube-shaped pastry and smeared one creamy end of it through her curls and across her sex.

"Oh," she groaned.

He pushed at her inner thighs and Izzie parted her legs, giving him the access he'd silently demanded. When he took a first, slow lick at the filling, thick and heavy in her curls, she came up off the floor.

"Oh, definitely sweeter," he said. He moved farther down, sliding his tongue over every inch of her, eating every drop of sticky cream as if it was the best thing he'd ever tasted.

Izzie was a quivering mess, shaking, panting, bucking. Desperate for more, she didn't know whether to beg or remain still for fear he'd get distracted from what he was doing.

He didn't get distracted. And before she knew what he was up to, she felt the flaky shell of the cookie scraping across her clit. She cried out again, feeling the climax build inside her. When he licked at her again, working her clit with his tongue and his lips—lathing, then sucking—she finally got what she'd been waiting for. Pleasure erupted through her, rocking her hips, sending a pulse of heat through her.

Nick didn't even pause, beyond muttering a soft "Yes," in acknowledgment of her orgasm. He just kept going, sliding the cannoli farther…following it with his tongue. Until finally he began working the delicacy between her drenched lips.

"You're not…you can't…" she gasped.

But he did and he was. He slid the tip of it into her wet crevice—sending a cacophony of sensations rushing through her. The roughness of the delicate shell, the smoothness of the filling, she'd never felt anything like it. It was wicked—erotic. A little outrageous.

And she loved it. "Nick…"

"I'm not quite finished with dessert. Though I'm just about full," he murmured.

She only wished she were.

She didn't get too impatient, however, because she was too anxious to see what this supposedly "nice neighborhood guy" would dare next.

He wanted to keep playing, obviously. He slowly sunk the treat deeper, as far as he could, then gently tugged it out. He did it again, leaving Izzie to wonder how long it would take before the shell broke and the oozy cream filled her.

Finally, when she thought she'd die of the wild wantonness of it, he started working it out with his teeth, rather than his fingers. He nibbled off little pieces as it came out of her, whispering sweet words about how good it tasted… how good *she* tasted. How juicy and creamy she was.

His words were almost as arousing as his touch.

"Gotta make sure I got every drop," he whispered once the last of the cookie was gone. And he did, plunging his tongue into her and stroking—in and out—until she lost her mind and came again.

She threw her head back, closing her eyes, giving herself over to the rocking of her body, which seemed to go on forever. When it had finally eased up, and she opened her eyes again, it was to find Nick over her.

She lifted her legs, realizing his were bare. His lean hips brushed her inner thighs, and his thick cock lay heavy on her pelvis.

Whimpering, she looked down. "Let me see you."

"Feel me," he whispered, burying his face in her neck. He slid up and down, his cock separating the slick lips of her sex, hitting her clit at the perfect angle.

"See *and* feel," she insisted, sliding her arm between their bodies to reach for him.

She caught his erection in her hand, shocked at how big and hot it was. He'd already sheathed himself with a condom, but she could feel his pounding pulse through the rubber.

"You're bigger than that cookie," she said, nibbling on her lip as she acknowledged just how much Nick Santori had been hiding beneath his clothes.

He groaned and dipped closer, sliding into her a little at a time. "You're sweeter than that cookie." He pushed a bit more, easing into her with incredible restraint. "And you are definitely creamy enough to handle me."

She didn't doubt it. He'd aroused her half out of her mind and right now, she wanted him plunging to the hilt inside her. Grabbing his hips, she dug her nails into his butt and arched up for him. "Take me, Nick. Fill me up."

He seemed to forget about restraint because he did exactly what she asked, plunging hard and deep until Izzie howled at how good it felt.

He stretched her, embedded himself in her, then drew out and plunged again. "Oh, my God," she groaned. "This is amazing."

Better than amazing. It was absolute perfection. Worth every one of the years she'd waited for it.

Thrusting up, Izzie took what he gave and demanded even more. When she became too frenzied, he slowed the pace, showing so much control she wanted to sob in frustration. But he wouldn't relent, taunting her with slow, deep strokes and teasing half ones. He kissed her so often and so deeply she wasn't sure she'd remember how to breathe when she wasn't sharing the breath from his lungs.

Finally, though, she heard the tiny groans he couldn't contain. His hips thrust harder, more frantically, and she wrung as much as she could out of every stroke.

"I can't…oh, Izzie…"

"Do it," she ordered, feeling another climax building in her from the friction of their locked bodies. "I'll come with you."

That seemed to satisfy him—that he had her permission—and he finally lost his head and gave her the deep, pounding thrusts they both needed. Again. And again. Until he threw his head back and shouted as he reached his climax.

She found hers a second later and wrapped her legs tightly around him to ride it out.

As if knowing the floor was hard against her back, Nick scooped her in his arms and lay down, dragging her on top of him. They were both panting, gasping for air, and he kissed her temple, smoothing her hair away from her sweaty face.

"Izzie? I have to tell you something." His words were rushed. Choppy.

"Yes?"

Closing his eyes, he dropped his head back onto the floor.

"I'm going to call you Cookie until the day I die."

6

FUNNY. NICK HAD once thought that having absolutely mind-blowing sex with a woman would make her friendlier. At least more approachable.

No. Uh-uh. Not Izzie Natale. Because within *minutes* of their incredible lovemaking in the back of the delivery van, she was back to freezing him out, trying to act like nothing had changed between them.

After sex like that, he'd kind of expected to be invited in for a cup of coffee…if not dessert. Oh, man, he was *never* going to look at a cannoli the same way again.

But she hadn't invited him in. Hadn't answered him when he'd asked if she wanted to go get a bite to eat somewhere. And over the next couple of days, hadn't returned his calls. Hadn't even met his eye in the past couple of days.

The woman was killing him, she really was.

When he'd finally confronted her on the sidewalk in front of the bakery Friday afternoon, she'd erupted. "It was a one-time thing, Nick. It was fabulous, I loved it, but it's not going to happen again. Because if it does, then you're going to be *more* of a pain about wanting me to go get a pizza with you, or go visit the folks, and then the whole neighborhood will be congratulating poor little Izzie for finally landing her man."

She'd stalked inside without saying another word. She hadn't needed to. He got the message, loud and clear. She'd loved the sex, she just didn't want all the stuff that went with having a sexual relationship. Or any relationship whatsoever.

He thought about proposing that they just set up a weekly sex-buddy meeting in the parked van behind her shop, suspecting he could have her on those terms if he wanted her.

He didn't want her on those terms.

"Hell, admit it, you want her on any terms," he muttered aloud as he walked out the back door of Santori's that night. He hadn't even realized anyone else was there until he saw his brother Joe, who'd just parked his pickup in one of the empty spots in the alley. Fortunately, Joe hadn't heard Nick talking to himself and so wasn't dialing for the rubber-walled wagon.

"Hey, where you off to?" Joe asked as he hopped out and pocketed his keys. "I was going to take you up on that pitcher you owe me."

"I'm not very good company right now," he admitted.

Joe, who was the best-natured of all of the Santori kids, threw his arm around Nick's shoulders. "Then what better time to share a beer with your brother?"

He had a point.

"Okay. But not here," he said, looking back at the closed door to the kitchen. "I really need someplace quiet."

Joe's smile faded and he immediately appeared concerned. "Everything okay? Is there a problem?"

"No problem. Just a case of family overdose."

"I hear ya. Come on, let's go across the street."

Following Joe into a neighborhood bar on the corner, Nick ordered a couple of beers and paid the tab. If Mark had been sitting across from him, Nick knew he'd be getting one-liners aimed at making him say what was on his mind. Lucas would be doing his prosecutor inquisition. Tony would throw his oldest-brother weight around and try to browbeat him into talking. Lottie would jabber so much Nick would say anything to get her to shut up.

Joe just watched. Listened. Waited.

"Thanks again for pointing me toward the job," Nick finally said, filling the silence. The bar was pretty empty—it was too early for the weekend regulars, who'd be drifting in for a long night of drinking and darts before too long.

"How's that going?"

"Pretty well. I've only worked the past two weekends but the money's good."

"You still haven't told the rest of the family?"

Nick shook his head. "Just Mark."

Joe nodded. "Probably just as well. I know Pop and Tony are talking nonstop about you coming in on the business."

Yeah, they had been to him, too. Nick couldn't prevent a quick frown. Because managing a pizzeria was not the way he saw himself spending the next six months, much less the rest of his life.

"It's okay, Nick. Nobody can force you to do anything you don't want to do."

"Guilt goes a long way," he muttered.

"Don't I know it. But guilt didn't stop you from enlisting. It didn't stop me from picking up a hammer and learning construction. Didn't stop Mark from strapping on a gun or Lottie from…well, from doing whatever it is Lottie does."

"Like marrying a man who killed someone?" Nick asked drily, still not having gotten used to the idea that his new brother-in-law, Simon, had killed a woman, even if in self-defense.

"Let's not go there," Joe said with a sigh. "She's happy, and he's crazy about her."

True. Lottie and Simon's recent marriage had contributed to the 95 percent marital success rate in the Santori family.

"The point is, you can live your life the way you want to live it, and nobody will try to stop you." As if realizing he'd left Nick with one major argument, he added, "Except for Mama's crying. Which we're all used to and you can get past. You just need to figure out what you want to do, and go after it."

Good idea. And lately, Nick *had* been figuring out what he wanted to do, especially since he'd been working at the club. "An old buddy of mine from the service is putting something together with a couple of the other guys. They're talking about opening up a protection business."

"Professional bodyguard?" Joe asked, looking surprised.

"I have the military background for it and I like what I'm doing at the club."

Joe smiled. "Especially when the people you're guarding are very easy on the eyes."

"Like you'd *ever* look at another woman."

The twinkle in his brother's eyes confirmed that. "Hey, I'm not *you*. You're the single one. Have you met anybody, uh…interesting?"

Nick felt heat rise up his neck. Because that was a loaded question. He had definitely felt interest in the Crimson Rose. But now that he'd had Izzie—tasted her, consumed her, made love to her—he knew he didn't want any other woman. But he couldn't very well explain that to Joe…without hinting about what had happened with Izzie. She'd never forgive him if that little tidbit became common knowledge. "I guess."

"Their star performer?" Joe sipped his beer. "I hear she's one of a kind."

Clearing his throat, Nick sprawled back in the booth. "She is that."

"Have there been any more problems with her?" Joe sounded only casually interested, but Nick's guard immediately went up.

"Problems?"

"Threats, freaks trying to grab her?"

Nick sat up straight. "No. What are you talking about?"

"Didn't Harry even tell you why he hired you?"

He had, but only in the most general terms. Nick didn't realize Rose had actually been threatened. "What do you know?"

"Just what the guys were whispering about when we were working at the club. That there had been a few incidents that had disturbed Harry and scared the dancers. Especially the featured one."

Harry Black had said almost nothing about any specific threats. Rose had said even less. Why would they hire him and then tie his hands by not giving him all the information he needed to do his job? He just didn't understand it. "Maybe whoever was causing the problems got caught and the threat has been eliminated," he murmured, speculating out loud. "Because I haven't gotten any kind of specific heads-up."

Joe kept his eyes on his beer, for some reason not looking Nick in the eye. Which made him wonder about his brother's interest in the stripper.

He immediately discounted any suspicion that Joe was interested in the woman for himself. He was married to the sexiest kindergarten teacher ever born, and he adored her and their baby daughter. Besides, of all the Santoris—who'd been raised to equate cheating with a mortal sin—Joe was the very last one who'd ever stray.

"Well, if I were you, I'd stick close to the featured attraction at Leather and Lace. I think she might be more of
a target than she or Harry would like to admit." Shaking
his head, Joe added, "There are some really sick guys out
there who like stalking vulnerable women."

Suddenly feeling on edge, Nick nodded, anxious to get
to the club and question Harry Black. He didn't particularly want to confront Rose—not alone, anyway—but one
thing was sure. He had been hired to do a job: protect her.
It was about time he stop letting his physical response to
the woman interfere with doing that job.

And it was well past time for him to stop letting his
feelings for Izzie Natale consume so much of his attention
that he didn't even *realize* a stalker might be threatening
someone he'd been hired to protect.

That had to end. Starting right now.

So it looked like Izzie was finally going to get what she
wanted. Him…out of her life.

"HEY, SOMEBODY SENT you flowers."

Izzie hesitated, her hand on the doorknob of her dressing room. One of the other dancers, a young blonde with
a sweet smile and a killer body, approached her. "They
were waiting on the stoop at the back entrance when I got
here. Had your name on the envelope. I put them in your
dressing room."

Izzie's first reaction was a tiny little thrill as the image
of Nick's handsome face filled her mind. But it quickly
dissipated. Nick had no idea she worked with him every
Saturday and Sunday night.

Damn good thing. Because if he found out now, after
she'd had such incredible sex with him, he was going to
be mad. More than mad—irate. Especially because of how
insistent she'd been that it was a one-shot deal.

Boy did she wish it didn't have to be a one-shot deal.

She still got shaky and shivery and weak and wet thinking of that amazing interlude in the van. It had been the most intensely sensual experience of her life.

But not to be repeated. Never.

Not as Izzie. Not even as the Crimson Rose. Because now that he'd had her naked in his arms, it was all too possible that he'd recognize her as Rose. Dancing and interacting with him at work was going to be difficult enough. If she let him get close—the way she'd invited him to that night in her dressing room—there was no way she'd be able to keep her secret.

So tell him the truth.

The idea had merit and Izzie knew it. Part of her truly wanted to—it wasn't easy maintaining a double life with no one to talk to about it. He'd listen—she knew he would. And she even suspected he wouldn't judge her about what she was doing. Given the things he'd said about feeling so hemmed in by his own family and their expectations, she thought he might even understand. A little.

But telling him—bringing him in to her alternate life— would mean involving him deeper in her real one. Each secret shared would be another rope tied to her body, holding her down, dragging her back into the world she'd fought so hard to escape.

If he knew she was Rose, there would be no reason they couldn't get more involved, at least at work. That, however—a secret, sordid affair conducted in dressing rooms and closets at Leather and Lace—wouldn't be enough for him. She knew it down to her very soul. He'd insinuate himself in her daily life, start tangling her in the ropes of a relationship, make her fall for him even harder... so he would be even harder to leave.

No. She could not tell him.

"Rose? Didja hear me?"

Realizing the other dancer was waiting expectantly for

her reaction to the flowers, Izzie nodded. "Yes, thanks, Leah."

"Not a problem. It was pick 'em up or trip over 'em," she said with a cheery smile. Without the stage makeup and the sequins, the young woman looked so fresh-faced and wholesome an average set of parents would have asked her to babysit.

She'd been the first of the dancers to befriend Izzie when she'd first taken the job at Leather and Lace. The others had been slower to warm up, especially Harry's wife, Delilah, who'd been the featured dancer up until a couple of years ago when she married her boss. Now she served as a sort of warden to the others...and hadn't liked that Izzie wasn't interested in her rules and regulations. She *especially* hadn't liked that she couldn't get her husband to order Izzie to listen to her...and that the Crimson Rose had become hugely popular.

The rest of them had all come around, though, especially since they had all started bringing home more money every weekend that she performed.

"How did you get into this, Leah?" she asked.

The girl shrugged. "Typical story. My parents divorced, father split out West somewhere. Mom remarried an asshole who tried to touch me after she'd passed out on their wedding night."

Izzie instinctively reached out and put her hand on the other woman's shoulder. "I'm sorry."

"Hey, I survived. Stabbed him in the wrist with a fork and took off. Never looked back."

"Do you..." She didn't know how to proceed without seeming judgmental. It just seemed so sad to think of this young woman making this, dancing at Leather and Lace, her only career goal. For Izzie, it was a part-time thrill to stay in shape and save her sanity. Some of the women here, however, saw no other future for themselves.

"What?"

"Do you think you'll do something else when you get tired of this?"

Leah nodded, her blond curls bouncing around her pretty heart-shaped face. "I got my GED last year and I'm taking college classes. I'm planning to be a nurse."

"Good for you."

Hearing footsteps upstairs, Izzie glanced at her watch. It was only six—a couple of hours before her first number. Usually Nick showed up later than this. But hearing the deep male voice from upstairs, she immediately stiffened.

"That's our sex-on-a-stick bodyguard I hear up there."

"Damn," Izzie muttered, immediately whirling around. "Stall him if he comes down the stairs, okay?"

"You still playing the 'nobody can see me' game with him?"

Izzie nodded. "I *don't* want him to see me. Please help me."

The woman offered her a big smile. "You got it…in exchange for one of those flowers your secret admirer sent you."

"I'll do you one better," Izzie said as she pushed open her dressing-room door. She grabbed the vase and thrust the bouquet at the young woman. "You can have all of them. Just don't let him near my door."

Either Leah was true to her word, or else Nick hadn't yet ventured downstairs. Whatever the case Izzie had privacy for the next twenty minutes. Long enough to get her hair extensions clipped in place and put her mask on. Only after she'd yanked it into position did she realize she'd forgotten her false eyelashes.

"Damn Harry for not giving me a lock," she muttered, glancing at the closed door. If she took the mask off to put her lashes on, she risked Nick walking in on her. No, he hadn't exactly gone out of his way to be alone with her as the Crimson Rose, but she couldn't count on her luck lasting forever.

Frowning at her reflection, she did a quick evaluation, wondering if she really needed the lashes. Her eyes had disappeared. She looked like the Marquis de Sade.

"Need the lashes," she muttered.

She'd been putting false lashes on her eyelids for years, she could probably do it…well, not blindfolded, but *masked.*

"Sure," she whispered as she bent toward the mirror. Grabbing one lash, she dabbed special glue on it, then carefully reached into the eyehole of her mask and applied it.

"One down," she said as she blinked rapidly, pretty proud of herself.

The second one was a little trickier, mainly because it was hard to see out of the first heavily lashed eye. But she managed it. And a moment later, when she heard voices in the hall, she was very glad she hadn't taken the chance and removed the mask.

"Hey, Nick, how's it shakin', baby?" a woman's voice said. Loudly.

Bless you, Leah.

"I need to talk to Rose." He cleared his throat. "I mean, I need to talk to all of you, *and* Rose."

Huh. Still too chicken to see her alone.

She quickly squelched the thought. That man had the most incredible, powerful body she'd ever seen in her life. He was afraid of nothing.

Besides, refusing to see her alone was exactly what she needed him to do. Even if it wasn't what she *wanted* him to do.

Tightening the sash on her robe, she reached for the doorknob and opened the door. Nick's immediately looked over, stiffening when he saw her there.

He *so* didn't want to be attracted to her, his expression said it all. Knowing he didn't want anyone else made Izzie, the baker he'd made such incredible love to a few days ago, amazingly happy.

"I need to talk to you, and all the other girls, in the greenroom for a few minutes," he said. Without waiting to see if she was coming, he spun around and walked toward it.

Shrugging, Leah followed. So did Izzie. Once they were inside, Izzie realized all the other dancers—nine or ten of them—were already present, including Delilah with her two-foot-tall pile of red hair on top of her head and three inches of makeup on her face.

In varying states of undress, all the other dancers practically licked their lips when Nick walked into the room. She couldn't blame them. In his tough/bodyguard mode, he looked incredibly hot. Gone was any trace of the sweetheart who'd helped her deliver baked goods. Or the sensual lover who'd given her more orgasms in one lovemaking session than she'd had in entire previous relationships.

In their place was a frowning—scowling almost—man, dressed all in black, looking not only menacing but dangerous. And absolutely delicious.

"I asked you all in here to discuss your security."

"Let's discuss your ass," one of the dancers cracked.

"I'd rather talk about his shoulders."

"I vote for his co…"

"Ladies," another voice said as Harry entered the room. Rolling his eyes, he gave Nick an apologetic look. "Please go ahead, Nick."

Nick got right back on track, hitting them all over the head with the need for tighter security around the place. Though he was talking to everyone, he looked at Izzie so often, she knew she was the one on his mind.

There wasn't any reason to single her out. Well, not *much* reason. Yes, she'd had a few persistent customers.

One guy had lunged at her on the stage a few weeks back. Another had burst into her dressing room. And there'd been a few parking-lot lurkers who'd been chased away by one of the bouncers, Bernie, who'd been watching out for her since her first night. Long before Nick had come on the scene.

In this job, she'd expect nothing else. But Nick was relentless in his lecturing. He kept on about how they all needed to look out for one another, report anything suspicious. Yadda yadda. Izzie zoned out somewhere between "drive a different route home from work every night" and "have a buddy when you go to the restroom."

That one did spark an "I'll be your bathroom buddy, Nick" from one of the girls, a glare from Delilah and another long-suffering sigh from Harry.

Finally, though, the meeting broke up and the other dancers raced to finish getting ready. Izzie quickly ducked out of the room, hoping Nick wouldn't see her. She'd gotten about ten steps from her dressing room when she realized he'd followed.

"Rose, wait a minute."

She froze, but didn't turn around.

"I'm particularly concerned about you. The 'who's behind the mask' element puts you at higher risk. Some whack job might decide to try to find out for himself."

She glanced over her shoulder. "Thanks for the warning." *Now go away.*

Before she could look away again, she saw a dark frown pull at Nick's handsome face. "What in the hell?" he muttered, staring at her face.

Fearing he'd recognized her, she quickly lifted her hands to ensure her mask was still in place. It felt okay—but Nick was still staring at her, blinking in confusion.

"What?" she snapped. Remembering at the last minute that she needed to lower her voice to the sultry whisper he'd grown familiar with, she rephrased. "Is something wrong?"

He reached for her. Izzie immediately lurched back, almost tripping over her own feet. If she hadn't backed herself up against the wall, she would have.

"Careful," he muttered, still frowning. "It wouldn't look good on my résumé if somebody I'm supposed to be guarding trips and breaks her neck."

Right. He needed to guard her.

Not look at her. Not watch her. Not batter at her defenses with every flex of that body, every whiff of his spicy scent that filled her head whenever he was near.

God, this was hard. So much harder than it had been last weekend, when she hadn't *had* him. When she didn't know what he was capable of.

"You have something on your...it's..."

Shrugging uncomfortably, he reached for her again. This time, she stayed still. At least until he yanked at her eyelashes hard enough to jerk her eyelid off her face. "Ouch!" she yelped, slapping his hand away.

His hand was still stuck to the lashes so when she smacked him, she only ended up hurting herself more. As his hand flew away, he took the lashes with him, ripping them off her lid.

"I thought it was a bug," he said with an uncomfortable grimace.

She yanked her false eyelashes out of his fingers. "A *bug*? You thought I had a bug on my face?"

"It's not like you'd be able to tell if you did with that stupid mask on. Why do you wear it when you're not on-stage, anyway?"

Oh, boy. A question she definitely couldn't answer.

"You don't have to keep up this mysterious-woman act for the staff, do you? So why not take it off and take a deep breath?" Swiping a frustrated hand through his short spiky hair, he added, "Or at least put your damn false eyelashes on more securely?"

She almost growled in annoyance. *He* was the reason she'd had to put the lashes on through the eyehole in the mask. "I want a lock on my dressing-room door," she whispered harshly.

He glanced at the knob. "You don't have one?"

"No." Thinking quickly, she added, "And that's one reason I keep the mask on all the time. I have no place to go for complete privacy. A reporter who did an article on the club a few weeks ago came creeping around down here one day, trying to get a picture of the real me."

Nick moved in close, towering over her, burning her with his heat. Putting his hands on the wall on either side of her, he trapped her in. "Who is he?"

Izzie nibbled her lip, trying with every ounce of her strength not to throw her arms around his shoulders and her legs around his waist. Or to shove him away so he'd stop looking searchingly at her, seeing her eyes…how could he not recognize her eyes? How could he be this close and not know the smell of her body?

It was good that he didn't, she knew that. But it was also starting to tick her off.

"Just some reporter," she murmured.

"Have you had any problems with him since?"

"No, he hasn't been around since the story came out. Would you relax?"

"You tell me if you see him." Then, staring hard at her, he slowly pulled back, releasing her from the prison of his arms. An odd look appeared on his face, as if he'd suddenly realized just how close they'd been and wasn't happy at himself for it. Clearing his throat, he added, "I'm sorry I hurt your eye."

"It's all right." Slipping away from him, she headed again to her door, relieved to have escaped his scrutiny.

Good thing he'd let her go, because the longer he stayed so close to her, the more angry she was going to get that he didn't know her.

Especially because a mask would never prevent *her* from knowing *him*.

Huh. Men. So painfully unobservant.

"I hope you're taking me seriously," he said, that gruff, no-nonsense tone returning to his voice, his apology obviously done.

"I am, I am." She practically bit the words out from between her clenched teeth, ready to smack him if he didn't shut up and let her go get herself back under control. And fix her eyelashes.

"No more running out to your car alone to get something you forgot."

"Yes, your majesty."

"No more coming back upstairs and mingling close to closing time."

She seldom did that, anyway. Whirling around, she offered him a sharp salute, and snapped, "Got it, chief." Then, determined not to listen to another word, she spun on her heel and strode into her dressing room, slamming the door shut behind her.

It was only after she'd shut him out that Izzie realized how *stupid* she'd just been. Nick had annoyed her so much—both because of his overbearing protective bodyguard schtick and his inability to see what was right in front of his face—that she'd completely forgotten her role in this. The role she played as the Crimson Rose.

Because during those last three words, when anger had overtaken common sense, she'd forgotten to speak in her sexy, husky voice.

She'd been pure, 100 percent Izzie.

7

LEATHER AND LACE employed a few burly bouncers to watch the doors and to stand in the back of the crowd during the show. Their presence was mainly to inspire intimidation to keep the audience on its best behavior. And they did their job well, especially the tallest one, Bernie, whose beefy build concealed a guy with a deep belly laugh and a good sense of humor.

Nick, however, wasn't technically one of them. His job involved more than rousting out rowdy drinkers or breaking up any fights. He was there to make sure nobody touched the dancers. Especially Rose. And the bouncers were his backup.

He typically moved around during the performances—sometimes in the audience, sometimes backstage, sometimes downstairs. He kept a low profile, his eyes always scanning the crowd, looking for the first sign of trouble.

Tonight, he was standing close to the dance floor, in a shadowy corner just left of the stage. He couldn't say why. It wasn't as if he expected anyone in the front row to leap up and try to grab Rose or one of the others. Yes, it'd happened. But usually not until at least the second set, late in the night, when the patrons had consumed more than a few fifteen-dollar shots of top-shelf whiskey. And when they'd forgotten how big the bouncers were or how stupid they were going to feel having to call their wives to get bailed out of jail.

Tonight, Nick was close to the stage because he wanted to watch *her*.

Something had happened earlier, something that was still driving him crazy. Oh, she drove him crazy in any number of ways, already—mainly because of that blatant sexuality oozing off the woman. But this didn't have anything to do with her attractiveness, or Nick's reaction to it.

It was something else. Something he couldn't define. Ever since he and Rose had exchanged words outside her dressing room, a voice had been whispering in his head that there was something he wasn't seeing. Some truth he had overlooked.

He had replayed their entire conversation, thinking about every word, wondering what had seemed so *off* with it. Aside from her being such a smart-ass about the self-protection tips he'd asked her to follow, they hadn't been confrontational. Hadn't been unpleasant in any way, other than when he'd accidentally almost ripped her eyelid off.

So why are you so tense?

Good question. He was wound as tight as a ball of rubber bands, his jaw flexing, his hands clenching. His heart wasn't maintaining its usual pace, it was rushed, as if adrenaline had flooded his body.

When they introduced her, something *did* flood his body. Heated awareness. Maybe adrenaline, too.

She didn't spot him when she started, and from here Nick had a perfect view of every move she made. She was using the pole tonight, taking advantage of it to showcase her strength and flexibility. Not to mention inviting every man in the audience to imagine being the one she was writhing against, the one cupped between her incredibly long legs.

He tensed, then thrust away the flash of jealousy. It was none of his business what Rose did—in her professional life or in her personal one.

She'd begun removing her petals now, they fluttered onto the stage, one even wafting so close it was only about a foot away from Nick's corner position. Something made him step closer, to reach for it. Whether to give it back to her, or to save it as a souvenir, he couldn't say. Fingering it lightly, he stuck it in his pocket and kept watching.

When this close, he had a very good view of the Crimson Rose…a view of a trim waist made for his hands. Of supple legs he could almost feel wrapped around his hips. Of slender fingers that had tangled easily in his hair. A delicate throat for nibbling. Lush round breasts for cupping. And when she removed the petals covering those breasts, his mouth flooded at the image of sucking on those dark, pebbled nipples.

Every bit of her was familiar…to his eyes, and to the rest of his body. He knew what it would be like to taste her, to touch her, to hear her soft little moans of pleasure.

To hear her…

Her voice. That *voice*. That body.

"Oh, my God," he whispered, certain he'd lost his mind but unable to chase the thought away. Because as he watched the performer disappear behind the curtain after her dance, he saw a face behind that mask. A face he saw in his dreams every night.

Izzie's face.

"It can't be," he mumbled, staggering back into the shadow. He hit the wall in the corner and slid down it, bending over so his hands landed on his knees. Sucking in a few deep breaths, he kept his head down, thinking over everything he knew about Izzie Natale. And about the Crimson Rose.

She'd taken dance lessons throughout her childhood,

he remembered that. She'd gone to New York to become a performer. On the stage. She hadn't exactly said she'd been an actress.

My God, had she been a stripper at some high-end Manhattan club? And when she'd been forced to return to Chicago after her father's stroke, had she taken up the same profession here—wearing a mask so she wouldn't possibly be recognized?

Their bodies were so alike—how could he not have seen it before? Then again, he had never seen Izzie naked before, until two nights ago, so he couldn't possibly have known that her legs were as long and supple as a dancer's. That her hips were full enough to make a man hard just at the thought of getting his hands on them. That her breasts were big, high and inviting.

She'd hidden a lot behind the apron. So much that he hadn't registered that Izzie and Rose were the same height, had the same builds. Or that their hair was close in color—the length of Rose's obviously caused by some kind of hairpiece or wig.

Now it registered. But it still seemed impossible. Absolutely unbelievable that cute little Izzie, Gloria's baby sister…the girl who'd crushed the cookies for God's sake…was the woman driving men all over Chicago insane with lust.

Including him. *Especially* him.

At that moment, he knew it was true. He'd been reacting to Rose and to Izzie the very same way from the moment he'd seen each of them. With pure, undiluted want based on absolutely nothing but instinct and chemistry.

They were the same. His body had known that immediately. His brain had finally caught up.

Somehow, he managed to stay on the sidelines and finish doing his job throughout the long night until the club closed at 2:00 a.m. He stayed upstairs, sending one of the other guys down every so often to do a sweep outside the dressing rooms. He didn't trust himself to go down there and confront her yet.

If he did, it might get loud. And neither one of them might be ready to go back to work after they had the blow-out fight Nick suspected they were going to have.

It was definitely going to be a blowout, and probably not for the reasons Izzie would suspect. Yeah, it bothered him that his sister-in-law's kid sister was working as a stripper. But he was no prude, nor was he judgmental. He'd seen her act…she was not only good, she was damn good.

As someone who was—and might again be—Izzie's lover, he was not happy. Couldn't deny that. But again, not so much because of other men looking at her, but more because she was working in a very risky field. Putting herself in danger.

The real reason he was fuming was because she'd lied to him. She'd been deceitful, letting him chase after Izzie by day while Rose pursued *him* by night. The woman had nearly sent him out of his mind—for what? Some twisted game? A power trip?

He didn't know. He just knew he wanted answers. And when the club finally shut down and everyone began to drift away, he walked downstairs, determined to get them.

Nick knew she hadn't left yet, he'd been watching her car in the parking lot, which was emptying as everyone departed for the night. She usually left much earlier—since her last number took place around midnight. And it didn't take her long to get ready since she didn't bother taking her mask off before getting into her car and roaring away. Obviously for his benefit.

But she was still here. So he could only assume one thing: she was waiting in her dressing room, either hiding in the hopes that he'd leave first, or preparing herself for his arrival.

Because she had to know he'd figured her out. All she'd have had to do was look out at him in the audience during her second set and see the steam pouring out of his head. And the fire burning out of his eyeballs.

Reaching her closed door, he remembering she'd said it had no lock. He gave her a one-knock warning, then entered without waiting for an invitation. It wasn't like she had anything to hide…he'd seen her body, both as Izzie and as Rose.

"What do you think you're doing?" she asked, staring at him from across the room, where she'd been slipping a jacket on. She was dressed casually, in a loose, comfortable-looking pair of baggy pants and a tank top. If she hadn't been wearing the mask, she'd have looked just like the girl next door.

Like Izzie.

God, what a blind idiot he was not to have seen it before. The eyes were the same—though "Rose's" were shadowed by the mask. Those lips couldn't be denied. The shape of her jaw, the length of her neck. Everything about the Crimson Rose was Izzie under a sexy microscope. Everything about Izzie was the Crimson Rose in nice-girl trappings.

"What do you want, Nick?"

"You're here late," he murmured, stepping inside and shutting the door behind him.

"Um, yes, I guess so," she replied.

"You don't usually stay until closing time."

She tilted her head back, her chin up, displaying outright bravado. She was going to try to bluff her way through this, since she couldn't be certain she'd been busted. "One of the other dancers got sick and had to leave. I wasn't sure if Harry would need me to cover for her."

He hadn't. Nick knew that much. If he'd had to watch "Rose" in a third performance on the stage, he would have lost it. He didn't know that he'd have been able to keep himself from going up there and confronting her right in front of the audience.

She fell silent, just watching him. Waiting. Nick said nothing, not giving himself away yet. He wanted to see what she'd do. How far Izzie would go to maintain her secret.

God, it killed him that she didn't trust him. He had no illusions about why she'd put that mask on her face in the beginning. Her parents would be upset if they found out. He could even see why she'd kept quiet the first couple of times he'd worked here—before she knew she could trust him.

But now he was her lover. She'd trusted him with her body. She *should* have trusted him with her secret.

"Well," she said, "I guess it's time to go."

"So soon?" he murmured, leaning back against the closed door, blocking her escape. He crossed his arms and stared. "But this is the first time we've been alone in quite a while."

She licked her lips nervously. Nick almost felt that moist tongue on his own mouth and had to force himself to stay cool.

"It's late."

"I know. It's also nearly deserted. You and I might be the very last ones here," he said. Watching her closely, he saw the way she gulped as that truth dawned on her. They were practically alone in this big building. No one would hear if she decided to shout for help.

As if Nick would ever *hurt* her. He'd sooner cut off his own arm. That didn't mean, however, that he didn't intend to torment her just as much as he possibly could.

She was nervous, quivering, her whole body in minis-cule motion. And he knew why. He *could* just put her out of her misery and confront her on her deception, but some-thing made him string her along a little more. Maybe it was the way she'd been stringing him along. Maybe it was just because he liked seeing the wild flutter of her pulse in her neck. Plus hearing the choppy, audible breaths she couldn't contain.

He liked having her at a disadvantage for once. He also knew how to put her at more of one.

"So, Rose," he said, finally straightening and stepping closer, "about our very first conversation?"

She slid back, trying to increase the space between them again, but couldn't go far before hitting the folding screen. Nick pressed closer, relentless in his silent, stalking approach. "I've been giving it a lot of thought."

"You have?" she whispered. "I haven't been, not at all."

What a liar. "Really? Because I think by the way you watch me, you've been thinking about it a lot." Lifting an arm, he put it on the top of the screen, blocking her with his body. They were close enough for him to feel the brush of her pants.

"I need to go."

"I need you to stay." Tracing the soft line of her neck with the tip of one finger, he added, "I've changed my mind about your invitation."

Her mouth opened. "You don't mean…"

He tipped her mouth closed, sliding his thumb across her bottom lip. That juicy, full lip he had tasted the other night and wanted to lightly bite now. "You're very attractive, Rose."

"But…"

"I can't take my eyes off you."

Though she sighed at his touch, her soft body also stiffened. Her fists curled. She obviously didn't know whether to melt or erupt. It was all he could do not to laugh.

"You were so dead-set against it," she said in that hot whisper. "Why now?"

"Men can change their minds, too. You're all I've been thinking about for weeks."

The fists rose to her hips. The sultriness disappeared. She looked indignant, verging on angry. "Oh, yeah?"

"Most definitely." He dropped a hand onto her shoulder, feeling the flexing of her muscles. He kneaded it softly, easing away the angry tension, knowing he was only going to build it back up again. "I want to touch you, everywhere."

She shook under his hand.

"Want to taste you." Knowing how to make the top of her head blow off, both with lust and with fury, he leaned close. Moving his mouth to the side of her neck, he placed an openmouthed kiss at her nape, licking lightly at her skin, flavored the tiniest bit with salt from her energetic dancing. "Aww, Rose, do you know what I want to do to you?"

She just whimpered, not saying a word.

"I'd like to smear something luscious and sticky all over you, then lick it from every sweet crevice of your body."

That did it. Izzie/Rose shook off her half hungry, half worried daze and reacted with gut fury. She lifted one of those fists and whammed it toward his face. If Nick hadn't been prepared for it, he might have been caught in the jaw. As it was, he deflected the blow by grabbing her hand in midair.

He didn't let go, holding her tightly as she struggled to pull away. "Damn you, Nick Santori," she spat out, completely forgetting her sultry whisper.

"What's the matter, sweetheart," he snapped back, "you afraid to get a little oral?" Sliding an arm around her shoulders, still gripping her first, he added, "Or do you just like to *give* it rather than *get* it?"

"Put *anything* in my mouth and I'll bite it off."

"Oooh, rough. I like it." Tracing the opening in the

velvety fabric with his finger, he added, "I couldn't *fit* anything in your mouth with that thing on your face. Especially not my cock, *as you well know*." He pressed hard against her, pushing her back against the wall, grinding into her. Because while her actions and her continued deceptions drove him crazy with anger, her nearness was driving him crazy with lust.

He was rock hard for her, raging with need.

She whimpered and stopped wriggling for a second, her hips bucking toward his in response—once, then again. She lifted one leg slightly, tilting her pelvis so his bulge hit her in the spot she most needed it to. "Oh, God," she mumbled, "I get the point, you've got a lot to offer."

She'd whispered that, calming herself down, and Nick almost groaned at her determination.

She *still* hadn't quite let herself believe it had already gone too far, that her masquerade was over. Izzie had lost her temper at the thought that he'd play the same sexy, wicked games with another woman that he'd played with her the other night in the van. And she'd reacted with honest—if momentary—fury.

Now, having realized it, she was almost desperate to convince herself she could salvage the situation. She was hoping he *hadn't* been talking to Izzie, who knew firsthand what he had to give her since she'd taken him into her body the other night. And that he was instead talking to Rose, who was right now feeling the size of his cock as it pressed against her.

Bending to the side, he grasped her bent leg, gripping her thigh to tug her up for a better fit. She groaned as their bodies came together more intimately. He could feel the heat of her—her moisture—through her thin pants and his own. She was wet and aroused, flushed and ready.

Yet still too damn stubborn to whip off the mask and take him on open, honest terms.

"So you ready to play those kinds of games?" he muttered as he rocked against her, inhaling her little cries of pleasure.

"I don't like to be manhandled," she muttered through hoarse breaths. The excited pulse in her throat and the desperate tone in her voice made a lie of that statement. She liked it. A lot.

He bit lightly on her bottom lip. "Yes, you do."

She started to shake her head, but he kissed her, thrusting his tongue against hers, loving the silky feel of her mouth almost as much as he hated the scrape of the mask against his cheek. That mask was what finally brought him back to his senses. He didn't want the masked woman, he wanted the real one. The one who trusted him and exhibited honesty. And guts.

He'd had enough. Enough of the lying, enough of the deception. Even enough of tormenting her.

So he dropped her leg. "I think we're done."

She sagged back against the wall. Even with the mask he could see the way her eyes widened with shock. And hurt. *"What?"*

It wasn't easy to stay back, keep his hands off her, ignore the heat in the small room and the overwhelming smell of sexual want filling his head. But he did it. "I changed my mind."

Turning his back to her, he took one step toward the door. Then he heard her whisper, "You son of a bitch, you *do* know."

He put his hand on the knob. Glancing over his shoulder to meet her stare, he frowned and sighed. "Yeah, Izzie. I do."

Then he walked out.

FOR THE FIRST TIME in the nearly three months that she'd worked at Leather and Lace, Izzie called in sick Sunday night. She told herself she was a coward ten times over. But that didn't change the way she felt.

She couldn't face him. Not after what had happened in her dressing room Saturday night.

His anger had been undeniable. His revenge understandable.

But it was his *hurt*—that glimpse of sadness on his face as he'd looked at her over his shoulder before walking out the door—that had been the real punch in the gut.

He'd been pursuing her relentlessly for weeks and had finally caught her that night in the van. He'd been nothing but honest about what he was going through—with his family, his life, his attraction to her.

And she'd been lying to him from the first moment. Lying about her secret job, lying about her feelings for him. Lying about what she really wanted.

Hell, she'd even been lying to *herself* about those last two. She'd been denying her feelings for him though they had existed for as long as she could remember. And she'd pretended she wasn't dying for him physically when the thought consumed her every waking moment.

Even her parents had zoned right in on her mood when she'd gone to visit them Sunday. She'd tried so hard to paste on a smile, especially around her father, who was just now starting to seem like his old self. But her mother had immediately noticed something was wrong and had questioned her about it.

She'd covered…promising everything was fine.

One more lie to add to her list. She was becoming quite adept at it. And frankly, she hated herself for that.

"You deserve to feel this way," she told herself as she sat in the closed bakery a few evenings later. It was her quiet time again, when the café staff had left for the day but the evening kitchen and delivery help hadn't arrived. She was sipping a big, fattening cappuccino laden not only with whipped cream but a swirl of caramel. Feeling like absolute scum.

"Iz?" a voice called. A female one.

Turning on her stool, she saw her cousin, Bridget, enter through the employees' entrance in the back.

"Hey," Izzie mumbled.

"I've been calling."

"I don't usually answer the phone after hours."

Bridget frowned. "I mean your cell phone."

"Turned off." Izzie blew on the steaming coffee drink. "There's more if you want to make yourself one."

Bridget looked longingly at the mug and fresh whipped cream and got to work. She remained quiet as she did it, but Izzie saw the worried sidelong glances her cousin cast her way.

When Bridget had finished—topping her hot drink with a sprinkle of cinnamon—she took a seat on the opposite side of the counter. "You look like hell. You haven't been sleeping."

"Thanks. And you're right. I haven't been."

Bridget sighed. "Me, neither."

Finally looking seriously at her cousin, she saw the dark circles under her pretty eyes and the droop of her normally smiling mouth. It was an unusual combination. Bridget was not the cheerful, constantly giddy sort, but she was always quietly happy. And her face reflected that.

Not today, though. "What's wrong?"

"I hate men."

"I hear ya," Izzie mumbled, though her heart wasn't in it. She didn't hate Nick, not at all. She just hated that look of disappointment on his face. Hated how it made her feel.

Low. Rotten.

Yes, she'd had a reason to keep her identity hidden from most of the world. But once she'd let Nick lay her down in the back of that van and do things to her that would cause a real good little Catholic girl to faint of shock, all masks should have been torn away.

"I don't understand them."

Sensing her cousin was talking about one man in particular, Izzie set aside her own emotional misery. "What's going on?"

"It's that guy at work I mentioned a few weeks ago. Dean."

"The new salesman?"

Bridget nodded. "I finally met him for coffee one day, kind of figuring it was our first date. But obviously I totally misread him. He made it clear he was just interested in getting to know a coworker. And he hasn't asked me out again."

Izzie frowned, disliking the look of unhappiness on Bridget's face. "Have you made it clear you're interested?"

"I went out with him, didn't I?"

"Yes, but did you make it *clear* that you were looking at him as more than just a coworker?"

"How was I supposed to do that?"

"I don't know—flirting, smiling, brushing up against him. All the typical weapons of the female romantic arsenal."

"I...don't suppose I did. We talked mostly about business...at least when I wasn't griping about my landlord."

"So, he might not even know you're interested in him *that* way. Which means, you need to let him know, then figure out if he gave you the brush or retreated out of self-preservation."

Bridget blinked. "Self-preservation?"

"Some men won't make a move on a woman unless they're sure she's interested. It takes a lot of self-confidence."

Self-confidence like Nick's. It had taken a boatload of

it for him to keep pursuing her when she'd kept turning him down.

"Is that what *you* would do? Make it more obvious?"

"Yeah. I would."

Her cousin mumbled something, then cleared her throat. "You know, I'd think you're right. But there's something about Dean that makes me think he's not quite as nice and shy as he seems."

Izzie instantly stiffened. "Has he done anything to you?"

"*Done?* Oh, goodness, no. He's barely looked at me since the day we went out. But there have been one or two times when I've caught him staring at me—with this, oh, God, it sounds so stupid, but I'd swear he looks almost *hungrily* at me when he thinks I'm not looking."

"Hungry's good. If it's coming from someone you *want* to want you." Not just a roomful of horny men turned on by a naked dancer. Her audience sometimes annoyed the hell out of her. Sometimes it seemed like dancing naked alone would be better than dancing naked in front of a crowd. Of course, she wouldn't get *paid* for that. A definite drawback.

"Not if he constantly hides it. And there's more, he sometimes just comes across so much harder—tougher— than this nice, quiet, soft-spoken salesman. It's almost like he's trying really hard to be on his best behavior."

Izzie didn't like the sound of that. Guys who tried that hard to be on their *best* behavior had to be pretty *bad* during their not-quite-best behavior. She said as much to her cousin, but Bridget waved away her concerns.

Though they talked a little while longer, Izzie couldn't keep her mind on anything. Her cousin noticed her distraction and tried to get her to talk about it, but she wasn't ready to.

It wasn't that she didn't trust Bridget to keep her secret. Or that she feared her cousin would be shocked by it. But the truth was, it didn't seem right for Bridget to be the one she talked to about this. Not when Nick was the first one who'd realized what she was doing on Saturday and Sunday nights.

She wanted to talk to him.

She wanted him. Period.

She just didn't know if it was too late to get him. Judging by the way he'd slammed out of her dressing room Saturday night, she greatly feared it was.

IT TOOK EVERY OUNCE of willpower Nick possessed to avoid going into Natale's Bakery that week. Something inside him insisted that he go up there and confront Izzie now that he felt at least moderately calm. Unlike the way he'd felt Saturday night at the club.

Something else demanded that he stay away, let her figure out what the hell it was she wanted from him and clue him in when she was ready. Maybe he'd accommodate her. Maybe he wouldn't. It depended entirely upon what she wanted: Him in her life, him out of her life? A secret affair, or a public one? A lover…a friend?

There were a lot of different possibilities. He honestly wasn't sure which he was most hoping for. The only thing he knew he wanted was for Izzie to come clean with him about everything. Then they could figure out the rest.

He assumed it would take a while. Considering she'd called in sick from work Sunday night, he had the feeling she was going to avoid the confrontation for as long as possible. But, unless she quit working at the club, she wasn't going to be able to avoid him forever.

Quit working at the club. He couldn't deny that his first reaction had been to want her to.

He didn't want other men looking at Izzie. He didn't want other men fantasizing about her. And he most certainly didn't want anyone getting fixated on her…fixated enough to stalk her, threaten her or hurt her.

Once he'd calmed down, though, he realized he understood exactly why she'd gone to work at Leather and Lace. It was probably for the same reasons *he'd* gone to work there.

She was every bit as out of her element in this old-new environment as he was. Fitting in about as well as he did.

Fitting in…hell, what he was doing right now was proof he didn't fit in. It was Thursday night and he was holding a brown paper bag clutched to his side. Walking to his building, his eyes scanned side to side in the hope that he didn't bump into his parents or another elderly relative who'd rat him out.

Chinese carry-out was probably grounds for his mother to call for an exorcism. Especially since he'd refused yet another doggy bag full of calzones and Pop's lasagna tonight. If he bit another piece of pasta, he was going to explode like the giant marshmallow man in *Ghostbusters*.

"Tough," he muttered, his mouth watering for the kung pao chicken he could smell from the bag. Not to mention the egg rolls, fried rice…he'd bought enough to feed an army.

Nick knew a little something about clandestine missions. Enough to know that when you were on one, you accomplished as much as you could the first time, in the hopes that you could delay going back. And a big bag of food meant leftovers. Enough to last a week or so, meaning no more dangerous, secret excursions to Mr. Wu's for a while.

Unless, of course, he had unexpected company for dinner. Female company. Like the female standing right outside his apartment door, her hand lifted to knock.

"Izzie?" he mumbled as soon as he stepped off the elevator, wondering not only how she'd gotten into the building, but also how she'd found out where he lived.

She whirled around, her eyes wide and bright. She hadn't knocked yet, which meant she hadn't quite prepared herself to face him. He'd caught her off guard.

Nick tried not to wonder what this meant, tried to remain casual. Tried not to notice how curvy and inviting her body looked in her tight tank top and sexy short skirt.

It would be like not noticing an earthquake shaking your house down around you. She was just too beautiful to ignore.

As they continued to stare, he finally murmured, "Hi."

"Hi."

They said nothing else for a moment. Long enough for him to notice the smudges of shadow beneath her pretty brown eyes and the paleness in her cheeks. She was practically biting a hole in her bottom lip as she tried to figure out what to say.

He couldn't help taking pity on her…at least taking pity on that gorgeous lip before she bit a hole right through it. Shifting his bag to his other hip, he walked to the door and lifted his keys to the lock. "You hungry?"

She glanced at the bag. "No pizza?"

"Nope. I've got egg foo young, lo mein, couple of different chicken dishes, you name it."

"Oh, God, feed me," she exclaimed, following him into the apartment with a smile on her face.

Once inside, she tossed her purse onto his couch, a large one that dominated the small living area of the very small apartment. He didn't mind—compared to sharing a barracks with twenty other guys, this was pure luxury. He'd picked the place because it was clean and high, with a great view of the college a few blocks away. And he'd barely started furnishing it, figuring he'd get the most important things first.

Big comfortable reclining leather couch. Big TV for watching football. He could live for a while on that…plus the huge comfortable bed dominating his bedroom.

A flow of warmth washed through him at the thought of that bed. He'd imagined Izzie in it many times. He'd *dreamed* of her in it many times.

Now, here she was. So close he could smell her perfume and hear her breaths. Like a fantasy come to life.

"Minimalist, huh?" she asked as she stared pointedly at the couch and the big-screen TV.

"I'm working on it."

He couldn't believe how normal they sounded. Like two old friends getting together for dinner. Considering the last two times they'd been alone they'd been either fighting or practically ripping each other's clothes off, he figured that was a pretty good trick.

"I, uh, wanted to…"

"Save it," he muttered, not wanting to start their discussion yet. "I'm hungry. Let's eat first."

Relief washed over her pretty face as she followed him into the kitchen. When she lifted something up onto the counter, he realized she hadn't come empty-handed.

"Peace offering." She pointed toward a six-pack of beer.

"Are we at war?" he asked, repeating a question she'd once asked him.

"We've been doing a lot of battling."

Yes, they had. And he, for one, was tired of it.

Getting some bowls, plates and silverware, he spread all the food out on his small kitchen table, and they each loaded up, smorgasbord style. "Where…"

"Do you mind the floor?" he asked.

Shrugging, she followed him into the living room, watching as he sat down in front of the sofa, stretching his legs out in front of him, with his plate on his lap. It wasn't quite as easy for her, since she wore a skirt.

Nick forced himself to focus on his food, not on her long, sexy legs so close to his on the floor. Picking up the TV remote, he flicked the power button, then channeled up to a station playing soft music. It was background noise, filling the silence that grew thicker as they ate…as they drew closer to the conversation they both knew they were about to have.

When they'd finished, he took their plates into the kitchen. She followed, working on putting away the food. Within a few moments, there was nothing left to do—no dinner to eat, no dishes to clean—nothing to do but face each other.

"I don't want to do this," he said, surprising them both.

"Do what?"

"Fight with you. Do battle. Whatever you want to call it."

She shook her head. "I don't want to, either. But I need to tell you… I need to get this out."

Crossing his arms, he leaned back against the kitchen counter and waited. "Okay."

She closed her eyes, then spoke in a rush. "I'm sorry I was dishonest with you about being the Crimson Rose. At first, I didn't trust you—didn't trust *anyone*. I'm sure you know that my parents wouldn't be happy about what I'm doing, and I don't want to do anything to add to my father's health problems."

"I understand that." He did. It made perfect sense for her to go incognito at her risqué job. "But once you and I…"

"I know." She raked a hand through her brown hair, which was loose around her shoulders tonight, rather than up in its usual ponytail. "I should have told you immediately. Instead I panicked and pushed you away."

"Yeah. I gotta say, I felt pretty damn humiliated when I figured it out. I should have known you."

"I *am* a performer. I know about portraying someone else."

"About that…when did you start in this line of work?"

"Stripping's not my line of work. Dancing is. I was with the Rockettes until a year ago."

"You were one of those kick-line chicks?"

She glared at him. "It's harder than it looks."

"Right. Tough life dancing with giant nutcrackers and Santa Claus." He quickly put his hand up. "I'm joking. You must have been damn good to make it."

"I was," she said with complete confidence. "But I got bored with it and went with a modern-dance company in Manhattan. Then came the injury. Then came Dad's stroke. Now I'm here."

Her life in a nutshell.

"And now what?" he asked, knowing that was the question he really wanted answered. Where was she going from here? Where did she see him fitting into that?

"I don't know. Right now I'm biding time, trying to figure out what I want." Her jaw tightening, she continued. "But it's not the bakery, and it's not the neighborhood. It's not Gloria's life—a repeat of my mother's. And it's not my sister Mia's life as a hard-ass lawyer with tons of drive and no happiness."

"I understand," he murmured.

Nodding, she said, "I'm sure you do. If anyone would, it's you." The tension easing from her shoulders, Izzie walked across the small kitchen, covering the distance between them in a few short steps. Putting her hand on his chest, she looked up at him, her eyes bright. "Which is why I have to repeat this—I am sorry, Nick. Please say you'll forgive me."

He hesitated, then offered her a short nod. Appearing relieved, she began to pull her hand away, but he covered it with his, not letting her go. "Where do *we* go from here?"

She hesitated, so he pressed her. "We can't be just friends."

"We can't be a couple."

Their eyes locked. They both said the same four words at exactly the same moment. "We can be lovers."

Nick chuckled as Izzie smiled. Tightening her fingers in his shirt, she scraped the tips of them along the base of his neck. "Where I'd *like* to go right now is into your bedroom to see if it's furnished any better than your living room is."

Lifting her hand to his mouth, he pressed a warm kiss on the inside of her palm. "Oh, it is, angel. You bet it is."

8

MAKING LOVE TO NICK in the back of the van had been erotic and spontaneous and incredibly hot. It had also been a week ago and in that week, Izzie had begun to wonder whether it had really been as amazing as she remembered.

As soon as Nick led her into his bedroom, turned her to face the mirrored door of his closet and slowly began to kiss her neck, she knew it had been. He was so slow—so patient—so deliberate. The man had incredible control and he had used it to drive her absolutely wild.

Izzie had flipped the light switch on as soon as they entered the room, determined to see all, savor all, enjoy every minute of this experience. When Nick studied her in the mirror, consuming her with his eyes, she was very glad she had. She liked watching him watch her. Liked having his eyes on her. And she wanted to watch everything he did to her.

"You've been driving me absolutely insane since I saw you that night in the restaurant," he whispered, his lips hovering just above the sensitive skin below her ear.

"You've been driving me insane since you landed on top of me on the cookie table."

He turned her to face him. "Izzie, I'm sorry I didn't..."

"I was a kid. You needed to wait until I caught up a little," she said with a smile.

He glanced down at her, his stare lingering on the scooped neck of her shirt and the clingy fabric hugging her breasts. "You caught up a lot."

She reached up and unfastened the top button of his shirt, then moved to the next. "Oh, more than you know," she whispered, feeling incredibly free. A sensual woman capable of knocking him back on his heels the way he'd knocked her back last week.

Their first time together had been about him overwhelming her senses. Tonight it was Izzie's turn.

She was not going to lie back and *take* the pleasure he wanted to give her, she intended to *give* with every lustful molecule in her body. He'd offered her an experience she would remember until the day she died. Now she planned to do the same.

Using the one thing she did best.

She quickly scanned the room, thinking ahead. "Where'd that come from?" she asked, pointing to an old-fashioned straight-backed chair in the corner. It, a simple, immaculately clean dresser and an enormous four-poster bed were the only things in the room. The chair didn't look at all new like the rest.

"My parents insisted on giving me stuff…. I had to take *something* and there's no room for it in the living room."

"It won't fit with that TV that's more suited for the Jolly Green Giant's living room," she said with a low laugh. Licking her lips, she pointed to the chair. "Go sit down."

One of his eyebrows rose, but he obeyed, watching with interest to see what she was up to. Izzie glanced around the room, looking for a radio, a boombox, something.

No luck. Nick's bedroom was nearly empty, with just the furniture and a smaller TV on the dresser. There wasn't a piece of clothing on the floor, or a speck of dust anywhere. It was nearly Spartan…military, she assumed. And it lacked the warmth she knew Nick possessed.

She hoped that someday he allow that warmth to spill free and become part of his home as well as a part of his life.

"You got me where you wanted me," he drawled from the chair. He put his hands behind his head, his fingers laced, and leaned back against the wall. His sleeves were rolled up to his elbows and his forearms bulged and flexed. His big strong legs were sprawled out in front of him and for a second, Izzie was tempted to climb right onto his lap.

She could unzip his jeans, tug them out of the way, release that big erection she could see from here. It would be delicious to slip her panties off, lift her skirt, then slide down onto him to ride him to her heart's content.

Not yet. First she needed to delight his senses the way he'd delighted hers last week. He'd focused on her sense of touch and smell—she could still inhale and remember that sweet, cheesy filling he'd smeared all over her. And her body tingled at the memory of his lips and tongue removing that filling.

They'd played games with food. She intended to whet his taste buds with something else.

The sight of her body.

Suddenly remembering what he'd done with the TV in the other room, she grabbed the remote control and turned on the bedroom one. Punching in a few numbers—familiar, since she liked listening to the same station at her own apartment—she landed on a channel that played sultry Latina music.

Because luck was a woman, the song was a slower one with a sultry backbeat and a sensuous rhythm. Easy to dance to.

"What are you…"

"Watch me," she whispered. *Watch me and I'll make you burn.*

She began to move, closing her eyes and letting the music roll through her. Since childhood Izzie had had an affinity for music—all types of music. It had always made her want to move. To sway or to spin, to leap or to bend. She just had a dancing gene that demanded release whenever the right beat hit her ears and rolled on down through her body.

This one was perfect for seduction.

Keeping focused on her own instincts—giving herself pleasure by the simple act of moving—she knew Nick would gain pleasure, too. At first she simply danced. Her eyes still closed, she threw her head back and tangled her hand in her hair. Rocking her hips, she gyrated against an imaginary partner, sliding down and up against an invisible thigh, quivering under the touch of a hand that wasn't there.

She heard Nick groan softly. Licking her lips, she slid her hand down her own body. Her hips still rocking, she touched her stomach, then slid her hand lower, resting her fingertips on her pelvis. Her other hand she moved across her chest, scraping her nipples, already rock hard in anticipation and excitement.

"Izzie…"

"Shh."

She didn't look at him, didn't let him distract her. Instead, she tugged her top free of her waistband. Flicking at the snap and pushing down the zipper of her skirt, she rocked until the thing fell to the floor. She kicked it out of the way, never losing the beat, her body in constant, sensual motion.

Her top came next. She dragged it up—slowly, so slowly—letting the fabric fall back an inch for every two she raised it. She could hear Nick's ragged breathing over the music. Could hear her own heart pounding in her chest, too. Every move she made was an invitation and a promise.

She pulled the top off, sensual even when untangling her hair from the material. Clad in nothing but a skimpy bra and thong panties, and her high-heeled sandals, she bent over and swung her head, letting her hair fly free.

"You're killing me here," he whispered.

"So take care of yourself. Get ready for me," she replied, coming closer—but not too close. "Do what you *want* to do when you watch me dance."

"I want to *have* you when I watch you dance."

Tsking, she shook her head in disbelief, still swaying like a woman being sexually aroused by the touch of the musical notes on her body. "Pretend you don't know you're going to have me, Nick. Let me see what you'd do then."

She turned around, her back to him, returning her attention to her dance. Bending at the waist, she put her hands on her thighs and did a booty rock that she knew would drive him out of his ever-loving mind.

His low groan told her it had worked. But Izzie ignored it.

Grabbing the end post of Nick's bed, she used it, hooking one leg around it and bending back. The wood was hard against her swollen sex, but she needed it—got off on it—rubbing up and down in a way she never rode the pole at the club.

"Izzie," he whispered hoarsely.

She glanced over and almost smiled in triumph. He'd finished unbuttoning his shirt and it hung from his shoulders.

Even better, his jeans were open, his briefs pushed down. And his hand encircled his huge erection.

"Yes. Imagine it's *me* touching you," she told him.

He never took his eyes off her, beginning to stroke,

up and down, his movements timed to match her strokes against the bedpost. But when she let go of it, he didn't stop.

"The bra," he ordered.

"Just as the customer desires," she whispered, taunting him with every bit of her sexuality.

She unfastened the bra, dragging out the moment before it fell away to reveal her breasts. This usually marked the end of one of her numbers, but tonight, Izzie was just getting started. She touched herself, showing him the way she wanted to be touched. Crossing her arms—her hips still rocking—she cupped each breast. Capturing her nipples between her fingers, she tweaked and rolled. The pleasure she gave herself—and the way Nick reacted to it—sent pure liquid want rushing to her sex, already dripping with readiness.

Hearing Nick clear his throat, she glanced over and saw he held a twenty dollar bill in his hand. He was enjoying this game. Getting into the fantasy.

"You have something for me, mister?" she asked, almost purring the words as she danced closer, wearing nothing but her skimpy panties and shoes.

"Uh-huh. But you have to work for it."

She moved again, closer, stepping over one of his legs to straddle it. She lowered herself closer to his thigh, rocking a few inches above it. Her breasts swayed close to his face. "What'd you have in mind?"

He leaned up, his mouth moving toward her breast.

"Uh-uh, no touching," she said, easing back a little. "I can touch you…you can't touch me."

"Those the rules?"

"Uh-huh."

"Not sure how long I'll be able to obey them."

"You'll just have to keep your hands busy *elsewhere* until I say you can break them."

He flexed his hand again, lazily working the erection

that still jutted out of his unfastened pants. "That means the rules *will* eventually be broken?"

She bent down again, low, brushing her silky panties over his strong thigh. "If you're very, very good." Her mouth watering, she inched closer, so her leg could brush against all that male heat. He instinctively arched toward her, branding her with that ridge of flesh that had given her such intense pleasure last week.

She wanted it. Badly. In every way it was possible for a woman to take it.

"You want a lap dance, mister?" she asked in her heavy, Crimson Rose whisper.

His eyes narrowed. "I didn't know you gave them."

"I don't. But you're an extra-*special* customer."

Izzie had never done this particular type of dance, but she figured she could fake it. Frankly, she didn't think Nick would care if she didn't get it exactly right.

So she went with her instincts. With both hands on the back of the chair, she swayed over him, brushing her breasts against his cheeks, shivering at the delicious roughness of his skin. She danced above him, writhing just above one leg, then the other, then straddling both. He watched with glittering eyes, groaning with need as she taunted him—coming close, so close—then pulling away.

"Gonna have to break that rule soon, lady," he growled.

"We'll see."

Driving them both closer to the brink of insanity, she dipped lower than she'd ever gone, until the silky wet fabric between her thighs met his arousal and set them both completely on fire. He grabbed her hips, helping her rock up and down on him until they both moaned with the pleasure of it.

"You're touching," she said.

He thrust up harder, the hot tip of his erection easing

into her, bringing her silky panties along. "I'm going to be touching you a lot more in a minute."

Oh, she liked playing these wicked, sexy games with Nick. It was unlike anything she'd ever done with anyone before, and Izzie sensed she could be happy playing bedroom games with him and *only* him for a very long time.

"But you still haven't paid me." She licked the side of his neck, biting lightly on his nape. Feeling the scrape of the bill against her skin, she pulled away just enough to watch him slip it into her panties. "Big tipper."

"You're worth every penny."

"I think maybe you should get a little bonus for being such a good customer."

She needed a little bonus herself. Needed to do something she'd been aching to do since she'd first seen him take off his pants in the back of the van.

Sliding back, she lowered herself to the floor, then moved between his thighs. She reached for his hand, covering it with hers, mimicking his slow, easy movements up and down his erection. Eventually she pushed his hand away, pleasuring him with her fingers and her palm. Encircling him as best she could, she slid down to the base of his shaft, then eased back up. She trailed her fingers across the thick, bulbous head to moisten them with his body's juices, then repeated the motion.

But it wasn't *quite* enough. Izzie inched forward, wetting her lips with her tongue.

"Iz…"

"Let me," she murmured.

She didn't wait for permission. Kneeling between his spread thighs, she drew closer, flicking out her tongue for a quick taste of the sac pulled up tight beneath his erection.

He jerked up, thrusting harder into her hand, which still encircled him. Izzie didn't stop. Parting her fingers to make way for her mouth, she licked her way from the base of his shaft all the way up to its tip. "You taste so good, Nick," she whispered before flicking her tongue out to catch more of that fluid dripping out of him.

"So do you." Still sprawled out before her, he tangled his hands in her hair. "But I'm hungry. I want some, too."

Mmm…mutual oral pleasure. She'd love to savor that experience with Nick. But for right now, she wanted to concentrate on him. So, ignoring his comment, she moved over the thick, pulsing head of his cock and took it into her mouth. As she sucked, he hissed. The deeper she went— taking as much as she could—the louder his groans.

Shifting around for better access, Izzie began to slowly make love to him with her mouth, getting off on hearing *him* get off. She slid up and down, taking more with every stroke, wanting to swallow him all the way down, though he was, of course, much too big for that. But she gave it her all, focused on his sounds of pleasure, the smell of sex rolling off his body, the feel of his hands delicately stroking her hair and the back of her head.

"Ride me, Izzie," he whispered, not demanding but pleading. "Come up here and take me."

Take him. Izzie had never had a man beg her using those words, though she, herself, had spoken them. She found herself liking the sensuous power of it. He didn't just want her, he *needed* her. Was desperate for her.

With one last little suck, she pulled her mouth away and looked up at him. He was staring down at her, his dark brown eyes gleaming with want. Reaching for her shoulders, he began to tug her up and repeated his plea. "Take me, Izzie."

Offering him a half smile, she rose to her knees. She was nearly naked, but Nick was still half wearing his clothes. So she reached for his waistband and pulled his pants and briefs down. He lifted up to help her, kicking his shoes off and his clothes with them. His shirt fell off his shoulders with a simple shrug, and now the tables were turned—she was the only one wearing a stitch of clothes.

It was, of course, a tiny stitch. And as she rose to her feet, Nick didn't take his eyes off it. Reaching for her hips, he tugged her closer until he caught the elastic seam of her panties with his teeth. Nudging them down, he tasted her with two quick, heart-stopping flicks of his tongue. Her clit swelled against his lips. "Please," she whispered, not knowing what she needed more—for him to lick her into an orgasm, or to tear her panties off and plunge down onto him.

"Since you asked so nicely," he murmured, returning his mouth to her most sensitive spot. Taking her hips in his hands, he pushed the panties down and nuzzled in deep in her curls.

Feeling a climax rocket through her, Izzie threw her head back and groaned. She was still groaning when Nick tugged her down over him. He glanced at his jeans. "My pocket…"

"We're safe," she assured him since she was on the pill. "As long as you're comfortable with that."

"Oh, I am so comfortable with that," he muttered hoarsely. "I cannot wait to feel you wrapped around me, skin to skin."

Straddling him, her toes on the floor, Izzie rubbed against him, loving the tangle of his chest hair on her rock-hard nipples. Nick dipped his head down to suck one of them, hard and demanding. "Ride me," he ordered, his mouth still at her breast.

She eased onto him, taking the hot tip into her wet channel a little at a time. He was right—skin to skin was incredible. She could feel every beat of his pulse through his velvety smooth erection.

"Can't…take much…" he said through choppy breaths. As if he'd reached his breaking point, he squeezed her hips and thrust up, impaling her hard and deep. "Oh, Nick," she groaned, shocked at the full intensity of it.

It took her a second to catch her breath, he filled her so deeply. But when she did, she had to move. Had to slide up and then ease back down. She rode with slow strokes, her arms on his shoulders, looking down into his face as he stared up into hers.

Nick lifted one hand and cupped her cheek, drawing her toward him. Covering her lips with his, he kissed her deeply, sliding his tongue in and out of her mouth in strokes matched by the ones deep inside her core.

The kiss went on and on, slowing or growing frenzied in mirror reactions to the movements of their bodies. Izzie rode him, took him as he'd demanded, using muscles she didn't even remember she had to stretch out their pleasure.

Their position was perfect for pleasing her both inside and out. And within moments, the friction on her clit provided her with another mind-blowing orgasm.

Finally, though, her legs began to weaken. She wasn't sure how much more she could take. As if he knew, Nick wrapped his arms around her, cupping her backside, and rose from the chair.

The strength of the man defied description.

Still buried deep within her, he continued kissing her as he walked the few steps to the bed. He dropped her on her back, coming down with her, and took over control.

"Yes, Nick," she gasped, her legs around his lean hips.

He didn't reply. He was gone now, mentally just *gone,* at the mercy of his wildly plunging body. Izzie held on for the ride, whispering frantic words of pleasure, telling him how much he pleased her.

Until she, too, was incapable of words. Together they lost themselves to the power of it until Nick shouted and came deep inside her, sending Izzie spiraling over the edge again, too.

BRIDGET HAD BEEN thinking about her cousin's words nearly all night Thursday. So much so that she barely slept and climbed out of bed long before her alarm went off Friday morning.

If there was one thing Izzie knew, it was men. And if she thought Bridget hadn't been sending out strong enough signals to Dean, she was probably right.

Izzie would make her interest more obvious.

So that's what Bridget would do.

That morning, she dressed for work a bit more carefully than usual. Her regular workday attire was typically a pair of pastel capris or a pair of slacks and a blouse. Today, she shimmied into a yellow skirt that cupped her butt like she'd sat in a tub of butter. Pulling a tight white tank top on with it, she glanced in the mirror and was surprised at what she saw.

She didn't look much like Bridget, the nice, smiling bookkeeper. In fact, she looked sexy. She had curves…nice ones. Her breasts were high and shapely, highlighted by the scooped neck of the tank top. And while she didn't have especially long legs, they looked pretty good in the skirt.

Feeling almost armored for battle, she donned a light-weight sweater—which she intended to remove as soon as she saw her quarry—and headed to work. She wanted to get there early so she could get used to walking around the office in the minuscule skirt and high-heeled sandals without tripping and making a fool of herself.

Usually, she was the first one at the dealership, any-way. The lot didn't open to customers until ten o'clock, with most of the sales staff showing up around nine…a half hour or so after her regular starting time. By the time she got to the lot, it was only seven-thirty, an hour early even for her.

The inside was dark, as expected, and as she entered, she reached for the switch to turn on the bank of overhead lights. But before she did it, something caught her eye…a sliver of light coming from beneath the door to the business office. Where *she* usually worked.

She supposed she could have forgotten to turn the light off last night when she left. But she was still cautious as she approached. This was a pretty safe area, but occasional robberies certainly weren't unheard of. She wasn't about to open the door and surprise some junkie looking for a petty cash box.

When she got to within a few feet of the nearly closed door, she heard a voice from inside. She tensed for the briefest second, then recognized the voice and relaxed.

It was Dean. He'd obviously shown up early for work. Though she didn't hear whoever he was talking to, she figured someone else must have come in early, too.

Too bad. Had he been alone, she might have been able to put her "send stronger signals" plan into action. If, of course, she had the nerve, which was questionable.

Reaching for the knob, she paused when she heard Dean speak again, answering a question she hadn't heard asked. That was when she realized the conversation was one-sided. He was talking on the phone to someone.

Not wanting to eavesdrop, she stepped away, catching only the snippet of a comment Dean made. Something about a deal going down. Sounded like their star salesman had landed another buyer—one who liked to close deals very early in the morning.

When she heard his voice stop, she figured she'd see if he was done, and knocked once on the door. Feeling a little foolish—since she was, in essence, knocking on her own office door—she pushed the door open and stepped inside.

"Good morning, early bird," she said.

He jerked his head up, so surprised he dropped his cell phone right onto the floor near her feet.

"Sorry, didn't mean to startle you," she said. Normally,

she'd wait quietly and let him pick up the phone himself. But Izzie's words kept ringing in her ears. So instead, she carefully bent at the knees, reaching down to pick it up for him. She kept one hand on her skirt, to hold it in place, but Bridget couldn't deny that it slid up several inches, high on her thighs, despite that.

Still appearing shocked, Dean didn't say a word. His narrowed eyes were locked on her thighs. His jaw was visibly clenched and he breathed over parted lips.

He looked...hungry. Just as she'd seen him look at her once or twice in the past. More than that, he seemed dangerous. Not nice Dean looking at a pair of woman's legs, but wickedly sexy Dean looking at a pair of woman's legs and imagining them wrapped around his waist.

She could do that. She could definitely do that. Whether it was what Izzie would do or not.

It is.

"Here you go," she said, handing him the cell phone.

He took it from her, their fingers brushing lightly. Standing, he stuffed the phone in his pocket. His lean face looked weary, as if he hadn't slept well.

"So, was it worth your early trip in?" she asked, knowing she sounded coy. She couldn't help channeling Izzie a little bit. "Everything...satisfactory?"

His pale blue eyes narrowed. "What do you mean?"

"I mean, did you get whatever deal you're working on taken care of this morning?"

He nodded slowly. "The deal. Yeah. It's all good."

"Good. You might set another sales record this month."

With a casual manner she had never suspected she could pull off, she tossed her purse onto her desk, which was laden with files, legal paperwork and financial stuff. Holding on to her courage, she slipped her sweater off her shoulders. She had to move close to Dean—very close—to reach the coatrack on the wall. Her arm brushed against his as she lifted the sweater onto one of the hooks.

"Bridget…"

Smiling, she turned and glanced up at him. "Yes?"

He wasn't looking at her face, his attention was focused lower. On the scooped neck of her tight spandex tank top. The heat in his stare warmed her all over and she felt her body reacting to it. A lazy river of want flowed through her veins. She clenched her thighs in response to it. But there was no way to disguise the way her breasts grew heavier, her nipples hardening to twin points that poked against her shirt.

He noticed. Most definitely.

Swallowing hard, he growled, "Why are you dressed like that?"

"Like what?"

"Like you're trolling for men at a club rather than working with a bunch of used-car salesmen and wrench jockeys at an auto shop?" he asked, his tone harsh.

Bridget instinctively stepped back. A little hurt. A little confused. "I just…" *Channel Izzie. WWID?* Taking a deep breath, she tilted her head back and jutted her chin out. "What business is it of yours what I wear to work?"

He reached for her, grabbing her arm as if he couldn't help himself. "Put your sweater back on."

"*Make* me."

His whole body tense with frustration, he lifted his other hand and grabbed her other arm. Bridget wasn't sure what he was going to do—shake her or haul her into his arms and kiss her.

She was most definitely hoping for option two.

She should have been intimidated, maybe even scared given his size. But she already knew he wouldn't do anything to hurt her. He was attracted to her, she was sure of it now, and he just didn't know what to do about that attraction since they were coworkers.

"Either take your hands off me or do something with them," she snapped, still thinking the way her cousin would.

"Damn it, Bridget."

But before he could do either one, they heard the sound of voices coming from right outside the door. They weren't, it appeared, the only two who'd arrived to work early.

Dean instantly released her and stepped away. He shook his head, as if to clear it, and eyed her warily. Finally he said, "I really think you should put your sweater on."

Bridget hid a smile, liking the tiny thrill of power she felt at having this big handsome man react so strongly to *her*. Crossing her arms in front of her chest—which pressed her breasts even higher and harder against her top—she shook her head. "I don't think so, Dean. If you don't like the way I'm dressed…I suggest you don't look at me."

Knowing her bravado wasn't going to last for much longer, she sashayed past him, out onto the showroom floor to greet the other salesmen who'd arrived. Leaving Dean watching her with eyes that blazed like the sun.

Izzie had spent the night in Nick's arms, but she'd slipped away early—around dawn. Knowing the bakery would open soon, he didn't protest.

He wanted to, of course, but he kept his mouth shut.

Izzie's whole reason for being here in Chicago was her devotion to her family's business. He wouldn't even think of interfering with that. Because he *liked* her working at the bakery. Right here close by.

As for her other job, at the club? Well, that, Nick had to admit, might be a tougher proposition. He hadn't yet been tested, but he didn't imagine it would be easy watching the woman he was absolutely crazy about take her clothes off for a roomful of other men. Especially since he'd almost certainly be picturing what had happened last night, when she'd taken her clothes off only for him.

It had been the most unbelievable night of his life. And he had to wonder how she'd had the strength to get up and walk this morning considering he'd spent so much of the night between her legs.

Izzie wasn't the only one who had to go to work. Nick had promised Tony he'd help him handle the delivery of a new wall oven at Santori's. So after showering, he got dressed and walked the few blocks up to Taylor. He passed right by Natale's on the way, but, mindful of Izzie's feelings, he didn't pop in. It felt strange as hell to walk on by and not say hello to the woman he'd made love to in so many wild, different ways the night before.

But she wanted their relationship to remain entirely between them. Meaning he couldn't single her out, couldn't grab her hand in public, couldn't ask her to do so much as walk across the street with him.

"This is gonna suck," he muttered aloud as he reached the restaurant. He had no idea how long he'd be able to maintain this secret, nighttime-only relationship with Izzie.

He only hoped she'd change her mind. That she'd realize she didn't have to give up *herself* to become part of a relationship with him.

A relationship. Yeah. He wanted one. He was falling for her in a big way, just as he'd suspected he could when he'd seen her looking so bored and aloof on the other side of Santori's all those weeks ago.

It was pretty ironic, really. He was starting to think he really could have found the perfect woman. He was already falling in love with her. And a union between them would absolutely delight everyone in both their families.

But Izzie didn't want one.

"Women," he muttered as he pushed into the restaurant.

His brother Tony, who'd been standing right inside the door, greeted him with a clap on the back. "Can't live with 'em…but they're sure as hell better than living alone."

As usual, his larger-than-life older brother coaxed a smile out of him.

Fridays were usually busy at Santori's, so the day flew by quickly. And, as usual, the rest of his family started drifting in after their workdays had ended. By eight o'clock, all of his brothers were here with their wives and kids, as was his sister, along with her new husband. Those two were cuddling like the newlyweds they were. Though he'd been skeptical, given what he knew about Simon Lebeaux's shady past, even Nick had to admit the two of them were obviously crazy about each other.

Besides, if Lebeaux could put up with his mouthy little sister, he had to be one hell of a strong man.

"Come on, take a load off," Mark said to Nick as he emerged from the kitchen, where he'd been helping his father.

"Yeah, I guess my slave-driver boss will let me knock off now," he replied, glancing over his shoulder at Tony, who stood in the swinging doorway.

"Not boss…partner," his brother reminded him with a grin.

Uh, no. Not in Nick's opinion. But he still hadn't wanted to have that conversation.

His siblings and their families took up several tables in the restaurant—tables that would probably have been appreciated by the paying customers lining up near the front counter. But Mama would never dream of shooing them out to free up the space. She clucked around, ordering them all to eat, cooing over the grandbabies and beaming when Noelle, Mark's wife, offered to let her feel the baby kicking in her stomach.

In Nick's opinion, that was *Twilight Zone* stuff. But *all* the women got into it, and Mark looked like he thought it was the coolest thing since Optimus Prime and the Transformers. Nick, however, was freaked by the very idea. The only thing he wanted to feel moving around inside a woman was his own cock. A baby? Forget it.

Unless the woman was Izzie.

The thought was crazy—bothersome, even. But it wouldn't leave his head.

"Hey, look who's here," Gloria called, waving toward the front door. "My baby sister! How you doin', Iz?"

Nick immediately swung around, seeing Izzie at the counter.

"Ah, Isabella, you haven't been to see me too much. What's wrong with you, eh?" Mama said as she bustled over. She cupped Izzie's face in her hands, pressing a kiss on her forehead, then grabbed her arm and dragged her over.

Smacking Lucas on the shoulder, she said, "Move over and make room for Gloria's little sister."

"Yes, ma'am," his older brother said with a grin. Luke was the next oldest above Nick and Mark and, as a prosecutor, was used to ordering other people around. But, like all of them, he couldn't refuse a command from their bossy mother.

"How's everything, Iz?" he asked as he stood and moved his chair out of the way. "You remember Rachel, right?"

Izzie nodded, smiling at Luke's pretty blonde wife, the only fair-haired one of the bunch. A die-hard Southerner, she'd somehow made herself fit in so well that Nick couldn't imagine what the family would be like without her.

Fortunately, the room Mama had forced Luke to make was between his chair and Nick's. Rosa Santori stole an unused chair from a nearby table and slid it in place, nearly pushing Izzie down onto it. Which had Nick ready to kiss his mother's hand, even though Izzie looked less than happy.

"I was just picking something up for dinner on the way home from work," she said, sounding almost dazed at how quickly she'd been shanghaied into a family dinner.

He understood the feeling. His mother was a power-house.

"Such a silly girl," Mama said. "You will eat here, with the family. You're one of us!" Trying to squeeze past her to get back to the kitchen, Mama said, "Scooch over a bit, eh?" and she pushed on Izzie's chair until it was so close to Nick's their thighs touched under the table.

Nick would lay money that his mother had done it on purpose. When he saw the smirk on her face as she left to check on dinner, he knew it was true.

Everyone wanted them to hook up. *If only they knew...*

"Hey, *Isabella,*" he whispered from the side of his mouth.

She kicked him under the table.

"So, how do you like being back in Chi-town, Izzie?" his brother Joe asked. "Guess it's pretty tame and unexciting after your life in New York. You must really need a creative outlet."

There was a surprising twinkle in Joe's eye. As he and Izzie exchanged a long stare, Nick began to have a suspicion that Joe knew a little more than he'd let on about Izzie's nighttime life. Remembering the way Joe had steered him toward the job, and had been so adamant about Nick taking care of the "featured dancer" at Leather and Lace, he had to wonder if Joe had seen Izzie there during the renovations.

"It's okay," Izzie replied. Smiling, she added, "I'm just busy trying to avoid resuming my cannoli addiction. They're my absolute weakness."

Everyone at the table laughed. Except Nick. Because there'd been a sultry purr in her voice and he believed she'd been speaking only to him.

When he felt her hand—concealed by the red-and-white-checked tablecloth—drop onto his leg, he was sure of it.

There was something really hot about having a woman you were supposed to just be casually friends with feel you up under a dinner table. Especially when that table was filled with curious family members who would love to see any sign of interest between the only two singles there.

Izzie was careful. So they definitely didn't see her hand creep up his leg to trace the outline of his dick. That, he assumed, would be taken as a definite sign of interest.

He was going to make the woman pay for her sensual torment. Right now, however, he was enjoying it too much to try slipping his hand down to beat her at her own game.

The conversation soon resumed, Izzie falling into it as if she'd never been away. She traded barbs with his brothers, reminisced with his sister Lottie about their school days.

She fit. She just fit. Like a normal neighborhood girl.

But no normal neighborhood girl he knew would be working Nick's zipper down, reaching in and pulling him free of his trousers. She definitely wouldn't be brushing the tips of her wicked fingers across his cock, arousing him until he hardened into her hand.

This was incredibly dangerous. If someone dropped a fork and bent over to get it, they'd get an eyeful.

But Nick didn't give a damn. Maybe he and Izzie couldn't be the "normal" couple the neighborhood would like to see. Somehow, though, this was *better*. Having an erotic secret…

and acting on that secret in public where they could be exposed, was mind-blowing.

It made him hot. It made him desperate.

It made him finish his dinner quickly and declare himself so tired he had to call it a night.

And thankfully, Izzie found an excuse of her own, followed him out the door and led him to her place for another long night of the wildest sex he'd ever had.

9

"HOW ARE YOU FEELING, Rose? All better?" Holding the back door of Leather and Lace open for her early Saturday evening, Harry watched her closely, as if worried she wasn't up to dancing tonight.

Izzie had to stop for a moment to wonder why. Then she remembered. *Crap.* She'd called in sick the previous Sunday night. Probably really leaving him in the lurch.

"I'm fine, Harry," she said as she walked past him into the building, watching him shut and lock the door behind her. Security had improved around here ever since Nick had been hired. "I am so sorry about last Sunday night."

Harry waved an unconcerned hand. "Hey, don't worry about it, something wicked had to be going around for three of you to get knocked on your butts."

"*Three* of us?"

Harry nodded. "Leah got sick Saturday night."

"I remember."

"She came back in Sunday evening, was here for two hours, got sick all over again and had to leave. So did Jackie."

Jackie was Leah's dressing roommate. Whatever was going around had obviously nailed both of them.

Izzie was about to open her mouth to confess that she

really had not been sick—just cowardly. But before she could do it, the back door was unlocked from the outside and opened again. She knew before she even saw him that Nick had arrived.

She recognized his warm, masculine scent. And her nipples got hard. Oh, yeah, it was definitely Nick.

His gaze immediately went to her, hot and appreciative. She'd had to leave his bed early this morning to go to work at the bakery. But right before she'd gone, he'd whispered how much he looked forward to seeing her tonight in her dressing room…which now, he'd made sure last weekend, had a lock.

She'd shivered all day, thinking of that first night he'd been in there, when he'd seen her naked reflection. *Mmm.*

"Nick," Harry said with a nod. He looked back and forth between the two of them. "No more mask, Rose?"

Smiling, she shook her head. "I've decided I trust him."

Nick returned the smile, the two of them sharing a silent intimacy that excluded Harry, though he stood right beside them. Finally, though, Nick broke the stare and addressed their boss. "Everything looking okay so far?"

Harry nodded. "Been kind of a quiet week. Last night was the slowest Friday we've had in a while." Glancing at Izzie, he added, "But I bet the crowd will be roaring back to see you."

"Are you short-staffed again?" she asked, wondering if Harry would need her to dance an extra set.

He shook his head. "Everybody's here, sound and healthy."

"What do you mean?" Nick asked, a frown furrowing his brow.

Harry began to explain about the sick dancers, which made Izzie feel guilty again. Especially when he groaned over how hard it had been to tell Delilah, his "retired" wife, that she wasn't in shape to go on in their place. Oy.

She wouldn't have wanted to see the redhead's expression during that conversation.

Something else she didn't want to do was have to look Nick in the eye and admit she'd called in sick rather than face him last weekend. She figured he knew that much, but didn't particularly feel the need to confirm it.

Excusing herself, she headed to her dressing room. The door wasn't locked, but she immediately noticed the dead-bolt, which had not been there the previous weekend.

"You sneaky man," she whispered with a smile as she dropped her purse and keys on the vanity. She could think of several wicked ways Nick could help her kill time between her numbers.

Of course, being the hard-ass guy he was when on the job, she suspected he might resist her. That was okay. Izzie had found she was pretty good at working around his resistance.

Having stood most of the day at work, she wanted to relax before going onstage. Kicking her shoes off her feet, she pulled her chair out from under the makeup vanity and sat down at it.

She immediately heard a cracking sound, but didn't register what it was until the chair broke apart beneath her, sending her crashing to the floor. "Son of a bitch," she snapped as she lay still on the tile. The back of her head had scraped the concrete block wall on the other side as she'd fallen. She rubbed at it, shocked to see a few flecks of fresh blood on her fingertips.

"Izzie? Are you all right? What was that noise?" Nick asked as he burst into the room.

He swung the door open so hard he almost hit her with it. An inch closer and she would have taken a flat piece of oak square in the face.

"Oh, my God." He immediately dropped into a squat beside her. "You're hurt."

"It's okay," she insisted, slowly sitting up.

He put his hand under her arm to help her. "What happened?"

"My chair broke," she admitted, almost embarrassed about it. She'd never fully gotten over that chubby-girl terror of breaking a chair in public.

"Is that blood on your fingers?" he asked, his voice so taut it almost snapped.

She lifted it to the back of her head again. "Yeah, I scraped my head on the wall when I fell."

"You need to go to the hospital." He rose and tugged her up, too. "Come on, I'll take you right now."

"No, Nick, I don't. I didn't bang my head, I promise. I just scratched it on the way down."

He frowned, obviously not believing her.

"Check and see for yourself. I swear, it's nothing but a scratch." She turned around, tilting her head back so he could see the spot where the blood had come from.

Nick gently pushed her hair out of the way. Izzie watched him in the mirror, seeing the frantic expression on his handsome face. And the way his jaw clenched as he tenderly examined her.

He was worried about her. Truly afraid for her.

"See?" she asked softly.

"Looks like a scratch," he admitted.

"Good."

"But that doesn't mean you're not hurt anywhere else. God, Izzie, what the hell happened?"

She gestured toward the remains of the chair, in pieces at her feet. "It fell apart as soon as I sat on it." Glaring at him, she added, "No big butt jokes."

He rolled his eyes. "As if." Stepping away, he ran his hands up and down her arms. "You're sure you're not hurt anywhere else?"

She was hurt elsewhere. Her hip was killing her from

where she'd banged on the floor. But thankfully, she hadn't landed on her bum knee. "I'm okay."

Nick shook his head, muttering something, then bent down to examine the pieces of the chair. It was a sturdy rolling one that easily slid around when Izzie needed to reach something on the vanity. But it had fallen apart into several pieces.

"This doesn't make any damn sense." His tone was curt, all business now. "How could it just fall apart like that?"

"I have no clue. Maybe it was just defective."

Nick didn't even look up. He was poking around in the pile, picking up a couple of screws and staring at them hard.

"Rose? Nick? Is everything okay? Somebody heard a crash."

Glancing at the door, she saw Harry Black, and, right behind him, one of the bouncers. They both stared wide-eyed from her, down to Nick and the broken chair.

"Are you okay, honey?" Harry asked.

"Can I help you up?" the bouncer, Bernie, her self-appointed watchdog, asked.

"I'm fine. Just a little mishap."

"She could have been badly hurt," Nick barked.

"But I wasn't," she murmured, trying to calm all three down. If Nick was like a protective lion, Harry was like a fatherly teddy bear. And Bernie was like a big grizzly somebody had poked with a stick. They all looked equally upset.

"It's okay, I swear. Just an accident. Now, if you don't mind, Harry, could you find me another chair? I need to get ready to go on." The older man nodded and backed out of the door, taking Bernie with him.

Glancing at Nick, she added, "You need to get to work, too, making sure everything is safe and secure for me to perform."

He slowly rose, his eyes locked on hers. "Are you really worried about something, or are you trying to get rid of me?"

Izzie offered him a cocky grin, put her hand on his chest and pushed him toward the door. "I'm trying to get rid of you. I have to be onstage in an hour, and with you in here oozing all that hot man stuff, I'm going to be tempted to test that lock and seduce you."

His eyes twinkled. But his frown remained. "You're not going to seduce me into forgetting you could have been hurt."

"And you're not going to bully me into forgetting I have a job to do."

He reached up and cupped her cheek. Izzie couldn't help curling into his hand, loving the roughness of his skin against her own. "I would never bully you into doing anything, Izzie."

They hadn't yet talked about her job. They'd officially been secret lovers for two wild, passion-filled nights, and she hadn't had a chance to even ask him if he was going to have some kind of macho problem with her dancing. Now he'd opened the door for the question.

"Are you going to be all right upstairs, watching me?"

He brushed his thumb over her jaw. "I love watching you."

Nibbling on his finger, she murmured, "I meant, will you be okay watching everyone else watch me?"

His jaw stiffened and his dark eyes flashed. But he didn't pull away. Instead, he drew closer, tipping her head back so sweetly, so tenderly, she knew he was still worried she could be hurt. "Izzie, I can't promise anything because I haven't experienced it yet. But I can tell you this…I know and want the real you…both sides of you. The Rose and the woman you become when you walk out of this place every Sunday night. I'm in this with *both* of you."

Without saying anything more, he bent down and covered her mouth with his, kissing her sweetly and tenderly. Then, with one more brush of his hand on her face, he turned and walked out.

As IT TURNED OUT, Nick did not have to test himself to see how he'd handle watching Izzie strip for other men. Because before she ever went onstage, Nick was forced to deal with a couple of punks who didn't understand the rules of a place as upscale as this one. One of them had made a move on a waitress, another had lunged at a dancer. Nick and Bernie plucked the guys up and dragged them out the front door, where, high on liquid courage, they'd both tried to put up a fight.

Maybe it was the residual anger he'd felt at seeing the blood on Izzie's fingertips. Or maybe it was the rage that flooded his head at the thought that it could have been Izzie the prick had grabbed, but as soon as the guy threw the first punch, Nick reacted harshly.

He'd had a few fights in his day, both before his military days and during them. And it was painfully easy to take down a drunk. The fight was over almost immediately after it had begun. Bernie dispatched of the drunk's friend just as quickly and the two of them nodded to each other in appreciation for the backup.

"Thanks, man," Bernie said.

"Not a problem."

Bernie shook the bleary patron. "I think this is the same prick who grabbed Rose a month ago."

Nick's jaw went rock hard. If the man hadn't already been in Bernie's firm grip, he might have found a reason to throw another punch. But he was a fair fighter and wouldn't do something so out of bounds.

Unless the guy got free…then all was fair.

The guy didn't get free, Bernie had a tight grip and

had begun chewing him out for harassing Rose. That incident had obviously been a more serious one than Nick had been led to believe, because Bernie hadn't forgotten a moment of it.

Because things had gotten physical, Nick decided to cover his own ass as well as the bouncer's and the club's, and called the police. He wanted this thing on record, now, when there were plenty of witnesses who'd seen both the assault on the female workers inside, and the provocation in the parking lot.

It was just his bad luck that Mark heard the call to Leather and Lace and decided to respond. Nick saw his brother get out of his unmarked car and saunter over, smiling widely. "Get in a fight without me?"

"Just doing my job," Nick replied, trying to figure out a way to get Mark to leave without going inside the club. If he was on duty, it wouldn't have been an issue—his brother was too good a cop to go inside a strip club while on duty. But he knew Mark's hours. No way was he working this late on a Saturday. "What are you doing here, anyway?"

"I heard it on the scanner. Noelle was already in bed—that woman goes to sleep by eight every night now. So I thought I'd head on over and see if you were okay."

"You know this guy?" one of the officers asked.

"My baby brother," Mark replied, his dimples flashing.

"By ten minutes," Nick said, shaking his head.

It took about an hour to clear up matters outside. Nick had stayed near the entrance, far from the stage, but he'd gotten reports from the bouncers about what was going on inside. So he knew when Izzie had performed...and when she was finished.

She'd done her first number and wouldn't be back on for at least an hour or two. Long enough to get rid of his brother.

"Come on, let me buy you a beer," Mark said once the last of the police cars pulled away.

"I'm working."

"Okay, then you buy me a beer." Not taking no for an answer, he threw his arm across Nick's shoulder and tugged him into the club. "Come on, I've never been in this place."

"Noelle probably wouldn't like it."

"I'm visiting my twin at work. No harm in that, is there?"

"Depends on whether you visited me blindfolded."

"I'll keep my back to the stage," Mark said. "Seriously, we haven't talked in weeks. I know something's going on with you."

His twin was right. They had been…disconnected. Not just because of what had been going on with Nick and Izzie, but also because his brother was about to become a father. Mark had changed. He had different priorities, talked a different language, looked at the world a different way.

Noelle and their baby were his family now. Oh, sure, he loved the rest of the Santoris, but he'd crossed that threshold from son and brother to husband and father.

Nick was the only one of the Santori siblings who had not.

"Let's sit out here," Mark said, nodding toward a couple of low, round tables in an outer chamber between the lobby and the main lounge area. They were out of view of the stage.

Nick wasn't surprised. Mark was a good husband. Like the rest of their brothers.

"All right." Gesturing to one of the waitresses, he ordered a club soda for himself and a beer for his brother. Returning to the table, he sat down across from his twin. "Can't be away for too long, though."

Mark settled back into the leather chair. "Nice."

"Yeah, it is."

"Good fringe benefits?"

Holding back a smile, Nick just shook his head.

"Hey, I'm married, these days are long gone. Throw me a bone."

"Throw me one," Nick replied before thinking better of it. "Tell me what it's like."

Mark frowned, obviously confused by the question. "It?"

"Marriage. What's it like being tied down, committed?"

Those deep dimples that had charmed girls from the time he was two years old flashed in Mark's cheeks. "It's the best. Noelle's everything I ever wanted."

"Yeah, but how'd you know what you wanted?" Nick muttered as he lifted his drink and downed half of it.

Chuckling, Mark admitted, "I didn't. I think it was more of a case of meeting her, and *knowing* that whatever I eventually did figure out I wanted for my life, she'd be part of it. It was always her. Everything else fell into place around her."

Somehow, that made a lot of sense to Nick. Because even though he'd been thinking of dozens of reasons why he and Izzie couldn't make it work—the primary one being that she didn't *want* it to—he couldn't help hoping it would. Because, as Mark had said, he suspected she was the one. That whatever else happened in his life, whatever direction he went in, whatever he chose, he'd want her to be a part of it.

Surprisingly, his brother didn't press him about why he was asking so many questions. Probably not because he didn't care—or didn't suspect there was a reason behind them. But because he knew Nick well enough to know that pushing for answers usually only made him clam up tighter.

Nick appreciated the courtesy. And realized yet again just how much he'd missed his twin.

"Hey, Nick, we got a live one at the bar," a woman said.

Glancing over, Nick saw one of the waitresses, who was rolling her eyes. "Serious?"

"Not yet. But he could be if he's not handled right."

"I'll be there in a minute." Addressing his brother, he added, "Is there a full moon out tonight? The crazies are out."

Mark stood. "Yeah, including me. I must be crazy to be out here with you instead of home in bed with my wife."

Feeling better than he had in the hours since Izzie's accident with the chair, Nick reached out and grabbed his brother for a quick hug. Mark's eyes widened. He was the demonstrative one, not Nick. "What's that for?"

Nick shook his head. "I don't know. Give it to your wife."

"I've got plenty of my own to give," Mark said with a grin. "But thanks just the same."

The rest of the evening went by quickly, with more of the same insanity to deal with. Nick hadn't been kidding— the crazies were out tonight, and a lot of them had decided to show up at the club. The bouncers had had to forcibly eject more guys in this one evening than he'd seen them eject in the past month.

The only positive thing about keeping so busy was that Nick missed the Crimson Rose's final performance of the evening, too. He hadn't even realized she was on until he heard the thunderous applause, whoops and whistles of her audience. But at that point, he'd been outside, doing a sweep of the parking lot to make sure none of their uninvited patrons had decided to come back.

Fortunately, they hadn't. But there were still other issues to deal with, like his conversation with Harry about Izzie's broken chair. She had called it an accident…and it might have been one. But he wasn't taking any chances. He and Harry had talked about adding security cameras to the basement area of the club, to hook into the system already covering the upstairs. Izzie's accident had confirmed the idea for both of them.

Just in case.

Saying goodbye to Harry, he headed downstairs, glancing at his watch. It was after two, the club was closed, everyone drifting out. But he knew she'd have waited. She wouldn't have left without seeing him. Partly because she'd want to see his reaction to her act. Partly because she knew he'd kill her if she'd walked out to her car alone.

"Iz?" he asked, knocking lightly on her dressing-room door.

She opened it immediately. "Hi." She was nibbling on her bottom lip and her hands were clenched in front of her. Rather than being dressed to go home, she wore just a slinky robe. Thankfully, though, the mask and hairpieces were gone.

"You doing okay?"

She nodded, then looked at him through half-lowered eyelids. "Um, so? What'd you think?"

He reached for her and drew her into his arms. "I didn't see you dance."

"What?"

"Sorry, other stuff was going on."

"I heard there were some problems."

"Yep."

She fisted her hands and put them on her hips. The pose did really nice things, like pulling her short pink robe apart at the neck to reveal the lush upper curves of her breasts.

"You're telling me you just happened to have to deal with various crises during the exact times I was onstage? And that was simply coincidence?"

She might not believe it, but it was true. At least, he

thought it was. He guessed he could have done the parking-lot sweep a few minutes earlier or later. He hadn't evaluated his decision before. But now, looking back... well, maybe something inside him had made sure he didn't have to see other men looking at the beautiful body of the woman he considered his.

"You're *sure* you're going to be all right with this?" Her chin went up. "I won't be able to handle it if you go all Cro-Magnon man and try to drag me by the hair back to your cave."

"You woman. Me man," he said, slipping his hands down and parting her robe farther. He nuzzled into her neck, breathing in her essence, realizing twenty-four hours had been far too long to go without making love to her. "Me got heap big appetite."

She swatted at his shoulder. But she didn't back up. "You're such a dork."

Nick had *never* been called that, or anything like it, in his entire life. Ass maybe. Jerk. Cold-hearted pig, on one occasion. But never a dork. And it surprised a laugh out of him.

She delighted him. Simply brought every good feeling that existed inside him out into the open.

"God, I love being with you," he muttered, unable to help revealing a little bit of what he was feeling.

"I know, I feel the same way."

She didn't admit that easily, the words had come haltingly out of her mouth. Which made Nick value them that much more.

He moved his mouth down, sampling her collarbone.

"Did you put that lock on my door yourself?" she whispered as she tilted her head farther, silently begging for more.

He nodded, continued to kiss and lick, lower now, to the curves of her breasts, beautifully bare under the robe.

"Let's use it."

"My thoughts exactly," he murmured.

He didn't let her go, he simply reached back and flipped the lock, then dipped down lower to lick his way down her to her pert nipple. Flicking it with his tongue, he waited until she was quivering to cover it with his mouth and suckle her.

"Mmm…more."

Nick stroked her sides, his thumbs meeting near her belly button and scraping lower to tease the top edge of her pretty pink panties. With one last sweet suck on her breast he moved down her, following the path his hands had taken.

Izzie moaned softly, swaying on her feet. Nick kept her steady as he kissed his way down the front of her body. The soft robe brushed his face. So did her soft skin.

"Do you know what I wanted to do to you the first time I came into this room?"

She tangled her hands in his hair as he dropped lower, kneeling on the floor in front of her. "I think I have an idea."

He pressed his face in her belly, licking at that tender bit of skin right above her pelvic bone, slowly pushing her panties down as he dipped lower.

"Did it involve that nice big flat surface in front of the mirror?" she asked.

Smart girl. "Uh-huh." Gently holding her hips, he flicked at the panties, watching appreciatively as she shimmied out of them. The robe fell, too. Under the bright light-bulbs ringing the mirror, he was able to see every glorious inch of her. But he wanted to see more—didn't want his view blocked even by her pretty brown curls. So he turned her and edged her back until her bottom brushed the edge of the vanity top.

"Wait," he said, suddenly remembering her accident.

Wrapping his hand around the edge of the vanity counter, he tugged at it sharply, testing the shelf's sturdiness. It remained firmly in place, well secured into the wall.

"Good," she murmured. Rising on her tiptoes, she slid onto the vanity, parting her legs just the way he wanted her to.

Someone had brought her another chair, and Nick grabbed it, sitting on it directly in front of her. Reaching for her knees, he slowly pushed them apart, watching a pink flush rise through her entire body.

She made no effort to resist. Confident. Sensual. Incredibly seductive. She knew what he wanted and she wanted it, too.

He pushed her legs farther, until he could see the glisten of moisture on the sensitive slit between her legs. "Do you have any idea how beautiful you are?" he asked.

It was a rhetorical question. She couldn't possibly know how beautiful she looked to him, wanton and aroused, opening herself up so he could pleasure them both.

He couldn't wait any longer. With a low groan of need, Nick dropped his face to that sweet, warm spot. He lapped at her in one slow, long lick, feeling her thighs quiver beside his face.

Izzie tilted up for him, inviting him farther, and he sampled her again. "You taste just as good without the cannoli, Cookie," he mumbled.

She managed a choppy laugh. "Don't call me Cookie."

"Can't help it." He nibbled his way up to catch her erect clit between his lips. He played with it even as he scraped his fingers across her swollen sex. She was drenched and ready to take whatever he wanted to give her. Wanting that warm, wet flesh wrapped around part of him while he continued to savor her with his mouth, he slipped a finger inside her.

"Mmm," she groaned. "More. More of everything."

He complied. Licking harder and sucking deeper, he slid another finger into her, then slowly moved them in and out, timing his strokes to her helpless moans.

With one more swirl of his tongue on her most sensitive spot, Izzie cried out and climaxed. He wanted to be part of that climax, to experience the spasms of her body as she clenched and shook. Standing, he tugged his shirt up and off, then unfastened his belt and pants and pushed them down, out of the way.

When he looked up again, Izzie had slid down to stand before him. He frowned. "I wasn't *nearly* done."

Her eyes sparkled. "Neither was I." Then, with an Eve-like smile on her face, she turned around, facing away from him, until they were both looking in the mirror. She slowly bent forward, putting her hands flat on the vanity, curving that sweet ass back in pure, unspoken invitation.

His pulse roared. "You're sure…"

"Oh, I'm *very* sure," she promised him. She was still smiling, her eyes still glittered in avarice and hunger. "It's *your* turn to take *me,* Nick."

Remembering the way he'd begged her to take him the other night at his place, he nodded in lazy agreement. "Oh, honey, you can't imagine how much I want to take you like this."

Making love to her face-to-face—watching her incredible eyes widen with pleasure, and her sweet mouth fall open on every long sigh—was amazing. He knew he'd never tire of doing it.

But the idea of taking her like *this*—with raw, hot passion—excited him beyond reason. He'd be able to see her expressions in the mirror, be able to plunge deeper than ever before until he imprinted himself somewhere deep inside her. Deep enough that, perhaps, she might never want to let him go.

"Nick," she begged, "please." She arched again, those

long dancer's legs putting her curvy butt directly in line with his cock. She backed into him as he moved forward to her.

He held her full hips in both hands, bending a little so he could see her sweet entrance and ease his way into it. She hissed and arched, trying to take him deeper, but was powerless. His hands held her firmly, he was setting the pace.

And he planned to go slowly, wanting to savor every second of the experience.

"Give it to me," she begged, watching him with desperation.

He smiled at her in the mirror and thrust forward a tiny bit. Rewarded by her gasp and the flare of her eyes, he pulled out again. This time, she didn't beg for more, she simply licked her lips and watched, trusting him to make it good.

He didn't make it good. He made it amazing. By the time he finally sank all the way into her tight heat, Izzie was whimpering. And by the time he began to lose his mind and thrust wildly, in and out, over and over, she was practically sobbing.

He thought they were alone in the building. But he couldn't be sure. "Izzie…" he said, slowing to ease out of her, to calm them both a little "…wait."

"Don't stop."

"I'm not stopping, sweetheart," he said. Then he stopped. She whimpered, watching him, then realized he was turning her around. "I have to kiss you, Iz," he murmured.

She twisted in his arms to face him, twining her arms around his neck and one leg around his waist. Plunging his tongue in her mouth, he tangled it with hers keeping his eyes open so he could stare into her beautiful face. Lifting her back up onto the vanity, he went right back into her, deep and fast, knowing this last stretch would be a quick, pulsing one.

"Sweet heaven, you amaze me," she whispered against his mouth as he filled her again.

"Amazing. Yeah."

Those were the only words he could manage. Wanting to be connected with her everywhere, he kissed her again, wrapped his arms tightly around her body and drew her up against him.

Stroking and thrusting, he rocked into her with every bit of himself, her cries of pleasure echoing sweetly in his ears. And when he finally heard those cries turned into desperate gasps as she climaxed, he let himself go, too, erupting inside her until he was completely empty.

"HEY, HOT STUFF, you're looking delicious again today."

Bridget jerked her head up, blinking the columns of numbers out of her brain as someone stepped into her office Sunday afternoon. She knew it wasn't Dean…he didn't speak to her like that, which was good. She wanted him to notice her, wanted him to realize she was interested in him. But she definitely didn't want a man who'd speak to her so coarsely.

"Oh, hi," she said, seeing one of the salesmen standing in the doorway. The guy, Ted, was a middle-aged divorcé with a phlegmy chuckle. He also had what she and her friends in middle school used to call Roman hands and Russian fingers.

He was grabby. Touchy. But he'd never gone too far beyond pats on her shoulder. She hoped that wasn't about to change.

Ted wore his usual ugly striped sports coat over a dingy dress shirt and a red tie. In other words, he looked a mess. Usually, she saw him as a kind of sad guy whose wife had dumped him. He was smarmy and coarse, but had never given her any reason to be wary of him personally. Now, however, goose bumps prickled her body and tension throbbed in her temple.

She didn't like the look in his eye.

"You dressing like that just for me, hot stuff?" he asked as he sauntered into the office.

"I think that question would be called sexual harassment," she said as she stared hard at him, hoping he'd take the warning as a threat and get out now, before he'd gone too far.

When he smiled and pushed the door shut behind him, she had a sinking feeling he'd *already* gone too far.

Damn. She should have left an hour ago. It was four o'clock, an hour after the dealership closed on Sundays. And she had to assume everyone else had gone home. Ted hadn't been around since this morning. Judging by the whiff of alcohol she caught wafting off him, she figured he'd gone for a long lunch at a local bar.

Dean, why didn't you show up? She'd thought for sure he'd be here. He'd worked every weekend since he started. That was the only reason Bridget had come in herself today…to see him!

It had been for nothing. She'd worn another short, sexy skirt that she'd bought at a cute local clothing store last night. That, with the silky sleeveless shell that draped across her curves invitingly would have been enough to get the man's temperature rising. And he hadn't even been here to see it.

Instead, Ted was. *Ick.*

"Girl, you have been hiding your light under a bushel." He stepped closer. "It's closing time. Let's go have some fun."

"No, thank you," she said, her tone icy. She stuffed her paperwork into a drawer. Normally, she'd be more tidy. Today, she was in a hurry. She wanted out of here.

"Aww, come on, sweetie, I know there's no man in your life. You must be lonely. Why don't you let me keep you company?"

She'd rather keep company with a dead skunk. "No, Ted."

Hopefully that firm tone would get the message across and he'd get out of her way and let her leave. But as she stood, Ted stepped between her desk and the door, right in her path. "You know you really want to stay."

"No. I *really* don't."

Trying once again to be like Izzie, she fisted one hand, retrieved her purse and tried to walk past him.

He grabbed her arm. "Not even a few minutes' conversation?"

"Not even that," she insisted, jerking her arm away.

Her angry tone and the heat in her eyes must have finally gotten through. Because Ted went from stupid drunk trying to *score* to angry drunk trying to *control* in one blink of her eyes. Without warning, he put both his hands on her shoulders and pushed her back. Bridget stumbled over her own high-heeled sandals, landing on her butt on the edge of her desk.

"Perfect." Dropping his hands onto her thighs, he crudely pushed her legs apart and forced his way between them.

"Let me go!"

"Not yet, hot stuff."

She reached around on the desk behind her, hoping she'd left her scissors or stapler out, but all she managed to grab was a small desk clock. Wrapping her fingers tightly around it, she swung, but only managed a glancing blow to Ted's shoulder.

His nostrils flared even as his eyes narrowed in anger. "Playing hard to get?"

"Let me go or I'll scream."

"Nobody to hear you, pretty thing," he said, any hint of charm gone from his voice as his true nature emerged.

Before she could say a thing—or think what to say—Bridget heard something that sounded like an angel. But it was no angel.

It was Dean Willis. *Roaring*.

"Get the hell off her you son of a bitch."

Suddenly he was. Ted was lifted off her and tossed to the side of the room. Bridget saw him land hard against the wall and crumple to the floor. He yelped in either fear or pain. Or both.

He had reason to be afraid. Dean was already reaching for him, his face red, his body emanating danger. "You're dead."

Ted's bravado when facing her disappeared under this new threat. Before Dean could even grab him, he'd launched himself to his feet and run out the door, leaving the two of them alone. The whole thing—from Ted's entrance to his speedy departure—had taken place in under three minutes.

Her head was spinning. Breathing hard and shaking a little, she mumbled, "Thank you so much."

Dean swung around to look at her, that blood rage still evident on his face. His blue eyes were like matching chips of ice. He looked as much like a cute, nice-guy car salesman as she looked like Xena the Warrior Princess.

No. This was not gentle, good-natured Dean. This was a dangerous man in a high fury. And her shivers of fear turned to shivers of excitement.

"What the hell happened?"

Still sitting on the desk, she could only shake her head. "He obviously had been drinking. He came back and caught me alone. It's the first time he's ever…I mean, he's a creep, but I never thought he'd…"

"Maybe if you'd wear clothes that didn't scream 'do me' men wouldn't try."

Bridget's jaw dropped and she stared at him in shock. "What did you say to me?"

"Look at you," he snapped, stepping closer. He pointed to her legs, still splayed open on the desk.

Bridget tried to jerk them back together, but Dean stepped between them before she could do it. With absolutely no warning, he plunged his hands into her hair and bent to cover her lips with his. He thrust his tongue in her mouth, tasting her, devouring her. His body was hard against hers, his hips between her thighs, and Bridget couldn't even try to deny the absolute flood of heat that roared through her in response.

She wrapped her arms around his neck, tilting her head to kiss him back just as deeply. And for a long, heady moment, they made crazy, wild love with their mouths.

Then the moment ended. Dean let her go and staggered back a few steps. "Bridget, I'm…"

She put her hand up, palm out, to stop him. Sliding off the desk, she straightened her skirt and said, "Don't. Okay? Just don't say anything. I wanted that. Maybe I *needed* it just so I could wash Ted out of my memory. I didn't exactly jump up there and part my legs—he pushed me."

Dean instinctively swung his head to look at the door, that tense rage returning.

"He's long gone. Thank you for coming in when you did."

He ran both hands through his hair, his anger finally draining away. "I'll take care of him, Bridget."

"Marty will deal with him." She stepped closer, offering him a tremulous smile. Because now there was no doubt that Dean's interest in her was one of more than friendship. That kiss—and his body's hard, instinctive reaction to it—told her he wanted more. Maybe as much as she did. "I guess that makes you my hero, huh?"

Dean stared at her, his eyes softening, the tension easing. Reaching for her, he pulled her into his arms. But this time, he didn't attempt to kiss her. His embrace was pure, sweet comfort. He held her tightly, running his hand up and down her back. "I'm sorry. Sorry for what he did... sorry for what I said."

"It's all right. You were angry." Tilting her head back, she smiled up at him. "I thought it was kinda sexy."

For a second—a brief one—she thought he was going to smile back. To laugh, then lower his mouth to hers and kiss her again, gently this time.

But it didn't happen. Instead, Dean sighed heavily and his mouth drew tight. "I'm also sorry for kissing you. I should never have done that."

"I've been wanting you to..."

He put his hand up to stop her. "Don't. It was a mistake, Bridget. A big one. And it won't be repeated."

She gasped, unable to believe he was rejecting her. *Again.*

"What is your *problem?*" she asked, completely indignant.

He just shook his head. "I don't have a problem. I just can't...don't want...hell, Bridget, this just can't happen." As if needing to convince himself, as much as her, he reiterated.

"It *won't* happen."

10

WHEN NICK MANAGED to get through another evening at Leather and Lace *without* watching her dance, Izzie got a little nervous. She didn't want to ask him about it over the next few nights since they were having such an amazing time doing wildly sensual things to one another. But she couldn't help wondering.

On Sunday night, he'd been too *busy* to watch her dance. Or so he'd claimed. He'd conveniently had to go put out another fire in the club every time she was scheduled to go on.

Suspicious. She didn't want to be, but she was.

He'd said he could handle it…but he wasn't acting like he even wanted to try.

It wasn't that she didn't understand. In fact, putting herself in his shoes, she'd have to say she'd probably have a major problem with other women looking at *her* naked man with covetous eyes, thinking of ways they could have that incredible body and handsome face.

Her man. Her man? Oh, God, had he somehow become *her* man?

Sitting in her apartment, she realized that yes, at some point in recent weeks, Nick *had* become her man.

Maybe it had been when he'd made love to her in the

back of the van. Or when he'd cared for her after she'd fallen in her dressing room. Maybe it was because of his sexy smile and the intimate way he watched her when he thought no one was looking.

Maybe it was even because of the way she'd felt every single time she'd woken up in his arms.

Those predawn moments. Yeah. They'd probably done it.

Because each time it had happened—whether at his apartment, or hers, she'd had to lie there and watch him sleep. Study the line of his jaw and the curve of his cheek. Wonder how a man could have such a sensuous mouth and still be so damned tough. Note the small scars on his body, and his tattoo, and grieve for the things he must have gone through as a soldier.

Yes. In those moments, her heart had opened up. And she'd let him in just as surely as she'd let him in her body.

There were moments when she allowed herself not to care. To even consider whether they could make this crazy relationship of theirs work. *Maybe a masked wedding...the Crimson Rose and the sexy night watchman.*

That was *so* lame.

But it was no more crazy to think about than the idea of an official union between Izzie Natale and Nick Santori of Taylor Street.

"Would that really be so bad?" she whispered. She'd been telling herself it would, but at moments like this, she had a hard time remembering why.

"I need sugar," she mumbled as she headed for her kitchen, dying for something sweet. She'd been so good at the bakery and tried to resist temptation, so she never brought any of that stuff home. At moments like these, though, she regretted it.

Nick had called a while ago, saying he'd be leaving the pizzeria in an hour and would come by. She glanced at her watch, wondering if she had time to run to the corner market. She was so desperate she'd go for a packet of Ho Hos at this point.

Before she could grab her shoes and dash for something to binge on, her cell phone rang. Glancing at the caller ID and recognizing the New York City number, she immediately began to smile, now knowing another sure-fire way to escape—at least mentally—from her troubles.

"V!" she exclaimed as she answered.

"Girl-*friend!*" was the reply. "It has been for-*evah,* where have you been?"

Plopping down on the sofa, Izzie kicked her feet up and leaned back, so happy to hear a voice from her old life, she wondered if fate had sent Vanessa's call as some kind of mental gift. Vanessa was a good friend from her Rockette days. The striking, long-legged African-American woman had been Izzie's roommate on the road and the two of them had hit it off from their very first hotel stay, when they'd both decided to call for room-service French fries at two in the morning, despite the matron's orders to go to sleep by eleven o'clock.

"I'm still in Chicago."

"Still doing that bakery thing?" Vanessa asked, sounding completely shocked. "I can't believe you've lasted this long."

"Join the club. I sometimes forget I haven't spent the past seven years with my arms in cookie dough up to my elbows."

"How's your father?

"Getting better every day, already pestering my mother to let him go back to work."

"That's great. And as soon as he does you can quit."

Yes, she could. Why that idea would send a shot of sadness through her, Izzie didn't know. It wasn't as if she liked working at the bakery. Even if she *had* made friends with all the staff, gotten on a first-name basis with their restaurant clients and the regulars who stopped in every day for breakfast.

Well, maybe she did like it. A little. But certainly not enough to want to stay there permanently.

Vanessa laughed softly. "And then you can come home. You still thinking of choreographing, or teaching?"

She had been, though, not as much lately. But she didn't tell Vanessa that.

Fortunately, her friend quickly moved on. "You've got to come back soon. You are so missing out." Launching into an explanation of all the things that had been going on—with the Rockettes, and in her personal life, Vanessa soon had Izzie laughing so hard she had to wipe tears from her eyes. The other woman was a wild one, and the ballsi-est female she'd ever known.

The stories were entertaining, particularly when told with Vanessa's flair. But even as she laughed, Izzie couldn't help wondering whether her friend was truly happy. She sounded a little…empty. Lonely. Bored.

Which made Izzie suddenly remember the way she'd been feeling right before she'd hurt her leg.

Very much the same way.

All the things Vanessa had been describing were things Izzie had been doing the past few years in New York. She missed none of them. Honestly, all she really missed were her friends and her apartment. The lifestyle she'd already begun to outgrow even before she'd been forced to leave it.

Going back to it didn't sound very palatable.

She shook off that crazy thought—not go back to her life? Insane. Like she had anything better going on *here?* "So which guy did you shove in the fountain?"

"The French dude. Pierre from Paris. Only, I think his name was probably really Petey from Poughkepsie or something. He wasn't French any more than my dry wheat toast was French this morning." Sighing, her friend added, "Why do men suck so bad?"

"Not all of them," she said before thinking better of it.

Vanessa caught the tone in her voice and leaped on it. "Talk. Who is he? What's he do? When did you start doing him?"

Having had no one to truly confide in since she'd been here…about her feelings, her relationship with Nick, even a bit about her sexy weekend job, she found herself spilling all of it to Vanessa. She must have talked for a solid five minutes without letting her friend get a word in. Finally realizing that, she whispered, "You still there?"

Vanessa murmured, "Oh, honey. This is serious."

Yes. It was. Very serious.

"This Nick, I remember you talking about him."

Izzie was afraid of that. Nick had always been—for her—the dream guy she'd never landed.

Now she'd landed him. She just didn't know if she was going to get to keep him. Or if he even *wanted* her to, considering he hadn't been able to bring himself to watch her dance again at the club.

"He might be a man worth settling down for, Izzie. Giving up your dancing…wait, what the hell did you say is the name of this place you're dancing at?"

She should have known that would interest her friend more than any potential romance. "It's called Leather and Lace."

"Holy shit, girl, you're strippin'."

"Yeah. I'm stripping. And I'm having the time of my life." Well, the stripping wasn't giving her the time of her life. Nick was. But she'd already talked enough about Nick.

Vanessa demanded all the details on Izzie's secret life, not sounding the least judgmental, and asked a bunch of questions. "That sounds like *fun*. You know, I've thought about taking a strip-dance exercise class they offer at my health club, but there's a waiting list."

"You're joking."

"No, honey, I'm not. It is the hottest thing going—there's a three-month-long list to get in this class and everybody I know is putting their name on it. If you come back, you need to teach me how and maybe I'll retire and we can start a school somewhere. Teach housewives how to shake their booties."

Izzie laughed softly at that silly idea. Then she thought of the word Vanessa had used. *If.* "What do you mean, *if* I come back? Why wouldn't I come back?"

Vanessa grew very quiet, as if working out what to say. Knowing her friend was streetwise in a way Izzie never had been, she very much wanted to hear it. Anything Vanessa put this much thought into had to be worth hearing.

Finally, her friend murmured, "Why would you come back here when the life you really want is there?"

"You think I want to be a *baker* for the rest of my life?" Izzie protested, shocked that her friend would even suggest it.

"I don't know whether you want to be a baker or a stripper. A pizza-delivery gal or a ballerina. All I know is that whatever you end up wanting to do, it'll be tied up with that man you've loved for half your life."

Izzie's jaw dropped. She flinched so hard the phone fell onto her lap. Scrambling to get it, she heard Vanessa's words echoing in her head. Especially because they'd come so quickly—mere minutes—after Izzie had been tearing herself apart to try to figure out just what she felt for Nick.

She really shouldn't have had to think about it so hard. She knew what she felt for Nick. It was the same thing she'd always felt for him, only deeper now, adult. Sensual. Mature.

Forever.

Vanessa was right. She loved him. Part of her knew she should resent that, since it had been what she'd feared—and why she'd thrown up walls between them when he'd first pursued her. But she already knew she didn't regret it. How could she regret feeling so emotionally alive for the first time in years?

"You still there?" her friend asked when Izzie finally brought the phone back up to her ear.

"I'm still here."

Vanessa chuckled. Then, in a very low voice, she added, "I better be in the wedding."

Then all Izzie heard was the dial tone.

"HEY, LITTLE BROTHER, when are you gonna come talk to the business lawyer with me and Pop?"

Nick stared at Tony, who'd followed him out the front door of Santori's Friday afternoon. He'd been planning to head up the block to Natale's. He had a real taste for cannoli. The fresh kind that could only be found in Izzie's kitchen.

Or in Izzie. But that was another kind of decadent dessert altogether.

"I dunno, Tony, I really haven't thought about it."

His brother frowned. "I don't get it. I thought it was all set. You know how much Pop wants to retire completely."

"Bullshit."

Chuckling, his brother nodded in agreement. "Okay. We know he won't ever get outta that kitchen until they pry his wooden spoon out of his hand for his own funeral. But I know he's hoping to get you settled."

Get Nick settled. It sounded so archaic. And constricting.

"If you're worried about coming in as a financial partner rather than just a working one, I am sure willing to let you buy in with some of that money you said you saved while you were in the service."

Honestly, that had been one of Nick's big concerns. He didn't want anyone covering his way, he liked to pay his fair share. And if he were seriously considering going into business with Tony, he would absolutely insist on those terms. He did have the money, he did have the desire to get involved in a successful business and help it grow.

But that business was not a pizzeria. He knew it in his heart. He just hadn't figured out how to tell the family that yet. "I haven't made any decisions."

Tony met his stare, obviously trying to figure out what was going on in Nick's head. Nick thought about how best to put into words that he didn't want the life his family had mapped out for him. But before either of them could say anything, Nick spotted Izzie walking up the street, coming up behind Tony. Considering his big brother was a mountain of a man, she probably hadn't even seen Nick yet.

The sight of her face brought a stupid smile to his. But he didn't give a damn. At least, not until his brother turned to look over his shoulder at whatever had made him so happy.

"Whoa-ho," Tony said, when he looked back at Nick. "Izzie? It's *Izzie?* Holy shit, Gloria's gonna love this."

"Gloria's not going to know about this," Nick muttered. Izzie was not twenty steps away and if she heard what they were talking about, she'd probably bolt. Then ignore him for the next week until he could work his way around her defenses again.

Damn, but the woman was prickly.

"Why not? Cripes, the family's been wanting you two to hook up forever."

"That's the problem. Izzie isn't the kind of woman who likes to do what's expected of her."

Maybe that's one reason they got along so well. Because Nick felt exactly the same way about his family. He just hadn't been able to make that clear to them yet.

"Okay, I won't do anything to jinx it. But I don't know how long I'll be able to keep it from Gloria." Tony grinned, shaking his head back and forth. "The woman can get anything out of me with her sexy…"

"Don't want to hear it," Nick smoothly interjected. He continued to watch Izzie, realizing the exact moment when she spotted him. A quick grin flashed across her face. But when she saw who was with him, the grin disappeared.

"Hi, Tony. Nick," she murmured, reaching them. She sounded so cool and calm. As if she hadn't been in a huge tub of warm bubbles and cold champagne with him twelve hours ago, loving each other until the water got cold and the champagne got flat.

God, what a night. Another amazing one in Izzie's arms. He didn't know what he'd ever do without them.

"How's it going, little sister?" Tony asked, giving her a one-armed hug. "Sorry I couldn't make it to lunch at the folks' house Sunday. Work—it kills me." He glanced at Nick and wagged his eyebrows. "If only I had a partner to take up the slack."

Nick managed to suppress a sigh. Then he turned his attention to Izzie. "I was just on my way to the bakery. I'm jonesing for something sweet."

She chuckled. "I was last night, too. I almost dashed out and got a Ho Ho to tide me over until you…" She quickly snapped her mouth shut, remembering Tony was there.

His oldest brother had never been the king of tact. In fact, his wife affectionately called him Lunkhead. Well, *usually* affectionately. Right now, however, Tony managed to pull it off. "Well, it was great seeing you, Iz, but I have to get back to work. Nick, you're gonna swing by the bank after you go up to the bakery and grab us some of Izzie's fabulous cannolis?"

They had plenty of cannolis left in the restaurant, but,

he assumed, it was the best Tony could do on such short notice. "Sure, Tony. You bet."

They both watched Tony go back into the restaurant, with breezy hellos and good wishes to every customer he passed on the way back to the kitchen. When they were alone on the sidewalk, Izzie continued to stare at the glass restaurant door. Finally, she murmured, "He knows, doesn't he?"

Nick nodded. "Yeah."

"How?"

With a helpless shrug, he told her the truth. "He saw the look on my face when I saw you walking toward me just now."

She finally tore her gaze off the door and directed it toward him. Staring into his eyes, she searched for the meaning of what he'd said.

He didn't try to hide it. He was in love with Izzie and his eyes affirmed that, even if his mouth didn't.

He just didn't know if she'd *want* to see the truth there.

He understood why she wouldn't. Putting the reality of their feelings out there meant they had to deal with them. It meant she could accuse him of breaking their "secret lovers" deal and freeze him out of her life again.

It could also mean she'd acknowledge that she was falling for him, too. And that maybe they could make something work between them. Something good. Right.

Permanent.

"I can't handle this, Nick," she whispered, appearing stricken. "He'll tell Gloria."

"Not intentionally."

"And she'll blab to the known universe and the neighborhood will have me married and fat before winter and my parents will be eyeing a perfect little row house for us right up from theirs, getting our future kids on the waiting lists to go to Sacred Heart and St. Raphael's."

She sounded pained, as if the very idea of living that life devastated her. He understood why. Because he didn't want it, either. Any of it. Oh, he wanted Izzie, no doubt about it. But as for how they lived? Well, it wouldn't be like anything anybody on Taylor Street would understand.

But before he could reassure her, Izzie shook her head and started walking. "I can't talk about this now. Not here."

He fell into step beside her. "Tonight."

"I'm going to my parents' tonight. My sister Mia's coming into town for the weekend and I had to promise to come for dinner—which I can't do tomorrow or Sunday."

In a normal relationship, she'd ask him to come with her. In a normal relationship, he'd do it.

They weren't normal, of course.

"Call me when you're done and I'll meet you at your place."

She hesitated, glancing at him from the corner of her eye. "I need a little time, Nick. Just a little time. Can we… maybe take a break until tomorrow?"

One night. She wasn't asking for much. But the thought of going without her tonight nearly killed him.

"All right, Izzie." He caught her arm, holding her elbow before she could stalk away. She looked frantically from side to side, as if to see if anyone was watching, but Nick didn't release her. "Don't panic," he ordered her. "Don't see trouble where there is none."

She flashed him a grateful smile, murmured, "I'm mentally kissing you goodbye," then tugged her arm free and walked away.

He mentally kissed her goodbye, too, until she disappeared into the bakery.

SPENDING FRIDAY NIGHT with her family actually turned out to be a very good experience. Izzie had been half dreading it, since she'd felt like an alien among all of them since the day she'd gotten home. But something about this gathering was different. Maybe because Mia was home and therefore got a lot of the attention. Or because Gloria's boys were there—the grandsons always caused everything else to cease to exist for her parents.

Or maybe it was just because Izzie forced herself to relax. Not having to talk a lot meant she didn't have to watch every word she said. Didn't have to worry about letting something slip regarding her dancing—which they all assumed she'd given up entirely because of her knee.

Not being so on edge actually allowed her to relax and, to her shock, even enjoy herself.

She was still mulling it over the next day, remembering the smile on her father's face as he talked about returning to work soon. When he told her he'd been talking to his brother—who was about to retire—about coming to work with him at the bakery, Izzie began to see a silver lining in the cloud of her life. With another member of the family coming in to the business, the pressure would be off Izzie to stay involved. Maybe she could get back to something like a real life of her own.

Whatever she did—staying in Chicago or going back to New York, continuing to strip or giving it up—loving Nick or letting him get away—she knew she did not want to be a baker for much longer.

Nick tried reaching her a couple of times Saturday but she'd missed his calls. Not intentionally—the first time she'd been in the shower and the second she'd been waiting on customers at the bakery. By the time she had a minute to call him back, he'd been the one who hadn't answered.

Still, not having spoken to him for more than a day—since that tense moment on the street when she'd realized Tony had stumbled onto the truth of their relationship—she was a little nervous. Heading to work at Leather and Lace, she immediately scanned the parking lot for his car, but didn't see it. She was early—probably two hours earlier than she needed to be, and she knew it was because she was hoping he'd be here.

"Hi, Rose," someone said as she came in the back door.

"Hi, Bernie. How's the week been?"

The bouncer shrugged, offering her one of his big boyish grins. "Knocked a few heads together, wiped up the ground with a drunk or two. You know, the usual."

Laughing, she began to walk past him.

But he stopped her with a hand on her shoulder. He glanced at the big canvas bag she carried, which was filled with some street clothes and supplies. "Can I help you in any way, Rose? Carry that? Get you some dinner?"

She shook her head. "You are so sweet, but no, honestly, I've got it." The guy had been tripping over himself to take care of her since her first night at work. If he'd ever made a move on her, she'd suspect it was because he was interested. But he'd never been anything but a nice—if overprotective—friend.

Still smiling as she walked toward her dressing room, Izzie acknowledged just how comfortable she felt here. The club staff was like a second family already. Bernie and Harry. Leah and Jackie and the other dancers. They were all people she cared about, who seemed to care about her.

She didn't *want* to give this up. Which was another reason she didn't quite know how to deal with Nick's seeming inability to watch her perform. It was as if ever since he'd become her lover, he no longer liked her doing her job.

That was how it *seemed*. But she couldn't be sure. "Maybe he really is just busy," she mumbled, trying to convince herself.

When she reached her dressing room, she put her new key in the new lock and twisted it. Before going inside, however, Leah stopped her. "Hey, I feel like I'm always picking up your presents!" the grinning girl said. She held up a gold-foil-wrapped box. "Yum. Have I told you how much I love chocolate?"

Izzie glanced at the box, looked down at her own full hips—at least an inch bigger than they'd been when she moved back from New York—and sighed. "Have I told you how much chocolate sticks to my hips and butt?"

The one plus was that the candies were chocolate-covered cherries. And she wasn't too crazy about them. If they'd been caramels, she'd probably be much more tempted to grab a fistful. As it was, she easily waved them away. "Take them out of my sight, would you?"

Leah clutched the box to her chest. "Woo-hoo! Remind me to watch for the next jewelry box heading your way."

Entering her dressing room, Izzie slowly slipped out of her clothes and put her robe on. She took her time—there was lots of it. Over the next hour, she got ready for her night. The chatter of women's voices from the greenroom couldn't drown out the sound of lots of footsteps walking in the lounge above her head. Customers were already pouring in, performers already onstage judging by the low bass beat she could almost feel reverberating in her chest.

The whole place felt alive and vibrant. Exactly the way *she* felt when she was here. The only other time she felt as good was when she was with Nick. What on earth was she going to do if he couldn't take her working here anymore?

"Don't think about it," she reminded herself as she glanced at her watch. She'd been here over an hour and he still hadn't come in. Which was making her very jittery.

Izzie forced everything else out of her head and finished putting on her makeup. Her audience might not see much of her face, but that didn't mean she didn't cover the stage makeup basics. She was puffing anti-shine powder on her cheeks when she heard a knock on her door. "Come in." Almost holding her breath, she let it out with a pleased sigh when she saw Nick. "Hi."

"Hi, yourself," he said. He pushed the door shut behind him, bent down and kissed her on the mouth. Quick,
hard…hot and sexy. "Been needing that," he said when he
finally straightened.

"Me, too.

"Want more later."

She grinned. "Me, too."

"Things are already heating up upstairs, but I wanted
to see you before it got too crazy."

Izzie turned away, slowly lifting the powder puff to her
face again. "Do you think it'll be too *busy* again for you
to be there during my numbers?"

Nick met her eyes in the mirror. "I don't know," he muttered. "I can't promise anything."

He was still hesitant, she heard it in his voice. Nick was
avoiding having to acknowledge how he really felt—was
going to feel—about her stripping. Izzie wanted to cry,
sensing she knew what that answer would be.

He'd hate it. Sure, he'd been fine with her taking her
clothes off when she was a stranger. But now that they were
lovers? Well, if he was like every other male of the species,
he was going to turn into the caveman he'd once jokingly
pretended to be and get all overbearing. He'd want her to
quit, he'd be surly and pouty until she did.

There weren't many men who'd be able to take having their girlfriend strip down to a G-string in front of
a bunch of strangers…why should she expect Nick to be
any different?

"I'm doing my best, Iz."

"Okay," she murmured, blinking rapidly against unexpected moisture in her eyes, welling up not because she
didn't understand, she *did*. But because she so feared what
this was going to mean when it finally came to a head between them.

"Oh, God, somebody get a bucket!"

Hearing the loud shout from the corridor outside her dressing room, Izzie immediately rose to her feet.

"Catch her!"

Nick flinched. "Wait here while I see what's going on."

She just rolled her eyes. "Yeah, right."

Following him out, she immediately saw a small crowd of a half-dozen dancers gathered around someone who was lying on the floor. Nick pushed through them, and immediately bent down. "Leah, what happened? Are you okay?"

"She's sick," someone said. "Like, all over the floor sick."

Poor Leah. She'd been ill last weekend, and now again. Izzie briefly wondered if the poor kid was hiding an unexpected pregnancy or something. Then, as the crowd parted and she saw Leah's face, she discounted that idea.

The pretty blonde looked like she was in misery. Her face was ghost-white, slicked with sweat, and she appeared too weak to even stand on her own. She looked absolutely nothing like the pretty young thing Izzie had run into a little over an hour ago. She had to have been hit with some kind of fast-moving bug.

Nick didn't waste time asking questions. He bent to lift the dancer, easily cradling her in his arms as if she was a child, and carried her into the greenroom down the hall. "Somebody get her a cold cloth."

One of the dancers rushed off to do as Nick said. The rest of them crowded around. Izzie couldn't say whether their avid interest was more on Leah's behalf, or because of the incredible sight Nick made playing hero. His muscular arms bulged and flexed, but he spoke so softly— gently—to Leah as he gently laid her on the lumpy sofa in the greenroom. He even brushed her hair out of her face.

It was enough to make the hardest of women melt. Even the half-dozen strippers surrounding the sofa.

Izzie, of course, wasn't surprised. She knew the tenderness the man was capable of. She also knew the way he'd been raised and imagined he'd have done the same thing if his little sister, Lottie, had been the one lying on that floor.

"What happened?" he asked Leah.

Leah groaned. "It just came over me out of nowhere. I haven't been nauseous or anything, then all of a sudden, boom."

"Have you eaten shellfish today?" someone asked.

"Or some old lunch meat?" asked another.

Leah shook her head, gratefully accepting a wet clump of paper towels her dressing-roommate, Jackie, had brought her. She pressed it to her forehead and replied, "I had a salad for lunch, then nothing until I binged on Rose's chocolates."

Seven heads swung around to stare at Izzie, seven pairs of eyes wide and curious. Maybe even a little accusing.

She opened her mouth to reply, wondering if they thought she'd done something to make Leah ill, but didn't have to. The sick dancer herself spoke up again. "I found them lying on the stoop when I got to work today, with Rose's name on them. She never even opened the box, she just gave them to me."

That seemed to calm everyone down. Everyone except Nick. Because while all the others turned their attention back to Leah, offering to get her some ice or to drive her home, he frowned and stiffened his jaw so much it looked ready to break. "Where are these chocolates?"

"My dressing room."

He looked up and stared at Jackie. "I'll get them," she said, quickly rushing out of the room.

It seemed ridiculous and Izzie didn't for one second believe Leah had been brought down by some kind of poisoned candy...intended for *her*. That was strictly *CSI* stuff and she absolutely did not believe it. Judging by the look on

Nick's face, however, she knew better than to say that. He was going to see for himself no matter *what* she thought.

"Nick, I just heard one of the girls is sick, what's going on?" Harry came rushing in the room, out of breath as if he'd just run down the stairs. The expression of worry on the older man's face had to make all his employees feel better—no one could accuse Harry Black of not appreciating and caring about his dancers. Which probably made him a rarity in this industry…and was probably why few dancers ever quit here for any reason other than to move on to a different career.

Seeing Leah, he hurried over. "Should we call 9-1-1?"

Leah shook her head. "I don't think so. But I do want to lie here for a little while, if that's okay."

"Oh, honey, don't you even think of getting up," another voice said. A woman's. Delilah had heard the news, too, and followed her husband to the greenroom. She sounded concerned—a rarity for her. "We can cover you tonight and someone can take you home if you want."

The room was getting crowded. But everybody made way for Jackie when she returned with the box of chocolates. "Here you go, Nick." Frowning, she put her hand on his arm and nodded toward the corner of the room.

Nick took the box and followed Jackie. They exchanged a few words, and whatever she said to him made his scowl deepen. He kept the box tightly clutched in his hand and Izzie wondered if he was going to crush it.

Harry joined them, murmuring, "What's wrong?"

Nick's reply was softly spoken, he obviously didn't want everyone else to hear. Jackie, having delivered whatever message it was that had gotten Nick even more fired up, called 9-1-1 after all, then went back to help take care of her friend. All the others hovered over Leah. Someone offered to get her a pillow for her feet, someone else offered a bucket for her head. That broke the ice a little and the group laughed.

Izzie didn't join them. Nick suspected someone had tried to slip her poisoned chocolates. Damned if she was going to stay out of that conversation.

Striding across to the two men, she asked, "Well? Satisfied that I'm not a mad poisoner's target?"

Nick didn't look at her at first. Neither did Harry. They were both staring intently at the open box of chocolates on the makeup table. One of the men had flipped over all the remaining individually slotted pieces in the package, so they were bottom-side up. And in the bottom of each, very easily visible, was a small hole.

Something that wouldn't have happened at the candy factory.

"Oh, hell," Izzie whispered.

It appeared someone had, indeed, tried to poison her.

And when Nick turned to her and said, "Tell me about the roses," she realized it might not have been the first time.

11

WHEN NICK REALIZED there were holes in the bottom of the candy, he saw red. And it wasn't the cherry cordial filling.

He needed to know more—especially after what Jackie had told him about some flowers Izzie had passed to Leah last weekend. But he didn't want to do it here.

"The police are on their way," he muttered to Harry. Then, without a word, he grabbed Izzie's elbow and pulled her out of the room, straight to her private dressing room.

She stumbled to keep up and he realized he might be holding her too tight. But he couldn't let go, couldn't release his grip. He wasn't letting her get more than six inches away from him…or letting anyone else get within six feet of *her*.

"Nick, calm down," she muttered.

"I'm calm." *Deadly calm.*

"No, you're not. You're volcanic," she said as they walked into her dressing room.

Nick shut and locked the door. The last time he'd locked the door to this room had been at the start of one of the most amazing sexual experiences he'd ever enjoyed. He really wished he was doing it for the same reason now.

He wasn't. He was locking the door to keep Izzie—the

woman he now knew he loved—safe from someone who'd tried to hurt her at least twice now. Maybe even more.

Looking down, he saw the new chair sitting in front of Izzie's vanity and the steam built again. He leaned over and smacked it with his palm, sending it crashing against the wall. It did not fall apart.

But that didn't ease his suspicion about the last one.

"Why did you do that?" she asked, her voice calm and even.

Good thing one of them was. "Just making sure our friend didn't sabotage another chair."

Izzie's pretty mouth opened into a perfect *O* as understanding washed over her. That, more than anything, seemed to finally make this situation sink in. She grabbed the edge of the table and sagged against it. "Someone really is trying to hurt me?"

He stepped close and wrapped his arms around her shoulders and tugged her against him. "I think so, babe."

"Why?"

"I have no idea. Why do stalkers do any of the crap they do?"

Tilting her head back to look up at him, she murmured, "*Stalker?* Why would someone wanting to get *close* to me only to do something as dumb as make me sick?"

He had a few ideas. There were a lot of men out there who liked to play hero. Maybe somebody was setting Izzie up to get sick or take a fall just so he could get near her by being the one who came to her aid. Who knew how some dark, twisted minds worked? "Maybe somebody was hoping you'd pass out onstage and he could say he was a doctor and come to your aid."

She blew out an impatient breath. "That's silly."

"But not impossible," he insisted. "Those flowers that came last week…Jackie said they were for you, but that you gave them to Leah?"

Narrowing her eyes, she nodded. "You think they have something to do with this?"

That seemed incredibly obvious to Nick. "You get a couple of anonymous gifts, and the person who ends up with them gets sick."

She quickly figured out where he was going. "Harry said Leah was sick Sunday night...."

"So was Jackie. They share a dressing room and both smelled and touched the flowers when they were putting them in a vase."

Izzie shook her head, obviously not wanting to believe it. He didn't blame her. It couldn't be easy for her to think someone out there had been targeting her.

Because it was absolutely *killing* him to think it.

"And you think there was something on the roses...."

"Could have been insecticide, roach powder, anything. They both got nauseous and dizzy, and went home with horrible headaches."

Nick didn't know a lot about common household pesticide exposure, but he sure knew about its military applications. He'd been trained in dealing with all kinds of chemical attacks and imagined the most basic symptoms would be similar.

Izzie finally slipped out of his arms, her lovely face taut and strained. Her mouth drooped and she shook her head, appearing almost...*hurt*...that someone would be after her.

But the hurt didn't last for long. As she stared toward the replacement chair, her frown deepened and her eyes narrowed. He saw the clenching of her jaw and knew she was working herself into a temper.

"The cowardly bastard." She smacked her hand flat against the tabletop, muttering a few more choice curses. "You find out who did this, Nick."

He liked the return of that fierceness. Izzie wouldn't let anything keep her down for long—it was one of the things he loved about her. Which he planned to tell her, just as soon as they got around to having that whole "I love you," and "I love you, too," conversation. Which would be soon, if he had his way. Very soon.

"I intend to. We'll start by questioning everyone to see if anybody noticed your anonymous gift-giver hanging around."

Though he didn't say it to her, Nick also intended to carefully watch the staff when he talked to them. It wasn't impossible that someone who worked right here at Leather and Lace was behind the attacks. An obsessed bartender, a jealous dancer who wanted Izzie's headliner spot. Maybe even a bouncer wanting to be her hero. Hell, maybe even Harry wanting to stir up a big news story as publicity for the club. He could see the headline now: Hottest Mystery Dancer in Chicago Stalked by Unknown Assailant.

It was possible. Anything was.

"I'll watch the crowd tonight and see if anybody acts suspiciously, or if I recognize some of the guys who come every night I'm on." Glancing at her watch, she added, "I have to hurry up."

That comment drove everything else out of his mind. Nick shook his head hard. "You're not going on tonight.

She lifted her mask, turning to the mirror. "Of course I am."

Nick met her reflected stare. "Like hell."

"It *can* be like hell in here if you force me to make it that way," she shot back. "Because if you say that again, we're going to be having a major fight."

Nick couldn't believe her. She'd just found out someone had likely tried to poison her and she still wanted to perform. "Izzie, you can't be serious."

"Oh, you bet I am. We're already down one girl with Leah being sick and I left Harry in the lurch last weekend." Her eyes flashing fire, she added, "Besides, *no one's* going to force me off the stage."

Her expression betrayed her sheer determination as much as her words did. And he had to wonder if they had a double meaning.

Because despite everything that had happened this evening, he hadn't forgotten what they had been talking about before Leah got sick. She'd basically asked him if he was going to watch her dance, and he'd hedged on his answer. He hadn't missed the shine in her eyes or the disappointment twisting at her mouth. But he hadn't been able to reassure her, because even Nick didn't know how he was going to react when that moment came.

"It's too dangerous."

"There are four big burly bouncers upstairs to make sure nothing happens," she insisted. Piercing him with her stare, she added, "Besides, you'll be there to protect me. Or *won't* you? Maybe there'll be something more *important* to deal with."

Nick now knew for sure she was referring to their earlier conversation. And maybe she had a right to.

But being a little slow to want to watch the woman he loved get naked in front of a bunch of other guys had absolutely nothing to do with his concern for her now. "It's not about that."

"Oh, yes, it is." Izzie stalked around the privacy screen. Given that it offered no privacy whatsoever, considering the mirror, that was a statement in itself.

A frank one...that the walls were going up between them.

"And frankly, I'm tired of asking you about it. You can watch or not, but the Crimson Rose is performing tonight."

She yanked her robe off, then, watching him watch her, dropped her bra and panties to the floor.

"Damn it," he muttered, as always unable to take his

ravenous eyes off her. She was just so incredibly beautiful. The woman stopped his heart every time he looked at her.

Izzie continued to ignore him, reaching for her G-string and pulling it on. Then she covered her dark, puckered nipples with those two ridiculous pink petals.

"Don't do this," he ordered through a thick, tight throat. "Not until we know you're safe." When she stepped out from behind the screen and lifted her chin in challenge, he added, "You don't have to go out there."

"It's my job."

"It's something you do part-time for kicks and to rub it in to your family and the world that you're not sweet little Isabella Natale anymore," he said, frustrated beyond belief at her stoic refusal to listen to reason.

She appeared stunned by his accusation. "How can you *say* that? My family doesn't even know I'm here."

"I know and that proves my point. You get your *secret* kicks out of it without ever having to face the consequences. You're not being honest to anyone—not even yourself—about why you're doing this and what you really want."

She jerked as if he'd slapped her. Closing his eyes and shaking his head, Nick wondered how he'd let this whole conversation spin so badly out of control so rapidly.

"You certainly are a fine one to talk," she finally said, her tone steely.

"What?"

"You accuse me of that, but you're doing exactly the same thing, Nick Santori. Stringing your family along with this idea that you're going to be singing "O Sole Mio" and slinging pizza dough with Tony and your father. Meanwhile, you hide your nights doing something exciting and dangerous at a place they would never approve of. I call that hypocritical."

He couldn't believe she'd turned things around on him like that. "That's ridiculous."

"So why haven't you told Tony you're not sticking around? Why haven't you told your father about this 'protection' business you're thinking of going into with your Marine buddies?"

Leave it to a woman to use something he'd told her less than a day ago in a fight against him. "That has nothing to do with whether you go out onstage and flaunt yourself in front of someone who wants to *hurt* you." But even as he said it, a small voice in his head whispered that she might be right. At least a little.

Not that he was going to admit that now...not when they still had the issue of her physical safety to work out. So he pushed on. "And I'm not onstage intentionally taking off my clothes to try to turn on a hundred strangers—one of whom might be trying to poison me."

She'd stiffened at the word *flaunt*. By the time he'd finished speaking, Izzie's face was as red as her mask. "Well, that's it, then, isn't it? We've finally gotten down to it."

"Izzie...."

She put a hand up to stop him. "I knew it would come to this, and now it has. You need to leave. I'm going onstage tonight. By the time I get back, I hope there will be a new lock on my door, for my own protection." Her chin quivered, her full lips shook. But she had one last thing to say. "And you most definitely will not have a key to it."

NICK WASN'T IN the audience. Izzie scanned the crowd for him throughout her performance, wondering if he'd be lurking in the shadows, watching out for her.

He wasn't.

It was over.

Somehow, she managed to not cry as she gyrated to the

music. Managed to not show the hungry-looking men in the audience that her heart was broken.

It shouldn't feel this broken, after all, she'd known going into this crazy, wild relationship with Nick that it would have to end badly. From day one, they'd wanted each other on opposite terms. He'd wanted the cute kid sister of his brother's wife, who worked at the bakery every day. She'd wanted the sultry, sexy bodyguard who guarded *her* naked body every night.

That he'd tried to put his foot down and forbid her from dancing the very *first* moment he had a convenient excuse emphasized that and more.

As she dipped and swayed and thrust and jumped on the stage, four words kept time with the music. They played over and over, keeping the 4:4 beat.

It can not work.

By the time she was finished dancing, Izzie was as much angry as she was heartbroken. Aside from being her lover, Nick was supposed to be the club's bodyguard. And yet when she'd been the most vulnerable—exposed—he'd been nowhere to be seen.

She'd have something to say about that the second she saw him. But that moment came almost immediately—he had been watching her back. Literally. He was standing, dark and predatory, in the wings just offstage. He'd been watching for her to come off…out of a direct line of sight to center stage. So he *hadn't* watched her dance. And he most certainly hadn't experienced watching her dance with the rest of a big male audience.

Nothing had changed.

"I'll escort you to your dressing room," he said, his jaw as stiff as his shoulders. *"Rose."*

She didn't even respond as she slipped her robe on over her nearly naked body, then sailed past him toward the stairs. She didn't need his help, she didn't need his approval.

Yes, she needed him. But she'd learn to do without him, just like she'd done without him all those long, lonely teenage years when she'd pined for the man.

Of course, never having had him might have aided her then. Now that she had?

Izzie feared she was never going to get over Nick.

"Ahem." As they reached the bottom of the stairs, Harry stepped out of the greenroom.

"Everything okay?" Nick asked, instantly on alert.

"It's fine," the older man said, but he didn't sound convinced. In fact, his voice was weak, his face a little pale.

Izzie reached out and put a hand on his shoulder. "Harry, what's wrong? Is Leah all right?"

He covered her hand with his. "Yes. Jackie called earlier; Leah's fine." He glanced over his shoulder into the quiet greenroom. He stepped out of the room and eased the door closed. "But I need to talk to both of you. Will you come with me, please?"

Hearing his urgency and seeing his very obvious concern, Izzie immediately went on alert. Something else had happened…maybe someone else was hurt.

"What is it?" Nick asked in a low voice, obviously realizing the same thing.

The man just shook his head, leading them back up the stairs to his small office, which was on the other side of the lobby. They took a private, back hallway—a good thing since Izzie still wore just her long silky robe. Whatever was bothering Harry, it had to be serious because he hadn't even offered to wait while she put some clothes on.

Harry's office was unpretentious and simple. Comfortable. Much like the self-deprecating man who occupied it.

But Harry Black did not look at all comfortable right

now. As he gestured them toward the two armchairs across from his desk, his hand shook.

Izzie almost held her breath, watching him sit down behind the desk. Before he said a word, he dropped his head forward and put it in hands. "I can't even look at you when I say this."

Izzie had no idea what the man could be talking about, but beside her, Nick sucked in a sharp breath. "You…"

Their employer immediately looked up, shaking his head. "No. Not me." Moisture appearing in his eyes, he continued. "It was Delilah."

Izzie suddenly got it. Delilah had been the one after her. She'd poisoned the chocolates—and perhaps the roses.

Nick muttered a foul word, but Harry didn't leap to the defense of his wife. She deserved their scorn. No, she hadn't succeeded in hurting Izzie, her target, but she had certainly made Leah miserable.

"Tell us," Nick said, leaning back in the chair and crossing his arms over his chest.

His eyes were narrowed, his expression forbidding. Izzie recognized that tension in his rock-hard body. It was a good thing Delilah Black was not here for a personal confession. A very good thing. Because if Izzie didn't rip her apart, Nick just might have.

"I thought she *wanted* to retire," Harry said. He had a dazed expression, the same one many men wore when trying to understand their wives. Izzie had certainly seen it on her father's face. "She seemed happy helping me with management."

"How long ago did she stop?" Izzie asked, feeling a sharp sense of pity for the man. She sensed Harry needed to build up to telling them the worst of it.

"A few years ago when she turned forty. Right after we got married." Opening his desk drawer, Harry reached in and grabbed a silver flask and a shot glass. He poured himself a drink, raising a brow toward Nick and Izzie to see if they wanted one.

Neither took him up on it. Izzie because she was already feeling queasy at the story Harry was telling them. Nick… well, probably because he was already on a low simmer in the chair next to her. Throwing alcohol on a slow burn could make it erupt.

"And what, she thought if she could get rid of your head-liner, you'd suddenly put her back onstage? That makes no sense," Nick said, disgust dripping from his words.

"Not to you. Not to me," Harry said with a sigh. "But to her." Growing slightly pink in the cheeks, he added, "I, uh, think there might have been a little more to it, though. I guess I talk a lot about you, Rose…Izzie," he clarified, calling her by her real name for the first time since he'd hired her. "And I think Dee got a bit jealous, thinking my interest was something other than professional." Almost blushing to the roots of his balding head now, he quickly added, "That wasn't at all true. I'm as proud of you as if you were my own daughter…but Dee didn't get that."

The man had never even looked at her the wrong way. Izzie didn't doubt he was being truthful.

"Was she responsible for the roses?"

Harry nodded, taking another deep sip of his drink. "She put some kind of bug powder on them. And before you ask, yes, she did the chair, too. I got her to admit to both of those things, as well as putting some kind of syrup—Ipecac—in the chocolates."

This time Izzie was the one to call the other woman a bitch under her breath. She simply couldn't help it. Again, Harry didn't make any effort to defend his wife.

"Why'd she come clean?" Izzie asked.

"I suspected as soon as I saw the box of candy. Dee loves that kind. And she came home with some of that syrup a couple of days ago, saying she wanted it on hand in case one of her nieces or nephews came over and swallowed something poisonous."

Nick shifted a little, his arms still cross, his body still rigid. "So you confronted her?"

Harry nodded. "And she confessed. When she saw how sick Leah was, she felt awful."

"Wonder if she'd have felt that way if it had been Izzie lying on the floor," Nick snapped.

He sounded very protective. Which made Izzie feel all warm and gooshy inside, even though she told herself that was stupid.

"I dunno," Harry admitted. "Maybe not."

Gee, it was nice to be liked.

Nick finally sat up and leaned toward the desk. Fixing a firm eye on Harry he said, "Have you called the police?"

The man slowly shook his head. But before Nick could confront him on it, he added, "I went to Leah first and told her everything. She and Jackie decided to press charges, and they made the call to the police themselves."

Nick relaxed. A little.

"I understand why that needed to happen." Tears rose in Harry's gray eyes and oozed a little onto his round cheeks. "But I couldn't be the one to turn my wife in."

Izzie reached over and put her hand on Nick's leg, sensing he was about to make another comment about Delilah. She squeezed his thigh, warning him not to. Harry was suffering enough. He didn't need to be told he was a fool for loving someone so hateful. "I understand," she murmured.

"I hope you do. And I hope you'll understand that I'm going to see her through this. She'll be facing assault charges."

"At the very least," Nick mumbled.

"I know this might make you want to leave, Ro…Izzie. But I wish you wouldn't." The man smiled weakly. "You're family."

Huh. If poison was the way Delilah treated members of her *family,* Izzie would hate to see what she did to her enemies.

"I know that, too," Izzie said, slowly pulling her hand away from Nick's warm thigh, already missing the contact. Already missing *him.* "You love her. That's what people who love each other do…they support one another, even when they make what other people might see as bad or foolish decisions." Hearing a quiver in her voice as the subject touched much too close to home, Izzie offered Harry a tremulous smile.

Nick she didn't even look at.

"Thank you for telling me, Harry. I'm going to go get ready for my next number." Without another word to either of them, Izzie walked out and went back to work.

And Nick didn't come anywhere near her for the rest of the night.

WHEN BRIDGET WENT back to the dealership on Monday morning, she looked for Ted, wondering if he'd have the nerve to show up.

He didn't. That was good.

Neither did Dean. That wasn't good.

Hopefully Ted had been scared off, either by Dean, or by the ramifications of his own stupid actions.

Hopefully Dean had *not* been scared off and was just stuck in traffic.

Bridget had spent all Sunday night wondering what on earth she was going to say to him—how she was going to climb that wall he'd erected between them after he'd kissed her so passionately in the office. But for nothing. He wasn't there.

She trudged through her day, going through the same song and dance with Marty about the books. She found problems. He waved them off as unimportant. A typical day in the life.

"I am so gonna quit this job," she muttered that afternoon.

Soon. Maybe she'd even give her notice today. After all, she'd only stayed to see if something was going to happen between her and Dean Willis. Judging by yesterday, it seemed pretty clear nothing was.

She went so far as to open up a document on her computer to type her resignation letter. She'd give two weeks notice, even though she had no other job lined up. She had enough of a cushion to be unemployed for a while. And if she didn't come up with another bookkeeping job quickly, she'd lay money that Izzie would hire her on at the bakery, just to pay the rent.

But before she'd typed so much as the date, Bridget heard a commotion—shouts, coming from the sales floor. Her first thought was that Ted had come back and was making a scene. But there were several voices, all yelling at once.

She grabbed her purse and threw it under her desk, then wondered if she should crawl under after it…this could be a robbery. But when the door to the office flew open and she saw a uniformed police officer, she didn't.

"Is anyone in here with you?" the officer barked.

"N-no. Just me."

"You need to come with me, ma'am."

Dazed, Bridget followed the officer, seeing all the other employees being herded together by other policemen. All of them were gathered just inside the front door, and Marty was shouting loud enough to break the glass in the windows.

Everyone was talking—demanding answers. Everyone but Bridget. She didn't have to. Because the second she saw Dean Willis—dressed in a perfectly fitted dark blue suit—talking to other dark-suited men right outside the front door, she knew what was going on.

He was no car salesman.

"Sir, you'll have an opportunity to call your attorney soon," one of the officers said, trying to calm Marty down.

It worked for a brief second, until Dean walked through the door. When Marty saw him with the rest of the investigators, he started ranting and struggling against the officer trying to handcuff him. Another one jumped in to help and between them they got the livid man into custody.

Dean looked her way once. His nice blue eyes were frigid. His smile absent. His tousled blond hair was slicked down and parted on the side—conservative, professional. And his clothes were immaculate, right down to his shiny black wing-tip shoes.

He could have been a picture from an FBI agent's handbook come to life.

The rest of the day went by in a whirl. She was questioned endlessly—never by Dean, who stayed away from her—but by his fellow agents. Apparently there had been a reason Marty hadn't wanted Bridget to do a good job with the books. They were never *supposed* to balance out. Because, if the agents were to be believed, Honest Marty's Used Cars had been bringing in and cleaning up a whole lot of dirty money for some pretty bad guys.

And she'd fallen right in the middle of it.

By the end of the day, Bridget was utterly exhausted. Ready to collapse, her throat sore from answering so many questions. She hadn't asked for a lawyer—had cooperated fully, believing that's what an innocent person *should* do. And she'd spent the past four hours in the conference room, going over months' worth of seized bank statements and ledgers with some FBI accountant, watching step by step as they built a case against her boss.

At first, she felt a little sorry for Marty. But not too

sorry. Especially when she caught snips of conversation about where the dirty money had come from. In her opinion, anybody who cleaned cash that had been earned off the sale of filthy drugs to kids deserved what he got. She was just sorry the creep had dragged her into the sordidness.

She'd seen Dean only briefly, when she'd been brought to tears by the relentless questions of the accountant. Dean had appeared out of nowhere, appearing behind the other officer's back, barking, "She's not a suspect, she's a witness. Treat her like one." Then, with one long, even look at Bridget, he'd left again to go back to work with the other investigators.

Finally, when it was nearly dark out, Bridget was told she could go home. She'd be called in to help again—and, likely, to testify—but for now, she was free.

Free. Great. She was free to go home, look back on this horrible day—on these past few horrible weeks—and think about what a damned *fool* she'd been.

Dean had *used* her. He'd feigned an interest in her so he could build his money-laundering case against Marty. He'd played her like an instrument, obviously seeing the quiet, sweet-faced bookkeeper as an easy mark.

She hated the son of a bitch with a passion she'd never had toward anyone in her life.

That rage carried her down the block as she strode away from the dealership, heading toward her nearby apartment. Usually when she made the walk home, she kept her purse clutched tightly to her side, and constantly scanned for any possible danger. This wasn't a bad part of town—but as a young woman walking alone, she didn't take chances. Tonight, however, she practically *dared* anyone to mess with her. She felt capable of doing real violence.

"Bridget, wait, please!" a voice called.

Though she kept walking, she peered over her shoulder

to see who'd called her. She almost tripped over her own feet when she realized it was Dean. "Stay away from me," she snapped, picking up her pace.

He picked up his, too, chasing her down until he reached her. "Would you stop? I've been calling you for two blocks."

"Not real quick on the uptake, are you?" she said. "I don't want to talk to you."

"You have to let me explain."

"I don't *have* to do anything," she said, though she did finally stop and face him. "And you don't have to explain, I got it, okay? You were working undercover. I was the easy mark. Of course you'd come after me by any means at your disposal."

"It wasn't like that."

"Like hell."

"Just...calm down and let me explain. I did not mean to hurt you, and I definitely never meant to get personally involved with you."

"You mean that wasn't in the manual?"

"No, it wasn't. But I was worried, I felt sure early on that you were caught in something you didn't know about." He put a hand on her arm. "I was worried about you."

She shrugged his hand off. "Sure you were. I'm sure your concern was the reason you asked me out. And your fears that I was being used by my boss to help hide money was the only reason you kissed the lips off my face yesterday."

He closed his eyes, breathed deeply—as if for control—and tried again. "I lost my detachment where you were concerned."

Those were the first words he'd said that actually made her pause. Because he'd whispered them hoarsely, as if against his will. Like he didn't want to admit to the weakness.

And she believed him.

Not that it made a damn bit of difference. "Well, that's too bad for you then," she said, lifting her chin, amazed that her voice didn't even quiver. "Because I never want to see you again." She began walking again.

"Bridget, I know you're upset now. But I want to make it up to you. Soon, when you've..."

"When I've what?" she asked, swinging around again. "When I've calmed down? Well, keep dreaming, buddy. Because it's not going to happen. *Ever.*"

Dean met her stare, but didn't try to stop her this time when she turned again to start walking. He did, however, have one more thing to say, low, as if making a vow.

"I'm not giving up."

"Well, too bad for you," she snapped back, feeling both proud of herself for being so strong...and sad at having lost something she suspected could have been very special.

"Bridget...."

This time, she didn't turn around. And she didn't have to wonder what Izzie would do.

Bridget knew what *she* wanted to do.

So without a pause, she lifted her hand, flipped him the bird over her shoulder and kept on walking.

12

Izzie DIDN'T SEE or hear from Nick for six long days. The longest of her life.

Since she'd walked out of Harry's office Sunday night, Nick had apparently taken her orders to leave her alone seriously, because that's exactly what he'd done. He hadn't tried calling, hadn't popped in to the bakery, hadn't even nonchalantly walked by the shop and pretended not to look in at her.

That's what *she'd* done, at Santori's, but she hadn't seen the man at all.

"Why didn't you fight for me?" she whispered as she drove to the other side of town Saturday evening on her way to work. "Why did you listen to me and leave me alone?"

Why did you tell him to?

Good question. And Izzie was already forgetting the answer, though it had seemed so important Sunday.

Yes, she was still upset that he'd suddenly gone from an approving coworker to a disapproving lover when it came to her dancing. But maybe they could have worked it out. Maybe he wouldn't have reacted so badly to watching her onstage.

Maybe…hell, maybe she loved him enough that she could have quit and never regretted it.

But he hadn't given her the chance.

In the six days since she'd seen him, Izzie was questioning a lot of the choices she'd made. After accusing Nick of living a lie, too, she'd realized that she was tired of living one all the time. So she'd actually begun to share her secret. Only with her sisters and her cousin so far, but it was a start.

And they'd been remarkably supportive. Even Gloria who had, to Izzie's utter shock, admitted that she'd love to see her perform. Honestly, it felt as if a weight had been lifted, and she'd decided then and there to start thinking of how to work her daytime life into her nighttime one. Slowly…a little at a time. But she might just have to find a way to do it.

Because if Nick ever *did* come back after her, she wanted to try to find a way to make all the pieces of both their lives fit.

Performing again…that caused more stress. Izzie couldn't deny a small amount of trepidation when she arrived at Leather and Lace Saturday night. This was her first time back since last Sunday, the night of Delilah's confession—and her arrest. She hadn't talked to Harry since and she was worried about what the older man was going through.

Bernie was waiting at the back door. "Hiya, Rose," he said without a smile. Obviously the mood around here was still dour.

"Hi. Harry around?"

He shook his head. "He hasn't been here much." Shaking his head, he added, "Wish he'd just ditch that witch and get back to work, this club ain't gonna run itself."

Izzie didn't say anything. She honestly didn't want to think about what she'd do in her boss's situation. He was a man who loved his wife…warts and all. Should he be faulted for that? Maybe. But it wasn't her place to judge.

The dressing rooms and greenroom were pretty quiet for a Saturday night, any chatter between the dancers was going on quietly. Just as well. Izzie didn't feel very social. There was only one person she wanted to see…only, she didn't know what on earth she'd say to him when she did.

I miss you. I love you. Please love me as I am and let's work it out.

All of the above.

He never appeared. She didn't see him downstairs, and he certainly didn't come to her dressing room. Izzie went through the motions getting ready, tense and anxious… but for nothing.

By the time she was ready to go on, she was seriously wondering if she'd made a mistake in coming in at all. Her heart was not in it. Not tonight. "The show must go on," she reminded herself as she walked upstairs and took her place backstage.

She'd like to think she gave her audience her all, but as she began removing her rose petals in time to the music, she knew her heart wasn't in it. Her heart was in little pieces, scattered around Nick Santori's feet. Wherever he may be.

Usually, Izzie ignored the audience as she performed— it was part of her "mysterious appeal" as Harry had described it right after she'd started working here. And he'd been right.

Tonight, however, something caught her attention. Rather, some*one*. Normally, all were still when she performed—including the waitresses. But now, someone was walking from the back of the room straight down the center aisle toward the stage.

It was a man. A dark-haired, dark-eyed man.

A *familiar* dark-haired, dark-eyed man.

"Oh, God," she whispered, stumbling a little.

Because it was Nick. A Nick like she'd never seen before.

Though he wore his typical on-the-job tough-guy uniform of black pants and tight black T-shirt, he was carrying a bouquet of roses. A huge bouquet of them. He was also smiling, his eyes locked on her, apparently not caring that she was dancing nearly naked onstage in front of a bunch of strange men.

And for the first time in her entire dancing career, Izzie did something entirely unprofessional. She committed the cardinal sin. She stopped right in the middle of her number.

"Nick," she whispered.

He had reached the edge of the low stage, which was about as high as his midthigh and was staring up at her. The look in his eyes…oh, God, that look. He was smiling broadly, adoring her with his gaze.

He not only looked approving, he looked absolutely enraptured. "Hi, Izzie," he said, his voice low, intimate, just for the two of them.

The music slowly faded away into silence. The audience began to murmur. One man yelled something like "Down in front," but he was shouted down by several others who obviously wanted to see what would happen next.

She'd like to know that herself.

"Hi," she whispered. "Uh…what are you doing?"

His smile widened. "Watching you."

"I noticed."

"You're wonderful."

She nibbled her bottom lip. "Thank you."

"I could watch you dance every night and be a happy man."

"Who couldn't?" someone from a nearby table called.

Nick never even glanced over, not distracted. Instead, he lifted the bouquet and offered it to her. Izzie took it, bringing the flowers up to her masked face and sniffing the heady fragrance permeating the red blooms. "They're beautiful."

"I figured roses were your flower."

"Good call." Laughing a little, she asked, "Is there some reason you gave them to me here? And right *now?*"

He nodded. "I wanted you to know how proud I am of you and how much I love seeing you dance. No matter who else is here."

He'd said it. He'd put it into words. Exactly what she needed to hear. "Oh, Nick, really?"

He nodded. "*Really.* I have more to say. But not here." He glanced over his shoulder at all the men leering at them. "Some things were not meant to be done in front of an audience." Then he looked back up at her. "And the next thing I want to say to you can't be said when you're wearing that mask on your face."

She shivered, anticipation rolling through her. Oh, how she hoped she knew what it was he wanted to say to her. That it involved talk of a future. And a lot of uses of the word *love*.

"I'll meet you downstairs in two-and-a-half minutes," he said. "I've timed your song…that's how much you have left."

"You're on," she said with a broad smile as she clutched the flowers close to her body and slowly backed away from the edge of the stage. She put the flowers down right in front of the curtain, where she could easily retrieve them.

Nick turned around and walked back the way he'd come. From where Izzie stood, she could see every man in the place turn to watch him go. Most were regulars who had to have recognized him. And probably all of them wanted to know exactly what he'd said to her…and what he meant to her.

That was easy to explain. *Everything.*

Nodding toward the crew member on the side of the stage, Izzie waited for her song to resume. Now she danced joyfully, the way she hadn't in a very long time. And she smiled during every moment of it.

As soon as the last notes of the music played, Izzie grabbed her flowers and darted toward the wings, pausing only long enough to stick her arms in her robe before tearing toward the staircase. She took the cement stairs two at a time, almost stumbling. But even if she had, it would have been okay. Because Nick was waiting at the bottom of them, staring up at her.

He would have caught her. She knew that, from now on, he would be there to catch her.

"Come on," he murmured, taking her hand. He twined her fingers in his, then lifted them to his mouth to press a soft kiss on them. "Let's talk privately."

She followed him, easing against his body, her curves fitting perfectly in his angles, as if they were two pieces of a puzzle. When they reached her dressing room, Nick opened the door and held it for her, then followed her inside.

"Thank you again for the roses," she murmured as she put them on the makeup-strewn counter. They'd already begun filling the room with their heady perfume and she inhaled of it deeply.

"You're welcome." He immediately added, "You were right."

"About?"

"Everything," he admitted evenly, making no effort to hedge or share blame for what had happened between them. Even though Izzie knew she bore some of the responsibility.

"We both…"

"No, Iz, let me finish, please. You were right to accuse me of living the same double life I'd accused you of.

You had legitimate reasons, with your father's health and your, uh…"

"Being a stripper?"

He grinned. "Yeah. That."

"I told Gloria and Mia."

His eyes widened. "Really? How'd they react?"

"Better than I expected." Much better. But she'd fill him in on that later. "It's a first step, anyway."

"I know. I made that same step. I told my father and Tony that I wasn't interested in the business. And what I am interested in doing."

"Being a bodyguard?"

For the first time since he'd walked up to her during her dance, Nick looked a little hesitant. He glanced to the side, and scrunched his brow. "Well…not exactly."

Immediately on alert, Izzie crossed her arms. "What did you do? Tell me you're not going to be a cop like your brother!"

He shook his head, as if appalled at the idea. "Not a chance. As it turns out, Harry's going to need to take a step back from this place to deal with Delilah's legal situation."

Not a surprise.

"And he asked me if I'd manage it."

Izzie couldn't prevent a shocked gasp. *"What?"*

"There's more."

Still stunned at the very concept, she waited, mouth agape.

"He needs an infusion of cash…I think he anticipates a lot of legal bills. I have money I've been socking away during all the years I bunked with Uncle Sam. So I've just become a part owner of this club."

That was so unexpected, Izzie couldn't help sinking down to her chair in absolute shock. "You're serious?"

"Very serious."

"You're going to work *here*."

"Uh-huh. You okay with that? Working with your husband?"

"Oh, I'll love…" His words sunk in, banging around in her head. "*What* did you say?"

He smiled. "I thought diamonds would go well with roses."

Izzie remained still, in a stunned silence, as Nick reached into his pocket and pulled out a ring. A gold one. With a big fat diamond on top of it. "I'm going to slide this on your finger, but not until you take that mask off your face."

Dazed, she reached up and unfastened the clasps of her mask, one on each side of her head. The slow-motion feeling of the moment continued as she drew the red velvet away, letting it fall to the floor at her feet.

He reached for her hand, drawing her up to stand in front of him. "I love you, Izzie Natale. I love you, Crimson Rose. And I want you both in my life from this day on," he said, his voice serious and unwavering. His expression was every bit as serious—as proud and determined as she'd ever seen him—as if he placed more value on this moment than he had on any other.

She certainly did. Because this could be the moment when her life changed forever. When, as silly as it sounded, all her secret dreams—the ones she hadn't even acknowledged to herself—might actually start coming true.

"Whether we stay here, or go to New York, whether you work at the bakery or take off your clothes for a living…I'll follow you. I'll lead you. I'll stand beside you." He reached up and cupped her cheek, brushing his fingertips over her skin in a caress so tender it brought tears to her eyes.

"Be with me. Always."

Now the teardrops gushed. Izzie seldom cried, but, at this moment, it was absolutely the only reaction she could manage. "I will, Nick. I love you so much. I've loved you for so long, I can't remember what it felt like to *not* be in love with you."

Reaching for him, she twined her arms around his neck and drew him toward her. She rose on tiptoe, touching her lips to his in a gentle kiss that gradually deepened. Their tongues sliding together in delicate intimacy, their bodies melted together. They shared breaths and promises not yet made but never to be broken, making a bond in that deep, unending, heady kiss that would last forever.

It was the most beautiful kiss of Izzie's life. Because she was kissing a man she'd loved forever…and his amazing mouth had just given the same words to her.

When they finally paused, Nick smiled down at her. "Are you really going to wear my ring?"

She stuck out her hand. "Starting now. Lasting forever."

Once he'd slid it on, she stared at the beautiful, glittering stone and gasped at the beauty of it. "Oh, thank you for waiting for me," she whispered to him.

"Thanks for pulling me on top of you on that table of cookies to let me know how much you wanted me."

Izzie glared at her new fiancé. "I did not pull you on top of me."

"I'd have to say you pulled, Cookie."

Reaching for the sash to her bathrobe and slowly unfastening it, she smiled a wicked, sultry smile. "Nick? You want to see what's beneath this robe?"

His eyes glittered in hunger and need. "Oh, you know I do."

He reached for her, but Izzie put her hand over his, stopping him. "Then I have one piece of advice for you. *Don't* call me Cookie."

Epilogue

Three Months Later

THOUGH THE COLD WINTER air outside buffeted the city with an early blast of winter, inside Leather and Lace, everything remained *hot*. As usual.

The club was packed this Saturday night, every table full, mostly with men, but a few daring women were in the audience, too. Leather and Lace had started earning a reputation as a "couples-friendly" club and more pairs were coming in. Laughing and partying as they entered…quite often whispering and cuddling seductively as they left.

Nick had thought that a fine idea…until tonight when he'd looked up and had seen his brothers Joe and Luke walk in, their wives on their arms. That had given him a momentary heart attack, but once he'd sat and had a drink with the quartet, he'd realized something: Rachel and Meg were excited beyond belief, not at all judgmental and certainly not jealous that their future sister-in-law was about to strip in front of a bunch of men…including their husbands.

He hadn't understood it at first, until his brothers had confessed that their wives—as well as Tony's wife, Gloria, and Nick's sister, Lottie—were all taking the pole-dancing classes Izzie was now teaching at a Chicago dance studio. Mark's pregnant wife was on a waiting list for a future class.

He had to grin every time he thought about it. Now that she'd stopped working at the bakery, Izzie had found herself a full-time job teaching the housewives and professional women of Chicago how to stay healthy while learning to be ultra-sexy.

"I can't wait to see her. I mean, she's done her routine for us at the gym, but to see her here, in front of an audience...oh, sugar, just you watch and see what I'm going to be doing in a couple of months." Rachel leaned close to Luke, curling her arm around his, and whispered something that made his brother cough into his fist.

Okay. This appeared to be a good thing. And obviously Izzie was aware they were coming, so he didn't have to go track down his fiancée—and star performer—and give her a heads-up.

Leaving his family to their drinks, he ran another sweep of the room, touching base with Bernie and the other bouncers. He'd had to hire another bartender to work on weekends and both guys were rushing around pouring shots of high-end liquor and now, making froufrou drinks for their female patrons.

Harry would be proud, if he'd been here to see it. But the man had come in less and less, leaving the management to Nick.

"Hey, boss, somebody to see you," one of the bouncers said.

Glancing up, Nick saw four men approaching the bar. Even if he hadn't known them, their postures and bearing would have told them they were brothers in a way that only those who'd been *there* would understand.

"Semper fi, man." He nodded to the first, recognizing the black hair and even stare of an old friend...a good man to have at your back when the situation turned rough. Reaching for the extended hand, Nick shook it, saying, "Been a long time, Joel."

The man nodded. He'd gotten out four years ago, just before Nick had been deployed to Iraq. "I figured I'd come in and see why this was so much better than coming to work with me."

As Nick greeted the rest, another of the men, also an old Marines friend, glanced toward the stage where one of the girls was doing her thing. "I think I'm catching the vision," he mumbled.

"What can I say?" Nick shrugged. "I've settled down, become respectable." His mouth widening in a grin, he added, "And the little woman didn't want me doing anything as risky as working security with you guys."

Joel's big shoulders moved as he chuckled. He had a pretty good sense of humor considering he was one tough son of a bitch.

Nick gestured to one of the hostesses, asking her to get his friends a good table. But before they walked away, he murmured, "Seriously, thanks for offering to let me in. But I'm pretty happy with what I'm doing."

Joel nodded. "Got it. Still, if you ever change your mind…" He reached into the pocket of his black leather jacket and pulled out a crisp white business card.

Nick read it. Then he looked back at his friend, offering him a short nod. "I'll keep it in mind."

Reaching out with his elbow bent and arm up, Nick grasped the other man's hand again in a brothers-of-the-field handshake, then watched the group head to their table.

He could have been one of them. Hell, he and Joel even *looked* like they were in the same line of work since they were both dressed in black from head to toe. Old habits sure died hard.

But he didn't regret it. He hadn't been lying when he

said he liked what he was doing. A lot. Maybe not forever, but for now, working with Izzie doing something nobody had ever expected either of them to do was suiting him just fine.

"What time you got, Bernie?" he asked the bouncer, who stood nearby, on constant, vigilant guard.

"Eight-twenty," the other man said.

Hmm…about forty minutes before the Crimson Rose's first performance of the night.

Forty minutes. That *might* be enough time to tell the woman again how crazy he was about her. And how very glad he was that she'd stayed in Chicago with him.

When he got downstairs, walked into her dressing room and caught her standing behind her screen wearing nothing but her G-string, however, he reconsidered that idea.

Forty minutes wasn't going to be enough. Not nearly.

"Hey, lover." She smiled at him in the mirror.

He smiled back. "Hey, Cookie."

Never taking his eyes off her beautiful face, Nick reached behind him and closed the door, flipping the lock to keep the world *out*. And to shut them *in* the wild and sultry one he thrived on with the woman he loved more than life.

* * * * *

COMING NEXT MONTH FROM

 HARLEQUIN®  *Blaze*®

Available May 21, 2013

#751 I CROSS MY HEART • *Sons of Chance*
by Vicki Lewis Thompson

When Last Chance cowhand Nash Bledsoe goes to investigate smoke at a neighboring ranch, the last thing he expects to find is a super sexy woman. But he hasn't got time for a relationship, especially with *this* female. Still, where there's smoke, there's fire....

#752 ALL THE RIGHT MOVES • *Uniformly Hot!*
by Jo Leigh

Whether it's behind the wheel of a sports car or in the cockpit of a fighter jet—or in bed!—John "Devil" Devlin has never faced a challenge like gorgeous spitfire Cassie O'Brien. Challenge accepted!

#753 FROM THIS MOMENT ON
Made in Montana • by Debbi Rawlins

Every time gorgeous cowboy Trace McAllister flashes his signature smile, the ladies come running. But street-smart Nikki Flores won't let another handsome charmer derail her future...which is definitely not in Blackfoot Falls.

#754 NO STRINGS...
by Janelle Denison

Chloe Reiss wants Aiden Landry, badly! But because of a no-fraternization rule at work, the only way they can indulge their passions is to do it in secret. Unfortunately, even the best-kept secrets don't always stay that way....

HBCNM0513

Love the Harlequin book you just read?

Your opinion matters.

Review this book on your favorite
book site, review site, blog or your own
social media properties and share
your opinion with other readers!

REQUEST YOUR FREE BOOKS!
2 FREE NOVELS PLUS 2 FREE GIFTS!

red-hot reads!

YES! Please send me 2 FREE Harlequin® Blaze™ novels and my 2 FREE gifts (gifts are worth about $10). After receiving them, if I don't wish to receive any more books, I can return the shipping statement marked "cancel." If I don't cancel, I will receive 4 brand-new novels every month and be billed just $4.74 per book in the U.S. or $4.96 per book in Canada. That's a savings of at least 14% off the cover price. It's quite a bargain. Shipping and handling is just 50¢ per book in the U.S. and 75¢ per book in Canada.* I understand that accepting the 2 free books and gifts places me under no obligation to buy anything. I can always return a shipment and cancel at any time. Even if I never buy another book, the two free books and gifts are mine to keep forever.

150/350 HDN F4WC

Name	(PLEASE PRINT)

Address	Apt. #

City	State/Prov.	Zip/Postal Code

Signature (if under 18, a parent or guardian must sign)

Mail to the Harlequin® Reader Service:
IN U.S.A.: P.O. Box 1867, Buffalo, NY 14240-1867
IN CANADA: P.O. Box 609, Fort Erie, Ontario L2A 5X3

Want to try two free books from another line?
Call 1-800-873-8635 or visit www.ReaderService.com.

* Terms and prices subject to change without notice. Prices do not include applicable taxes. Sales tax applicable in N.Y. Canadian residents will be charged applicable taxes. Offer not valid in Quebec. This offer is limited to one order per household. Not valid for current subscribers to Harlequin Blaze books. All orders subject to credit approval. Credit or debit balances in a customer's account(s) may be offset by any other outstanding balance owed by or to the customer. Please allow 4 to 6 weeks for delivery. Offer available while quantities last.

HB13R2

SPECIAL EXCERPT FROM

 HARLEQUIN®

 *Blaze*®

New York Times bestselling author
Vicki Lewis Thompson is back with three new,
steamy titles from her bestselling miniseries
Sons of Chance.

I Cross My Heart

"Do *you* like an audience?" Bethany asked.

If he did, that would help cool her off. She wasn't into that. Of course, she wasn't supposed to be feeling hot in the first place.

"I prefer privacy when I'm making love to a woman." Nash's voice had lowered to a sexy drawl and his blue gaze held hers. "I don't like the idea of being interrupted."

Oh, Lordy. She could hardly breathe from wanting him. "Me, either."

She took another hefty swallow of wine, for courage. "I have a confession to make. You know when I claimed that this nice dinner wasn't supposed to be romantic?"

"Yeah."

"I lied."

"Oh, really?" His blue eyes darkened to navy. "Care to elaborate?"

"See, back when we were in high school, you were this out-of-reach senior and I was a nerdy freshman. So when you showed up today, I thought about flirting with you because now I actually have the confidence to do that. But when you offered to help repair the place, flirting with you didn't seem like such a good idea. But I still thought you were really hot." She took another sip of wine. "We shouldn't have sex, though. At least, I didn't think so this morning, but then I fixed up the dining room, and I admit I thought about you while I did that. So I think, secretly, I wanted it to be romantic. But I—"

"Do you always talk this much after two glasses of wine?" He'd moved even closer, barely inches away.

She could smell his shaving lotion. Then she realized what that meant. He'd shaved before coming over here. That was significant. "I didn't have two full glasses."

"I think you did."

She glanced at her wineglass, which was now empty. Apparently she'd been babbling and drinking at the same time. "You poured me a second glass." When he started to respond, she stopped him. "But that's okay, because if I hadn't had a second glass, I wouldn't be admitting to you that I want you so much that I almost can't stand it, and you wouldn't be looking at me as if you actually might be considering the idea of…"

"Of what?" He was within kissing distance.

"This." She grabbed his face in both hands and planted one on that smiling mouth of his. And oh, it was glorious. Nash Bledsoe had the best mouth of any man she'd kissed so far. Once she'd made the initial contact, he took over, and before she quite realized it, he'd pulled her out of her chair and was drawing her away from the table.

Ah, he was good, this guy. And she had a feeling she was about to find out just *how* good….

**Pick up I CROSS MY HEART by
Vicki Lewis Thompson, on sale May 21,
wherever Blaze books are sold.**